THE GRAVEYARD GIRLS

BOOKS BY RITA HERRON

THE
GRAVEYARD
GIRLS

RITA HERRON

bookouture

Published by Bookouture in 2025

An imprint of Storyfire Ltd.
Carmelite House
50 Victoria Embankment
London EC4Y 0DZ

www.bookouture.com

The authorised representative in the EEA is Hachette Ireland
8 Castlecourt Centre
Dublin 15 D15 XTP3
Ireland
(email: info@hbgi.ie)

ISBN: 978-1-83618-590-1
eBook ISBN: 978-1-83618-589-5

To my wonderful, kind, loving husband and best friend, a great father to my three kids and a super Pop to our eight grandchildren.
I lost a piece of my heart the day you went to heaven. Every day I miss your smile, your voice, and holding your hand through life. Fifty years of friendship and love was not enough. A hundred wouldn't have been enough.
I see your face in the clouds and hear your sweet voice in my mind. Until we meet again...
You and me and me and you and that's the way it'll always be, just like we promised. Love you forever and ever and always.

PROLOGUE

The scream woke sixteen-year-old Ida Bramble at midnight, a scream that sent goosebumps skittering up her spine.

The wind beat at the window panes, rattling the glass. Rain drops splattered the surface in patterns that resembled spiders.

She clenched the edges of her comforter and shivered, then froze. Maybe she'd imagined it. Maybe her daddy was right and she was a little touched in the head from the time she fell off Hangman's Ridge onto the jagged rocks below. He'd warned her not to wander around in the dark. But she thought she'd seen a lost kitty and had run after it.

She remembered the sharp pain stabbing her in the back when she fell. Her leg twisted, a bone poking through the skin.

She hadn't imagined that. But the body she'd just seen... maybe she had imagined it was a person. Or maybe she'd been dreaming.

After living by the graveyard where her daddy worked digging graves and making pine boxes for the indigents all her life, you'd have thought she would have gotten past the scary dreams, running from the dark shadows, hearing the cries of the dead and seeing ghostly shapes in the night.

But she hadn't.

Breathing out to control her anxiety, she closed her eyes and listened to the eerie sounds. The wind wheezing, a hollow empty sound filled with sadness and questions about the people buried by their old clapboard house.

But then... another scream pierced the air. This one so shrill she thought her bedroom window might shatter.

A shiver started deep inside her and wouldn't let go. Her fourteen-year-old cousin Hetty, who'd been living with her and her daddy since her own parents died, rolled over in bed and jerked up, then startled awake. Hetty's choppy black hair was tangled around her pale face. Her eyes were huge and glassy with fear.

Hetty had heard the scream, too.

Terrified, Ida eased aside the covers and planted her feet on the cold wood floor. Her leg throbbed and her knee buckled. She grabbed the edge of the metal bed to steady herself then rubbed her thigh to ease the kinks as she limped to the window.

The curtain was flapping in the January wind seeping through the cracks, an icy chill sweeping through the already cold room.

Hetty tiptoed up behind her and clenched Ida's arm. Her whisper came out in a shaky puff. "What was that?"

Ida had a bad feeling she knew. That this was *real*, not a figment of her imagination.

She caught the fluttering curtain with fingers stiff from the cold and held it aside just enough to see out. Hetty stared over her shoulder, her bony body trembling against Ida's back. The half-moon was barely visible through the winter clouds, leaving the desolate woods and graveyard dark and filled with an ominous sea of shadows.

Ida squinted through the snake-like limbs of the oaks, her stomach churning.

"Oh, God..." Hetty's voice cracked.

Ida's fingernails dug into the windowsill as she saw the back of a man in a dark coat and ski cap dragging what looked like a girl's body toward the deserted section of dead land bordering the graveyard. Land parched and destroyed by a coal mountain fire that had been burning underground for years. Toxins from it had taken lives and driven people away, leaving it looking like a ghost town.

Locals had dubbed it No Man's Land because neither man nor animal nor plant could survive on it.

Suddenly the figure halted and turned and stared at the house. At the window.

Ida grabbed Hetty's arm and pulled her down to hide. Had he seen them?

Hetty hunkered into a ball and Ida curved her arms around her as if she could protect her.

She knew who that figure was. So did her cousin.

If they tried to stop him, they'd end up in the ground just like the girl was going to.

ONE

Green Gardens Cemetery

Fifteen years later

He jammed the shovel into the ground with all his force, his adrenaline pumping as he watched the tears streaming down the young girl's face.

Horror filled her wide brown eyes as she silently pleaded for him to let her live. Her lower lip quivered and a moan escaped her as she struggled with her bindings.

"Beg and fight all you want, honey," he muttered as he tossed dry dirt, stones and weeds into the pile that would cover her once he put her six feet under. "Ain't nobody out here but the dead." He gestured toward the deserted area and the woods. "Not even the wildlife can live on this toxic land."

Steam oozed from the parched ground surrounding him where the coal mine fire still burned. A fire that had destroyed people's homes, taken lives, and still sizzled years after it had erupted and turned Brambletown into a ghost town.

It was the perfect graveyard for his victims. If anyone dared to venture here and happened to find the graves, the heat would have sped up decomposition to the point of destroying identities and evidence.

Though he was always careful.

Except for that first time.

That had been a pure spontaneous act of rage.

It had also been his most satisfying kill.

Laughter bubbled in his dry throat, and he tugged his ski cap lower over his head and adjusted the bandana around his face. He'd learned to hide in the shadows. To be methodical.

To sit and watch quietly and choose the perfect moment.

Still, the need to repeat the killing ritual simmered inside him just like that fire that filled the air with the scent of gases, charred earth and death.

He dug another foot, the shallow grave becoming deeper and deeper. She kicked at the dirt, sending dust and pebbles flying. Anger tore through him and he yanked her by the hair and dragged her toward the hole.

She pushed and fought, but he shoved her into the ground. She clawed at the dirt sides of the hole he'd dug, but he pressed his boot on her chest and held her down. Smiling, he stooped down then wrapped the scarf around her throat and pulled and tightened it until her eyes bulged and rolled back in her head and she gasped for a breath. Her body spasmed and jerked, arms falling limply by her side.

He removed one of her shoes, then shoveled the first clump of leaves and dirt onto her face. Her death stare disappeared beneath the dirt as he covered her and said goodbye.

TWO

DAY ONE

Crooked Creek

Two weeks later

The sharp trill of Detective Ellie Reeves' phone jarred her from a peaceful sleep. Her boss, Captain Hale. Six a.m.

Not a good sign.

She reluctantly rolled away from Cord McClain where she'd been snuggling against his back. She missed his warmth already.

The phone trilled again and she held her breath as she answered the call. "I'm here, boss."

He cut straight to the chase. "Unidentified body found near Green Gardens Cemetery in Brambletown. I need you and McClain up there ASAP. Their police department is so small they don't have a crime team or detective."

"You know small-town sheriffs don't like others horning in on their territory?"

He grunted. "I know. But considering the fact that fifteen years ago a young girl disappeared from that town and the case was never solved, rumors spread that the sheriff in charge of it dropped the ball. And his son is sheriff now."

Sounded like a challenge.

She rubbed her temple. The last couple of months had been blessedly peaceful and free of crime. She'd almost grown accustomed to the quiet in town and living a half-normal life. Almost.

But a spurt of adrenaline shot through her. She thrived on working a case.

And Brambletown was an interesting place with a rich history of death. Only twenty minutes away. Not peaceful. Not serene. Famous for the coal mountain fire that had destroyed homes, the land, and killed so many people.

There the leafless trees looked gnarled and lifeless. And she'd heard about the hillbillies, moonshiners and meth labs in the remote areas.

"Detective?" her boss asked. "You understand?"

That he thought the police might be incompetent. "Yeah, on it."

She turned to wake Cord but he was lying on his back staring at her with an odd expression in his smoky brown eyes.

He was still harboring secrets from her. Secrets he kept buried deep inside.

No matter that they'd spent the last few months together, he still didn't trust her. That stung and made her want to shake him and promise that he could trust her with anything.

But she had to be patient.

He tunneled his fingers through his sleep-tousled shaggy dark hair. "You caught a case?"

His voice was thick and gruff and so damn sexy she wanted to curl back into his arms and ignore the call. But she couldn't do that so she nodded instead. "Body found near Brambletown. Boss wants us up there now. You know the area?"

Cord's face paled. "Yeah."

Shoulders tensing, he swung his long legs over the side of

the bed and stood. She stared at the back of his T-shirt knowing he had scars underneath that he refused to show her in the daylight. But she felt them at night in the dark when she ran her fingers across his chest and his broad back.

"What's wrong, Cord? Do you know something about that town?"

His expression turned hooded. "Just that it's had its share of trouble."

But he seemed bothered by the mention of it. "I wish you'd talk to me," she said as she pushed away the covers.

"Let it go, El," he growled. "We need to get to work."

Dammit. He'd shut her down like he always did when she tried to get him to open up.

But he was right. Work called and she needed to focus.

THREE

Green Gardens Cemetery

Twenty minutes later, Ellie parked at the graveyard where local police were already on the scene. She darted a glance toward Cord, who'd lapsed into one of his brooding silences.

Odd that the graveyard was called Green Gardens when nothing about the land here was green. She knew the history of the area. Brambletown was named after the numerous Bramble family members who'd occupied the semi-remote area for decades.

Gray storm clouds had rolled in, hovering over the desolate, parched terrain, making the area look even more eerie. The little white church on the hill still sat, obviously vacant, paint peeling, trees dead, the faint sound of praise hymns lingering like a ghostly cry from the heavens mourning the dead.

Yet someone had recently created a memorial for those lost due to the fire and now tourists and residents had come to either honor or gawk at the stone markers in front of the church on the hill.

Distaste soured her mouth. Morbid curiosity seekers, Ellie thought. Some people even collected murderabilia, a hobby she didn't quite understand. She saw enough horror in her work not to want to have the evidence at home in a glass case to display as if honoring the demented killers' tools of the trade.

She quickly scanned the area. "Is the land still toxic?" she asked Cord.

Cord shook his head. "Toxins are thought to be farther north and the area has been cordoned off and warnings posted. The cemetery has been tested and proven safe. Although people have reported still seeing steam oozing from the ground at times from the heat below."

Ellie breathed out in relief and climbed from her Jeep.

Cord followed, their doors closing and echoing in the silence created by the lack of wildlife; forest creatures no longer lived on the land. There had been controversy about how the toxins had been handled and people were up in arms for the government to do something. But change took time and the government bigwigs didn't see this run-down town as a priority.

The local sheriff's car was parked by the edge of the grave-yard, but as they walked toward the cemetery, Ellie noticed the sheriff and a couple of his officers were actually pacing a deserted section of woods bordering the graveyard. An area with dry grass, dead weeds and rotting, downed trees.

An officer met them at the edge of the woods and identified himself as one of the deputies. Ellie made the introductions, and he led them toward the cordoned-off scene. "Who found the body?"

Deputy Newberry gestured toward a thin man with a goatee sporting an expensive-looking camera. "Says he's a wildlife photographer."

"Did he see anything? Anybody around?"

The deputy shook his head. "No, but I doubt he would

have. Judging from the situation, the body may have been here a while."

Ellie gave a small nod and they walked toward the sheriff, a medium-built guy with short brown hair and a scruffy jaw. His police-issued shirt strained across his broad chest and his khaki pants looked a size too small. She pegged him as an athlete in high school. He'd replaced his father as sheriff, so who knew if he was qualified to do the job or if he was a shoo-in because of his father.

"Sheriff Clint Wallace," he said, his expression hidden by a hat. "No need for you guys to get involved. Brambletown is my territory. I can handle it."

Sensing he didn't like his authority questioned, she gave a nonchalant shrug. "I get it. But our boss said you need our ERT."

She gestured to the crime team van that rolled up and parked. Four investigators climbed out and began to collect their kits from the van.

"While they get ready, tell us what you found."

His broad jaw snapped tight. "See for yourself. That dumb-ass memorial has brought in all the crazies."

Ellie didn't comment. His attitude probably spoke for half the people around here, who didn't like outsiders and wanted the past to stay buried. "Any idea who the body belongs to?"

"Not a clue. We haven't had any trouble around here in years." He patted his belt where his baton hung and then his holster. "Now this."

"You're talking about Ruth Higgins, the girl who disappeared from Brambletown fifteen years ago?" Ellie asked.

A frown pinched his face. "What do you know about that?"

Ellie's pulse jumped at the sinister look in his eyes. "Just what I've read about Brambletown's history."

Lieutenant Williams, head of the ERT, led the group toward her as Cord met them to discuss the search.

Anger flared on the sheriff's face and she remembered her boss's comment about his father. Was he annoyed they were invading his space or did he know more than he wanted to share?

FOUR

Ellie studied the sheriff, noting the defensive expression on his face. Judging from his looks, he might have been about Ruth Higgins' age when she went missing, which would put Ruth around thirty if she'd survived. Did the remains they'd found belong to her? "Did you know Ruth?"

He shifted. "Of course. We went to the same high school and her daddy owned half the town. Besides, her story was plastered all over the news."

"What do you think happened to her?" Ellie asked.

He shrugged. "Who knows? She probably ran away to escape this hellhole."

Yet he'd stayed. Interesting.

"I'd like to see the body and talk to the man who found it." She gestured toward Cord. "Ranger McClain works with me on a task force created by the governor to solve crimes along the trail. He's going to look around in the woods."

"Don't contaminate the scene," the sheriff snapped. "We may be country here, but I don't want the area compromised."

A muscle ticked in Cord's jaw. "I know the drill." Body rigid, Cord set off with the ERT into the woods to search.

Sheriff Wallace directed Ellie to the gangly man who'd found the body. He stood beneath a crooked pine tree watching as the ERT photographed the scene.

"I'm Detective Ellie Reeves," she said.

He shook her hand limply and she noticed a scar marring his arm and hand, a burn scar. Red pocked skin on the upper right side of his face near his hairline indicated another burn. Dirt stained his fingernails. Had he touched the crime scene? Or the body?

"Your name?"

"Emanuel Black," he said, his voice flat and toneless.

"The officer mentioned you're a wildlife photographer?"

"Yeah. Focus on nature, the woods and mountains. Remote areas always intrigue me."

"What were you doing here?" Ellie asked.

"Came to see the memorial," he said. "Got some pictures then decided to take a walk."

"You know the history of the land?"

"Sure do." He gave a nod. "I grew up around here but moved away after that fire." He indicated his scars.

Sympathy for him warred with her professional need to treat him as a suspect. "That must have been traumatic."

"Yeah, lost my family in the blaze." Rage seeped into his tone as he glanced at the memorial. "This memorial is a little too late and the people's families weren't even compensated."

He definitely sounded bitter. "I'm surprised you'd come back."

He stared across the land. "Curious to see if it was as bad as I remembered."

"So you were taking pictures?"

"Yeah. I wandered past the gravestones by the church and went to take pics of the destruction. I wanted to see for myself if what they say is true, that no wildlife or plants survived out here."

Judging as far as Ellie could see, it looked more harsh than she'd imagined. "Go on."

"Started getting dark so I headed back. It was really hard to see what was in front of me and I didn't have a torch. I lost my footing when I stumbled over a rock." His bony shoulders slumped slightly. "When I looked down, I thought I saw what looked like a bone protruding from the dirt." His voice remained monotonous but there was an odd flicker in his wideset eyes as if finding the body excited him. "I assumed it was an animal that died out here, but then I saw what looked like a human hand. That's when I called the sheriff's office."

"Did you touch the bones?"

He shook his head vehemently. "I raked away a little dirt and brush to see what was there. When I realized I was right, I stepped away."

Ellie regarded his thin pale face, his loose-hanging clothes and tattered shoes. "We're going to need your prints and to take casts of your boots."

He glanced at her and she noticed his eyes were two different colors, one a hazel and the other a disturbing dull gray. It was called heterochromia. Some superstitions claimed the condition was a sign of evil.

His thin lips twitched. "You think I had something to do with this body?"

"Just following protocol, Mr. Black. Your prints are required in order to rule you out as a person of interest."

His gaze settled on her, cold and serious, and sent a quiver up her spine. Sometimes the person who found the body was actually the killer. In order to throw off the police or out of morbid curiosity needing to relive the crime, a perpetrator often returned to the scene and inserted himself into the investigation.

She angled her head toward the sheriff. "Take the memory

card from his camera. Maybe he caught something on it that will give us a lead."

<h1 style="text-align:center">FIVE</h1>

Ellie turned back to Black. "Sir, we'll need you to stick around town for a while. We might have more questions later."

His eyes narrowed to slits, then a tiny smile twisted his lips, making the burn scars on his face redden. "Of course."

Ellie gestured to the sheriff. "See that ERT prints him and collect a DNA swab." She lowered her voice. "Also get a shoe print." If Cord found footprints in the woods, they could compare.

"You don't need to give me orders," Sheriff Wallace growled. "I know how to run an investigation."

Ellie barely resisted rolling her eyes. Gawd. Men and their egos.

Thankfully a car engine sounded, and she glanced back to see the medical examiner's car approaching. "That's our ME, Dr. Laney Whitefeather," Ellie said. "I'll show her to the scene."

The sheriff stayed with Black and motioned one of the crime techs to come over, while she hurried to meet Laney. Dried leaves crackled beneath her boots, the scent of death suffusing the air as the wind picked up. Above storm clouds gathered, heavy and gray, making it urgent they recover the body and process the scene before the clouds unleashed rain and washed away evidence.

Laney slid from the vehicle, tugging on her rain slicker, her reddish-brown hair secured at the nape of her neck with a leather tie. In one hand she held her crime kit while pulling latex gloves from the pocket of her jacket with the other.

They traded hellos, then Laney quickly glanced up at the memorial in front of the little church on the hill with a frown. The sight of those stones and their proximity to the toxic land wasn't lost on either of them. "What do we have here?"

Ellie indicated the photographer. "The man with the camera, Emanuel Black, found bones. I haven't seen them yet, but ERT is photographing the area and Cord and crime techs are searching the woods."

Behind Laney, a young man in his twenties appeared wearing jeans and an ERT cap, his name tag reading Tad Phelps. "This is my new forensic anthropology assistant," Laney said then introduced Ellie. "He's here to assist in recovering the remains."

Ellie gave a nod of understanding. The bones had to be carefully extracted to ensure evidence wasn't destroyed or compromised in the process. "Let's go see what we have."

Laney and Phelps followed Ellie across the barren ground to the crime scene tape where the sheriff's deputy stood guard.

The sheriff might seem ornery, but at least he'd followed protocol to preserve the scene.

Dusk had set in, although she'd heard this land was bathed in a perpetual gray and she believed it. Leaves and dead brush dotted the ground, but it was obvious grass hadn't grown here in a long time. The dirt seemed dry, the Georgia red clay hard and packed.

They paused by the deputy and surveyed the scene, the

sight of a finger poking through the soil confirming Black's story. Three more fingers were also evident.

A shudder rippled through Ellie. Looking at skeletal remains was never easy.

"I'll retrieve our equipment, lights and a tarp to spread the bones on as we recover them," Laney's assistant said.

Thunder rumbled and Laney glanced up at the darkening sky. "Set up a tent to cover the grave from the rain."

Her assistant nodded, then Laney adjusted her head lamp, knelt and surveyed the bones. "Definitely human although at this point we can't be sure there's an entire body here until we dig it up."

Ellie's mind was racing. An image of Ruth, a teenager with bright blue eyes and silky blond hair, taunted Ellie. They needed to find out how old the bones were. If they were from a teenager. Although it was possible Ruth's abductor had held her captive for years, which would make her older.

If so, why kill her now?

SIX

Cord carefully skirted the cordoned-off area, knowing preserving evidence was key in identifying the body in that grave and learning how the person ended up dead.

Unease knotted his neck. He also knew other people were buried here in these woods.

But that was his secret to keep. And something he never wanted Ellie to know about.

Fifteen years had fallen away the second he heard Ellie mention Brambletown. He'd been on his own during his teenage years, grateful to have escaped his abusive, evil foster father. He'd learned how to blend into the wilderness, to move around to avoid being detected, to go unnoticed. To live in the shadows of civilization.

To see and not to be seen.

He knew things about the Bramble family, too. Had witnessed Earl Bramble's abusive ways toward his daughter, Ida, and his niece Hetty.

Then that one night...

Thunder rumbled above, lightning streaking the dark sky. It had been cold and storming then, too. The screams had barely been discernible over the thunder, but he'd heard them. Then he'd gotten closer...

His heart raced as he dove deeper into the wooded area and although he told himself to stay away, his feet refused to obey. Several minutes later, he recognized the spot. A cluster of rocks that looked like a devil's claw sat next to an overhang. Sweat beaded on his neck as he moved toward it. Memories tore into him like a raging storm ripping him apart inside.

Had he done the right thing back then?

Something shiny glittered near the rock formation and he strode toward it. Seconds later, he stopped and raked his gloved hand across the dirt.

His breath stalled in his chest as he realized what it was. A silver pocket watch.

For a moment, he considered burying it so deep no one could find it.

Ellie's voice in his head and the training he'd had working with her was a reminder that even the smallest piece of evidence could lead to the truth. To a killer.

His phone buzzed. Ellie.

Slipping the watch into his pocket, he answered. "Yeah?"

"The ME's here and they're excavating the scene. We've confirmed there's a body in this grave. Dr. Whitefeather just examined the skull. Appears to be female. A teenage girl."

The words hung in the air. It could be Ruth Higgins.

Cord swallowed hard. His secrets tormented him. Sooner or later reckoning day would come. Then the dominos would fall. And the past would catch up to him and bite him in the butt.

He pressed his hand over his pocket where the busted watch felt like a heavy weight.

That reckoning day might be here sooner than later. Worse, when it did come, he would almost certainly lose Ellie.

SEVEN

A wind gust tore Ellie's ponytail from its holder, but she clawed through the tangled strands and secured it again. Laney and her team were working slowly and meticulously to remove the bones and spread them on the tarp to transfer them to the morgue for analysis.

Decomposition had progressed to the point where the hair, skin and soft tissue was decaying. The heat from the ground, insects and lack of embalming had sped up the process. The autopsy would take longer but her forensic team was topnotch and hopefully in a few days they'd have an ID and Ellie could notify the family.

Her stomach clenched. The fact that the poor girl had been dumped in the wilderness near toxic land without a proper burial broke her heart. Whoever had put her here had no regard for her at all. So far, they'd found no personal effects which might indicate an accidental death and that the person who buried her actually cared, like a family member or friend instead of a cold-hearted sadistic monster.

"Her clothes have mostly disintegrated," Dr. Whitefeather said. "And there's no indication she was wearing shoes. But there is something that resembles a scarf in the grave so that might be helpful."

Ellie's heart stuttered as she scanned the ground, which was covered in sticks and dried brush. Had the girl been killed in these woods? Had she been running from her attacker?

"We need to determine if this was the kill site. If she was held nearby, she might have been on foot trying to escape. But he caught her and killed her here."

"Will get you everything I can find," Laney agreed.

The local news van rolled up and news anchor Angelica Gomez climbed out. Impeccably dressed as always, her gold blouse accentuated her black suit and her curves. Today her long dark hair was held at the nape of her neck by a gold clip that matched her blouse.

"Detective Reeves," she said as she and her cameraman, Tom, approached. "Looks like you're busy again."

Ellie nodded. She and Angelica had butted heads at first but through working together over the last few cases they'd developed respect for one another and learned they were half-siblings. During her downtime lately, they'd even shared meals and long talks.

"No close-ups of the bones," Ellie said as Tom began to set up his camera. Ellie had given press conferences with them before, but she still hated appearing in front of the camera.

She also tried to protect the scene and viewers by omitting gory details and images, especially when family members hadn't yet been notified. And at the moment, she had no name to release.

"Are you ready to give a statement?" Angelica asked.

She wasn't, but the town would hear about the discovery of the remains soon anyway and hopefully if the victim lived in town, someone might come forward. Back at the station, she'd check missing persons reports as well but she needed more details on the victim's age, size, and possible race or ethnicity to narrow the search.

Laney would also compare DNA to Ruth's.

She stepped in front of the excavation site then swallowed hard as Angelica began.

"This is Angelica Gomez, coming live to you from Brambletown with this breaking story. Just this morning, we highlighted the memorial which was created in front of the Little White Church on the Hill at Green Gardens Cemetery where many people who lost their lives in the toxic coal mountain fire are buried. Locals, tourists, historians and families of those who died were present as the memorial was unveiled. Unfortunately, tonight we're here for a different reason." She gestured to Ellie. "Detective Ellie Reeves?"

Ellie cleared her throat. "Early this morning human skeletal remains were found buried in the woods neighboring the cemetery. At this point we don't have details or an ID on the body but once the medical examiner completes the autopsy, we'll know more." She inhaled a breath. "If anyone has information regarding this discovery or reported a missing person lately, please call the local police in Brambletown or the sheriff's office in Crooked Creek."

Out of the corner of her eye, she noticed Sheriff Wallace's frown as he spotted Cord walking back toward them.

The sense that the sheriff knew more than he was saying, that he looked worried, hit her. She'd have her deputy research him and see if he had any secrets hiding in his closet.

EIGHT

The Green Thumb, Brambletown

Twenty-nine-year-old Hetty Bramble pushed her choppy black hair out of her face then looked down at her scarred hands. Her short blunt fingernails were as broken and brittle as she felt inside. Some said she still had the goth look she'd sported as a teenager, but she didn't care. She was not interested in pleasing anyone but herself, much less in attracting a man.

She walked through the nursery she now owned with pride, sniffing the plants and rose bushes and knowing that soon the azaleas would bloom.

After the way she'd been raised, taken in by her uncle Earl when her parents died, then being forced to help him build the pine boxes for the indigents, pull weeds and clear spots for the graves, who would have thought she'd enjoy digging in the dirt, spreading fertilizer over the ground and tending to the flowers in the graveyard?

Uncle Earl had seen her as his work horse, and never let her forget that he'd given her a home instead of sending her to foster care. He hadn't been so selfless though. He'd wanted her parents' money, what little there was. And she'd never seen a dime of it.

Sometimes she wondered if she would have been better off in the foster system. But she did have her cousin Ida to lean on so that made it bearable.

As morbid as the graveyard was, it was all she'd ever known. It had been home to her, an amusement park for her and Ida as children. They'd played hide-and-seek behind the gravestones, and sometimes pretended the graveyard was the jail. They'd chase each other and any other kid who wanted to play, pretending to be the graveyard police, then make an arrest and throw the kid in a grave until they paid to get out. Of course, to lure the kids into playing, first they'd had to make up a story about what fun they'd have and not let on the exact nature or rules of the game.

At night they played ghosts in the graveyard. Sometimes the mischief got in them, and they robbed flowers and left them on people's doors to freak them out or played spooky music and sounds when visitors came just to scare them away.

Half of the Bramble people, including drunk Uncle Billy Bob and their mean as a snake cousin Luther, were buried there. Her mama and daddy and granny were spending eternity in a section called the Garden of Peace although there was nothing peaceful about the cemetery.

A sarcastic laugh escaped her as she walked out to her pick-up truck. Only time her mother had ever had any peace was the day they put her in the ground.

Although the sound of shovels hitting rock echoed in her ears constantly, she took comfort in gardening and tending the graves herself. Some folks thought she was daft because she talked to the dead and sang them old gospel hymns her mama used to sing to her at night.

With all the haunting memories between those rows of

headstones and vases of plastic flowers, she tried to atone for her sins, for the dark things she and Ida had done, and make the ground look cheerful for the families who visited.

She lifted the bin of fertilizer to store in the back of her pick-up and started to carry it outside, but the rain stopped her. Fertilizer smelled like death anyway, but when wet it knocked her head off.

A gray Lincoln pulled up beneath the awning and nosy Nell Nickerson waved to her as she got out, tugging her raincoat around her meticulously groomed outfit. That woman had hired hands do her bidding and had never touched dirt with those hands much less a scrub brush.

"Hetty, good Lord, did you hear the news?" Nell's eyes looked like giant saucers about to fly out of her head.

Hetty wrangled in her irritation and when Nell's wandering eyes fell to Hetty's arms, she yanked her long sleeves down to cover old bruises.

She didn't want to play guess what with this gossip monger, but Nell wouldn't quit until she spilled whatever seed of a rumor had her body preening with excitement. "No, what now?" Probably one of the bunco ladies' teenagers wore a whore dress to prom. Or some boy knocked up a girl or got busted for weed or meth. Meth labs were popping up in every corner of the mountains like weeds in a flower garden.

Sheriff Wallace didn't seem too keen on shutting the labs down and turned a blind eye. Hetty always wondered if he had a stake in them himself.

"I heard they found a body up yonder at Green Gardens Cemetery," Nell chirped. "Might be that girl Ruth."

Hetty went bone still, her breath trapped in her chest.

A body found at the graveyard where all the bad things happened? Where her uncle had worked? Where she spent her days now?

Was Nell goading her or was that a fact?

Was it Ruth Higgins, the girl Uncle Earl was accused of killing?

NINE

Atlanta, Georgia

A cold chill washed over Tilly Higgins as the reporter's words echoed in her head.

An unidentified body has been found here in Brambletown this evening. Police are at the scene and will reveal more information as it becomes available.

Her breathing quickened as she started the engine of her trusted Red Escape, left Atlanta and headed into the mountains. She'd run away from Brambletown years ago to escape the stigma and suspicion surrounding her family.

After her sister, Ruth, disappeared, both her brother and father had been treated like suspects.

Although most people believed Earl Bramble had killed Ruth.

Everyone in town had their version of an Earl Bramble story, all sordid and ugly.

As mayor, her father had had several run-ins with him. During one of his drunken benders, Earl had crashed his car into the Soap and Suds car wash and her father banned him from using it again. Earl had retaliated and trashed her father's office the next day, earning him a few days in a cell.

Memories of the way her family had been torn apart by rumors and doubt in the weeks following Ruth's disappearance made her breathing quicken.

When Tilly left town after high school, she'd vowed never to return to that godawful place. But here she was on her way with a fist-sized knot in her stomach, her emotions in a tailspin and perspiration soaking her wavy auburn hair. She lifted the tangled strands and fanned herself with one hand while gripping the steering wheel with the other.

Determination kicked in. Revisiting her hometown would serve two purposes, she reminded herself. Ruth's case had gone cold over a decade ago. But if this body was Ruth's, she might finally get answers about her disappearance.

She could also cover the story of the memorial recently erected and add that credit to her resume.

Although she expected folks back home would think she was strange because of the subject matter she chose to write about.

Travel writing. But not exotic beaches, glamorous cities or desirable foreign locales. She focused on murder tourism, an oddly popular interest that had gained her followers and landed her a regular column for the *AJC*'s online paper.

Considering the nasty emails she'd received from her estranged father, Edward, who accused her of keeping their painful past alive, he would agree about her job being morbid.

Her mother, Gina... she released her venom by ignoring Tilly and her brother, Hayden, all together. They'd been invisible in the Higgins home.

As mayor, Edward had been the pillar of Brambletown before his older daughter, Ruth, went missing. Respected. Intelligent. Educated in a world where blue-collar workers and miners dominated. Where the Bramble moonshine kept the men happy and college was not an expectation for the girls. A factory worker or secretarial job would suffice, and a doublewide was supposed to be a girl's dream come true.

Her parents were different though. Educated and hard-working.

Her mother created a social scene with the garden club, but she thought she was better than the other ladies because she had a two-story Georgian house on acreage and they lived in modest brick ranches with pint-sized yards. Her husband was the mayor while theirs managed the grocery store, the hardware business, construction and other jobs deeming them a class below the Higginses.

The hierarchy dropped another notch with the Brambles. Their old clapboard house by the cemetery, thrift store clothes, run-ins with the law, and dirt-coated hands landed them in the white trash category.

All through high school, Tilly had wanted to leave the town. She was a geek, a book nerd. She didn't belong in Brambletown. Didn't fit.

Beautiful blond Ruth with the striking blue eyes, a year older than her, had excelled in school. As the pet of the family, their parents were planning her future at any cost.

At night, she and Ruth had shared dreams of what their lives would look like once they graduated. Ruth was set to be valedictorian without even studying, which had earned her the nickname *Brains* and not in a flattering way. Although she made up for it with her notorious flirting and friendships with the cheerleaders.

When the football quarterback Clint Wallace asked her out, she'd been ecstatic and suddenly became a member of the popular crowd. Except it also made her the enemy of some of her female classmates, especially Hetty and Ida Bramble. Apparently Ida had a crush on Clint or was it Hetty? Tilly couldn't remember and didn't care.

A knock-down-drag-out fight between the three at the Dairy Queen had caused an uproar. Her father had defended Ruth, and Hetty and Ida were suspended for three days, which only created a bigger rift between Ruth and the Bramble girls. After that, it was one nasty prank after another.

Then perfect Ruth started to rebel. Staying out late. Sneaking out to meet boys. Letting her schoolwork go. Their parents blamed it on the mean girls at school. Wanted her to get away from the clique and focus on her education.

But on a freezing, snowy and stormy night, after a tense dinner on New Year's Eve, Ruth disappeared.

Her family imploded. Her father and brother were both questioned. The suspicions and gossip destroyed them.

They still had no answers about what happened to her.

Yet here she was, pushing sixty miles, winding around the switchbacks that wove through the foothills of the Appalachian Trail, an endless sea of trees and trouble back to the place where it all went wrong. Rain fell in a near blinding haze, her tires slipping on wet asphalt as she hugged the curves. Her windshield wipers screeched back and forth in tune to her raging heart, and a war raged in her head. Nerves gathered along her spine and she slowed. Maybe she should head back to Atlanta where she was safe.

No, a body had been found at that creepy graveyard and she had to know if it was Ruth.

Fifteen years of not knowing, wondering, fearing and imagining what her sister might have suffered at the brutal hands of whoever had taken her, had nearly stolen Tilly's sanity.

Fifteen years of living under the suspicion that her own father or brother might have been responsible.

If Ruth was actually alive, where had she been? Had she run away with some secret lover? Or had someone abducted her?

And if she was dead, as Tilly feared, who killed her?

Memories tugged at her, clawing at her with truths and secrets that she'd somehow lost in the cluttered attic of her mind. The family arguing over dinner that night. *Her* birthday dinner.

Ruth shoving her slice of cake at her mother and telling her it tasted like mud. Her father finally losing it with her and ordering Ruth to her room. Hayden insisting he was going out and his father shouting at him.

Tilly blindly sitting in silence, angry and hurt with all of them for ruining the only day of the year she received any attention.

The disappointment and pain pulled at her like she was a worn-out rubber band that wouldn't break.

But she was breaking. Had been for months now.

The nightmares dogged her like demons. Could she really face them?

Long ago, her therapist had suggested that making peace with her past might help her heal. Give her closure. That perhaps the mystery of her sister's disappearance was the reason she was obsessed with murder cases and unsolved crimes in other small towns.

If she learned the truth about what happened to Ruth, maybe she could glue her fractured family back together.

Find forgiveness for herself.

She passed the Welcome to Brambletown sign swaying in the wind with a grimace. A coffee shop had been built on the corner and she swung into the parking spot, tugged her raincoat on and ran to the entrance. A bell tinkled over the door and as she stepped inside, curious eyes turned her way. They probably weren't accustomed to strangers around here—or did someone recognize her?

A quick scan of the room and she instantly saw Nosy Nell Nickerson. Her daughter Trina had been prom queen, and Nell bragged about Trina's acceptance into an Ivy League school, which only fueled Trina's justification for her condescending attitude toward her female classmates.

Hushed whispers followed Tilly as she made her way to the coffee bar to order and she winced when she heard someone say, "That's that Higgins girl, ain't it?"

"She ain't been back in years."

"Bet she heard about that body they found."

"Wonder if it's her sister."

Tilly's chest tightened, but she held her head high. She was not the same shy teenager she'd been when she lived here.

No, she was an adult, a survivor, a success in her field.

And she was going to fix the broken side of herself by getting answers about her sister.

The truth lay somewhere in the foothills of these mountains.

And she would dig it up with her bare hands if she had to.

TEN

Ida Bramble Jones stared at the mushy leftovers on the stove in disgust. Normally she didn't mind cooking but today she'd had a bad headache that was quickly morphing into a migraine.

The scent of burned beans wafted to her and she grabbed the pot and dumped them in the trash.

She hated her life.

After the scandal over Ruth Higgins' disappearance when her father was accused of killing Ruth, Ida thought the gossip and stares would never die down. At times she'd wanted to disappear herself and run from Brambletown where every Bramble man she'd ever known was a loser. No wonder the town treated them like trash. They were no more than poor dumb hillbillies with a reputation for drinking, fighting, cussing and causing trouble. Accusations that Earl had killed Ruth had flown from day one.

They'd even locked him up for a few days. But lack of evidence and the fact that Ruth's body had never been found forced them to release him. Two days later, her daddy had gone missing, which made him look as guilty as sin. As if Earl Bramble had killed Ruth and run off to escape incarceration.

She breathed out a sigh just like the day she had when he'd left. Having him out of their lives had been a relief for her and her cousin Hetty.

Hetty had sometimes helped their father in the graveyard when they were little. Now she owned her own business, a nursery and gardening center named The Green Thumb. Barely having graduated high school, Ida had been desperate to get out of her house and away from the cemetery. Although for some reason she hadn't been able to leave town. The graveyard where they'd grown up was all she and Hetty had ever known.

Worse, Ida had stars in her eyes that Joe Jones, a semi-fit guy at the time who worked for their father doing maintenance on the cemetery grounds, would give her a better life. Ha.

He'd crawled in her pants and knocked her up. They'd had to get married.

But he turned out to be a sexist, a slob and a hypochondriac, a mama's boy who wanted her to practically wipe his fat ass.

At least he had a job. That was more than most Bramble men. Although he'd worked for Earl at the graveyard in high school, afterward he'd landed a job driving a delivery truck for a national chain of discount stores. Now he was gone a lot of the time so she and her fifteen-year-old daughter, Kat, had the place to themselves, and on those nights she could sleep without his pig-like snoring rattling the window panes.

She scraped the burned ends of meatloaf Joe had left on his plate into the trash, then lowered her Melmac dishes into the hot soapy dishwater to soak. Wiping her hands on the kitchen towel, she rubbed at her throbbing leg. When the rain came, it hurt like a mother, a reminder of the accident that had mangled her leg to the point that she had a bad limp now and had to prop it up on a pillow at night to ease the pain.

Rain hammered the tin roof of her doublewide, mingling with the rumble of her husband's notorious snoring that sounded like the roar of a tornado. His old hound dog whined at the door to get in the bedroom, and she called Kat's name. Kat was parked in front of the TV glued to some teen show she probably shouldn't be watching. But Ida gave all her fighting energy to Joe and lacked the bandwidth to argue with her daughter so she gave in. "Kat, put Rufus in the room with Daddy."

Kat huffed and rolled her pale green eyes but dragged herself over to the door, opened it, ushered him inside then made her way back to the TV.

Ida's phone buzzed, and she checked the number, praying it wasn't one of the debt collectors or the power company warning that they were about to turn her power off because she was two months late paying. Joe kept swearing he'd get to it when he got his check, only she had no idea when that would happen.

Not a bill collector. Hetty.

Old familiar anxiety rose like fiery ants in her gut. She and Hetty rarely talked, the distance between them filled with a mountain of secrets, lies and blame.

If Hetty was calling, she had a reason.

The phone trilled a third time. Taking a deep breath, she answered with a mumbled hey.

"It's Hetty."

"I know. What do you want?"

"Have you seen the news?"

Ida glanced at the TV. When the hell did she have time to watch television? "No. Why?"

"They found a body near the graveyard. Police and reporters are there now."

Ida sank into the kitchen chair and wiped at the sweat beading on her forehead with a dishtowel as she stared out at the night sky. For years, she'd been terrified this day might come.

That the nightmare from her teenage years would start all over again. And here it was about to blow up her life again.

ELEVEN

Green Gardens Cemetery

From the shadows of the rocks and trees, he watched the police scour No Man's Land for clues he might have left behind. But they would find nothing. He had been careful. Besides, the recent rain would have muddied the scene and washed away any signs he was there.

He aimed his binoculars toward the medical examiner and her coworker in the white lab coat. They were using head lamps and equipment to excavate the girl's bones. Adrenaline surged through him. He hadn't meant for her to be found so soon but it would raise the stakes if the town was on edge. The idea of wandering through the streets with the locals undetected while he watched the fear grow on their faces, especially the young girls and their mothers, exhilarated him.

A smile curved his mouth at the sight of that detective's frown. Detective Ellie Reeves. He'd seen her on the news before. She was known for tracking down killers but even she wouldn't pin this on him. After all, he had gotten away with murder before.

More than once. And he would do it again and again and laugh at her as she failed.

He turned in a wide arc, his pulse racing as he stared into the woods. That coal mountain fire had made the graveyard here famous. But little did anyone know that the surrounding area was a graveyard of his own making.

That more bones dotted the parched land. And more would go in the ground to keep those company.

A limb crackled and footsteps echoed in the distance. He went stone still and held his breath as he listened. Brush rustled and he aimed his binoculars to the right. A shaggy-haired man in a ranger's shirt pointed a flashlight his way.

He hunched behind a big boulder and waited until the guy passed, then decided to get the hell out of here. He could always come back and visit the graves another time.

He smiled at the thought.

TWELVE

By the time Ellie and Cord left, exhaustion tugged at Ellie's body. She'd grown complacent the last few months and reveled into sinking into bed with Cord, making love and falling asleep in his arms.

Tonight, he seemed closed off though. Distant.

Although questions about the case still plagued her. Who was the girl in the grave? How long had she been there?

Hopefully the ME would answer that tomorrow.

"You said you knew that area," she said, fishing for information. "Care to elaborate?"

Cord's jaw tightened and he glanced out the window at the falling rain which was casting more shadows on an already glum night.

"No," he said bluntly. "Everyone who grew up in this area knows about Brambletown, its close proximity to the coal fire and the story about Ruth Higgins' disappearance."

"True," Ellie said. Having been close to Ruth's age at the time of her disappearance, Ellie had heard about the case, too, and had been interested in what happened to the girl. Her parents had also been freaked out and at the time kept her on a tight leash, warning her about going out alone and not speaking to strangers.

But she'd been so busy with her own teenage problems, fighting for her independence and annoyed at her adopted mother Vera's overprotectiveness, that she'd stopped asking about Ruth.

Now she understood their reasons for being nervous, but not back then.

Little had she known that Vera had given her biological son up for adoption and that he'd turned into a psychopath who wanted revenge against Vera. Revenge by killing Ellie.

Pain at the memory gnawed at her, but she pushed her emotions aside. That time in her life was over. Now she had to focus on finding answers for another family and a young girl who'd been killed by an unknown predator.

The winter wind beat at the car, the rain turning to sleet and slowing her down as she maneuvered the curvy mountain road.

"I know you have things you don't want to talk about," she said softly as she drove through town. "But you can tell me anything, Cord." She slid her hand over his and felt him tense.

"Cord?"

His jaw tightened. "I'm beat tonight, El. Just drop me at the station and I'll clean up at my cabin when I get home and we can regroup tomorrow."

Disappointment caught in her throat. "Cord?"

His breath heaved out and he squeezed her hand as she pulled up beside his truck.

"Are you sure you don't want to come to my house?" Dammit, she hated the plea in her voice.

His gaze met hers for a moment, longing, worry and indecision in his eyes. Then he cupped her face between his hands, kissed her thoroughly and seemed to change his mind about coming over. "I'll meet you there."

Ellie's heart hammered. She wouldn't push him to talk tonight though. She just wanted his arms around her.

But one day she hoped he'd open up to her. That he'd trust her enough to confide his secrets.

THIRTEEN

Tension knotted every cell in Tilly Higgins' body as she crossed the railway tracks that took her onto the road leading to her childhood home. Whereas the land looked desolate and dry at the cemetery, in fall and spring foliage was abundant and colorful in the community where she'd grown up.

The kids at high school had joked about which side of the tracks you lived on. The difference was obvious; the middle class thrived, their houses double-storied Colonials and timeless ranches that were well kept, the properties boasting lush green grass and flowers in the spring. Of course, now in the heart of winter, leaves had fallen and the bare limbs swayed in the wind.

Night had descended and traffic was minimal as she veered up the two-lane road that led through a tree-lined street. Her family's house still sat at the end on two acres with a private circular drive and gated property. Her father had once suggested selling it, but her mother insisted on keeping the house in case Ruth returned home. Her reasoning: How would Ruth reach them if they were gone and the house belonged to someone else? She'd even insisted on keeping the landline with the same number in case Ruth called.

Painful memories flooded Tilly as she parked in the drive. The house looked empty and quiet, even sadder than it had when she'd left. For a moment, she considered driving to a hotel, but she might find something inside to help unravel the mystery, so she parked.

She'd been young and traumatized by Ruth's disappearance, her parents' anguish and grief, the suspicions surrounding them, and then the horrible rift between her brother and her father. It had started long before her birthday dinner though. Hayden had argued with their father over everything. By fourteen, he'd started sneaking beer and hanging out with the wrong crowd. His grades had dropped and when their father suggested college to him, Hayden had shouted he wasn't going.

Ruth seemed to enjoy watching Hayden get into trouble and egged him on. The night she disappeared he'd stormed out after the dinner and hadn't come home till late. The next morning their father grilled him over where he'd been, but Hayden just shrugged and said he was with his friends. But he had that sneaky look in his eyes that Tilly noticed when he was lying. His story kept changing, too.

When she'd confronted him, he'd exploded, yelled at her to leave him alone and put his fist through the door.

And her father... his eyes were bloodshot, his temper more on edge than she'd ever seen.

After that, she'd steered clear of her brother and her parents. All that mattered to her parents was Ruth anyway.

They hadn't once called or visited when she was in college.

Get off your pity pot, girl. Go inside and face the music.

She stared at the window to Ruth's bedroom, and for a second thought she saw the shadow of her sister's heart-shaped face looking at her. Her eyes that had once been bright and blue now looked dull and seemed to be begging for peace.

Inhaling a deep breath, Tilly tugged her jacket hood over her head, grabbed her purse, computer bag and suitcase and hurried to the front door. She inserted her key in the lock and jiggled it, grateful it hadn't been changed. Again, in case Ruth came home.

The door squeaked open, a cold emptiness enveloping her. She flipped on the foyer light and scanned the entryway into the living room and kitchen. Everything was just as she remembered. A shiver ripped though her, and her chest squeezed.

The family portrait still hung on the wall in the hall. Ruth's smiling face stared back. Yet she also saw the mischief in her sister's eyes. Her parents thought Ruth was a perfect angel. Until she'd rebelled herself. Even then they'd defended her.

But Ruth had another side. Her parents conveniently glossed over that and wouldn't tolerate a disparaging word against their oldest daughter.

A hollow loneliness permeated the air as Tilly closed the front door and locked it. Her footsteps echoed in the silence as she rushed to adjust the thermostat. A second later, the furnace rumbled to life although it would take hours to heat the house to a comfortable temperature.

Shoulders hunched from the cold, she took a quick sweep of the downstairs. Dust motes fluttered in the frigid air and a musty odor served as a reminder that the house had been closed-up and uninhabited for a while. Although she suspected her father occasionally came back to check on the house, probably looking for signs Ruth had been back.

Returning to the foyer, she hauled her luggage up the stairs.

Tilly's bedroom door stood ajar, and she rolled her bag inside. Nothing had been touched in here. Dust coated her wooden dresser, and her Jenny Lind bed was still covered in the same purple comforter she'd chosen when she was ten.

Notepads and spiral notebooks were stacked on her desk where she'd done her homework and dabbled in writing. At one point her English lit teacher asked them to keep a shadow journal and she'd enjoyed recording her thoughts and the observations of classmates.

Maybe there was something in there that might offer a lead. Someone, maybe one of the other students, had to have known something.

The Bramble sisters definitely had a grudge against Ruth and vice versa. Hetty was quiet and withdrawn and looked like a vampire with her choppy short black hair and pale skin. Her clothes were often dirty and stank of fertilizer and potting soil, her fingernails permanently stained and black.

Tilly felt sorry for her and Ida. Not only did Ida have a pronounced limp and a gap between her two front teeth, but she struggled in school and couldn't outrun the gossip about her father's drunken escapades.

Ruth nicknamed Hetty and Ida the Graveyard Girls and the name stuck.

Trembling at the memory of the knock-down-drag-out fight between the Bramble girls and Ruth at the DQ, she walked to Ruth's room. A hollow emptiness swelled inside. Ruth's queen bed was neatly made with a satin white comforter and her big stuffed teddy bear lay against the pillow. One of her teenage boy band posters hung on the wall then her gaze was drawn to a photograph of Clint and Ruth, then one of Ruth in her cheerleading outfit. On a small white board above the desk, her parents had listed their cell phone numbers. No dust motes in this room. In fact, it looked pristine.

The police had turned it inside out searching for clues as to what happened to Ruth, but there were no signs of that now.

She knew her parents had moved further north of Brambletown to a nice area called Finch Gardens but had never visited them. Did they pay someone to come in and clean Ruth's room regularly?

She closed her eyes to stem the tears threatening, and when

she opened them, in her mind she could still see her teenage sister plopped on the bed on her phone, twirling the end of her cornsilk-blond hair around one finger as she giggled and flirted with Clint Wallace before she'd disappeared.

Where are you, Ruth? What happened that night?

The image faded and the news report taunted her. *Are you the girl the police found in the graveyard?*

FOURTEEN

DAY TWO

Crooked Creek

Cord didn't deserve Ellie.

But damn if he wouldn't cut his own arm off to save her if she needed him to.

He rolled over in the dark and stared at her, memorizing every feature of her beautiful face so he wouldn't forget her if—or when—he lost her.

And he would lose her. He had no doubt about that.

The past would eventually catch up to him. Either that or the guilt for keeping secrets from her.

But lying in the dark with her warm soft body spooned against him, he couldn't help but savor the moment. Though fear tied his stomach in knots.

This new case... he knew more than he'd said. For a minute, when he'd seen that body and where it had been found, he hadn't been able to breathe. He'd been swept back to the horrific life he'd led. To his mistakes. To his reckless self when he'd dared death to claim him.

He'd thought Ellie might have seen that fear, that he was

hiding something. Her all-knowing eyes detected things about cases that others didn't see.

Saw things about him that no one else had ever been privy to.

She'd seen good in him. Good, for fuck's sake.

Looking into her strong face and hearing her tell him she cared about him made him *want* to be *good.*

Made him want to keep her here tucked in his arms, safe from the world and the pain he feared he'd cause her.

She turned and her long lashes fluttered as she opened her eyes and looked up at him. "Morning," she whispered.

Emotions clogged his dry throat, but he forced out a smile. "Morning."

She licked her lips and traced a finger along his jaw, rousing his body with a need so fierce that his blood felt hot.

But her cell phone burst to life, the shrill ringtone of her boss piercing the silence.

Her lips turned down into a frown as she answered.

Cord felt a sudden loss as she slid from bed, butt naked, a glorious sight.

Then she disappeared into the bathroom, and he heard the shower kick on. A second later, she popped her head around the corner. "We have to go. We can save time if you join me."

A seed of flirtatious hope softened her voice, and he wanted to comply. To watch the water cascade over her sensuous body.

But he reached for his shirt and jeans. "I'll meet you at the station."

Disappointment darkened her expression, but he shrugged on his shirt as he considered how much worse that disappointment would be if she saw the ugly truth about him.

She watched him a minute and he knew she was hoping he'd change his mind, but she'd promised not to push him. And he wasn't ready to give up this dream, to destroy her illusion of him. Not yet.

Maybe tomorrow he'd get up his courage and confess his sins.

Maybe.

But not today. Today, he wanted to hold onto her for dear life and never let her go.

FIFTEEN

Ellie met Cord, her boss and deputies Shondra Eastwood and Heath Landrum in the conference room at eight a.m. While they helped themselves to coffee and pastries Landrum had picked up from the Corner Café, she tacked pictures of Green Gardens Cemetery on the whiteboard then added shots of the area locals called No Man's Land where their victim's body had been discovered.

"Morning, everyone. Our quiet reprieve has ended. Yesterday, female skeletal remains were found by a travel photographer named Emanuel Black who claimed he grew up in the area and was in Brambletown to see the memorial honoring victims of the coal mountain fire. According to him, his family died in the fire and he sustained burns himself. I asked him not to leave town in case we needed to speak to him again."

"Is he a person of interest?" Deputy Eastwood asked.

Ellie gave a small shrug. "At this point, it's difficult to say. But it's possible he committed the crime then returned to watch us investigate or distract us." She glanced at Landrum. "Deputy Landrum, see what you can dig up on him and his past."

"On it," the deputy said, making a note on his pad.

"Was there anything helpful on the memory card of his camera?" Ellie asked.

"Not really," Deputy Landrum said. "He did photograph the area where he found the remains, but didn't catch anyone running or lurking around in the shots."

A dead end, Ellie thought.

"Dr. Whitefeather and her forensic anthropologist assistant should be working on the autopsy today, so we'll know more then. She did speculate that the girl was a teenager but not how long the remains had been there so hopefully she can narrow that down and get us an ID."

Captain Hale addressed the room. "Everyone know the history of Brambletown?"

Deputy Eastwood nodded and spoke up, "Some folks are lobbying for the government to finally clean up the toxins. The killer may have left the body on that land to draw attention to the cause or speed up decomp and throw us off with the timeline."

The captain frowned and popped a mint in his mouth. "The fire and toxins aren't the only problem in Brambletown."

"I didn't grow up around here. Fill me in," Deputy Landrum said.

Ellie responded. "Fifteen years ago, a teenager girl named Ruth Higgins, the mayor's daughter, disappeared from Brambletown. Police investigated and searched but her body was never recovered. They speculated she was murdered but found no proof."

"There's miles and miles of untamed land where her body could have been dumped or buried," Cord said. "Or she could have simply run away."

"True, and the police considered every theory, but eventually the case went cold."

Shondra rolled a pen between her fingers. "Do you think our body is the Higgins girl?"

"I don't know," Ellie said honestly. "Again, we're waiting on an ID. It's possible it's Ruth or also possible it's someone else. It has been a decade and a half since Ruth Higgins disappeared. If the cases are related, it might suggest a repeat offender. If so, where has he been? Serial predators usually don't wait that long in between kills." She took a sip of her coffee then set it down. "This may be an isolated event so let's start with identifying the girl, then locating her family and friends. They may know something about how she wound up dead in the mountains."

She angled her head toward Deputy Eastwood. "Shondra, while Landrum looks into Emanuel Black, pull all the files on the investigation into the Higgins girl. In town, we may come across some of those questioned in that investigation and if so, I want to know background information in advance."

"Copy that," Shondra said.

"So far no missing persons reports have come in from Brambletown so if the body isn't Ruth, the girl may not be a local," Captain Hale said.

"I'll search missing persons reports across the state," Ellie said. "Shondra, once I look at those and you study the files on the Higgins' investigation, let's head to Brambletown and talk to the locals. Ranger McClain, arrange a search team, expand the search grid and look for anything in those woods that seems suspicious. A button off a shirt, cigarette butt, soda can, something that could have belonged to the killer."

"ERT combed the area," he said gruffly.

She narrowed her eyes. "I know, but they might have missed something. Even the smallest clue could help us figure out what happened in those woods."

SIXTEEN

Brambletown

Tilly couldn't survive without her coffee. The diner she'd stopped at when she'd first driven into town didn't serve a vanilla latte with oat milk, but black would do. Hell, any coffee would do. As long as it was caffeinated.

Decaf was for the wusses. Or for those who'd slept eight hours, not those like her who spent half the night tossing and turning and tearing up the sheets with nightmares and images of her dead sister's face.

She threw on sweats, yanked her layered, wavy hair into a low knot at the base of her neck, grabbed her keys and hurried from her room. She passed Ruth's where she'd spent half the night combing through the high school annual and the love letters Clint Wallace had sent Ruth—gawd, those had been sickening. She couldn't believe her father hadn't burned them and tossed the ashes over a cliff. He had been so protective of Ruth. Almost possessive as if she was some prize to sit on a shelf and show off.

Ruth would have been mortified if she'd known the police had seen the letters, especially since Clint was the sheriff's son.

When questioned, their mother had pointed out their father's obsession with Ruth which had triggered suspicion toward him. Had he been too attentive toward Ruth? Had he been...

Tilly squashed the vile thoughts. She'd barely survived the accusations against her father and brother, and the rumors had definitely created a chasm between her parents. But according to her research, her parents were still together in Finch Gardens.

Back then, she'd cut them slack over their arguments though. Even a stable happy couple would have trouble overcoming the stigma of those allegations.

At least the rain had died down during the night, but a winter chill hovered in the air. Or maybe it never left this part of the mountain, not with all the death and decay the area had seen.

Her car engine chugged to life, and five minutes later, she headed toward town. With no fast-food chains in these parts except for the DQ, she found the small diner on the edge of Brambletown, a place called Daisy's Diner that had been there at least twenty-five years, and ducked inside. The place had been given a facelift though, and at odds with the age and deterioration of other businesses, looked bright and cheery. During her high school years, the drab diner was struggling. Today it was hopping with locals and tourists, probably drawn to the memorial. Coffee cups and plates clanked and rattled as people enjoyed stacks of pancakes, sausages and plump homemade biscuits with southern ham and red-eyed gravy.

Her mouth watered but her stomach protested. Coffee was about all she could stomach this morning. Pleased to see lattes on the menu, she ordered one along with a bagel then dropped some cash on the bar. Cradling the to-go cup in one hand, she snagged the bagel then headed out the door, hoping no one recognized her. She wasn't ready for the locals' scrutiny—not yet.

But the time would come when she would have to face them.

For now, she intended to lie low, do some poking around and exploring before she opened Pandora's box. No doubt worms would slither out. Or snakes, rattlers that might strike when she lowered her guard.

With all the hype about the discovery of that body, she drove toward the graveyard. Morning shadows from the bare trees hovered over her as if she was plunging into an unknown abyss.

Last night, police would have combed the area. This morning, a police presence already existed and crime scene tape flapped in the wind.

Her stomach twisted as Ruth's face flashed behind her eyes. Had they identified the body from yesterday?

She turned into the drive for Green Gardens Cemetery and spotted the memorial. She half expected Hetty and Ida Bramble to be wandering through the rows of graves.

This morning though she spotted a lone older woman carrying a quilt and a picnic basket toward a grave that overlooked the small pond and fountain.

Her breath stalled. It was Ms. Maeve, her very own kindergarten teacher. A sweet funny woman who'd first piqued Tilly's interest in storytelling. At the fall festival, she'd told ghost stories, regaled folklore and relayed stories of the town's history.

Tilly slid from her car and walked to the edge of the graveyard, then stood in the shadows and silently watched, not wanting to disturb her.

Ms. Maeve's long gray hair blew gently in the wind around a face gaunt with age, sorrow and loneliness. She had no family left, no one to come with her, no one to sit and hold her hand or wipe the tears from her eyes as she wept.

Tilly edged closer, then stepped behind a tree, unable to drag herself away.

Ms. Maeve gently spread plastic on the ground by her husband's grave, then covered the plastic with a homemade quilt featuring a wedding ring design. Next, she opened her picnic basket and pulled out a coffee and a muffin. Her bones creaked as she lowered herself onto the quilt, one gnarled hand cradling her coffee cup. She took a slow sip, then swirled it in her mug and looked inside as if it held some relief to her despair.

Eyes brimming with grief and love, she placed one hand on the grave marker. "Hey, honey, happy fiftieth. I love you. Just as we promised, you and me and me and you and that's the way it'll always be."

Her voice quivered as she spoke, and she traced her fingers over her husband's name, which was etched above a carving of two hands intertwined.

Tears filled Tilly's eyes.

Her sister's disappearance had ripped her family apart. Had torn her in two. Had caused her to distrust everyone. To shield her heart.

But Ms. Maeve had the deepest kind of love for her husband.

Tilly's heart squeezed and a longing stirred deep inside her. Would she ever experience a love like that?

SEVENTEEN

Hetty Bramble despised winter and the decay it caused to an already half-dead area.

It was difficult enough to keep the parched land alive in the summer and spring and fall but cold temperatures and recent rains destroyed all her hard work. Still, she felt called to do her best to spruce up the graveyard for the families who came to mourn their lost loved ones.

She spotted Ms. Maeve's little sedan then saw her in the distance at her husband's grave. The sweet lady was one of them. She came every weekend to sit with her deceased husband and toast the years they'd shared together. Usually Sunday mornings with her coffee. And Friday nights with her Chardonnay.

Hetty had never come close to marriage herself. She'd measured every man she met against Earl Bramble who'd been mean and as prickly as a porcupine. Long ago, she'd decided she didn't need a man in her life. Ever.

Especially after Ruth Higgins had stolen Clint Wallace

from her. She thought Ida secretly wanted him, too. After all, all the girls did.

He never was yours or Ida's, Hetty, she reminded herself. Ruth was pretty and vibrant and had nice clothes whereas Hetty was homely, wore hand-me-downs and had no chance of getting out of Brambletown. Ruth was set on a path to UGA with a scholarship, not that she'd needed it because her rich daddy, the mayor, would have forked over tuition, room and board, an expensive wardrobe and a fancy new car. But Hetty's future had been tied to the graveyard with no way out.

Hetty patted the dash of her jalopy of a pick-up truck. It had taken her scrimping and saving to buy when she was seventeen, but a tiny smile tugged at her lips. She was damn proud of it because she'd bought it all on her own.

Once Ruth disappeared, she'd thought Clint might finally notice her, but he'd been so smitten with Ruth he had a stick up his butt. He'd also been questioned about her disappearance but his daddy made certain any suspicion toward him was swept under the rug.

Tugging her ski cap and work gloves on, she climbed from the driver's side, walked around to the truck bed and hauled a bag of fertilizer from the floor. Although the ground was still damp from last night's rain, she wanted to get this fertilizer spread before the ground became too hard to absorb the nutrients.

It was too early for flowers, but it would help revive what little grass there was, and she tried to keep the common area where the angel statue stood decent. Once Ms. Maeve left, she'd spread some across her husband's grave in hopes for some green to appear in spring.

As she walked toward the angel statue, she noticed a red Ford Escape parked down the hill. She didn't recognize it, and she knew what everyone in town drove. Curious, she squinted to see who it belonged to.

A familiar-looking woman in sweats emerged from behind a tree a few graves over from Ms. Maeve.

Although it had been years since she'd seen her, she instantly recognized her.

Tilly Higgins, Ruth's sister.

A curse word spewed from her mouth, and she dropped the opened bag of fertilizer. A gust of wind picked up, swirling it in all directions. A nervous laugh rumbled from her as she wiped it from her face and spit it from her mouth.

Yep. Doomsday was here. Tilly Higgins was back in town. And the shit was already hitting the fan.

EIGHTEEN

Crooked Creek Police Station

While Cord left to meet his coworker Milo and conduct the search of the land by the cemetery as Ellie requested, she settled in her office, hoping Laney worked quickly and established an ID on the body soon. Without it, her hands were tied. Once she had it, she would know who to contact, look for her family and question friends and possibly arrange a tip line for information.

She booted up her computer, then plugged in what little information she had at this point—female between the age of thirteen and sixteen. Next, she ran a search for missing persons reports fitting that description. At least a dozen names popped up across the United States, so she narrowed her search to Georgia which cut the list to three names.

She clicked on the first one—fourteen-year-old Ansley Pollock from Augusta, Georgia. Her mother reported her missing after she'd spent the weekend at a summer camp. Later her body was found in a wooded area near the gorge where she'd fallen over a ledge and hit her head on a rock.

Ellie sighed and moved on.

The second name belonged to sixteen-year-old Jacey Ward, a brunette who lived in Watkinsville, Georgia, outside of Athens, home of the University of Georgia Bulldogs. She pulled up the police report and read interviews of the parents. Apparently, Jacey had been defiant, obsessed with boys and had been sneaking to the college campus and crashing fraternity parties. She hadn't been seen in months. Campus police, working in tandem with the local police, had cleared the young men in the frat houses and exhausted all leads to date.

Currently Jacey was still missing. Her middle-class parents had been described as loving and appeared to provide a stable home. They were also relentless about keeping the case open and had offered a reward of $50,000 to anyone who led them to their daughter. They continued to call weekly for updates.

Although if Jacey had disappeared from Watkinsville, how would she have wound up here in the North Georgia mountains?

The third name on the list was thirteen-year-old Bonnie Sylvester from Cleveland, Georgia. Mother died at birth. Father abandoned them. She'd been missing for three months and was in foster care where the foster parents claimed she ran away. Ellie thought about Cord and his foster care experiences and wondered if the girl had been placed in a good home or an abusive one as Cord had. Scrolling on, she saw the foster family had been questioned. They described Bonnie as unruly and difficult. The police had marked the investigation as a dead-end case of a teen runaway.

Emotions welled inside Ellie. Was it a dead end because Bonnie had no family looking for her? No one who cared enough to post a reward for information leading to her return?

"Don't worry, Bonnie," she whispered. "You're not going to be lost in the system. I'll find you."

NINETEEN

Special Agent Derrick Fox had been on leave since December while he recovered from a back injury sustained working the last case. But he was bored out of his mind and antsy to return to field duty. He didn't care if the doctor was on the fence about signing off on his request. Doctor be damned. Nothing was going to keep him tied to a desk or from doing his job.

"Listen, man, don't push it," his partner, Bennett, said over the phone. "Take a vacay. Go fishing. Get laid."

Derrick gritted his teeth. Sipping a martini on a hot beach sounded tempting considering the winter weather, but the mountains were calling his name.

Because of Ellie...

Dammit, Fox. She's with McClain now and you have to accept it.

"A body was found in Brambletown," Derrick told Bennett. "I saw the press conference."

Bennett sighed. "That's not your problem. Besides, I know

that detective got under your skin, but there's other women out there. What about Lindsey, the mother of your godchildren?"

Derrick ran his fingers through his hair. "I told you she was my friend's wife. Every time I look at her, I see him." *And that he took his life and I could have saved him if I'd stayed closer in touch.* He sure as hell didn't want to fail the guy's family. Besides, Lindsey wanted her husband back and he would only be a temporary filler.

"His death wasn't your fault."

Damn, Bennett knew him too well.

"Your buddy was in a bad place," Bennett said. "When someone reaches the point where they're suicidal, when they've made up their minds, you can't save them. It's a tragedy, but you have to accept it and move on."

"Which is what I'm trying to do with work." Derrick opened his laptop. "The history of Brambletown has always been on my radar because of that fire and the government's resistance to take responsibility and clean up the toxins. A lot of people died because of it. And now someone built a memorial for them." He sighed. "Some people are protesting it. It's triggering all kinds of emotions. Which could create a hostile environment, especially with skeletal remains being discovered on the premises. A new investigation in the area might stir up the fact that they never pinpointed who was responsible for that coal fire." He hesitated, then continued down that line of thought. "And if the person who abducted or killed the Higgins girl is still around, it could be dangerous."

"Is that why you want to get involved? To protect that pretty detective?"

Derrick went stone cold still. He hadn't thought about it like that. "Ellie doesn't need or want my protection," Derrick said grimly. "But the case is intriguing." He swallowed hard as he looked down at his computer where he'd been searching for cases of missing teens. There were too many of them across the states, some runaways, some abductions. "Besides, if the victim is from out of state, it becomes a federal case. And the mayor did assign me to head up the task force to investigate crimes on or related to the AT."

Ellie's face flashed in his mind, but he banished it and forced himself to turn back to the missing persons reports. At least five across the U.S. running from South Georgia to North Carolina to Tennessee.

Once he finished digging into them, he'd head to the mountains.

His interest had nothing to do with Ellie. Absolutely nothing at all.

TWENTY

Ellie tapped the steering wheel as she passed the Welcome to Brambletown sign. The country road leading here had been winding with switchbacks, the muddy roads slick, causing her to drive at a snail's pace.

"No ID on the girl yet," Ellie told Shondra. "But I sent Dr. Whitefeather the names of two missing teens so she can request DNA and dental records. That's a start. Hopefully we'll have an answer soon." She tilted her head toward Shondra. "Now tell me about this town. I've already met the local sheriff, Clint Wallace. A heads-up, he didn't exactly roll out the welcome banner."

Shondra arched a black brow. "Not a surprise. His father was sheriff at the time Ruth Higgins went missing. And according to the police reports, Clint was dating Ruth and questioned in her disappearance."

Ellie worked her mouth from side to side. "Interesting. He didn't mention that when we talked. Was he a person of interest?"

"He was questioned. Claimed he had no idea where Ruth was that night. His father quickly cleared him from the list of suspects."

"I bet he did." Most fathers would do anything to protect their sons. "Go on."

"Ruth's father, Edward, was mayor and also questioned. According to the case notes, he and his wife, Gina, were extremely distraught. Others stated that he was possessive of Ruth and didn't approve of her dating."

Ellie tucked that tidbit away in her mind as Shondra continued. "His other daughter, Tilly, was a year younger than Ruth and was described as shy, bookish and frightened. Said in her statement that her sister snuck out that night. Tilly thought Ruth might have been meeting Clint Wallace, but Ruth claimed she wasn't and wouldn't tell her who she was meeting. Apparently, Ruth and Clint had broken up the day before."

"Goes to motive."

"Right. Although Clint's buddies gave him an alibi." Shondra tapped the file. "Ruth and Tilly's brother, Hayden, was known as a hothead and picked fights. A week before Ruth disappeared, he got into a brawl with Clint Wallace and sent Wallace to the hospital with a broken finger. Their mother, Gina, gave Hayden an alibi, said he got along great with everyone, and that he was home that night. But his alibi was shaky. The family fell apart after graduation and he joined the Army."

Sounded like the family might not have been so perfect behind closed doors.

"There's more," Shondra said. "The Bramble girls, Hetty and Ida, butted heads with Ruth over Clint and they got into a catfight with Ruth at the Dairy Queen. Witnesses stated it was quite the scandal, that hot fudge, cherries and sugar cones were flying everywhere."

Ellie pictured the scene and bit back a smile. Teenagers did run on high emotions.

"Were they angry enough to kill her though?"

Shondra shrugged. "Apparently the Brambles had a bad reputation in town. Their father, Earl, was known as a drunk who had a violent streak. Rumors spread that he killed Ruth and got rid of the body."

"Was he arrested?"

"Sheriff Wallace brought him in but had to release him due to lack of evidence and no body. Shortly after that, Earl Bramble disappeared himself."

"Which made him look guilty as hell," Ellie said.

"And the reason Sheriff Wallace finally shut down the investigation. With no body or witnesses and Bramble in the wind, the whole mess just died down."

"And remains unsolved," Ellie surmised. "Although our current case may have nothing to do with the past, it's nice to have some background on the players in town."

Still, Ellie didn't like unsolved cases, especially if a minor was involved. Or crimes that occurred in the same town, especially a town already mired in the deaths of multiple victims from the fire, and the disappearance of a teenager that had drawn national attention fifteen years ago and put Brambletown on the murder tourism map.

TWENTY-ONE

Daisy's Diner, Brambletown

Ellie's phone buzzed as she parked at Daisy's Diner with its yellow striped awning, checked curtains and tablecloths, which were visible through the front window. Seeing the ME's number, she quickly connected.

"Laney."

"I know I said it would be a while, but I requested records for the two girls you called me about and one of them was a match. The girl we recovered is Bonnie Sylvester."

Ellie closed her eyes on a sigh. Poor girl. She'd been abandoned by her family, ended up in foster care and now dead. She'd never had a chance at life.

"You're sure?"

"Yes. Her DNA and prints were already in the system. And I obtained her medical and dental records to confirm. Sending you a current pic, one that was posted on the news when she first went missing."

"Thanks. I'll pass it to Sheriff Waters and let him handle Angelica and the news report."

"You planning to set up a tip line?" Laney asked.

"Yes. it's protocol." Ellie watched people exit and enter the diner. Sheriff Clint Wallace stepped inside with a pretty brunette. "What else can you tell me?" she asked, turning her mind back to the case. "Cause and time of death?"

"COD appears to be strangulation. TOD is not precise, but my best estimate is that she's been dead at least a couple of weeks, maybe longer."

Ellie considered the timing of the girl's disappearance. She was reported missing three months ago. So where had she been during the time between her disappearance and her death?

"Laney, can you tell if she was held hostage? Did she sustain other injuries?"

A tense silence fell between them for a long minute.

"Laney?"

"Again, it's difficult to say for certain, but I reviewed her medical records. She sustained injuries that were old, a broken arm at one point and a broken finger, but the doctor's report stated that she'd fallen down a flight of stairs in her previous foster home. The incident was reported to DFACS. Therefore, she was transferred to another home."

"We need to question that family," Ellie said.

"There's something else, Ellie. We found a shoe deep in the grave but only one. About the strangulation—the red scarf in the grave was the murder weapon."

Ellie struggled to block the image of a man strangling the girl to death from her mind. "DNA or prints?"

"Sorry. No."

Meaning he'd worn gloves. "I'm in Brambletown now and will show Bonnie's photo around. See if anyone saw her."

Anger sparked Ellie's determination. That girl had no one advocating for her. No one posting a reward. No one who seemed to care if she lived or died.

Ellie's chest squeezed with emotions. *She* cared.

I'll find out who did this to you, Bonnie. I promise. And I'll make them pay.

TWENTY-TWO

Ellie phoned the sheriff in Crooked Creek, Sheriff Bryce Waters, and filled him in on the identity of the girl.

"All right, I'll give a press conference, circulate her pic to all law enforcement agencies across the state and set up the tip line," he agreed.

"Thanks. Deputy Eastwood and I are canvassing the town, Ranger McClain is searching the site where the remains were found, then I'll contact the original investigator of Bonnie Sylvester's case and the foster parents."

"Copy that. Let me know if you need more backup."

Special Agent Derrick Fox's face taunted her. He'd been her partner on the last few cases. But he was still recovering from an injury and the situation between her, Cord and Derrick had ended on an awkward note. She'd have to handle this one on her own.

She thanked Bryce, then ended the call and turned to Shondra. "I'll check the diner if you want to canvass store clerks and business owners."

Shondra nodded. "On it, Detective."

Ellie smiled, grateful to have Shondra on her side. They'd spent a lot of time together through work and she'd become a friend, not just a coworker.

Ellie exited the Jeep and Shondra slid out and headed to the Dollar Store next door. Smart thinking. If Bonnie had been homeless and come to this town on her own before being murdered, most likely she'd had very little money, so she might have shopped there for basic toiletries.

A chime tinkled above the door as she entered the diner, and she was struck by the field of bright yellow daisies painted on the mural on the far wall. An odd contrast to the desolate parched land surrounding the graveyard. Daisy was obviously using her namesake to inspire cheer and hope into the near-dead town.

A buttercup-blond woman with a beehive hairdo and a smile as big as Texas stood behind the diner counter laughing at something one of the customers said. From her nametag and demeanor, Daisy.

A quick sweep of the room and Ellie spotted Sheriff Clint Wallace seated in a booth in the corner with a young woman draped all over him. A teenage waitress with bright purple and orange streaks in her brown hair popped over with a pad and pen to take their order.

Voices rumbled through the crowded room, and she forced herself not to react as heads and stares turned her way. The damn press made it impossible to investigate incognito. Small-town rumor mills and TV, which was probably the prime entertainment here, meant everyone in town probably knew her name and her reason for being in Brambletown.

Which could prove helpful or give people time to fabricate alibis and hide whatever they knew or didn't know. The sad truth was that most people flat out didn't want to get involved.

Especially if they harbored secrets of their own.

To keep the peace with local law enforcement, she crossed the room to the booth where Clint Wallace was accepting an iced tea and smiling at the young waitress. The girl was just a teenager but even she gave him a flirtatious wink as she waltzed away.

Ellie rolled her eyes, then pasted on a stony expression as she stopped at the table. The moment Clint saw her, he threw his shoulders back in a defensive gesture. "Detective," he said grimly. "I didn't expect to see you so soon again."

Ellie narrowed her eyes, ignoring the irritated sigh the woman emitted. She obviously didn't appreciate her date being interrupted.

"Trust me, it's strictly official business," Ellie said. "I won't be leaving until the murder in this town is solved."

His jaw tightened. "My people can handle it."

"Maybe so, but like I said earlier, I'm not leaving until we get justice for the victim." She folded her arms across her chest, chin raised. "And just so you know, I have information to share."

His brow shot up at that.

Ellie glanced pointedly at his lunch date. "We should speak in private."

He squeezed the woman's slender hand. "Be right back, Vanessa."

The woman emitted an exasperated sigh. Ellie ignored her and led the sheriff toward the hall across from the restrooms.

"We IDed the remains recovered near the cemetery," Ellie said.

Surprise streaked his eyes. "So soon?"

"Yes. I sent the ME some names I pulled from missing persons reports and she was able to access medical and dental records and compare DNA and prints. One name popped." She angled her phone toward the sheriff, careful to watch his reaction. "Her name is Bonnie Sylvester. Thirteen years old, in foster care, disappeared three months ago from Cleveland, Georgia."

"Jesus. Thirteen?" He cut his eyes away as if he couldn't bear to look at the photo of the girl.

"Do you recognize her? Maybe you saw her in town."

He shook his head. "No. Probably should talk to the foster family."

"Heading there when we leave here. I'm also going to speak with the investigator in charge of her case in Cleveland. But I want to show her photo around town first. Maybe someone has seen her."

"If she had no family, what would she be doing here?" Sheriff Wallace asked.

"She could have been on the run," Ellie suggested. "Looking for a safe place." Instead, she'd run into the hands of a killer. "Can you and your crew look for abandoned cabins or properties in the area where she could have holed up?"

"I was going to suggest that," he said, his tone irritated.

"I figured as much," Ellie said, offering him a saccharine smile.

Without another word, he turned and headed back to his lunch date, seemingly in no hurry. What if the killer was hiding out in one of those places now?

She needed extra manpower. Frustrated, she phoned Deputy Landrum, explained and asked him to come.

"Be there ASAP," he said.

"Thanks." She ended the call then headed to the counter where Daisy was serving two teenagers burgers, fries and milkshakes.

"Did you hear they found a body?" the pale black-haired girl said.

The sandy-blond girl grabbed the ketchup and dumped some on her fries. "I know. I wonder who she was."

"Maybe that girl from way back when," the first girl muttered.

Ellie cleared her throat, and the girls turned, eyes widening at the sight of her badge. "Hi, ladies," Ellie said then introduced herself. "Daisy."

Daisy gave her an anxious smile as the teens turned away from her. "Detective, I figured you'd stop in here sometime," Daisy said.

Of course she would. Local diners were the hub for gatherings and gossip quickly floated from one table to the next.

"Who are the girls?" she asked Daisy as the teens dug into their chili fries.

The sandy blond is Carrie Ann Parker," Daisy replied. "The pale brunette is another Bramble. Kat Jones."

Bramble? Ida had been pregnant in school and married Joe Jones. It must be their daughter.

Daisy fluttered her fingers to her throat. "Did you identify that poor soul from the woods?"

"We did," Ellie said. "That's the reason I'm here. Her name is Bonnie Sylvester. She was a foster child from Cleveland." Ellie pulled her phone, accessed Bonnie's picture, then addressed Daisy and the girls.

"Have any of you seen her around town?"

Carrie Ann eyed the photo with a squinted look then shook her head. "Don't think so."

"Not really. It's a small town, if there was someone new, they'd stick out," Kat said. "And she's not one of us."

"Daisy?"

"Afraid not. Can't remember names worth a flip, but faces stick in my mind. I'd remember if she came in here."

Ellie knew it was a long shot. If Bonnie had managed to make it this far from Cleveland, she might have laid low to avoid detection. Especially if she didn't want to be sent back to her foster family. "Well, if you think of anything or remember her, please let me know."

"Sure will," Daisy said, her friendly smile slipping back in place.

"The picture will be posted on the news, so tell your friends to pay attention," Ellie told the girls.

They nodded and Ellie moved on, canvassing the room. But no one in the diner claimed to know Bonnie or have seen her.

Emanuel Black, the man who'd found Bonnie's remains, sat in the back corner deep in concentration over his laptop and sipping a beer. She caught his eye as she approached and he lowered his laptop screen.

"Detective?"

"Mr. Black," she said. "I identified the remains you discovered in the woods."

An odd look washed over his face, one Ellie couldn't quite read.

Ellie flashed the picture. "Her name is Bonnie Sylvester. She was thirteen years old. Do you recognize her?"

Black leaned forward and studied the photograph with an intensity that almost unnerved Ellie. When he righted himself, he ran a finger over the scar on his forehead, then shook his head no.

A tense second passed, then Ellie thanked him. "If you remember seeing her somewhere, please call me."

"Of course," he said matter-of-factly.

The door to the diner opened and the bell tinkled. A family of four entered, then a woman in her thirties with a bedraggled, low ponytail and a flannel shirt dusted with flour. She made a beeline toward the girls, rubbing at her leg, drawing attention to her limp. Wincing in pain, she stopped at the bar and addressed the black-haired teen, her voice sharp.

"Kat, you have to come home now."

Kat rolled her eyes on a sigh. "But Mom, Carrie Ann and I were hanging out."

"I'm not going to argue with you, girl. Get your butt up and let's go or else."

Ellie's brows shot up. What did she mean *or else?*

Kat slammed her backpack on the bar then tossed it over her shoulder and rolled her eyes. "I told you she'd freak out, Carrie Ann. She's so *weird.*" Pouting, the girl dragged her feet and shuffled behind her mother out the door.

The other teen frowned. "Call you, later, Kat. Let me know when you get out of house jail."

Ellie bit back a laugh at the girls' dramatics, then crossed to the bar to Daisy again. "That was Ida, wasn't it, Daisy?"

"Sure was." A frown tugged at Daisy's lips. "That woman's always been hell on wheels and got some kind of temper." She mopped her forehead with a napkin, dabbing at the sweat beading above her brows. "And her daughter's just like her."

TWENTY-THREE

Tilly Higgins pulled her Braves baseball hat lower over her forehead to shield her face as she watched Ida Bramble storm in and make a scene with her daughter at the counter.

Tilly remembered high school. Ida had been pregnant when Ruth disappeared, but no one knew it at the time. She married Joe shortly before the baby came.

After the scandal that summer and the suspicions cast on her father, Earl, Tilly would have expected Ida to flee town like she did. But she supposed her roots ran deep in the heart of this dreadful town.

The daughter, a pale girl with hair the color of soot and a short skirt that rode up her butt, stomped behind her mother, as rebellious as Ida and Hetty had been. Tilly almost laughed at the irony. *Karma's a bitch, Ida. You reap what you sow.*

Except Tilly hadn't been one of the mean girls and look how her teenage years had gone.

All because Ruth had been a mischievous flirty girl who the boys all wanted and female classmates envied.

Not Tilly. She'd been the mealy, mousy, invisible little sister who no one ever noticed and probably didn't remember.

She buried her nose in her phone as the detective continued combing the room asking questions about the murder case she'd come to investigate. She'd heard they'd IDed the girl in the grave.

It wasn't her sister.

A mixture of relief and sadness filled her. The fact that it wasn't Ruth meant there was a slim possibility her sister was still alive. Although Tilly had lost real hope of that years ago. The disappointment each time a report surfaced of the discovery of an unidentified dead girl was too much to handle. Over and over her parents had their hopes raised, only to have them brutally crushed.

She still wanted answers though. Tomorrow she'd start digging around, pushing people to talk. She'd already obtained a copy of the police report from the original investigation.

She pulled it from her briefcase and skimmed through it one more time. There had to have been something the cops had missed. Someone they hadn't even looked at as a suspect or dismissed too quickly.

Either that, or someone in town knew who'd taken Ruth and was covering for them.

TWENTY-FOUR

Briar Ridge Mobile Homes

Kat was sick and tired of living in this divey trailer park. Mama said it wasn't bad when she and her daddy first moved in, that there was a pretty view of rolling hills from the ridge. She found that hard to believe. All you could see now were briar patches for miles and miles. She'd learned the hard way that snakes and rodents roamed though the weeds. A rattler almost bit her once and it scared her so bad her knees knocked every time she stepped close to the bushes.

When she was little, she'd seen monsters hiding in the thicket at night.

She despised her mother's shenanigans, too. She was always embarrassing her. Yelling at her one minute then the next wanting to live vicariously through her because her own teenage years sucked.

Kat knew the history. The gossip. All the kids around her had grown up with it. The horror of the coal mountain fire and the toxins. The people fleeing town to be safe. The fight between Hetty and her mama and that girl that went missing.

Her cheeks burned at the thought.

But no, her parents had stayed for some reason as if they were so accustomed to misery they'd forgotten how to live. Were they just plain stupid?

Sometimes she worried she'd been exposed to toxins and as she got old, she'd have some weird disease where she'd start having seizures or go crazy or have boils on her body like some of the rumors claimed.

She shivered at the thought, slammed the trailer door shut and shoved at the mountain of magazines her mama had piled by their old vinyl couch, knocking them to the floor.

"Kat, you better get yourself under control," her mama yelled. "And take off those damn red Converses before your daddy sees them. He says they make you look trashy."

Kat huffed, ran into her room and closed the door to pout. If it was up to her daddy, she'd wear a tent so none of the boys could see that she was finally starting to grow boobs.

She looked down at the little mounds with pride. She'd been waiting a long time for them to pop out and had almost given up hope. Her mama had big knockers, as Daddy called them, but poor Hetty was flat as a pancake.

Mad at her mama and afraid she'd devise some plan to keep Kat from going to the winter dance where she hoped Seth Simmons might finally notice her, she went to her closet and dug out her mother's old computer. She'd found it hidden in the cedar chest where her mama kept the quilts her grandma had made.

Mama wouldn't have hidden it if something juicy wasn't inside. Maybe something about Ruth Higgins. Or... some dirt Kat could get on her mama to use as leverage the next time her mama tried to ground her. Proof that once upon a time Ida Bramble had been as scandalous as the gossip claimed, not a nagging hag as her daddy called her.

Even fifteen years later, the fight between her mama and

Hetty and Ruth Higgins was infamous. Shame dug at Kat's insides. Good grief, a photo of it was even included in the yearbook that year. There was also a memorial to that bitch Ruth, according to her mama, who'd bullied her and Hetty and thought she was better than them cause her daddy was mayor and they had a nice house.

Kat crawled to the corner on her beanbag chair, opened the computer and realized she needed a password.

She thumped her fingers on her temple in thought then decided to try the obvious, her mama's birthday. It worked, so she dove in, searched the files and realized her mama had once kept a shadow journal. She was shocked her mama had enough smarts to do so.

Or maybe like in Kat's own English class, it was a requirement.

Curious, she clicked on the link, saw a picture of Green Gardens Cemetery and the title *The Graveyard Girls*. Her pulse jumped as she began to read the first entry.

If her mama knew what happened to Ruth or Kat's granddaddy, maybe she'd written about it in here.

TWENTY-FIVE

Ellie stopped at a table of ladies having lunch and asked their thoughts on the Brambles.

"Earl never had much sense," one woman said. "Flunked out of school in the ninth grade. That's why he dug graves."

"He was a stutterer, too," an ancient-looking woman muttered.

A thin gray-haired lady chirped, "One time someone accused him of burying their sister in the same pine box as her mama."

A woman they called Nell tsked. "I heard he made that girl Hetty sleep in one of the pine boxes."

Ellie shuddered at the very thought. She'd been claustrophobic as a child and during one case, the killer she was chasing locked her in a coffin. She still suffered nightmares from the experience.

A middle-aged plump woman added, "Right after Earl disappeared, my husband, Roy, said he saw Earl sneaking into the junkyard after dark. The next day an old pick-up truck was missing and so was the cash he kept in the cash box."

"Did the police ever find the truck?" Ellie asked.

"Don't reckon so," Nell said. "But there were other times Earl was sighted over the years. One time Norma Jean thought she saw him prowling in her backyard but by the time the sherif got to her house, he'd hightailed it out of there. We were all terrified he'd come back and start trouble again."

"And it looks like he did," a bony woman gasped.

Ellie showed them Bonnie's picture. "Take a good look, ladies. Have you seen her?"

A chorus of no's and head shaking followed.

If Bonnie had come to Brambletown on her own, she'd stayed under the radar. Either that, or the killer had murdered her in another location and transported her body to dump at the graveyard.

Maybe someone in Cleveland where Bonnie had lived with her foster family would have some answers.

TWENTY-SIX

Cleveland, Georgia

Ellie phoned Cord and asked him to meet her in Cleveland at the foster family's house. But as she entered town, she and Shondra drove to the police station first.

Unlike Brambletown, Cleveland was a quaint little mountain town and a hot tourist spot. Home to Babyland General Hospital where the Cabbage Patch Kids were born, families flocked there to witness the "births" and take home their favorite dolls, complete with printed birth certificates.

While Shondra went to canvass the local businesses, Ellie tugged her jacket around her and climbed the steps to the police department. A fifty-something receptionist with a nametag that read Mildred greeted her. Ellie identified herself and explained the reason for her visit.

"Oh, my, I'm so sorry to hear about that poor girl," Mildred said. "She had a rough life."

"Did you know her foster family?" Ellie asked.

"Just that the foster father was a jerk. And the wife, well, the few times she came into town, seemed like a mousy little thing that had nothing to say."

"Did you sense they were abusive to the foster children?" Ellie asked.

Mildred twisted her mouth to the side. "It's possible. Although I don't think the investigating officer found proof of it."

"I'd like to talk to that officer," Ellie said.

Mildred nodded, lifted the phone from its cradle and punched in a number. "Officer Novak, a detective is here to talk to you about Bonnie Sylvester."

A minute later, a tall brown-haired man she guessed to be early thirties appeared, his uniform fitting snugly over his taut stomach. "Officer Novak," he said then offered his hand.

Ellie shook it and identified herself.

"I saw the news report about the Sylvester girl," he said as he escorted her through a set of double doors to an office that was as neatly kept as his military haircut. "I was sorry to hear she was found dead."

"Murdered," Ellie said. "The ME said she was strangled."

Novak winced and arched a brow. "Sexual assault?"

"Thankfully no indication of that."

The officer's desk chair squeaked as he leaned back in it and studied her. "How can I help you?"

"I'd like to see your report on the investigation. But first please give me a quick summary. Who did you question, and did you have a working theory or a specific person of interest?"

"I'll have Mildred print you a copy of the report," he said. "Of course, we issued an Amber Alert and searched the town. We questioned the foster parents first. They insisted that Bonnie was difficult, that she didn't get along with the other foster kids, that she'd run off a couple of times before but usually came back. Mr. Wiley insisted that was the reason they waited three days before reporting her missing. But we believe he only filed the report because of the caseworker. She paid them a surprise visit and the girl wasn't there, then she insisted they file the report. Another boy in the house told her Bonnie had been gone three days."

"Did you think Bonnie was abused?"

He picked up a pen and rolled it between his fingers. "I suspected the man abused the kids and his wife, and so did the social worker but we never found proof. That said, she had the other kids removed from the house and struck the Wileys from the foster family list."

"How did they take that?"

"Not well," he said gruffly. "She believed they were just in it for the money. Funds stipulated for the children were used to enhance their own personal lifestyle. Expensive TVs, phones and other tech equipment were in the house. But the kids wore thrift store clothes, tennis shoes with holes and slept on ratty sheets."

Ellie sighed in disgust. "What did the teachers and school counselor have to say?"

He ran a hand over his cleanly shaven jaw. "That Bonnie was a smart girl, studied and made good grades, but she was shy, awkward around the other kids and kept to herself. The counselor said she didn't talk about her foster situation, but once said she was going to find a way to go to college."

Emotions gathered in Ellie's chest. The odds had been stacked against Bonnie from the beginning yet she'd had potential.

Only her dreams had been squashed when someone took her life.

TWENTY-SEVEN

Cord had only touched the surface of his search across the land near the graveyard. There were so many deserted areas providing optimum places to hide that the task seemed overwhelming.

He should know. He'd hidden in the shadows of the mountains as a teen. Had even combed this same land and remembered the day Ruth Higgins disappeared. The debacle between the Bramble girls and her had been the talk of the town. And when their father disappeared...

He shut out the memory of that day as he wound around the mountain road to Cleveland. The address for the Wiley family was on the outskirts of town. He didn't know exactly the reason Ellie wanted him to come along to question them, but he guessed it was because of his background. Maybe she thought he'd have some insight on the foster family.

Naturally they were suspects in the Sylvester girl's homicide.

Bitterness swelled inside him at the idea that they might have hurt her. But he knew firsthand it was a real possibility.

Trees swayed in the raging wind, tossing leaves and twigs

across the road. A limb cracked and broke off, sailing in front of his truck and he swerved to avoid it. His tires churned over the still damp asphalt from the rain the night before, but he veered onto the narrow dirt road leading to the Wiley house.

The mile-long drive seemed to be going nowhere but also highlighted the fact that the place was tucked deeply into the woods out of sight where anything the family did might go unnoticed.

Memories of his own foster father's cruel abuse bulldozed his mind, causing him to sweat. He'd lived above a mortuary, another place that had been out of sight.

For good reason. It had given the son of a bitch the opportunity to do whatever the hell he wanted to do to the corpses without drawing suspicion.

Just like this house in the woods offered Bonnie Sylvester's foster father the freedom to abuse the vulnerable children he was supposed to protect.

TWENTY-EIGHT

Pigeon Road

On the drive to the Wiley house, Ellie called the social worker Sally Emerson who'd handled Bonnie's placement.

"Gosh, I'm so sorry to hear about Bonnie," the young woman said. "She'd already been in five different homes when she was placed there. I inherited her case from my former coworker who retired of burnout."

"And Bonnie got lost in the process," Ellie muttered.

"I'm afraid so. I wish she'd have come to me sooner and told me if something was going on with that family. But she didn't trust anyone, including me."

Because no one had ever given her a reason to trust them.

"What can I do to help?" Sally asked.

"Tell me about the family. Did you see signs of physical abuse with Bonnie?"

A hesitant pause. "Some bruising occasionally. But she told me the same story a lot of counselors get. She fell down the steps. She tripped on the rug." Her breath rattled out. "I sensed the foster father favored the boys in the house."

"She was probably afraid to speak up," Ellie said.

"Yeah, in a lot of cases when victims report abuse, if they aren't removed from the home, the abuse worsens."

"Exactly. Plus, Bonnie was a sensitive girl. Once she'd been moved from home to home, families assumed she was difficult, which made it even more challenging to find a family who wanted her."

"Exactly."

"Did she mention a place she might go if she ran away? Some place she felt safe or wanted to visit."

"Once she mentioned college, but she didn't specify a certain one." Sally's weary sigh echoed back. "Frankly I think she was so busy fighting to survive that she just kept things to herself. Said one time she didn't want to jinx things."

Ellie bit her tongue. Yet Bonnie hadn't survived.

"If you think of anything that might be helpful, please give me a call."

"I will," Sally said. "Please find whoever did this. I... somehow feel responsible. Like I missed something and let her down."

"I'm sure you did the best you could. The system is broken and I realize you're probably overworked," Ellie said, although excuses didn't keep innocent kids safe. "But I promise to get justice for her."

Ellie reached the graveled road to the Wileys' house, assured Sally she'd keep her posted then steered the Jeep up the drive. Her tires spit gravel as she spotted Cord's truck parked in front of the house. Thankfully he'd waited on her as she'd requested.

But his was the only vehicle.

She pulled up beside him then slid from the driver's side. The wind swept her ponytail into a frenzy, the winter chill intensified by the isolation of the dingy clapboard house.

"Find anything at the graveyard?" Ellie asked as he walked toward her.

"Nothing useful," he murmured, a lock of his shaggy brown hair falling across his forehead. His look seemed guarded and he didn't make eye contact. Then again, he'd had a bad experience in foster care. Her heart ached for him. Bonnie's situation was probably resurrecting his own trauma.

Ellie gestured toward the house. "Seen any activity?"

"No. Place looks deserted."

Ellie pressed her hand over her weapon as they crept up the path to the front porch. Pigeons had roosted on the windowsill, their droppings evident. The wood was rotting, paint peeling, the steps squeaking as she climbed them. She and Cord exchanged wary looks as they crossed to the front door. She opened the screen, knocked and identified herself. "Police. Anyone home?"

Silence accentuated the echo of her voice. A bad feeling nagged at Ellie as she pushed open the front door.

The entryway was small and led to the living room and tiny kitchen. Faded orange linoleum covered the floor and the walls were a dull gray. A musty, damp odor wafted toward her. Mold maybe.

As far as she could see inside, the house was empty. Bare of furniture.

She scanned the living room and kitchen and realized the rooms had been cleared out.

"They're gone," she murmured.

"Probably saw the news about Bonnie's body being found and knew we'd come knocking."

Why would that have scared them away... unless they'd killed Bonnie?

TWENTY-NINE

The itch to take another girl was driving him crazy. But it was too dangerous to abduct one in town or to return to the graveyard at the moment.

Adrenaline heated his veins. The cops and that ranger were all over the place, swarming like flies. And there were the visitors and tourists who'd come to see that damned memorial. He'd been totally against it for a lot of reasons but most of all because it stirred up the gossip about the disappearance of the Higgins girl. The gravestones had drawn media attention and now the Sylvester girl's body had been discovered, the town was once again thrust into the limelight.

Not what a man like him needed to stay under the radar.

Laughter caught in his throat. No worries. He had a giant hunting ground along the AT, little towns where no one would even notice a stranger passing through.

He had that kind of face. That kind of demeanor.

That side that no one knew about. Not even the people closest to him.

THIRTY

Although the Wileys were gone, Ellie called a team to process the house. "I want prints, DNA, anything else you can find. Look for signs of an altercation and blood. Also look for notes, bills, something that might indicate where they were going."

She called Deputy Landrum and filled him in. "Start searching for an address where the Wileys may have gone. They'd probably be renting and staying off the radar."

"Do you have an idea when they left?"

Ellie scratched her head as Cord ducked outside to look around the property. "No. Could have been shortly after the foster kids were removed from the home. Check DMV records and see what kind of vehicle they drove, then issue a BOLO for the car and an APB for the couple."

"Copy that."

She thanked him, then ended the call and walked outside to find Cord. He was standing at the edge of the woods, looking through the trees with a scowl. Her boots crunched gravel as she closed the distance between them. When he turned to face her, he was holding something in his gloved hand.

"I found this lying in the grass by the pond."

Ellie's pulse jumped. The letter B dangled from a silver chain. Was it Bonnie's?

"Bag it and we'll see if it has Bonnie's prints on it. And if we're lucky, maybe the killer's."

"Copy that," he said gruffly. "We should drag the pond."

"But we have Bonnie's body," Ellie said.

Cord gritted his teeth. "I know. But other kids lived here, too..."

Ellie rocked back on her heels, her suspicions roused. Damn. He was right.

"I'll call and set it up."

If she found out the Wileys had killed Bonnie or hurt another child, she'd hunt them down and cage them like dogs.

THIRTY-ONE

His palms grew damp, his breathing erratic with excitement as he placed the red sandal on the shelf with his other trophies. All the pretty red shoes... all the pretty girls who wore them.

Red, the school colors. Red, like roses.

Red, the color of blood streaming onto the floor like a river...

He kissed his finger then gently traced it over each shoe as he counted them, whispering the name of each girl they belonged to.

The young faces and bodies, teasing and tempting... Their images flooded his mind, the sound of their screams taunting him, their bodies going limp as they gasped for their last breath.

He moved along the row until he ended at the first shoe he'd brought here and ran his hand over the stiletto heel.

Slowly the memories thrust him back in time. To the cold musty closet where he'd spent most of his childhood nights.

Darkness surrounded him in the tiny closed-in space where his mama had locked him. "Don't come out or you'll get it." The sound of the lock clicking screamed in his ears. The light from the keyhole faded as panic engulfed him. The furnace clanked somewhere in the silence. But the heat didn't seem to reach the closet and made it feel like an icy cave. He slid back against the wall and felt the heel of one of his mama's shoes stab him in the back.

Shivering, he yanked her wool coat from the hanger above and buried himself in it then wrapped her red scarf around his neck. It stank of sweat, cigarettes and stale whiskey. Threadbare, the coat hardly warmed him, but for a while he covered his head with it, hoping to drown out the sounds outside the room.

Footsteps clattered. Glasses clinked and rattled. The stereo erupted with the whine of some country two-step song. Clack, clack, clack. Boots pounding the wood floor in time with the twangy sound.

Then a shriek. Something shattered onto the floor. Dishes breaking. His mother's groan.

Terrified, he uncovered his head, crawled to the door and peeked through the keyhole.

The man growled and his mother giggled, a sickening sound that made him want to puke. Then the man threw her onto the kitchen table. Pouncing on her, he tore at her clothes. Shoved her backward. Her head hit the table with a whack. Her shoes flew off and hit the floor.

The man rammed at her, knocking the chair over. Gripped her around the throat.

She screamed but he kept going, pounding and grunting and...

Bile rose in his throat, and he crawled back into the corner, pulled the coat back over him and tried to shut out everything. But in his mind he could still see those red shoes dangling from her feet through the crack in the door... The red shoes... The man smacking her as she screamed.

THIRTY-TWO

Briar Ridge Mobile Homes

Kat scrolled through one of her mama's journal posts, intrigued. All her life she'd thought her mama was just a dumbass country girl who'd married a loser and both of them were boring and lame.

She'd gotten knocked up with her when she was a teenager, barely graduated high school, and they were so broke she never shopped anywhere except Goodwill and garage sales. At the grocery store, she bought day-old bread, off brands and coupon shopped. Once she heard Mama telling Daddy they'd make it big time when they could afford real beef hotdogs instead of the mystery meat ones you had to slather with ketchup and mustard just to choke down.

Once a year, Mama and Aunt Hetty ventured to the outlet mall in North Georgia to Christmas shop but that was as far as either one of them had ever traveled. It was as if they had glue on their shoes and rot in their brains.

Kat rolled her eyes and continued to read her mama's rants:

I hate being a Bramble. Everyone knows Daddy is a mean drunk and now he's been arrested again. This time for stealing from the dime store to buy moonshine. Apple pie is his favorite.

The. moonshiners are hillbillies you don't want to mess with. Course if you cross them they can't go to the police. No... they'll come after you themselves.

Last week I saw a big scruffy one covered in tats outside my window. I know Daddy owes them money. I'm scared to death they'll kill me to teach him a lesson.

They're nasty, foul-mouthed, tobacco chewing, sorry recluses with the mentality of a gnat and the horniness of a dog in heat. Incest is as common as the weeds that choke the vegetable garden, squashing the zucchini that desperately tries to push though the hard Georgia red clay.

The law is no better, as useless as a butter knife trying to saw through a raw potato. Instead of turning the other cheek as Preacher says on Sundays, they turn a blind eye to whatever happens behind closed doors. A person's business is his own, Daddy growled the other night through a mouthful of pinto beans, fat back and cornbread. Keep your mouth shut or I'll shut it for you for good, he told Hetty.

Everyone knows me and Hetty live in the slums. That we come from dirt, that Daddy tends the graveyard. Digging graves by night and making pine boxes for the poor by day.

That's how we got dubbed the Graveyard Girls by that bitch Ruth. That and the things we've seen and done this hellish hot summer.

We saw too much.

We said too little.

And we played hide-and-seek with a killer.

THIRTY-THREE

Ellie left Cord to supervise the dragging of the pond while she drove to the police station. The captain and deputies had gone for the day but she needed to know more about the Wileys. Everything was pointing to them as Bonnie's killer.

Once she issued the APB for them, she left a message for the social worker who'd handled Bonnie's case to call her. She wanted any information the woman had on the family, if they had other relatives or another address where they might have gone.

Next, she ran a background check and searched for information on their past. Mr. Wiley had grown up in the mountains with a single mother who cleaned houses for a living. After dropping out of school, he worked at a body shop but a back injury forced him to take disability.

His wife had lived in close proximity to the toxic land and had been in and out of the hospital in her twenties with depression issues. Ellie dug a little deeper to see how serious her illness was, but medical reports were confidential and she'd need a warrant to look at them.

Her phone buzzed and she connected. "This is Detective Reeves."

"It's Sally Emerson," the social worker said. "You left a message?"

"Yes," Ellie said. "I went to the Wileys' house but it was literally empty."

"So they moved?"

"Looks that way. Do you have any idea where they'd go? Did they have other family?"

"Not that I know of," Sally said. "I remember the subject came up when they were first interviewed."

"I see Mrs. Wiley had a history of depression. Didn't that factor into the decision to approve them for foster parenting?"

"Yes, but the social worker who first met with them overlooked it because Wanda's depression stemmed from being unable to have children. Apparently, she was affected by the toxins in the area like so many other women and it created health problems. Notes on the couple indicated that at first the woman was ecstatic to be a parent."

Ellie considered that. If the Wileys had wanted a family, would they have hurt Bonnie? "You said 'at first.' Did things change?"

"Yes. I don't think they, especially the husband, were prepared for children with problems or special needs. Once we placed a little girl with a learning disability with them, but Mr. Wiley lost his patience and verbally abused her. She cried all the time so she was removed. We found a better place for her with a former teacher."

"And they described Bonnie as difficult," Ellie said, seeing a clearer picture.

"Yes, she was shuffled around a lot. Her mother was a meth addict and Bonnie exhibited signs of those effects."

"Did Bonnie use recreational drugs?" Ellie asked.

"Not that we know of. But sometimes drug babies have impulse control issues and are hyper emotional. Bonnie could be a really sweet girl, but she got lost in the system, and the constant moves made it more difficult for her to trust adults and form friendships. That's why it seemed feasible that she ran away."

Ellie massaged her temple. "But if Marv Wiley had no patience with that behavior, he might have lost his temper and silenced her."

"It's possible," Sally said, her tone concerned.

Ellie pinched the bridge of her nose, praying Cord didn't find another dead child in the pond. "Did any other children run away or disappear while under the couple's care?"

"I did see a note from the first social worker who dealt with the Wileys. She indicated another girl ran away about two years ago, but police ruled it just that. There's nothing else in the file about it."

Ellie made a note to have Deputy Landrum do a deep dive into that situation. There might be a pattern with the Wileys.

THIRTY-FOUR

Tilly walked through her childhood home, memories bombarding her in each room she entered. She'd spent two hours cleaning it, dusting and sweeping, and trying to ignore the stains of childhood spills on the floor and the measuring stick on the wall where her parents had recorded hers, Ruth's and her brother's growth progression.

For years she'd wondered where her brother was, if he was still in the military or out and getting into trouble or if he'd cleaned up his act. She'd tried to find him once but hit a dead end when she was told he'd been discharged after his first tour.

She'd also hoped her parents would reach out, but apparently they still blamed her for Ruth's disappearance. Guilt and pain seized her at the memory of their reaction toward her. Her father's accusatory glare and her mother's sobs after Tilly admitted she saw Ruth sneaking out the window.

"You should have come and gotten us," her mother cried.

"If anything bad happens to her, it's your fault," her father snapped.

Tilly studied the measuring stick again, wishing she could turn back time. Three weeks before Ruth left, her mother measured them, but Ruth had rolled her eyes, calling her mother silly.

Tilly almost felt sorry for her mother except that she allowed Ruth to get away with talking shit to her.

Ruth had been obsessed with boys, making friends on Facebook, clothes and makeup. Tilly followed her a couple of times when she snuck out which infuriated her sister. The memory was just as fresh as the day it happened.

Ruth's blond hair shined in the moonlight as she turned to Tilly. "Get lost, brat, you're going to mess things up for me."

Tears burned Tilly's eyes. She just wanted to be close to her sister. "But I want to come along."

A smug smile curved Ruth's lips. "I said get lost or I'll tell Mom and Dad you have no friends at school."

Tilly felt like she'd been hit in the chest with a hammer because it was true. She really wanted to be friends with Ruth like when they were little and used to play dolls and dress-up.

But they were so different now. She was tomboyish and shy, not the sister with great hair and boobs like Ruth. She'd just as soon curl up with a good mystery novel in the corner than attend a party and talk to people with no interest in her or what she had to say.

Still, for some reason she wanted her sister's approval. So she'd done what Ruth said and kept her secrets. And they'd both paid the price for it.

Guilt suffused her, and she shuffled past the kitchen, ignoring the tug of nostalgia of family dinners, Taco Tuesdays and holiday meals when the house had smelled like prime rib and her mother's rosemary roasted potatoes.

Although meals had been stilted. Her mother insisted they dress for dinner and berated them if they didn't use proper manners. Her father had been up and down from the table on work phone calls and never joined the conversation. As an adult now, she realized he'd ignored her mother. The only one he paid attention to was Ruth.

And that was before Ruth went missing. The night that had happened they'd become obsessed with finding her.

Her parents had been distraught. Her mother turned to vodka while her father became the bane of the police's existence, hounding Sheriff Wallace. More than once, he'd accused him of negligence. The two of them had disagreed over politics in the town, her father pushing to get the toxins cleaned up while Sheriff Wallace had dragged his feet.

Exhausted, Tilly carried a glass of Chardonnay to her bedroom, pulled on flannel pjs and crawled into bed. For a long minute, she lay looking at the dark ceiling. Staring into empty space. Listening to the sound of the furnace grumbling just as it had when she lived here.

Time rolled back as if it was a video on rewind...

The loneliness. The ache to be close to Ruth, to someone. Not to be the geek freak with the outgoing sister who she'd played Barbies and Candy Lane with at one time but who wanted nothing to do with her as a teen. She missed that big sister.

The warmth of the room finally lulled her into sleep and dreams carried her back in time.

Another sound... the window sliding up. Her sister's room across the hall.

Tilly clenched the sheets, her heart thudding. Heard whispers in the dark. Ruth's. A boy at the window calling Ruth's name. The quiet padding of footsteps. The squeak of the wood floor.

"Shh." Her sister's voice. Then a quiet giggle. And nerves that ripped through Tilly from the inside out.

Then silence except for the wind whistling through the open window as Ruth left for the night.

THIRTY-FIVE

Although Kat hated that damn graveyard where Hetty worked and the other kids talked about the ghosts roaming the cemetery, she was intrigued by the mischievous games her mother played with Hetty. It was hard to imagine the two of them as *humans* much less kids.

They were old and such a drag now. Hetty's fingernails were always covered in dirt and she smelled like fertilizer or chicken shit.

Her mama's skin was dry and wrinkled and in the summer she smelled of the tomatoes she soaked in hot water to can. When winter came, she coated her chapped face and lips in Vaseline so she looked like a greased pig.

Her daddy ruled the roost, as the old biddies in town whispered.

Yeah, he thought he was king of the house, but he was a bully. She had no idea why her mama stayed with him except she didn't have a job and Mama claimed she stayed because of Kat.

That was just an excuse because she was too afraid to leave.

Kat lifted her chin, her stubborn streak kicking in. She refused to ever let a man run her life like that.

Downstairs, she heard her mama talking on the phone. "Oh, my word, Hetty, I can't believe this is happening. It feels like before."

Kat knew she was talking about Ruth Higgins and the gossip in town.

Her mother's voice grew more hushed and worried, as if she didn't want anyone to hear what she was saying.

Curious, Kat decided to check out her mama's journal again.

Everybody at school thinks Ruth is all there is. She acts sweet to the teachers and must be a genius because she gets good grades but I've never seen her study. In class, she's too busy passing notes to Clint.

Today this happened:

Someone passed a note to me to give to Clint and I snuck a peek.

"Meet me at the DQ." Ruth's pink lipstick painted lips formed a kiss on the paper.

I wanted to gag.

Instead, I folded the note in my hand and stuffed it inside my book.

The bell rang and Clint walked out with his buddies. Ruth tossed me a gloating smile as she followed.

I rolled my eyes, then hurried to meet Hetty in the hall and tell her what I did. She giggled and we decided to go to the DQ and watch Ruth's reaction when Clint didn't show.

We got there first and I ordered a hot fudge sundae and Hetty got her usual Dilly Bar. We settled in a booth and stared at the door. Several kids from school piled in, laughing and talking and placing orders.

Ruth pranced in with her cheerleader friends, scanning the room for Clint. The cheerleaders ordered ice cream cones and Ruth a milkshake. They gathered at a table and Ruth kept her eyes glued on the door.

Ten minutes passed. Then fifteen.

Then Clint loped in with the flyer on the cheerleading squad, Mindy Winterbottom, and the two of them ordered chocolate cones. Ruth gaped at him, eyes darkening with fury.

When they settled into a booth, Ruth walked over to them. "What the hell are you doing, Clint? I thought you were meeting me."

Her sharp tone brought the chatter in the room to a halt as everyone turned to watch the drama.

Clint wrinkled his nose in confusion. "Huh? Why did you think that?"

Ruth folded her arms below her boobs. "Because of the note I sent."

"What note?" Clint asked, obviously dumbfounded.

"The one I passed to you in class," Ruth said shrilly.

"I didn't get a note," he stammered.

Ruth went so still you could hear a pin drop in the room. Then she slowly turned around and stared at me.

I couldn't help myself. I wanted to rub it in that I'd outsmarted her, so I gave her the same kind of snarky smile she'd given me in class. Rage flared in her eyes, and she suddenly charged toward me and Hetty.

"You did this. You took the note," she snarled. "You and your cousin are just stupid, white trash, Ida."

Some of the other kids laughed.

Shame ate at me. I couldn't help myself. Even if it was true, I didn't like her saying it in front of everyone. Steaming mad, I picked up my sundae and threw it at her. She shrieked, then opened her milkshake and dumped it on my head.

Some of the kids stood and circled us, egging us on. I

grabbed her hair and pulled it and Hetty smashed her Dilly Bar in Ruth's face.

Suddenly a food fight erupted and ice cream and whipped cream and cones were flying all over the place.

Kat sat back and couldn't help but smile. Her mama had been feisty back then. And Ruth deserved ice cream in her face.

But she went missing not long after.

Did her mama have something to do with Ruth's disappearance?

THIRTY-SIX

Ellie closed her laptop and rubbed her blurry eyes. If Bonnie was killed on the Wiley property, why not leave her body in the pond? Why take her to the woods by the graveyard?

A knock brought her attention to the door. Special Agent Fox poked his head in. Surprise caught her off guard. The last time she'd seen him he'd been injured and in the hospital, but tonight he looked rested and as handsome as ever. The dark blue shirt accentuated his bronze skin, and he wore jeans, which made him look more relaxed and less like a federal agent.

His deep brown eyes raked over her, a tentative smile tugging at the corner of his lips. "I thought you might still be here," he said gruffly.

She folded her arms. "What are you doing in Crooked Creek? I thought you were out of commission for a while."

He shrugged. "Not a desk guy."

She laughed. "I get that. Missing the action?"

"More than you know."

The timbre of his voice almost held an innuendo. But she let the moment pass. "Are you working a case?"

He nodded. "Actually, I came to discuss *your* investigation."

Ellie gestured for him to come in and he claimed the chair facing her desk. "You saw the news?"

"I did."

Ellie frowned. "One dead girl from Cleveland, Georgia, doesn't constitute a federal case."

"I'm aware of that. But hear me out," he said.

Ellie raised a brow. Now he had her attention. "Go on."

"While I was recuperating, I started looking into some cold cases and found several female teens missing across the states."

"That's not unusual," Ellie said.

"No, but there was a common element among them. Tell me, was Bonnie Sylvester wearing shoes?"

Ellie narrowed her eyes. "As a matter of fact, she wasn't. But we found a red sandal in the grave where she was buried."

Derrick ran his fingers through his thick dark brown hair. "Just one?"

"Yes. Cord is with a team now searching the area for the other one and for evidence. We went to question her foster family but they're gone and we're looking for them." She leaned back in her chair. "Why did you ask about her shoes?"

"Three of the missing girls I noted were found dead. All three were barefoot but one shoe was found and not the other."

"Are you suggesting the killer kept one of the victim's shoes?"

Derrick made a noncommittal sound in his throat. "Wouldn't be far-fetched. Often killers keep souvenirs to remember their kills. This guy might have a thing about girl's shoes."

Ellie considered his comment. "Shoe fetishes are common as feet and shoes signify sexual interest. But Bonnie wasn't sexually assaulted. Were the three others?"

"No. Perhaps he has sexual interest but doesn't rape the girls either because he's impotent or he was sexually abused himself. Sex doesn't actually get him off; it's the violence and satisfaction of the act of killing that does. Collecting the shoes allows him to relive the crime in his mind."

Ellie's phone buzzed so she checked the number. "It's Cord." She answered the call. "Hey."

"El, they finished dragging the pond. They didn't find any other bodies."

Ellie sighed in relief. "That's good news. Derrick is in town, Cord. He suspects our case is related to others he's investigating."

Cord cursed. "What do you think?"

"It's too early to tell. Let's meet at the station in the morning and take a look at everything he has."

A tense silence stretched over the line.

Finally Ellie broke it. "Cord?"

"Yeah, sounds like a plan." His breathing rattled out. "I'm beat. Heading to my cabin to clean up. I'll see you in the morning."

Ellie frowned at his clipped tone. He was definitely in an odd mood. But she didn't have time to dwell on it now. Bonnie needed her.

Derrick stood, his look hooded as he headed to the door. "See you tomorrow."

She grabbed her bag and coat and decided to go home herself. If Derrick was right, they weren't just investigating Bonnie's murder.

They might be looking for a serial killer.

THIRTY-SEVEN

Kat paced her bedroom for an hour, waiting until the living room grew quiet. Daddy wouldn't be home tonight. That was fine with her. Mama would tell him about her short skirt and he'd get mad and yell at her and... it wouldn't go well.

She peeked out the door and saw the lights flicker off downstairs which meant her mama was going to bed. Pulse pounding, she waited another twenty minutes, tugged on her jacket, boots and ski cap, then slipped down the hall.

On the way out, she grabbed a flashlight and tiptoed out the back door, closing it slowly so it wouldn't make a sound.

Seconds later, she stared into the night then snuck through the woods. Grabbing one of the shovels for protection as she passed her daddy's shed, she used the flashlight to illuminate the way toward the graveyard. A faint sprinkling of stars flickered through the darkness, the thin limbs of the pines waving like crooked arms trying to grab her.

Twigs snapped as a branch broke off, and she paused and

studied the dark abyss of land that stretched for miles and miles. "Don't you dare go in those woods," Mama always warned.

"It's too dangerous for young girls," Daddy said. "People say Ruth Higgins' body is out there somewhere."

Suddenly a shadow moved in the distance. The silhouette caught in a sliver of moonlight then disappeared. Brush rattled as the figure ran away from the graveyard. The temptation to follow whoever it was hit her so strongly that she gave chase. Wind gusts tore at the trees and a branch flew off in front of her. A noise sounded behind her and the woods blurred. The man, at least she thought it was a man, got lost in the shadows. Which way had he gone?

Brush crackled as she neared the tree where she'd seen him. Footsteps crunched brush and weeds shifted. She sensed movement and spun around.

Suddenly out of nowhere something struck her on the side of the head.

She stumbled and fell, flailing and clawing at the ground. Pine needles stabbed at her hands and she tasted dirt. Her breath panted out, but she pushed up to her hands and knees and saw boots running away.

Blood trickled down the side of her neck. She swiped at it and looked up, blinking to clear her vision. But he was gone.

Her heart pounded. She hadn't seen his face. Had he seen hers?

THIRTY-EIGHT

Worry gnawed at Cord as he drove home and let himself inside his cabin on the river. Normally the sound of the water rushing over the rocks in the back of his property calmed him. But tonight his insides were twisted into knots.

Fox was back.

Dammit.

He'd figured the agent would return at some point. Maybe even make a play for Ellie.

Perspiration broke out on the back of his neck.

Hell, that's the least of your concerns.

He walked to his closet, opened his safe and studied the contents. The pocket watch was still there. Cracked, the face shattered just like it had been during the struggle that night fifteen years ago. He'd searched for it then, but it had been so dark and stormy he hadn't found it. He'd also been young and stupid and hadn't covered his tracks.

But now he had. It was evidence and he should turn it in. He was betraying Ellie by keeping it here. Better she not know though or she'd be forced to do the right thing and investigate. The truth might not matter. It would be tainted with lies.

But Fox was a top-notch FBI agent with resources beyond the Crooked Creek police department's. If he started nosing around, if the Sylvester girl's death was related to the Ruth Higgins case, then he might dig up the truth.

See that Cord had crossed the line.

He was crossing it now, too.

Cord slammed the door to the safe in an effort to silence the guilty voice in his head and shut down the emotions gripping him like a vise.

Still, if he had to do it all over again, he would.

Maybe Ellie would understand...

He shook his head, then stripped his shirt as he went to the bathroom. His reflection stared back in the mirror above the sink, and he turned and surveyed the scars crisscrossing his back. Maybe she wouldn't care if she knew the truth about him. But what if she was repulsed?

Ellie was the only good thing that had ever happened to him. He couldn't chance losing her.

He turned on the water and cranked it up as hot as he could tolerate, then stepped inside and let the spray beat at his skin. Jaw tensed, he scrubbed hard to erase the dirt and sweat from his body.

But no amount of scrubbing could cleanse the darkness living deep down in his soul or the image of Bonnie Sylvester's skeletal remains from his mind. She was barely a teenager, should have looked innocent and living her life, not decaying in the ground.

A pain he understood well. He'd been that kid once, been left to the wolves. And he'd run away to escape them just like she had.

Only she'd run straight into the wolves' den and paid for it with her life.

THIRTY-NINE
DAY THREE

Ellie picked up breakfast sandwiches and pastries at the Corner Café to fortify the team for their morning meeting. The owner and Cord's former girlfriend, Lola, looked tired today and kept rubbing her pregnant belly. At one time Cord believed the baby was his and planned to marry Lola, but Lola lied to him about the paternity which triggered their break-up. She still hadn't divulged the identity of the baby's father, but Ellie hoped he'd stepped up to support Lola.

As she entered the station, she set the food on the counter in the conference room beside the coffee station, then poured herself a mug. By the time she organized her notes, the team was filing in. Derrick was first and grabbed coffee and a pastry for himself, then claimed a chair across from Ellie and placed his briefcase on the table.

Cord came next, took a ham and egg sandwich and seated himself near Ellie. The men acknowledged each other with a quick hello, the tension between them palpable. When they'd first met, the men hadn't gotten along but over the cases they'd investigated, they'd learned to respect each other's work ethic and skills.

Deputies Landrum and Eastwood trailed in along with her boss and Dr. Whitefeather. Morning pleasantries were exchanged then Ellie took the lead by placing Bonnie Sylvester's photo on the whiteboard.

"This is our victim," she said. "Thirteen-year-old girl from Cleveland, Georgia, whose body was found in Brambletown. She was a foster child, bounced from one home to the other, described as shy and had a difficult time making friends. Her last foster family, the Wileys, claimed she was defiant and ran away." Ellie placed their pictures on the board under the title Suspects. "I drove to their house to question them, but their house was cleaned out and they're in the wind. An APB and a BOLO have been issued."

She angled her head toward Deputy Landrum. "What did you find on them?"

He shook his head. "Not much. No remaining family members and no paper trail. No properties in their name, no credit or debit cards, and no luck locating their car yet."

"Keep digging." Ellie gestured to Shondra. "Deputy Eastwood canvassed people in Brambletown but no one recognized Bonnie. At this point, we have no information on how she ended up in Brambletown, if she'd been somewhere in town or if the killer snatched her in Cleveland or elsewhere and dumped her body in Brambletown hoping no one would find her.

"So our unsub could either live in Brambletown or another town. With all the curiosity seekers visiting the memorial, he could be hiding among them." Ellie turned to the ME. "Dr. Whitefeather, do you have autopsy results?"

Laney stood. "I do. COD was strangulation. Particulates on the red scarf found in the grave and ligature marks on her neck confirm it was used to choke her. No signs of sexual assault, but she did have bruises on her arms, chest and legs indicating she fought her attacker. Bruising on her wrists suggests her hands were bound at some point. Other signs are consistent with prior abuse dating back years."

"Probably from the Wileys." A muscle ticked in Cord's jaw. "How long did Bonnie live with them?"

"About nine months," Ellie answered.

"Nine months of hell," Cord muttered.

Ellie wondered if he was thinking of his own hell, but now wasn't the time to ask.

"Actually, some of the bruises were there longer than that," Laney said. "Striations on the bones indicate some have been there for years."

"Then prior, maybe long-term abuse," Ellie said in disgust. The poor girl had no kind of life and now she died before she had a chance to live. "There's one more detail." Ellie posted a picture of the red sandal on the board. "Bonnie was found shoeless although Dr. Whitefeather recovered a red sandal from the grave. And Ranger McClain found a necklace by the pond on the Wiley property. We're testing it for prints."

Her boss cleared his throat. "The lab called and confirmed the DNA matched Bonnie Sylvester's."

Ellie gestured toward Derrick. "Which brings us to the reason Special Agent Fox is here."

Derrick headed to the whiteboard with a folder in his hand. "During my time off, I did some digging into other missing persons cases and discovered several missing teens cases with similar elements to this one." He added more photos. "These girls' bodies were found. In each of these instances, the girls were strangled and one of the victim's shoes was found with the girls while the other shoe was missing."

A hushed silence filled the room as that information sank in.

"There are other instances where the girls' bodies haven't been recovered that might be related." Next Derrick added a photograph of Ruth Higgins. "Fifteen years ago, Ruth Higgins disappeared from Brambletown. Ruth's remains were never uncovered although one shoe was logged into evidence." He tacked the photo of a red boot on the board.

Ellie sucked in a breath. Was Derrick right? Were these more current murders connected to the Higgins cold case?

FORTY

Derrick shifted, averting his eyes from Ellie. She drove him crazy with her stubbornness and tenacity. That was also what he liked most about her. Whether he helped or not, she would handle this case with professionalism and compassion. And she'd put herself on the line if necessary.

He hoped it didn't come to that.

The innate sense to protect her and work as her partner again had overcome him the moment he'd seen her in her office crouched over the files, gnawing on her lower lip.

He wanted to erase that worry and kiss those damn lips.

That was not an option though. She was with McClain. Like his partner said, he needed to move on.

Stick with the facts. Focus on the investigation. If this was a serial offender, no telling how many girls the unsub might have murdered.

Derrick pointed to each photo of the victims who'd been found as he shared their background history. "I have spoken with the lead detectives on each of these cases. All four girls were from North Georgia.

One, fourteen-year-old Ansley Pollock from Augusta. Three years ago, she attended a youth camp where the group took a day trip to Tallulah Gorge. Counselors stopped for food afterward at a fast-food place, but Ansley never made it back to the bus. Her friend stated she left Ansley in the restroom and planned to meet her outside, but Ansley never showed. No one in the restaurant noticed her or anything suspicious, but the owner said it was jam-packed that day and more than one youth group stopped in, so I guess Ansley didn't stand out. The restrooms were in the back of the restaurant with an exit door close by, which someone had left standing open that day. Whoever abducted her probably left that way and had a vehicle waiting."

Derrick hesitated. "Although one person in the restaurant claimed they thought they saw a man fitting Earl Bramble's description outside earlier that day."

"Where was she found?" Ellie asked.

"In a wooded area not far from the gorge."

She was trying to connect the girls. "Was she in foster care?"

Derrick shook his head. "No, she was being raised by a single mom. Father died in Afghanistan."

He placed another photo on the board. "Victim two: Nineteen months ago, Kelsey Palmer, fifteen, from Helen. Parents deceased, so she lived with her grandmother. She disappeared on an outing during Oktoberfest."

"Again, a crowded place," Ellie said. "Which made it easy for the killer to hide in plain sight."

Deputy Eastwood waved a finger. "Were there security cameras in town?"

"Yes, local police reviewed footage but didn't find anything. I analyzed the police reports, and they were thorough in their investigation. Police finally decided she was abducted by someone traveling through town. She was found thirty miles away in a deserted area of the woods in North Georgia."

"So he snatches them, then strangles them and dumps them in deserted places," Ellie said.

Derrick nodded and added another photo. "Victim three, sixteen-year-old Tracy Cook from Dawsonville. Thirteen months ago. Lived with a single father. She was last seen at the convenience store where she worked as a cashier. Father was questioned and was cleared as he was at the hospital where he worked as a radiology tech. Manager of the store said Tracy clocked out and was going home. She left in her car, but her car was found two miles away in a ditch. Girl was later discovered on farmland outside of Dawsonville."

"Who found her?" Ellie asked.

"Owner of the farm. Seventy-five-year-old Gunther Stevens when he went out to feed the chickens. Wife claimed they were at church the night before and then came home to bed. They were ruled out. No cameras on the property."

"And last, victim four, fifteen-year-old Helena Mires from Ballground. Raised by a single mother. Rode her bike home from school every day but six months ago she didn't make it home. Her bike was found on the side of the road leading to her house. Three days later, her body was discovered six miles away in the mountains."

"All those victims were strangled?" Ellie asked.

Derrick nodded. "With red scarves. And they were all missing one of their shoes." He added photos of the scarves and shoes and wrote a question mark beside the word "Red."

Ellie couldn't deny the similarities.

"We don't know the significance of leaving one shoe and taking the other, but it's possible the color red triggers a past trauma," said Derrick.

"It's the color of blood," Ellie said simply.

Exactly what he was thinking. "Unfortunately, we have no suspects. But we believe the same person, the killer, was in all these places at one time. And that north North Georgia is his hunting ground."

FORTY-ONE

Ellie's stomach churned. If this killer was the same one who'd abducted Ruth fifteen years ago, there could be victims they hadn't found. The enormity of that and that they had no definitive persons of interest worried her even more.

She drummed her fingers on the table. "The fact that there are multiple victims in different locations could suggest that our killer either travels around or his job takes him to these areas."

"The work angle would definitely fit," Derrick agreed.

"But that's another needle in the haystack," Ellie said. "He could be homeless and moving around or his job involves travel, which could be anything from a traveling salesman to a writer to a truck driver, delivery guy, handyman, a traveling nurse, even Uber driver."

She gestured to Deputy Landrum who was their resident tech expert. "Landrum, start looking into that. Check with the detectives working the cases Agent Fox just added to the murder board. See if the families mentioned someone related to them or acquaintances who might fit those descriptions." It was a long shot but they had to start somewhere.

"On it," Deputy Landrum said. "Send me copies of the police reports, Agent Fox."

Derrick nodded. "My partner at the Bureau is searching the girls' social media, emails and texts for connections to one another. Maybe a teen chat room or something. Our killer could be a cyber stalker."

"Good point," Ellie said. They needed more manpower. The FBI had sophisticated technology and more expertise in doing that than their police department. "We need as much help as we can get."

"I'll ask Angelica Gomez here for another press conference," Captain Hale added.

Ellie didn't want to create panic, but if the news story brought in a helpful tip, it was worth it.

Derrick cleared his throat. "Detective Reeves, if our first victim was Ruth Higgins, I suggest we go to Brambletown."

"Agreed. Maybe someone remembered something that seemed unimportant at the time. Or if they've kept secrets, the realization that the kidnapper/killer may have not stopped with Ruth, might shake them up enough to talk."

Cord shifted restlessly. "If you need manpower to question locals, I'm in."

Ellie nodded. Cord had proven helpful on all the cases they'd worked together. Not officially being a cop might make it easier for some people to open up to him.

Time was not on their side. They needed answers before the killer struck again.

FORTY-TWO

Athens, Georgia

Jacey Ward shoved her fingers through her tousled hair as she slipped from the mattress on the floor where she'd been sleeping with her boyfriend, Cameron. He lay on his back in his boxers, arms and legs sprawled, snoring.

She dragged on her T-shirt and skirt, then slipped on her red boots. When she'd first met Cam, he'd been the guy of her dreams. Cute, buff, sweet and flirty. She'd met him with one of her friends at the local coffee shop and fallen head over heels in love.

The first time she'd snuck out of her parents' house to meet him at one of his friend's parties she thought she'd died and gone to heaven. All her friends were so jealous. Three months later, her parents had found out and grounded her for life.

But that hadn't stopped her. She'd run away with him. After all, she'd dreamed about attending UGA and he was in Athens, right where she wanted to be.

At first it had been romantic. He rented a tiny apartment and they hooked up all the time.

Until he'd turned to weed then cocaine with his buddies. She'd experimented once but drugs made her paranoid and she'd regretted it.

But Cam went down the rabbit hole and never came back.

His parents had cut him off money wise, then he'd lost the apartment and they started couch surfing with anyone who'd put them up. That didn't last long so now they stayed here in this hostel, packed in with some homeless guys who gave her the creeps when they looked at her.

Shame burned her face as she remembered what had happened the night before. One of them had tried to feel her up but she'd pushed him away. High as a kite, Cam had been mad. He was low on coke and suggested she sleep with the guy in exchange for a score.

She rubbed her cheek which still stung from where he'd slapped her.

Snores rippled all around the room where those guys had passed out. The scent of beer, cigarettes, pot, male sweat and vomit where someone had thrown up clogged the air.

What are you doing here, Jacey? If your parents saw you living like this, they'd be mortified. She was mortified, too.

For the dozenth time since she'd left, she wanted to go home.

But she looked down at her skinny frame and dirty clothes and wondered if her parents would want her.

Tears blurred her eyes, and she tiptoed toward the door. Maybe she'd persuade them to let her come back. She knew they'd been looking for her, had heard they'd offered a reward for her return.

Suddenly she felt someone behind her. She glanced over her shoulder. Cam. His foul breath turned her stomach.

"Where the hell do you think you're going?" he growled.

The anger in his eyes sent a chill through her. He'd been furious at her last night. Was he going to hit her again?

She licked her dry lips. "To get us something to eat," she lied.

His fingers closed around her wrist, nails digging into her skin. "With what? We're broke." A nasty leer colored his unshaven face. "You gonna do what I told you to do last night?"

She could hardly believe this scraggy, smelly cokehead was the guy she'd fallen for. And that he wanted to pimp her out for drugs.

She took a deep breath and offered him a smile. "I'm starving. I'll do whatever I have to do."

He stared at her for a long minute, then gave her a demeaning look. "Don't be long. And for fuck's sake, don't get knocked up."

She glared at him.

"And don't come back unless you have what I want."

"'Kay." Her heart pounding, she vowed never to come back. Clouds hovered above, the wind whirling trash along the sidewalk as she stepped outside.

Tears clogged her throat and blurred her vision, but she broke into a run.

The wind beat at her face as she jogged through the streets. She finally found a convenience store, ducked inside and combed the snack aisle until there was no line at the checkout counter and she got up the nerve to ask the clerk if she could borrow the phone.

The woman looked her up and down, then sympathy filled her eyes and she asked, "Is it local?"

Jacey nodded. "I need to call my folks."

"Of course, darlin'." The woman's eyes were kind as she handed Jacey the handset.

Jacey's finger shook as she stabbed her mother's phone number. She held her breath as the phone rang and rang. *Please answer, Mom. I need you and I want to come home.*

But voicemail picked up and she heard her mother's voice. "Sorry I can't answer right now. Please leave a message."

The beep sounded and she blurted, "Mom, it's me. I'm coming home."

As she hung up, the clerk was watching with curiosity, and Jacey's cheeks burned. She quickly turned and rushed outside into the night. She should have probably told her mother where she was and to pick her up. But her parents had been so angry with her the last few months she'd been at home. They'd also been fighting constantly between themselves, and she'd heard them talking in hushed voices about divorcing.

"Jacey is the problem," her father had said. "I think we need to send her away."

"She is tearing us apart," her mother agreed.

"I'll look into one of those group homes where they straighten out troubled kids," her father said.

Jacey's throat clogged with emotions. She hadn't wanted to be sent away. So she'd run away herself.

What an idiot she'd been.

Tears blurred her eyes, and she turned and ducked into the shadows, sat down on a cardboard box in the alley and sobbed like a baby.

FORTY-THREE

He stood beneath the UGA arches, wondering if his life would have been different if he'd had the opportunity to go to college.

But he'd been trapped with an ignorant mother with no money or motivation and told he was stupid and worthless his whole life. A smile curved his mouth though as he watched a pretty blond stumble from the bar across the street. The temptation to take her struck him like lightning zipping through his veins, but seconds later, a group of her friends joined her, staggering as they held each other up.

Too dangerous. Besides, he liked them a little younger before they'd spread their legs for half a dozen boys.

Adrenaline heated his blood. There were dozens of girls on the UGA campus every day. Pretty and vulnerable because they lived in youthful denial that predators lurked among the college crowd with their fake IDs, propensity to get trashed at the bars and loose morals. Free at last from their parental bonds, they were excited to test their independence and live on the edge.

He crossed the street, tugged his bulldog cap low over his forehead and headed down the street away from the hub of the party life where he'd parked his truck. Night had long set in, and clouds obliterated the stars, adding a layer of darkness that helped him go unnoticed by curious eyes. Nobody gave him a second glance.

He climbed in his truck and drove to the gas station, then filled up. As he finished, he heard something in the alley. A sick cat?

No... it sounded human.

He eased his way into the alley and spotted a teenage girl slumped on a cardboard box crying into her hands. She wore a Georgia sweatshirt and was younger than the coeds, maybe fifteen or sixteen.

He jammed his hands in his pockets and walked slowly so as not to alarm her, adopting a non-threatening expression and tone as he reached her.

"Hey, miss," he said as he paused by the corner. "Are you okay?"

Her eyes widened as she looked up at him, cheeks red and splotchy from her emotional outburst. She looked young and innocent yet haunted at the same time. His fingers itched to touch her, to pull the red scarf from his pocket. To feel his fingers close around her throat.

The red boots caught his eyes. A lot of the college girls wore the UGA colors of red and black.

Temptation stirred inside him.

"I just want to help," he said in a low tone. "Make sure you get where you're going."

She stared at him for a long minute, body trembling, indecision warring in her eyes.

He held up his hands as if to indicate he wasn't a threat. "It's dangerous for a young girl to be out here alone. I'll walk you where you want to go. Or I have my truck. I can drive you to the bus station if that's what you want."

Her breath heaved out. "I don't have money for a ticket."

He smiled and pulled some cash from his pocket. "Here, this should be enough."

She took it and clutched it in her hand as if it was her lifeline. She still looked wary but seemed to relax slightly.

"Why would you do that?" she asked in a shaky voice.

He shrugged. "I have a sister your age. If she was in trouble, I'd hope someone would do the same for her."

Footsteps sounded behind her, and she peered around the corner, then gave a nod. "A ride to the bus station would be great."

His heart began to pound, and he gestured for her to walk with him, making sure he didn't spook her by getting too close. When they reached his truck, she hesitated again and looked around. A shadow appeared on the sidewalk behind her, and she made a little yelping sound of fear, then jumped into the passenger seat.

Victory sent excitement through his veins, and he got in and locked the doors. The clicking of the lock sounded like music to his ears.

So would her scream when he got her to a deserted area and she realized she'd climbed in the car with a killer.

FORTY-FOUR

Brambletown

Tilly had managed to hide out from the Brambles and keep a low profile with the locals the day before, but if she wanted answers about Ruth's disappearance, she had to face her fears and dive in.

She spent the morning photographing the memorial, making notes on the names of those buried and interviewing spectators who'd visited to pay their respects. Some had no connection to the people who'd died at the hands of the coal mountain fire and toxins but were intrigued by the history; several others had lost family members and wanted to honor them. Many brought flowers and took photographs in front of the stonework. There were also a handful of locals protesting the memorial with picket signs saying the shrine to the dead was only driving another stake in their hearts and would incite people to move away again. Already the neighborhoods closest to the cemetery hummed with sadness.

One man with burn scars on his face and arms stood in

front of a marker etched with the name Thomas Franklin. Tilly paused and watched as pain contorted his face.

"I'm sorry for your loss," she said softly. "What's your name, sir?"

"Emanuel Black," he said bluntly.

She gestured to the marker. "Was he related to you?"

He jerked around, his eyes pinning her with anger. "No, my father is over there with my mother." He gestured toward the opposite side of the graveyard. "I think this man is one of the people responsible for the fire that killed them."

"I wasn't aware they'd determined that," she said. "Was he punished?"

Rage darkened the man's expression. "No, it was never proven. But that's going to change."

Tilly's heart went out to him although his tone alarmed her. She did understand what it was like for the truth to go unexposed. What was he planning to do?

He simply turned back to the stone, dropped a black rose on it and walked away.

Grief and devastation lingered after he was gone.

Shaken, she roamed the graveyard searching for Earl Bramble in case he'd died in the last decade and a half and his daughters had buried him at Green Gardens, which was filled with other Bramble family members.

No Earl Bramble though.

Which meant the bastard was probably still on the loose, hiding from the law. If he'd kidnapped Ruth and killed her, he knew where she was. And she wanted that information. But most of all she wanted him to suffer the way she and her family had.

FORTY-FIVE

Ellie's mind raced. "If these cases are related and Ruth was the first victim, let's start with the original investigation."

"I have notes on who was questioned and persons of interest," Derrick said as he moved to a second whiteboard.

"Please fill us in." Ellie said, not surprised he'd already done some of the grunt work.

"First case, Ruth Higgins. The primary suspect was Earl Bramble, the caretaker of the graveyard at the time. According to locals, he was a mean son of a bitch who may have abused his daughter, Ida, and niece Hetty, who moved in with them after her own father was killed in a tractor accident. Her mother died of cancer two years before that."

"He couldn't have been too bad if he took in his niece," Deputy Landrum interjected.

Cord grunted, his tone bitter. "You'd be surprised."

"That's true," Derrick agreed. "Although the girls never actually accused him of abuse, people claimed he was harsh and forced the girls, especially Hetty, to work long hours at the graveyard." He paused. "Later, when the sheriff was on the verge of making an arrest, Earl disappeared, making him look guilty."

"Of course, Ida and Hetty were suspects as well," Derrick continued. "Apparently, they got into a fight at the Dairy Queen with Ruth and had other altercations at school with her which earned the Bramble girls a bad reputation and school suspension."

"A couple of other kids stated that Ruth started the fight, that she was a bully to Ida and Hetty," Ellie added. "But Ruth's father was powerful in the town and may have misused that power to twist the story in his daughter's favor."

Shondra and Deputy Landrum were both taking notes, while Cord crossed his arms and remained stoic.

"Police also questioned Ruth's father, Edward, and her brother, Hayden. Mr. Higgins was mayor at the time and supposedly overprotective of Ruth. He especially didn't like her dating. According to Ruth's sister, Tilly, Ruth snuck out the night of her disappearance to meet a guy, but she refused to tell Tilly who she was meeting. Their brother, Hayden, had a drug problem and anger issues. According to other students, he didn't get along with Ruth either. He claimed he was at a friend's house the night Ruth disappeared."

"Clint Wallace, the sheriff's son was also on the list because he and Ruth were dating. Other students stated that Ruth had just broken up with Clint. Which could have given him motive to hurt Ruth. His father, Sheriff Chester Wallace, gave him an alibi by claiming his son was home all night."

"He could have covered for his son," Cord pointed out.

"True. But would he continue to protect Clint if he suspected he'd killed again?" Ellie rubbed her temple in thought. "We can't forget Earl Bramble. He was the primary suspect fifteen years ago and could have been moving around all these years and killed the other victims on our board.

"There have been several calls across Georgia over the years claiming they saw Bramble but he was never caught."

Cord pulled a hand down his chin. "Why return to the original crime scene to dump Bonnie Sylvester's body? It makes more sense that there's a copycat and he brought Bonnie's body to Brambletown to frame Earl."

Ellie had to consider all options. "Then we get started and talk to everyone again. We know Clint Wallace is sheriff now and his father still lives in Brambletown. What about the others?"

Derrick answered, "The Higgins family moved away to escape the media attention, but I don't have their current location. The daughter Tilly attended UGA and now works in Atlanta with the *AJC* writing travel pieces."

"I'll contact Tilly," Ellie said. "Shondra, see if you can find Mr. and Mrs. Higgins."

"I'm trying to track down the son," Derrick said. "He joined the military and received an honorable discharge. One arrest for a bar fight a few months later. Charges were dismissed because a woman there testified that he was protecting her from a stalker. But that's as far as I've gotten."

Ellie made a mental list of questions to ask. "We also have to question Ida and Hetty Bramble. It's possible they know where Earl is and have been covering for him all these years."

FORTY-SIX

After leaving the graveyard, Tilly stopped at Daisy's Diner and kept her head down as the hostess led her to a booth in the corner. The little café was filled with the lunch crowd and just as she ordered sweet iced tea and a chicken salad sandwich, Ida and Hetty Bramble rushed in from the cold.

She'd recognize them anywhere, although neither woman had aged well. Wrinkles around Ida's eyes made her look tired and her brown hair looked dry and brittle and needed a trim. She'd gained about thirty pounds and her sweatpants and sweatshirt were faded. Her limp seemed even more pronounced, her posture slumped as if she lacked the energy to hold herself up.

Hetty wore old coveralls, her short black hair so choppy it looked as if she'd cut it herself just as she had in high school. Her skin looked ghostly and sallow, odd since she worked outside at her gardening center. A colorful tattoo of fireflies dotted her wrist.

The temptation to flee the diner struck Tilly. But she

wanted answers, dammit, and running hadn't gotten her those before.

"Look, there's another news report about that girl they found near the graveyard," the woman seated in the booth behind her said. A hushed silence fell across the room as Daisy clicked the remote to increase the volume.

"This is Angelica Gomez coming to you from Crooked Creek where Detective Ellie Reeves, who is working in conjunction with the task force which includes Special Agent Derrick Fox and Ranger Cord McClain, has an update on the investigation into fifteen-year-old Bonnie Sylvester's death." She tilted the microphone toward Detective Reeves. "Detective."

"As we revealed before, Ms. Sylvester's body was found in Brambletown. We now have information that suggests her murder is connected to several other girls who have disappeared across North Georgia over the past few years." The detective shifted. "One of those is the disappearance of Ruth Higgins who went missing from Brambletown fifteen years ago. Ms. Higgins was never found but her case is being reopened. I promise the citizens of this state we'll do everything in our power to find out what happened to her, Ms. Sylvester and the other girls who may have also been victimized by the same perpetrator."

A photo of Ruth in her cheerleading outfit appeared, a giant red bow attached to her blond ponytail. In comparison, that morning Tilly had woken up with a pimple on her nose and hadn't wanted to go to school. Ruth had laughed at her.

Although she did have some good memories of her sister when she was little. Tilly was scared of storms and when she was small used to hide under the covers. But Ruth let her crawl in bed with her for the night. They'd cuddled together and Ruth told her stories to distract her. She missed that sister.

The detective continued by detailing and showing pictures

of four other girls whose bodies had been discovered in a similar manner to Bonnie's.

Tilly glanced at Ida and Hetty who both looked pale-faced and shocked. Tension radiated in the air, and she suddenly felt pulled toward them. They must have felt it too or sensed she was in the room because Ida's gaze met hers and she clutched Hetty's arm as she realized Tilly was back.

And the case was being opened.

Which meant police would question everyone involved, including them, and Tilly's own family. The nightmare of the past would start all over. Wounds would be reopened, gossip would run amok and their lives would come under scrutiny.

Just the thought of it transported her back in time to the night Ruth disappeared. She stared into her coffee, but in her mind she saw her childhood bedroom.

Tilly woke to the sound of footsteps across the hall then the screech of the window being opened. The bitter winter wind blasted her as she tiptoed into the hall and peeked into Ruth's room. Rubbing her hands over her flannel PJs, she shoved her tangled hair from her face and saw Ruth dressed in a skirt and red sweater. "What are you doing?" Tilly whispered.

Ruth jerked around and shushed her. Her blond hair was swept into a high ponytail and sparkly red earrings hung from her earlobes. "Going out," she mouthed with a smile.

A sliver of moonlight shimmied through the open window. "But it's the middle of the night."

Ruth stormed across the room to her, fists on her slender hips. Even angry, her sister still looked pretty. "I know what time it is, but I'm meeting somebody."

"Who?" Tilly asked. More than one boy at school had a crush on Ruth. The sheriff's son for one. Although they'd just broken up. "Clint Wallace?"

"No. It's a secret." Ruth squeezed Tilly's arm. "And you'd

better not tattletale. If you do, I'll tell Mom and Dad you have no friends at school."

Her sharp words cut through Tilly and tears stung her eyes.

"But going out at night could be dangerous, Ruth. Mom and Dad will—"

"What they don't know won't hurt them," Ruth said with a giggle. "Besides, I'll be back before they wake up and they'll never know."

Ruth surprised Tilly by giving her a quick kiss on the cheek. "Don't be such a worry wart and go back to sleep, sis. Tomorrow we'll watch a movie together. Your choice."

Tilly nodded. That would be fun, like old times.

With a little wave, Ruth pranced across the room and climbed through the window. Tilly noticed her sister was wearing her red knee-high boots, the ones that made her look an inch taller. The ones Tilly wanted to borrow but Ruth refused to share.

Shivering as another gust of wind whipped through, Tilly tiptoed to the window, closed it then hurried back to her room and crawled in bed.

Then she closed her eyes, shutting out the worry gnawing at her. Ruth would be fine. She always came out on top. She'd sneak back in the morning gloating at the fact that she got away with her secret midnight rendezvous.

And then she'd make popcorn and they'd huddle on the couch and watch a movie together just like they used to do when they were little.

FORTY-SEVEN

Given their tasks, the team disbanded from the conference room to their own offices and cubicles, except for Cord who remained to study a topical map of Brambletown, the graveyard and No Man's Land.

A call had come in about Earl Bramble, someone who claimed they'd seen him in Helen, Georgia, so Sheriff Waters left to check it out. If they found him, maybe they could end this killing spree of his and finally locate Ruth Higgins.

Ellie retreated to her office and called the *Atlanta Journal-Constitution* newspaper office to inquire about Tilly while Derrick used the corner area in her office to work on locating Ruth's brother.

A receptionist answered, "*AJC*. Jennifer speaking."

Ellie identified herself. "I need to speak to Tilly Higgins. I understand she works there."

"Yes, she freelances for us. But she's currently on assignment in Brambletown."

Tilly was in Brambletown. "Can you give me her contact information? I need to talk to her."

"Sure."

Ellie jotted down Tilly's phone number as the woman rattled off the numbers, then thanked her, hung up and phoned the number. The call went straight to voicemail so she left a message asking Tilly to return the call.

Tilly being back in Brambletown was no coincidence.

Was she trying to connect the dots between Bonnie's murder and Ruth's disappearance?

FORTY-EIGHT

Ida choked on her fried chicken as her gaze met Tilly's. A litany of curse words boomeranged in her head.

She leaned closer to Hetty and whispered, "Lord have mercy. You were right. Tilly's here. I hoped we'd never have to see her damn face again."

Ida wiped her mouth and reached for her sweet tea, washing down the chicken stuck in her throat.

"Bet she came about that body," Hetty muttered. "I heard she's some kind of reporter at the Atlanta paper."

The ice in Ida's glass clinked as she set her tea glass on the table. She had to admit Tilly looked better than she used to. She'd always lived in Ruth's shadow, but she was attractive now, not the mousy girl with her nose crammed in a book all the time. Her dark auburn hair looked soft and wavy, her skin clear, and without glasses, her brown eyes looked almost golden. Her sweater was neat, her jeans nice, not raggedy like hers.

Ida looked ancient in comparison. Some days she felt like she needed tape to lift her baggy eyes. And Hetty's skin was leathery from working in the gardening center and taking care of the graveyard. Most days she smelled like sweat and fertilizer.

Ida's stomach twisted into knots. "She's not our only problem."

Hetty rocked her chair back and forth in a nervous gesture. "You mean the dead girl and the cops?"

"Yeah. And did you hear who's working with that detective?"

"The FBI," Hetty said, her voice cracking.

Ida nodded. "That ranger, too. You remember him, don't you?"

Hetty scrunched her nose in thought but seemed confused. "Who is he?"

Sometimes Ida thought Hetty might be having memory issues, maybe early onset Alzheimer's. Or breathing in the fertilizer could be killing her brain cells.

"Cord McClain."

Hetty's eyes widened in panic as the realization dawned. "Shit, we have to avoid *him*. The police are going to be all over the place again."

Ida nodded, her stomach roiling. "They're gonna wanna know where Daddy is."

Hetty pressed her trembling hand over Ida's. "Then we tell them the same thing we did before."

The lie rose in Ida's throat as if it was yesterday. She had to swallow hard to get it out. "Right, we stick to our story."

"He left and we don't know where he is," Hetty finished.

Ida stewed for a minute. "Exactly. The less we say the better. If we start speculating or talking about him, they'll just ask more questions."

Questions neither one of them wanted to answer.

FORTY-NINE

The Grind

Ellie and Derrick headed into town to find Tilly and the Bramble girls. Operating on the theory that the killer might revisit Green Gardens Cemetery and literally be hiding in the midst of curious tourists, Cord offered to station himself near the graveyard and watch for suspicious activity.

Ellie's phone buzzed. Sheriff Waters. "Did you find Bramble?" she asked when he answered.

"No," Bryce said. "I did check the camera at the diner where the call came from and there was a man in a black pickup but his face was obscure. He took off headed east but I couldn't get a read on his plate."

Dammit. "Alert the law enforcement along that route to be on the lookout for him and that truck."

"Already done that," Bryce said.

Ellie thanked him and hung up. If one call came in, maybe there would be another.

Her phone buzzed again. Tilly. Ellie quickly connected.

"Tilly, it's Detective Reeves. I'd like to meet and talk about your sister's case. I can come to your house."

"No," Tilly said. "How about the coffee shop, The Grind?"

Ellie wondered if Tilly was hiding something at the house but agreed. She needed a read on the woman before making any judgments. "We'll head there now."

Ellie ended the call and plugged The Grind into her GPS, then headed toward it. "She sounded nervous when I mentioned her house," Ellie said.

"Probably dredges up bad memories," Derrick said. "She was only fourteen when Ruth disappeared and her family was put under the microscope."

"That's one reason I want to talk to her," Ellie said. "Maybe she's remembered something since then. Or perhaps she omitted details about that night or her family that could have been helpful." If she had, Ellie would find out.

Ten minutes later, she pulled into the parking lot for The Grind, an eclectic-looking coffee shop with an etching of a giant coffee mug beside an old-fashioned coffee grinder etched on the front window. Together she and Derrick exited the Jeep and walked to the door.

Ellie scanned the room. Much like the coffee shops in Atlanta, seating areas were situated for working and small couches and comfy chairs occupied the back wall near a stone fireplace. Like Daisy's Diner, it was actually quaint and inviting as if the owner wanted to add life to the fledgling run-down town.

The strong scent of chicory, hazelnut, vanilla and mocha wafted through the cozy space, surprising Ellie. Daisy's Diner and The Grind were both attempting to bring their businesses into the current century.

"What does she look like?" Derrick asked.

Ellie pulled the photograph from Tilly's column and tilted

her phone for him to see. His eyes brightened slightly and he scanned the room.

"She's back there by the fireplace," Derrick said, gesturing toward Tilly. "I'll get us some coffees if you want to head on back."

"Thanks. I'll take—"

"I remember what you like," Derrick said with a twitch of a smile.

He strode to the order counter and Ellie made her way back to Tilly who was fidgeting and rubbing her hands together as if she couldn't get warm. The woman was about her age and pretty with curves, glossy auburn hair, and wore a dark green sweater, jeans and boots.

Ellie introduced herself, then Derrick appeared with their coffee, and they exchanged pleasantries. Tilly hugged her coffee in her hands and took a sip, but Ellie saw her gaze rake over Derrick with appreciation. She obviously thought he was handsome, and something sparked in his eyes as he seated himself across from Tilly.

"I know why you're here," Tilly said, dragging her gaze from Derrick as she squared her shoulders. "Do you have new information about my sister's disappearance?"

Ellie licked whipped cream from her mocha. "Nothing concrete," she said honestly. "But I'm sure you saw the news and know we're examining her case to see if it's connected to Bonnie Sylvester's murder."

"Why do you think they're connected?" Tilly asked.

Ellie's heart squeezed at the hint of hope in Tilly's voice. "As we mentioned on the news, we discovered several other girls around your sister's age who've gone missing across Georgia over the last few years."

"But how can you tell it's related to Ruth when her body was never found?"

"We can't say definitively," Ellie said. "Can you tell us what happened the night Ruth disappeared?"

Tilly traced her finger around the rim of her coffee mug. "Ruth snuck out that night. I... was in bed and heard her opening the window in her room."

"Did she say where she was going?" Ellie asked.

"To meet a boy," Tilly answered. "I told the police that at the time."

Derrick sipped his black coffee. "Not that night, but the next morning when your parents realized she was gone."

Misery flashed in Tilly's eyes. "I know, I should have told them sooner. But... Ruth told me to keep quiet."

"You were just a kid yourself, Tilly," Derrick said, his voice thick with empathy.

Tilly gave him a grateful look.

"Did she say where she was meeting this guy?" Ellie asked.

"No," Tilly said. "She just said it was a secret. That she'd be back before our parents woke up and they'd never know she was gone. But if I'd told, she might still be here today."

"Don't blame yourself, Tilly. It's not your fault," Derrick said softly.

Tilly's gaze met Derrick's and Ellie realized they shared a connection, not just a spark of attraction. Guilt was a powerful emotion.

"Ruth was dating Clint Wallace, wasn't she?" Ellie asked.

"Yes, but they'd just broken up." Tilly cradled her coffee again. "I got the impression she was meeting another guy just to piss him off."

"Do you have any idea who? Someone from school?"

Tilly shook her head. "No. All the guys liked Ruth. It was the girls who didn't."

"You're talking about Ida and Hetty Bramble, aren't you?"

"Yes." Tilly's gaze scanned the room as if she wanted to make sure they weren't in the coffee shop.

"We know they got into a brawl with her," Ellie said. "Was there more to it than that?"

Tilly pressed a hand to her chest. "Look, I don't want to disparage Ruth. She's my sister and I loved her."

"I understand. But?" Ellie's voice was gentle. "If she was enemies with the girls or another boy, they might be involved in her disappearance," Ellie said. Although how that would connect them to the other victims on their murder board she didn't know. But if they were, she'd find out.

Tilly ran her fingers through her hair, sending the waves cascading over her shoulders. "The police went through all this before. Multiple times."

"I know but bear with us," Derrick said gruffly. "Sometimes fresh eyes see things that were missed the first go around. And if the same killer is at work now, we need to stop him before he takes another life."

Tilly sighed wearily. "Ruth was mean to them, made fun of them for not having nice clothes and for living by the graveyard."

Which would go toward a motive.

"But they were mean to Ruth, too," Tilly added. "They were jealous of Ruth and I think one of them had a crush on Clint."

"Do you think they were capable of murder?" Derrick asked.

Tension stretched in the air. "I... don't know," Tilly said. "But... even so... Ruth didn't deserve to die."

Derrick patted Tilly's hand. "I understand this is difficult. I lost my sister when I was young and it still haunts me."

Tilly sniffed, sadness radiating from her somber eyes. "It tore our family apart."

"Mine, too," Derrick murmured.

Derrick and Tilly locked gazes.

Sympathy for Derrick and Tilly filled Ellie. Guilt and anguish had driven his father to suicide.

She let the moment pass. "Please make a list of anyone else at school who might have been angry with Ruth, Tilly. Especially another boy?"

Tilly nodded that she would. "Again, why do you think Ruth's case and these others are connected?"

"We can't discuss details at this stage," Ellie answered. "When the police investigated your sister's disappearance, was there a particular place they searched?"

"Outside our house and the woods behind it," she admitted. "And I told them about the watering hole at the overhang."

"Why would you think they'd go there?" Derrick asked.

"It was the make-out spot for all the teenagers."

"Did they find any of Ruth's belongings?" Ellie asked.

Tilly shrugged. "Not her clothes, but I think they found one of her shoes. I thought she might have taken them off if they waded in the watering hole but it was freezing that night so I don't know."

"They only found one?" Derrick asked.

Tilly nodded.

"What kind of shoes was she wearing?" Ellie asked.

"Red knee-high boots," Tilly said.

Ellie and Derrick exchanged a silent look. Red shoes were part of the unsub's MO.

FIFTY

Green Gardens Cemetery

Hetty tended the snapdragons and pansies around the fountain at the entrance to the graveyard, grateful to add some color to the gloomy sight of the morose-looking graves.

Some people visited and took care of their family members' plots and brought flowers, but others had been abandoned to the elements and required her to spruce them up.

She enjoyed the feel of fresh dirt on her hands and the smell of the earth and tried to make the land cheerier, hoping in some small way she could atone for the things she'd done in this very place.

A few tourists wandered by the memorial, some snapping photographs and selfies, their morbid curiosity evident, while others searched the names, most likely looking for a friend or relative. That man with the burn scars was back today and was roaming the graveyard, photographing the tombstones.

Memories of running and playing chase through the graveyard at night struck her. She and Ida had played ghosts in the graveyard for fun and had jumped in the freshly dug graves to play hide-and-seek or spy on visitors. They'd used the hose to fill up a new grave and pretended it was their swimming pond.

They'd lured Ruth there once by slipping her a note signed with Clint's name and asking her to meet him. When Ruth showed up, they'd run up behind her, blindfolded her and pushed her into the grave then tossed dirt on top of her. Ruth told her father who'd stormed over to their house and yelled at them, then threatened that if they ever did that again, he'd have the sheriff arrest them.

That night their daddy made them sleep outside in the graveyard as punishment. All night they'd listened and watched for the ghosts people claimed they saw rising from the graves and emerging like dark silhouettes from the toxic land beyond.

Hetty glanced toward the woods with worry. Dammit, she wished everyone would leave so she could sneak in there and check on her spot. A truck pulled up and parked near the garden, then that ranger jumped out, shading his eyes with his hand as he scanned the area.

Hetty's stomach plummeted. Cord McClain.

She went bone still, their gazes locking as he recognized her. A nervous tremor rippled through Hetty. Having him back here took her back to the worst night of her life.

One she'd been running from ever since.

Finally she'd found peace through her nursery. But the ranger could blow it up in a skinny minute if he talked.

He gave a nod in recognition, then turned and headed into the woods. Their secrets lingered there in the shadows, secrets she wanted to keep hidden. Secrets he could spill. Ones that could destroy her and Ida.

What are you going to do about it, Hetty?

The answer came with no hesitation. *Whatever I have to.*

FIFTY-ONE

Ellie and Derrick stopped by Hetty's gardening center, The Green Thumb, and were told she was tending the graveyard so they found Ida's address and drove to her house, a trailer in the mobile home park that looked as if it could use some touches from Hetty's business. A cement birdbath looked ancient and unkempt with twigs and dead leaves overflowing it. The trailer needed new paint and a variety of ceramic rabbits dotted the flower garden which held dead flowers and weeds. Odd that her sister ran a gardening center, but Ida's place looked lifeless, as if it had been abandoned.

"Is Ida married?" Ellie asked.

"Yes, to her high school sweetheart, Joe Jones," Derrick said. "They have a daughter named Kat who's fifteen."

Ellie frowned. She'd seen Kat in the diner that day. "All our victims are between the age of thirteen and sixteen. Her mother must be worried."

"Probably," Derrick agreed.

Ellie knocked while Derrick surveyed the property like he

always did when he first arrived. Being constantly on alert for trouble and sizing up a place or situation went with the job, and Derrick was acutely observant.

He and Cord shared that trait.

The door squeaked open, and Ida stood there, wiping her hands on a kitchen towel. Her frizzy, dull brown hair looked damp with sweat and flour dusted her apron.

"Mrs. Jones, I'm Detective Reeve and this is Special Agent Fox. May we come in?" Ellie asked.

Ida's wary look skated over her and Derrick, then she bit her lower lip, nodded and waved them inside.

"Can I get you some sweet iced tea or something?" she asked as she led them to the kitchen. Dirty dishes were piled in the sink, yet homemade uncooked biscuits occupied a tray which looked ready to go into the oven.

"Tea would be nice," Derrick said.

Deciding the kitchen wasn't as clean as Ellie liked, she declined. Ida's hand trembled as she poured the tea and handed it to Derrick. They seated themselves at the table and Ida joined them, fidgeting with her apron.

"I'm sure by now you've seen the news about the body we found in Brambletown," Ellie said.

Ida nodded and stared at her flour-dusted hands. "You think her murder was related to Ruth Higgins' disappearance?"

"We do," Ellie said although she didn't intend to share the details. Both Ida and Hetty had to be treated like persons of interest.

"Well, I didn't know this girl Bonnie Sylvester."

"But you knew Ruth. Both you and your cousin had run-ins with her."

"Ruth was a snotty brat who thought she was better than everyone else," Ida said flatly. "But like I told the sheriff back then, I didn't kill her. And even if I had, I got my own family now. Why would I kill this other girl that I don't even know?"

That was a good question. There were also multiple victims to be accounted for who also had no connection to Ida. "You have a point," Ellie said. And statistically women serial killers were rare. "We understand though that your father was the primary suspect."

Ida tensed. "Along with Ruth's daddy and brother."

The ice rattled in Derrick's glass as he sipped the tea. "We'll also be talking to them."

"Talk to Tilly Higgins, too. She was jealous of her sister because Ruth left her out. I always thought she might have done it."

Ellie arched a brow. "We've already spoken with her." Even if she believed Ida or Hetty or Tilly hurt Ruth, why would they kill other young girls? It didn't make sense.

"Let's talk about your father," Derrick said. "He disappeared just when the sheriff was about to make an arrest, didn't he?"

Ida hissed between her teeth. "There was talk of that," she said. "But gossip spreads like fire on dry brush. That's how small towns work. Anytime something bad happens around here, people want to lay the blame on the Brambles." She fidgeted again, her tone bitter. "But I tell you what. There were a lot of sorry men around town back then and there still are. Sometimes vagrants or people running from the law hide here in the mountains."

Derrick spoke, "We'll definitely talk to the former sheriff and see what he has to stay about that."

Ellie leaned forward, studying Ida. "Ida, do you know where your father went when he left town?"

Her right eye twitched and she shook her head.

"Have you talked to him since or do you know where he is now?" Ellie asked quietly.

"No and no." Ida stood and folded her arms. "If I did, I'd say. We weren't exactly close and I sure as hell wouldn't have minded if he was locked up. Then police wouldn't be rehashing all this again."

She walked to the counter, took the biscuit pan and slid it in the oven. "Now, I've answered your questions. You need to leave."

She gestured to the door and Ellie and Derrick both stood. "Thanks for your time," Derrick said.

"If you do hear from him, please call me." Ellie laid a card on the table. "I understand you have a daughter the same age as the other victims so I know you want her safe from whoever this killer is."

Ida's face turned ghostly white. A smidgen of guilt washed through Ellie for frightening the woman, but she dismissed it.

With a predator on the loose and lives at stake, she couldn't play nice. Every second counted.

FIFTY-TWO

Hetty ducked into the woods and searched for Cord, not surprised to see the direction he was headed.

How many times had she checked on the situation herself? As much as she tried to banish the painful memories, they tortured her.

Forgetting had never worked though, only stirred up more anxiety that left her sweating and dizzy with nerves. Once she'd even blacked out for a few minutes, only she'd been awake. They called it disassociation.

It wasn't the first time she'd done that either.

She'd been afraid to tell the doctor, afraid he'd send her to the nut house. So she'd googled her symptoms and read about it. People disassociated from things that triggered trauma and were difficult to face. It was a little like amnesia only when she returned to reality, everything came rushing back like a thousand needles stabbing at her skull.

Sometimes the memories wiped her out to the point she had to go to bed for a day or two.

She couldn't let it happen right now. Not until she saw exactly what Cord McClain was up to.

Brush crackled and snapped below her feet, but she plowed her way deeper into the woods. By now she knew the line between the toxic and non-toxic land and wouldn't cross it. She wound to the right between a series of bare trees, then looked all around her, feeling lost and terrified, her rising anxiety starting to make her shake.

She stepped over rocks and maneuvered around a boulder then sidestepped a weedy patch filled with poison ivy. A half mile in and she recognized the vegetation and the narrow path leading into a thickly wooded stretch that made it hard to see more than a foot in front of her.

Suddenly a twig snapped behind her, and someone grabbed her and pulled her behind the tree. She started to scream, but a gloved hand pressed over her mouth. Her pulse pounded then a deep voice spoke into her ear.

"I'm going to let you go, but don't scream."

Hetty hadn't heard that voice in years, and she'd never thought she would again. But she recognized it. Cord McClain.

Emotions swirled through her. Now he was working with the police.

She gave a little nod then sucked in air when he released her.

"What are you doing out here?" Cord asked.

She hugged her arms around herself, trembling. "What are *you* doing out here?"

His eyes narrowed to slits. "My job, looking for more dead bodies."

"You think there're more girls?" Hetty said in a raw whisper.

He shrugged. "It's possible."

"What about what happened—"

"I know what I have to do," he said through clenched teeth. "Now get out of here."

The warning in his eyes sent her breathing into spasms and she turned and ran back through the woods to the safety of the graveyard.

FIFTY-THREE

In order to speed up the investigation, Ellie and Derrick decided to divide up.

She called ahead to verify that Sheriff Wallace was in his office so she could question him, and Derrick drove her Jeep to visit Clint's father, Chester, who'd handled Ruth's case.

Ellie found Clint Wallace in his office studying something on his computer.

"Thanks for seeing me," Ellie said.

"Did I have a choice?"

Why some smalltown sheriffs resented working with outside law enforcement baffled her. Two heads were always better than one.

"Did you see the press conference about the other girls' murders?"

"I did. I was making notes on the information you shared." He leaned back in his chair, and she sank into the one facing his desk.

"We have to consider that Ruth may have been this unsub's

first victim. Oftentimes, a serial offender's first kill is someone they know personally, someone they have a grudge against or who hurt them in some way."

His gray eyes fastened on her. "If you've read the file my father put together, you can see he was thorough and questioned everyone in town."

"Including you?" Ellie asked with an eyebrow raise.

"He questioned all the kids at school who knew Ruth."

"You were what, sixteen at the time?"

"Seventeen," he responded. "I was a couple years ahead of Ruth."

"And popular, I heard." Ellie offered him a smile, stroking his ego.

He gave a little shrug, but his chest seemed to puff up. "Girls go for the jocks."

Ellie wanted to roll her eyes. "How long had you and Ruth been dating?"

"About four months I guess."

Ellie maintained a neutral tone. "Things were going well?"

"Yeah."

"I thought she'd just broken up with you."

Unease flickered in his eyes. "We may have argued the day before but things were okay."

"What did you argue about?"

"She was jealous, you know. Wanted all my attention and accused me of flirting with other girls."

Ellie imagined him as a flirt, especially at seventeen. "So you *didn't* break up?"

"We just took a couple of days to cool off. I figured she'd come back once she did."

What a narcissist. "And you had plenty of other girls crushing on you."

Irritation tightened his mouth. "Where are you going with this, Detective?"

"It's on record that Ruth snuck out of the house that night to meet someone. Was she meeting you?"

He shook his head no. "I hung out with the guys," he said. "If you're asking for my alibi, it's in the report. Besides, I would never have hurt Ruth. The reason I became sheriff was because of what happened to her."

Hmm. Ellie wondered if that was true. Or if perhaps he chose law enforcement to keep the truth from being revealed. "If you weren't meeting her, do you know who she might have been going to see? Was another guy interested in her?"

"All the guys thought she was hot, but they knew she was mine and was off limits."

Ellie contemplated that. "Would she have hooked up with someone else to make you jealous?"

"If she did, I sure as hell didn't know about it," he said bluntly.

His defensive tone held a hint of anger. At her or at Ruth because he had suspected her of cheating? Or had he been bitter that she broke up with him?

FIFTY-FOUR

Derrick's research on the former sheriff Chester indicated he'd retired six years ago and after a quick election, his son Clint assumed office.

He and Ellie needed to canvass locals for their opinions of Chester, and when he spoke with Ruth's parents, get their thoughts on how he'd handled the investigation.

He scanned the property, which was almost cheery compared to the parched land by the graveyard. Although it was winter, evergreens added color and the lake offered an inviting view. Derrick wound around the curvy drive, which led to an older red brick ranch house. The yard was well maintained, shrubs neatly trimmed, and four rustic Adirondack chairs provided seating around a stone firepit.

Derrick parked and strode toward the front door, but footsteps crunched gravel and he swung his head to the side. Chester Wallace, dressed in a flannel shirt and worn jeans appeared, scowling. It was obvious from the square jaw, stature and deep brown eyes that his son was his spitting image. Except Chester had a good thirty pounds on his son and gray streaks threaded his brown hair.

Derrick introduced himself as the man approached.

"I figured you'd show up at my door sometime," Chester said. "This about the Higgins girl?"

"And the body found at the graveyard," Derrick said.

"Why do you think they're related? Ruth could have just run off, you know."

"That's possible," Derrick agreed. "But there are reasons we suspect the cases are connected."

Wallace walked to the porch and Derrick followed, both seating themselves in the chairs facing the lake. "What reasons?"

"Ruth's sister, Tilly, admitted Ruth snuck out of the house. I also know that one of her shoes was found."

"So?" Chester shrugged. "Maybe she lost it running away."

"But wouldn't she have realized it right away and retrieved it?"

Wallace shrugged. "Who knows how a teenage girl's mind works?"

"I think she lost it in a struggle or running from someone she was afraid of."

An irritated sigh rasped from Wallace. "I guess that's possible. But I did my diligence and questioned all the teens she knew, Ida and Hetty Bramble and their daddy who I thought and still think killed her. I also talked to Ruth's father and brother who were persons of interest. But I never could find evidence to make charges stick." He wheezed a breath. "Then Bramble ran off which suggested I was right about him."

"That seems logical," Derrick agreed. "I'm sure you questioned his daughters about his whereabouts."

"Course I did," Wallace said. "They claimed they had no

idea where he was." He pulled a hand down his chin. "But I can tell you this. Neither one of them seemed upset or worried that he left. Instead, I think they were relieved because it was a shit-show with the media and he was known as a mean asshole."

"Did you suspect he abused them?" Derrick asked.

"Sure did. But neither admitted it to me."

"How about your son Clint?" Derrick asked. "He and Ruth broke up shortly before she disappeared. Was he upset about it?"

"Maybe but he went out with his friends that night." He gripped the edge of the desk, temper flaring in his tone. "Besides my son was on the road to a football scholarship and he sure as hell wouldn't have killed Ruth over a breakup and destroy his chances. He also could have any girl he wanted at that time."

"Yet he never married," Derrick pointed out.

"His choice," Chester said. "He likes the single life."

"What happened to the scholarship?"

Chester's jaw tightened. "Blew his knee out in training. And after the ordeal with Ruth, all the questions and negativity, his head wasn't into sports anymore. In fact, that's one reason he got into law enforcement. He wanted justice."

"Did he? Or did he want to keep the case buried?"

Wallace shot up from his seat, knocking his chair backward, his eyes flaring with rage. "We're done here, Agent Fox."

"I'm not done until that case and the current one are solved." Derrick stood, his body just as rigid at the former sheriff's. "Was the shoe the only thing you found in the vicinity of where Ruth disappeared?"

Wallace narrowed his eyes. "What do you mean?"

"Did you find any clothing? Jewelry? A backpack or phone?"

"No, none of those things." Wallace scratched his head. "Come to think of it though, we did find a red scarf in the woods but the family said it didn't belong to Ruth."

Derrick's pulse jumped. There was another connection. "I need that scarf to check it for DNA and prints." The other scarves that had been found lacked DNA or prints, but if Ruth was the unsub's first kill, maybe he'd been sloppy and left evidence behind.

FIFTY-FIVE

Ellie climbed in the Jeep with Derrick and shut the door as she punched Deputy Eastwood's number. When Shondra answered, Ellie put her on speaker and explained about Derrick's conversation with Chester Wallace.

"Shondra, Chester's son Clint was dating Ruth before she disappeared although his friends gave him an alibi." Ellie fastened her seatbelt. "I need you to canvass locals and find out what people thought of Chester Wallace and the way he handled the investigation."

"Copy that," Shondra agreed.

Derrick spoke, "Ask if they thought he was thorough, made mistakes, if he'd cover for his son."

"Will do," Shondra agreed. "I'll leave in a minute. Texting you the address for Mr. and Mrs. Higgins, Ruth's parents. They live outside Helen now at a place called Finch Gardens."

"Great," Ellie said. "We'll head there after we question Clint's alibi."

"So where are we going?" Derrick asked as she ended the call.

"To see Vernon Stancil. He owns the body shop on the edge of town."

Derrick entered the address into the GPS and she maneuvered the curvy road. "Chester definitely was defensive of his son," Derrick said. "Clint was in line for a football scholarship. His father insisted Clint wouldn't mess that up. If Clint did something stupid, it's possible Chester would have covered for him so he wouldn't lose it."

"Makes sense," Ellie said. "Maybe Shondra will get some insight."

They arrived at the body shop where three vehicles in various wreckage stages sat in the yard awaiting repairs. They parked near the front entrance. Wind whipped around Ellie as she slid from the Jeep, the smell of oil and grease wafting from the building. A short chunky, balding man in coveralls stood beneath an old Ford which was on the lift.

"Mr. Stancil," Ellie called.

He turned with a scowl as if he didn't appreciate the interruption. "Yeah?"

In sharp contrast to Clint, who was still fit and muscular, this guy had let himself go. Hard to imagine the two men being friends in high school. Although it had been over a decade.

Ellie identified them and he wiped his hands on a grease rag and lumbered toward them. "What do you want?"

"We think the girl found in the woods by Green Gardens Cemetery might be connected to Ruth Higgins' disappearance so we're talking to people who lived here fifteen years ago," Derrick said. "We need to go over your statement about that night."

He made a clicking sound with his tobacco-stained teeth. "Like I told the sheriff at the time, I was hanging out with Clint. We went to the river for a while and had some beers."

"Clint was with you all night?"

Vernon chewed the inside of his cheek. "Yeah, that's what I told Sheriff Wallace back then."

The hesitancy in his answer triggered warning bells in Ellie's head, but she adopted an understanding tone. "That's what you told them. Was it true or do you remember things differently now?"

"Are you calling me a liar, lady?"

"It's Detective," Ellie said firmly. "And no. But I understand you and your friends were scared kids back then. Maybe you were underage drinking or experimenting with drugs and were afraid of getting in trouble, so you decided to come up with a story to protect one another." She waited a beat and watched him squirm. "Clint had a lot at stake so he'd want to avoid trouble. And his father was the law so he didn't want him to find out if he did something to jeopardize his scholarship."

A vein jumped in Vernon's bulging neck. "Well yeah, Clint was worried about that and his dad was one strict old man."

"Was Clint with you all night?"

A tense second passed. "I think so."

"What does that mean?" Ellie asked.

Indecision blazed in Vernon's gray eyes, but he finally answered, "Uh, maybe I passed out for a while. But when I came to, he was there."

Ellie and Derrick exchanged looks. "So you can't be certain he was with you all night."

Vernon shrugged. "It's not like I lied or anything."

"Withholding information in a criminal investigation is a federal offense," Derrick replied.

Fear replaced the anger in Vernon's expression. "What the hell? You want me to cooperate then you threaten me?" He jammed the rag in his coverall pockets. "I'm done talking."

Then he turned, walked back to the car, picked up a wrench and resumed working.

FIFTY-SIX

Green Gardens Cemetery

Cord hated the fear in Hetty Bramble's eyes today just as he had years ago. That fear had triggered his protective instincts and led him to cross the line that dreadful night. He was surprised she and her cousin Ida hadn't moved away from this toxic town a long time ago. They'd be better off if they had.

Although running away hadn't helped him escape his dark thoughts or memories. They haunted him everywhere he went. And just when he thought he'd outrun them and found happiness with Ellie, they'd resurfaced and were threatening to destroy it all.

Still, he and the Bramble girls had to keep the one they shared buried.

Ellie and Fox suspected there might be more victims buried here and he had a job to do. He continued to search the land beyond the graveyard, not surprised to feel the heat from the ground seeping through the soil. Areas had been cleared for toxicity but still held signs of what had happened underground.

He studied the terrain for disturbed land that might indicate a buried body and almost four miles in, he noticed some loose rocks on the hill. Stepping closer to them, his foot sent stones tumbling over the edge into a deep ravine. Curious, he narrowed his eyes and scanned the land below. Bare bushes and sticklike trees dotted the side of the ravine and thick dried brush was piled on one side.

His instincts kicked in. Most of the land was barren except for that one spot. Had the wind blown the debris together, or had someone created that pile to cover up something?

Suspicions racing through his mind, he analyzed the terrain for the best way down and found a less steep section than where he stood. After pulling on gloves, he began to make his way downhill. He grabbed tree branches for leverage to keep himself on his feet and minutes later reached the bottom of the ravine.

He crossed to the pile of brush, noting dead roots of a tree and dusty rocks strategically stacked near the brush. His heart began to pound as he drew closer.

The brush definitely had been piled there intentionally. His training with Ellie kicked in and he photographed the area from different angles, capturing an overview group of shots, then close-ups.

He panned his flashlight over the area, then knelt and peered through some branches. The stench of a dead animal filled the air, and he carefully removed more branches and sticks and placed them to the side, peeling back the layers until he uncovered the ground beneath.

His pulse jumped as he spotted something red, and he quickly yanked the remaining brush aside and discovered a scarf caught in a tangled vine.

Fox said the victims were found with a red scarf that was used to strangle them. His head reeled. If another victim was here, there could be more.

Dammit. They had to widen their search. But then they might find... the secret he wanted to keep buried.

The temptation to dig up the ground and see for himself hit him. No... this was not the area...

He reached his hand out to do it, but a war raged in his head. If there was another body here, Ellie would ream him out for breaking protocol and tampering with the scene.

Hell, he wanted to be the man she deserved.

But if Ellie learned what he'd done, he could lose everything.

What the hell was he going to do?

FIFTY-SEVEN

Ellie wound along the mile-long drive to Mr. and Mrs. Higgins' home, a pristine property north of Brambletown set off the road with river access. The mountain views and privacy were breathtaking, an obvious contrast to the town where their young daughter disappeared.

"They apparently have an entire garden area with bird-feeders catering to the gold finches that flock to the area in winter."

"The Higginses did everything possible to escape the toxic place where they lost Ruth," Ellie said.

"Yet they were toxic to Tilly," Derrick said defensively.

"You're right. Although they were in pain, they still had two other children who were suffering and needed attention."

Derrick nodded. "Maybe getting answers will give Tilly some closure and ease her guilt."

Had finding his sister done that for him? She hoped so although regret still nagged at her because her father was sheriff when Derrick's little sister disappeared and he'd dropped the ball working the case in order to protect her. That investigation had first brought Derrick to Crooked Creek.

"I'm sorry, Derrick. I... wish I could change the way my father handled things with your sister," she said softly.

"It wasn't your fault, Ellie, and we both know it." His gaze met hers, emotions flaring, but in a nano-second, he shut down and reached for the car door. "You helped me find closure."

But no peace. She heard that in his tone and saw it in the way he switched to work mode without blinking an eye.

Wind ruffled the evergreens and musical notes from the windchimes echoed from the wraparound front porch of the classic farmhouse on the hill. Though winter had stolen the vibrancy of the garden, she imagined colorful flowerbeds blooming in spring. A park bench offered seating and finches sang from the birdfeeders in the well-kept sanctuary.

It was a place to cherish nature and the beauty the mountains offered. But had the couple found solace here?

"What is the former mayor of Brambletown doing now?" Ellie asked as she and Derrick walked up to the door and rang the bell.

"Retired. Seems his investments paid off, and after Ruth's disappearance, he dropped out of the public eye."

The door opened and a slender brunette in her fifties dressed in a dark green, velour warm-up suit looked down at them.

"I'm Gina Higgins," she said with a tightness to her voice. "Come in."

She seemed very formal, Ellie thought, or just nervous, the latter of which was understandable. Gina led them to an elegant living room with a marble fireplace where Edward Higgins was perched in one of the wing back chairs. His wife took the matching chair. The man held a tumbler of what looked like whiskey in his right hand, his expression serious.

Derrick introduced them. "Thank you for seeing us. We understand this situation is difficult for you."

The man's steely gray eyes hardened. "You really have no idea. Just tell me if you found my daughter," he said curtly.

"No," Derrick said. "But I'm assuming you saw the news about the body discovered in Brambletown and that there may be other victims—"

"Yes, we're aware of that," Higgins barked. "Now you assume my daughter is dead and that monster Earl Bramble killed her."

His brute voice sucked the air from the room. Derrick waited a beat before replying. "We're not assuming anything, sir. But we are investigating that possibility. I know you both want answers about Ruth and what happened to her and we want to give them to you."

"By telling us she was murdered by some psycho." Mrs. Higgins abruptly stood and paced in front of the fire, her movements agitated.

"I'm so sorry, Mrs. Higgins," Ellie said softly. "I understand this is painful but we are trying to help."

"You know nothing," Gina Higgins said bitterly.

"Maybe so. But we were hoping one of you remembered details that you might have forgotten back then. We spoke with your other daughter, Tilly, and she said Ruth snuck out that night to meet someone. Do you have any idea who it was?"

"Tilly and Hayden were always so jealous of Ruth," the woman cried. "Ruth couldn't help it that she was prettier and more popular. The other kids were just drawn to her." Shivering, she rubbed her hands up and down her arms as if to warm herself. "Tilly was awkward and quiet and bookish. It was her fault the boys didn't want to date her."

Ellie swallowed hard, the woman's words painting a hostile picture of the family dynamics. Sympathy for Tilly filled her.

"That's pretty harsh of you to say about your child," Derrick said.

Ellie cut him a warning look.

Tilly's mother planted her dainty hands on her hips. "I'm simply being honest."

Anger sharpened Derrick's dark brown eyes, but he clenched his jaw and refrained from comment.

"What about your son, Hayden?" Ellie cut in.

"That boy was trouble from the time he was fourteen," the father said in a cold tone. "First vandalizing properties with that group of hoodlums from the wrong side of the tracks, then experimenting with drugs and indulging in fights. He'd been suspended so many times the school didn't want him. Hell, even the private schools I spent a fortune on refused to take him back." The ice in the man's drink clinked as he turned the glass up and tossed it back. "Ungrateful little twit. After my precious Ruth went missing, he didn't act like he even cared. That's when I gave him an ultimatum, either face charges or join the military."

"And he joined the army?" Derrick asked.

"He did. Maybe they made a man out of him."

"When was the last time you saw or talked to him?" Ellie asked.

"The night he left," Higgins said matter-of-factly. "Left a note and we haven't heard from him since."

"You haven't attempted to make contact?" Ellie asked. Anything could have happened to him in fifteen years. Or he could have changed. Derrick confirmed he'd joined the military but he'd been discharged. Where was he now?

FIFTY-EIGHT

"My daughter is not dead and my son certainly didn't kill her," Mrs. Higgins stated emphatically.

"How do you know that?" Derrick asked.

Gina's frail-looking hand fluttered to her chest. "I... just refuse to believe it." She motioned to Ellie. "Let me show you something."

Ellie and Derrick exchanged a look, then Ellie followed the woman up the winding staircase. Sadly, just because Gina believed her daughter Ruth was alive didn't mean it was true.

Gina led her past two bedrooms that looked as if they'd been decorated by an interior designer, then to a third bedroom. When she opened the door, Ellie's pulse clamored.

"This is Ruth's room. Well, not the one where we lived before. We had to move from that house because of all the press, but I replicated her room here."

Teenage décor filled the room. A soft white duvet, a teddy bear propped against the pillow, posters of a boy band, a bulletin board covered with pictures of Ruth and various girls from school, Ruth with her cheerleading team, and a photograph of her and Clint Wallace obviously dressed for Homecoming. A desk held old textbooks and a pink covered laptop.

"Did the police search Ruth's computer?" Ellie asked.

Gina seemed lost in memories as she ran her fingers over the bedding. Ellie's question jerked her back to reality, and her expression morphed from melancholy to anger.

"I'm sure the sheriff did," she snapped. "But I asked for it back. I wanted everything the same when Ruth returned."

Sympathy squeezed at Ellie's heart although the woman's attitude was disturbing. For the parents' sake, she wanted to be wrong about Ruth being dead and find her alive. Some kidnap victims had been held in captivity for years before being found or escaping. If that was the situation, she'd probably be traumatized. Neither scenario was good.

Although her experience, and the fact that a red scarf and missing shoe had been found indicated Ruth wasn't coming back.

"Mrs. Higgins, how did you think Sheriff Wallace handled the investigation?" Ellie asked.

Her shoulders sagged. "Well, I guess he did what he had to do, talked to all her friends. But he tore our family up with his attention on my husband and son."

"If she was abducted, who do you think would have taken her? Did Ruth mention anyone she had problems with?"

"Those lowlife Bramble girls. Everyone knew they were trouble and their daddy was an ignorant drunk."

Ellie forced a neutral expression at the woman's tone. Gina certainly didn't hold back her opinions. "What about a boy? I know she was dating Clint Wallace."

A faraway look settled in her tear-filled eyes. "Clint seemed like a nice enough kid, but he was cocky and possessive."

"Possessive? Why do you say that?"

She shrugged. "I heard Ruth talking on the phone to one of

her friends one night. She said he was jealous when she talked to other boys."

"Do you think he'd hurt her if he knew she was meeting someone else?"

Another shrug. "I don't know. According to the sheriff, he had an alibi."

Yes, according to the sheriff, Clint's father.

"Tilly said Ruth wouldn't tell her who she was meeting that night, but she said it wasn't Clint. Was there another boy she was interested in? One Clint was jealous of? Or one who might have been angry if she rebuked him?"

Mrs. Higgins threw her hands in the air, a sigh of exasperation escaping her. "How should I know? Teenage girls don't exactly confide in their mothers."

True, Ellie thought. She certainly had had her differences with her adopted mother, Vera.

"Now, I've answered these questions a hundred times before, and I don't want to discuss it anymore."

Ellie nodded in understanding. "The computer?"

Gina rubbed her fingers across the pink cover, held it to her chest for a moment then finally relinquished it. "Let's get this straight, Detective. I expect it to be returned in the same condition it was in when you took it. Do you understand? Ruth will need it when she comes home."

Ellie gave an understanding nod. "Of course." Her phone buzzed, and she checked the number. Cord.

She lifted a finger signaling she needed to answer the call, then stepped into the hall and connected. "Cord? I hope this is important. I'm with Ruth Higgins' parents right now."

"It is." His breath wheezed out. "I think I found another body."

FIFTY-NINE

On the drive to the graveyard, Ellie called the ME and an ERT. If Cord had discovered another body, they needed the remains to be removed properly and the scene preserved and processed.

She relayed her conversation with Ruth's mother to Derrick. "It's disturbing that she's created a replica of Ruth's room."

"People hold onto hope as long as they can," he said.

"I suppose so," Ellie said. "But it's also unsettling that she didn't have a designated room for Tilly or her son."

A muscle ticked in Derrick's jaw. "The couple obviously favored Ruth over their other two children," he said. "Mr. Higgins had nothing good to say about Hayden."

The family dynamics had to have affected Tilly and Hayden. "No wonder Tilly or Hayden never sought them out."

"I know. Ruth's disappearance destroyed the family just like my sister's did ours."

Emotions clogged Ellie's throat. She hated that her family had any part in that. Even if she apologized a million times, it wouldn't change things. But at least Derrick didn't resent her for it.

He checked his phone. "I have a message from Bennett." His expression darkened as he listened to the voicemail. "Bennett found out Hayden left the Army after his first tour. Apparently, he renewed his driver's license but hasn't tracked him down yet. No info on a car registration or address."

"Arrests?"

"One arrest for assault. Charges were dropped because the woman claimed Hayden was protecting her from the man who was stalking her."

Ellie wrinkled her nose in thought. "He could have moved off the grid after that kind of trouble," Ellie said. "And now he's avoiding the media and police."

Assault indicated he had a violent streak. Could Hayden have lost that temper on his sister?

SIXTY

By the time Ellie and Derrick arrived at the graveyard, Dr. Whitefeather and her forensic recovery team were waiting. The ERT pulled up behind them.

"Why does Ranger McClain believe he discovered a body?" Laney asked. "Did he find bones?"

Ellie shook her head. "He spotted a red scarf poking through some brush and dirt. If there are human remains in the ground, he didn't want to disturb evidence."

Laney nodded in understanding.

The three of them followed the coordinates Cord had sent, weaving around bushes and trees until they located the ravine where Cord stood waiting.

Ellie came to a halt and looked down. "Wait here, Laney, and tell the ERT to do the same while we scout out the situation. We'll call you if we find something, then you can join us."

"Copy that."

"I found the scarf in that pile of brush." Cord indicated the precise spot. "I've set up a rappel system for you and Fox to go down."

"Thanks." She and Derrick followed Cord's lead and minutes later, they'd mastered the decline and made it to the brush pile Cord had described. Shining flashlights onto the area, they studied the sight, and Ellie spotted the corner of the scarf. Cord had moved some tree limbs and weeds aside to reveal a mound of dirt that looked as if it could be a grave.

Ellie sighed. "We have to excavate the area."

She and Cord stepped aside, and she called Laney to send her crew down. Cord hiked up to help them repel down, bringing the ERT with him while Derrick began to comb the ravine for evidence.

Wind moaned and whined as the team worked, and Ellie's heart pounded as they slowly raked dirt aside and uncovered a body.

"My God," Ellie said as the face of a young girl appeared, eyes wide open in a death stare. "She hasn't been dead long."

"You're right," Laney said. "Her body may be out of rigor, but skin and flesh and muscle are intact. We may be able to glean more information from her autopsy and more quickly than the bones we found of the other girl. Time is on our side here for DNA."

"If that's true, then it means the killer was here recently," Cord said.

"Did you see anyone in the woods?" Ellie asked.

"No, if I had, I would have pursued him."

"Tell Agent Fox and the ERT, and start a grid search, Cord. If the unsub is close by, we might get lucky and catch him hanging around to watch the action." Some sick SOBs enjoyed watching the police chase their tails and relived the crime as the cops helped them play out their twisted cat and mouse game.

"Copy that." Cord headed toward Lt. Williams, the head of ERT.

Ellie sucked in a breath, frowning as the odor of death, raw dirt and the charred scent of burning coal beneath the ground filled her nostrils. She covered her nose for a minute and struggled to breathe in fresh air, but it was impossible. The body and the fact that there had been toxins here was a reminder that the land had been robbed of life years ago and so had its residents.

And now with teen bodies piling up...

Dread gnawed at her as she scanned the ravine then the miles of land beyond the graveyard. If the same killer had been dumping bodies here for over a decade, how many more were out here?

Ellie felt the tension radiating from Derrick as he crossed the ravine to her. Laney and her crew were documenting the layout of the body and ERT was snapping photographs before they removed the girl from the ground to transport her to the morgue.

"Another victim was dumped here?" Derrick commented, his brow furrowed as he approached.

Ellie nodded, still poised for sounds the killer was hiding in the woods as she allowed Derrick a visual of the victim. "Yeah, and this one's fresh."

The thought that they might have just missed the killer didn't sit well with Ellie. With the attention the area had received after Bonnie Sylvester's remains had been discovered, and the memorial drawing outsiders, along with the added law enforcement and tourists' presence, the killer had been bold to leave another victim in this location.

Derrick's hiss rent the air. "Dammit, that's one of the missing girls I told you about. The girl from Athens, Jacey Ward."

SIXTY-ONE

Shit, shit, shit.

That damn ranger had already found the girl.

He should have covered her better, but he'd heard footsteps and someone thrashing through the woods, and he'd had to get the hell away from her.

Sweat streamed down the back of his neck, soaking his shirt, and dirt still clung to his fingernails. He used his shovel as leverage as he ran through the acres of barren land.

Now he heard tree limbs crackling and brush rustling and knew others had arrived. They were combing the land for him. He had to keep running. Find a hiding place until they passed.

He wasn't done with his killing. And he couldn't get caught or they'd stop all his fun. Every time he took a girl, a sense of satisfaction and relief filled him as if he'd purged one more demon from his soul.

Before he'd killed her, she'd cried for her mama. Said her parents loved her. That they had money and would pay him if he brought her home.

God, how he could use the money. And if he took her home

safely, he'd be a goddamn hero. A chuckle rumbled from his gut. Him, a hero!

But he wasn't an idiot. Police would want to question him, ask details about how he'd gotten the information. The media would hound him.

That would be too chancy. He had a decent poker face but not that decent.

He stumbled, then veered to the right and followed the river until he found the small cave half buried in the mountain. No one ever came this way. There were signs posting warnings of the toxic land neighboring it. But he'd been here before and didn't believe in all that bullshit. It would take years of long-term exposure now the fire had died down before the toxins could kill him.

He stooped down and crawled into the cave, then packed dirt around the entrance so if someone did venture by, they'd think it had been closed up for years. The dark interior swallowed him, and he hunkered back against a rock to wait. In spite of the cold outside, warmth from the ground enveloped him and he curled into it and closed his eyes, reliving the kill in his mind.

He'd waited until they'd driven out of Athens and away from the UGA campus, then turned away from the city and made it almost twenty miles before she seemed to get worried.

She twisted her hands together and stared out the window, growing more antsy by the minute.

Finally she broke the silence with a haunted whisper, "Can I borrow your phone to call my mama?"

He cut his eyes toward her. "Sorry the battery's dead. Just tell me the address and relax."

She bit down on her lower lip. "That's okay. Just drop me at a gas station and I can call from there."

"No, no problem. I don't mind driving you."

Her breathing turned choppy as she stared at the darkening sky and realized he hadn't made the turn toward Watkinsville.

"This isn't the right way," she said, her voice tiny and frightened.

His pulse jumped at the fear in her eyes. She reached for the door handle.

Panic streaked her face. "Please just let me out and I'll walk," she whispered. "If you want money, my mama will pay you."

He cut the steering wheel and raced down a deserted road then swung his truck to the shoulder.

She yanked at the door handle, jumped out and began to run. Laughter bubbled in his throat, and he pulled the red scarf from his pocket and followed her. They were in the middle of nowhere. Chasing her would be fun.

He strode after her, picking up his pace as he spotted her ahead. She ducked behind some trees to hide and his laugh erupted, catching in the wind and boomeranging in the air.

"You can run, but you can't hide," he sang as he drew closer.

She darted from behind the tree, her feet sending dirt flying as she begun to run again. His heart stuttered when her legs buckled, then he jumped on her. She screamed and kicked and tried to escape, snatching dirt and gravel and throwing it in his face.

Anger seized him and he pressed his knee into her stomach to hold her down then slapped her hard, twice, until her eyes rolled back in her head and her arms fell limply to her sides. Rage and heat burned in his gut, and his first victim's face flashed behind his eyes, launching him back in time.

Wrapping the scarf around his fingers, he slid it around her neck and tightened it, watching the blood-red silk cut into the delicate skin of her pale throat as he tightened it. Her eyes flew open in terror and he smiled as she dug her fingernails into his hands to pry them loose. He welcomed the pain and continued to squeeze, tighter and tighter until her body jerked and convulsed as she gasped for air.

Seconds later, she lost the battle and she went still.

His breath panted out with exhilaration, and he loosened his hold, savoring the emptiness in her eyes and the tears drying on her cheeks.

Heart pounding, he looked down at those red boots and reached for one of them...

SIXTY-TWO

Ellie greeted Sheriff Clint Wallace as he made his way down into the ravine while Derrick stepped aside to review what he knew about Jacey's family.

"We found a fresh body. She's been dead less than twenty-four hours," Ellie told Wallace.

She studied him for a reaction, maybe a case of nerves to indicate he might have put the body there. His posture was rigid and a vein throbbed in his neck, but she couldn't decide if it was a sign he was involved, or simply a reaction to another body being found near his town.

The sheriff pulled his phone. "I'll have my deputies search the area."

"ERT is on it and so is Ranger McClain, but the more hands-on-deck the better." She pushed a strand of hair from her cheek. "Thanks to Special Agent Fox, we already have an ID."

Wallace lifted a brow. "That was fast."

"Agent Fox was already looking into reports of missing girls and she's one of them. Her name is Jacey Ward. She was thought to be a runaway."

Her heart melted as she recalled the pleas of the family for

Jacey's safe return. As soon as they left here, she and Derrick would have to make the notification. Dread filled her at the thought.

Laney and her crew worked meticulously to remove the girl's body, preserving evidence as they went. With gloved hands, Ellie bagged the red scarf to send to the lab.

As soon as they'd laid Jacey on the tarp, Laney performed a preliminary exam and pointed out the markings on her neck. "It appears she died of strangulation just like Bonnie Sylvester." Laney gently brushed dirt from the girl's face and hair, then lifted her sweater and exposed her torso for a preliminary examination. "See that bruising," she said as she gestured toward the dark discoloration. "He held her down, either with his knee or possibly his foot."

An image of the violent scene rolled through Ellie's mind like a horror show. Poor girl.

"We'll study it more closely. If it was a shoe, we might get something on her clothing or be able to discern the shoe size." She lifted Jacey's hand and studied it, then examined her fingers. "Some bruising on her wrists where he must have grabbed her, and it looks like particulates beneath her fingernails."

"Maybe she scratched him," Ellie said, hoping they'd get lucky and find DNA.

Laney carefully scraped beneath Jacey's nails and bagged the sample, then used tweezers to pluck a fiber caught in the mix and held it up to the light. "This could have come from the killer's clothing." She dropped it into an evidence bag as well.

Cord walked toward her holding something in his hand. A scowl deepened his dark brown eyes as he approached, then Ellie saw what he had in his gloved hand. A red boot.

"Found this in the brush. It must have come off when the killer dragged her into the ravine. "

Cord bagged the shoe and placed it with the other evidence

bags, while Ellie joined Laney again. "Was there another shoe in the grave or brush anywhere?"

Laney and her assistant both shook their heads. "She was barefoot just like the Sylvester girl."

The missing red shoes and the red scarf were definitely significant to the unsub. Ellie wanted to know exactly what they meant to him.

Derrick returned, his phone in his hand. He addressed Cord first. "Keep the search teams combing the area for more graves."

Cord clenched his jaw, looking wary as he glanced up the hill. "Copy that."

"Ellie, I have the address for the girl's family," Derrick said. "We should notify them before this reaches the media."

"Can you and the ERT team handle it here if we leave, Laney? The local sheriff may want to consult with you."

"Of course. I'll arrange the transport to the morgue and update you on the autopsy findings ASAP."

Ellie and Derrick used the repel line to pull themselves to the top and over the jagged edge of the ridge.

Minutes later, they were in her Jeep heading to Watkinsville to deliver the bad news to the Ward family. "We're about to turn this day into the worst one of that couple's life," she murmured, her heart aching as she steered the vehicle down the graveled drive to the highway.

She only wished she had the answer to the one question they'd want to know—who killed their lovely daughter?

SIXTY-THREE

Briar Ridge Mobile Homes

Kat ushered her friend Carrie Ann into her bedroom and shut the door.

"What's up?" Carrie Ann asked. "You sounded excited. Do you have a date?"

Kat winced. She wished she'd never told Carrie Ann she had a crush on the soccer team captain. All the girls did and he'd never even looked at her twice, much less talked to her. She lived in a trailer and her mama's scandal years ago still had tongues wagging. She couldn't wait till she was old enough to escape this horrible town and her skanky relatives.

"No." Kat pulled Carrie Ann to the bed where she opened her mama's old computer. "I found the laptop Mama had in high school. You know she and that girl who went missing got into a brawl at the DQ."

Carrie Ann bit her lip and glanced away for a minute. "Yeah, I heard about it," she said softly.

Of course she had. It was legendary in Brambletown just like the rumors that her grandfather Earl killed Ruth Higgins.

"But that's not your fault, Kat. You weren't even born back then."

Kat's cheeks flamed. "Doesn't matter. People still look at me and Mama like we're roadkill. When they found that girl the other day at the graveyard, I heard some old ladies in town say my granddaddy did it." She gestured toward the computer. "I thought Mama might have written about what happened back then in her journal."

"You think she knows where he is or... if he did it?"

Kat shrugged. "Maybe." She leaned closer and whispered. "She and her cousin Hetty used to play in the graveyard when they were little. If Ruth Higgins was murdered or buried there, they might have seen something."

Curious excitement glittered in Carrie Ann's eyes. "Then let's dig in."

Somehow it felt wrong to read her mama's posts, as if she was invading her privacy. But she couldn't resist. Mama and Hetty whispered things all the time and kept secrets. She wanted to know what they were.

Picking up where she'd left off, Kat clicked on the next entry. She and Carrie Ann put their heads together to read.

Today was the worst. When I opened my locker, dozens of tampons came falling out. It was lunch time, and the entire football team was passing by and the boys burst out laughing. When I stooped down to pick them up and shove them in my backpack, Ruth was watching me with a gleam in her eyes, and I knew she put them there to embarrass me. She's such a rotten bitch. Just because her daddy is mayor, she thinks she's better than everyone else.

It felt like hours that the other kids stared at me while I cleaned up all those damn tampons. Ruth smirked and started to walk away, and that pissed me off even more. So I ran over to her and dumped the tampons on her head. She yelled at me and the principal came by and saw what happened and ordered me to go to his office. Ruth just stood there and acted like some innocent dummy. In the principal's office, I tried to explain but he wouldn't listen and then he called Daddy and sent me home for the day.

Daddy was furious when he got there, and he smelled like whiskey and sweat and drove like a maniac, yelling at me the whole way home.

Sometimes I hate him and want to run away. Hetty and I planned it once, but that night Hetty smarted off to him and he slapped her. Now she's too scared to do anything but what he says. I used to think he was nice to let her live with us, but he's even meaner to her than to me and that wasn't the first time he'd hit her.

Daddy ordered me to go to my room and not to come out. I slammed the door and stayed there fuming and beating my pillow like I was beating Ruth.

Sometimes I get so mad at her, I want to kill her.

SIXTY-FOUR

"The Wards are divorced, but the wife lives here in Watkinsville and teaches at the elementary school," Derrick said as Ellie parked in front of a gorgeous two-story gray Victorian. Flowerbeds dotted the front lawn with pansies dancing in the breeze.

"Where's the father?" she asked as they climbed from her Jeep and walked up the steps to the front porch.

A fat black and white cat lay curled on the porch swing, and windchimes played a symphony as a gust of wind blew through. Derrick rang the doorbell and seconds later a woman in a blue sweater and black slacks opened the door. A blond golden retriever ran up beside her, barking.

The woman's eyes had looked bright when she opened the door, but her smile faded instantly when she realized they were police. She hushed the dog and Ellie introduced them.

"Why are you here?" she asked in a raw whisper as she strained to look over their shoulders. "Did you bring Jacey home?"

Ellie's eyes burned with unshed tears. "I'm afraid not."

Mrs. Ward's face wilted. "But… she called this morning and left a message that she was coming home."

Ellie swallowed back a sob. This part never got easier. "May we come in?"

The woman nodded shakily and led them through a set of French doors to a homey living room decorated in greens and cream colors. A fire burned in the stone fireplace. Several photos of Jacey at various ages were displayed on the rustic wood mantle.

Mrs. Ward sank into a club chair and her dog settled beside her as if to protect her.

"You said Jacey called and was coming home this morning?" Derrick asked.

Jacey's mother nodded, tears glistening in her eyes. "I was at my prayer group, but she left a message."

"Did she tell you where she was?" Ellie asked.

"No. If… she had, I would have gone and picked her up. I've prayed so hard for her to come back and… I… was hoping she'd be home by now and we could make up for lost time."

"Where is her father?" Derrick asked.

"We divorced a few months after Jacey left," she murmured. "He remarried six months later and moved to North Carolina. We haven't spoken since."

"According to the missing persons report you and your husband filed, you said Jacey ran away," Ellie said softly.

"She did." Her voice cracked. "William and I… had an argument the night before over Jacey."

"What did you argue about?" Ellie asked.

"She'd been sneaking out to meet this kid named Cameron and we thought he was a bad influence. Her grades were slipping, she was being defiant, and we'd even caught her with beer. William suggested we send Jacey to a home for troubled kids so they could straighten her out."

"Did she know you two discussed that?" Derrick asked.

Guilt flashed on her face. "I think she heard us. My husband thought she was ruining our marriage, and... I thought maybe some time apart would help, too." Tears dribbled down her cheeks. "That night she snuck out again and we didn't hear from her again." She rubbed the dog's neck and he leaned into her. "Until today that is."

"Do you know where she's been?"

Mrs. Ward shook her head. "No idea. I thought the police would find her quickly, but the days dragged on. At the time, I was relieved she didn't show up in a hospital or the morgue, so I kept hoping one day she'd come back on her own. She always talked about going to UGA and I couldn't believe she'd give up that dream for Cameron." A frustrated sigh escaped her. "After a while, the police became busy with other cases. I kept hounding them and promised Jacey I wouldn't give up. Then I heard her voice today and thought everything would be all right..."

"Do you mind if we listen to the recording?" Ellie asked.

"Of course not." Mrs. Ward pulled her phone and played the message.

Ellie's heart gave a pang. She'd hoped for some detail as to who Jacey was with or where she was but there was nothing except the sound of cars in the distance. "I'm so sorry, I can't imagine the pain you've suffered," she said softly as she handed the woman back her phone.

The woman smothered a groan then straightened as if she realized they had bad news. "Do you know where she is? Is she in jail or something?"

Ellie and Derrick traded a wary look. A second later, Ellie inhaled a breath, then gave the woman a sympathetic look. "We did find her, but I'm sorry to have to tell you that—"

"No." Mrs. Ward's face turned ashen. "Oh, God... no..."

A strained silence stretched as the truth dawned on the woman and she broke into heart-wrenching sobs.

Ellie hugged her, patting her back to soothe her. "I'm so sorry. I am. I promise we'll find who did this."

"We'll also notify your ex-husband," Derrick said softly.

Mrs. Ward didn't seem to hear them. She just collapsed within herself and ran from the room.

Ellie and Derrick waited a few minutes, but the sobs grew louder.

Ellie finally stepped to the bedroom door and knocked, then cracked it open.

"Is there anyone I can call for you?"

"No... I just want to be alone."

"A friend or family member?" Ellie said gently.

"No... please just leave..."

Ellie hesitated, her heart aching for the mother. She couldn't imagine losing a child. "All right. We'll inform you when Jacey's body is released so you can make arrangements."

Meanwhile, they'd find that kid Cameron.

SIXTY-FIVE

Sometimes I want to kill Ruth.

That line in her mother's journal echoed over and over in Kat's head. She checked the date. A week before Ruth went missing.

"Do you think your mother did something to Ruth?" Carrie Ann gasped.

Kat's stomach knotted. "I don't know." Her mind spun. Was her mother capable of that kind of violence?

Kat always pegged her as a weenie, especially when she and Kat's daddy argued. Now she knew her granddaddy had slapped Hetty, she understood why her mama shied away from fighting.

But Ruth... was more her size. And that girl had been mean to her and embarrassed her in school with the tampons and who knew what else.

Carrie Ann's eyes widened. "Maybe she tricked Ruth into going up to that graveyard and she pushed her or something and

Ruth fell, then your mama buried her there like that other girl they found."

Nerves gathered in Kat's belly.

"The police questioned her and Hetty," she said. "But they had other suspects and never arrested Mama so they must have thought she didn't do it. They thought my granddaddy did, but he disappeared."

"Would he have covered for your mother?" Carrie Ann asked.

Kat wrinkled her nose in thought. "I don't know. I doubt it. I think he was mean to her and we know he was to Hetty."

"Let's read more. If she did hurt Ruth, she might write about it in her journal."

Kat's finger hesitated over the computer keys. What if she discovered her mama had killed Ruth? Maybe her granddaddy left town to take the heat off of her?

No... from what she'd heard about him, he wouldn't do something that selfless.

Logic kicked in. "But even if Mama hurt Ruth, she wouldn't kill that other girl. It's been fifteen years since Ruth went missing. All Mama's done since then is live here in Brambletown, raise me and take care of Daddy." In fact, she'd gotten pregnant in high school and married Joe. Kat had heard her parents talking about it once, and her mama admitted she'd felt trapped but she did what she had to do.

"Go ahead, Kat," Carrie Ann said. "Let's read another post."

Curiosity overtook Kat's doubts, and she scrolled to the next entry.

Suddenly a knock sounded at the door and her mama stuck her head in. Kat quickly closed the laptop, then covered it with her throw blanket.

"Dinner's gonna be ready soon, Kat. Your daddy's home."

"'Kay," Kat said as her mama left.

Carrie Ann stood and grabbed her backpack. "If you find something interesting, call me."

Kat nodded, although her stomach was somersaulting as she and Carrie Ann walked into the kitchen. Her daddy lumbered in the door, looking sweaty and tired, and smelling like stale beer.

Carrie Ann must have realized he was in a mood. She lifted her hand in a wave and hurried outside, avoiding eye contact with him.

The TV was blaring, and a breaking news story interrupted the regular programming.

"This is Angelica Gomez coming to you with Detective Ellie Reeves of Crooked Creek Police Department." She angled the mic toward the detective. "You have news?"

"Unfortunately, yes, but not good news," Detective Reeves said. "Today another body was discovered near Green Gardens Cemetery. We have identified her as sixteen-year-old Jacey Ward from Watkinsville, Georgia." Her picture appeared on the screen.

Kat's mama's face paled. "Oh, my word."

"Do you think Earl's back?" Kat's daddy asked.

Mama sank into the kitchen chair with a thud and closed her eyes as if she might faint.

Her father whipped his head toward Kat. "I heard kids are going up there to take pictures by that memorial, but you'd better stay away from that place and the graveyard. It's dangerous."

Kat started to protest, but his sharp look stopped her cold.

"Your daddy's right," Mama said, her voice on edge. "Stay away from there, Kat."

"Do you understand, girl?" her daddy barked.

Kat gave a slow nod and glanced at her mother who was trembling so hard her knees were knocking together. Curiosity gnawed at Kat again. Was her grandfather still hiding out? Had he killed Ruth and now these other two girls? Did Mama know where he was?

Her father turned off the TV then walked back to the table. "Now, no more talk about that. Let's eat."

The chair rattled as he slid into it, and he wiped sweat from his face with his napkin then scooped up a ladle full of pot roast and a hefty spoon full of mashed potatoes and smothered it with gravy.

Bile rose to Kat's throat, her appetite vanishing as she remembered the picture on the news. Jacey Ward was close to her age. Daddy was right. The graveyard was dangerous.

It could have been her.

SIXTY-SIX

Pine Hill

Tilly finished her notes on the memorial, detailing comments people offered when she talked to ones visiting the graveyard.

Now that detective and federal agent had found another teenage girl's body, and they seemed to believe the same killer murdered her and Bonnie Sylvester. Which meant it was possible he'd killed Ruth.

Fear and grief balled in her belly. It had consumed her fifteen years ago and although she'd moved away, she couldn't outrun it.

She went to Ruth's room, memories bombarding her.

She remembered her mother sitting for hours in this room, hugging Ruth's stuffed bear while crying. Once Tilly found her curled on her side in Ruth's bed, Ruth's cheerleading outfit and soft sweaters spread around her as she pressed them to her cheek and sniffed them.

That day was burned into her brain. It was the beginning of the end of her relationship with her mother.

"Mom, come on out and let's take a walk."

Her mother ignored her and pulled Ruth's comforter over her.

Tilly walked over to the bed and started to sit on the edge, but her mother pushed her away. "No, this is Ruth's. Go away, Tilly, and leave me alone."

A sharp pang cut through Tilly at her mother's words. She understood her mother was hurting and frightened but so was she.

She'd tried a couple more times that week to reach her, but each time she received the same cold response. Day by day, her mother sank deeper and deeper into depression.

Eventually Tilly just stopped trying and disappeared into a shell herself.

If only she'd been able to help find Ruth. If only she'd told her parents sooner Ruth had slipped out. If only she'd insisted Ruth tell her who she was meeting.

Guilt eating at her, she searched Ruth's closet and found a box. She opened it and saw several spiral notebooks filled with school assignments. They obviously weren't sentimental to her parents, but she dragged the box into the middle of the room and began to flip through the contents.

Algebra and trig assignments filled one notebook while another held book reports, which Tilly recognized because she'd helped Ruth write them. After all, she was the bookworm while Ruth was the outgoing social type who barely skimmed cliff notes before a test.

She flipped through another one with history notes, but the next one made her perk up. Ruth always liked to doodle. In this one she'd sketched rough drawings of flowers and animals, then a heart with her initials and the initials CW in the center, an arrow drawn through it.

CW for Clint Wallace.

Tilly drummed her fingers on the page. Ruth claimed she

wasn't meeting Clint that night and he insisted he was with his buddies.

But what if Ruth changed her mind and decided to make up with Clint? What if Clint had lied? His friends would have covered for him.

Back then, Tilly never would have gotten the nerve to talk to Clint, much less question him or call him a liar. But she wasn't a scared kid now.

Determination renewed, she hurried to the living room, snagged her keys and went to her car. Tonight, she'd make Clint look her in the eye and tell her what happened between him and her sister.

SIXTY-SEVEN

While Ellie handled the press conference to update the public and ask for help in finding the unsub, Derrick located Jacey's boyfriend Cameron's family. His mother lived in Monroe, Georgia, but his father died three years before.

He called the mother, but she didn't pick up so he left a message, then tried the work number listed for her at a gift shop in Monroe.

"Gifts Galore," a woman said in greeting.

"Hi, this is Special Agent Derrick Fox. I need to speak with Tamara Boyd. Is she working today?"

"Yes, she's ringing up a customer at the moment. Do you want me to have her return your call?"

"Actually I'll hold."

"All right."

Soft piano music wafted over the line, filling the silence as he waited. Meanwhile, Derrick pulled the missing persons report on Cameron. He was eighteen now, technically an adult.

An officer named Denton had assumed the lead and essentially ruled Cameron as a runaway. At fifteen, he was arrested on misdemeanor charges of marijuana possession and underage drinking. His parents bailed him out twice, then his father died and four months later, he ran away. He was seen at an ATM twice pulling cash from his mother's account until she notified the bank to cease payments.

The music faded as a woman's voice broke into his thoughts. "This is Tamara."

"Special Agent Derrick Fox, ma'am. I'm sorry to bother you at work but I need to talk to you about your son."

A tense beat passed, then the woman's heavy sigh. "What kind of trouble is Cam in now?"

The frustration and worry in her tone roused Derrick's sympathy. "We don't know that he's done anything wrong, but I want to talk to him about Jacey Ward, the teenager who ran away with him."

"Look, like I told her mother and the police, I begged him to leave that girl alone just like I tried to get him help for the drugs. But after his father died, he was so angry, I couldn't reach him." Her breath wheezed out. "Maybe I'm a terrible mother but I refused to let him have drugs in the house and then cut him off financially because I couldn't stomach what he was doing with the money."

"I understand and there's no judgment here. Do you have any idea where Cameron is?" Derrick asked.

"No," she replied in a pained voice. "I haven't heard from him in two years. But I think about him and pray for him every day. I... keep hoping that one day he'll show up and we can be a family again."

"I hope that works out for you," Derrick said sincerely. "What kind of car was he driving?"

"An older model black Pathfinder."

"Thanks. If you do hear from him, I need you to call me ASAP."

"What's going on, Agent Fox?"

"Unfortunately, Jacey Ward's body was found. She was murdered, and your son may have been the last one to see her alive."

Mrs. Boyd gasped. "Good heavens. You don't think Cam k... killed her, do you? Just because he uses drugs doesn't mean he'd hurt anyone."

Derrick held his tongue. In his experience, drugs could cause a person to behave erratically and out of character. The desperation to buy and have another fix sometimes drove them to violence. Drugs laced with chemicals could also cause side effects such as memory loss.

"Just please call me if you hear from him. He may not have hurt Jacey, but he might have seen the person who did."

SIXTY-EIGHT

This case was getting to Ellie.

She needed a reprieve, a night with Cord. She picked up two fried chicken dinners from the new restaurant in town, Home-Grown, which marketed their meals as locally sourced. They utilized produce and eggs from local farmers along with the chickens raised and processed in Gainesville.

The moment the restaurant opened, people swarmed there for homemade biscuits, fried chicken, country fried steak, and pork chops. The salads were enormous and daily vegetables included mashed potatoes, collards, black-eyed peas, glazed carrots, sweet potato souffle and Brussel sprouts. Their peach cobbler was giving Lola a run for her money at the Corner Café.

At least thinking about the food allowed her a momentary distraction from the grisly images of Jacey Ward being left in the elements where animals could ravage her remains. Sympathy for the girl's family made her hands shake as she let herself in her house and set the food containers on the counter.

The house was chilly from the winter winds outside, so she

turned on the gas fireplace to ward off the chill, then hurried to her bathroom to shower. She reeked of sweat, death and dirt from her hike in the woods to the crime scene. She set the water to a steamy spray, climbed in then scrubbed her body and washed her hair. A quick rinse then she dried off, pulled on sweats and towel-dried her hair, leaving it loose for the night.

Hoping to eat with Cord, she gave him a quick call. He answered on the third ring. "Hey, I picked us up dinner. Just wondering when you'd be here."

A tense beat passed, and his voice sounded guttural when he finally responded. "I'm going to keep searching for a while so go ahead without me. I'll probably head to my place at some point and crash but it'll be late."

Ellie bit down on her lip. Why did it feel like Cord was avoiding spending time with her outside the job? "Is something wrong, Cord? Ever since we started this case, you've been... quiet." And moody like he'd been when they'd first started working together.

"Everything's fine," he said. "I'm just trying to do my job. If there are other victims in the woods, I want to find them."

Ellie massaged her temple. "I know, the case always takes precedence. I want to find out who killed the girls, too. I... just miss our nights together."

A long beat passed. "So do I," he murmured. "We'll get back to us when this is over."

He hung up but worry still gnawed at her. She hoped they got back to *them* but he needed to open up and stop keeping secrets for them to have a future.

Her stomach growled again although the idea of eating at the moment turned her stomach. Battling frustration, she poured herself a generous finger of her favorite vodka, carried it to the couch, opened her laptop and sipped the vodka while she accessed her files on the case.

She downloaded the pictures of the latest crime scene she'd

snapped, then created a new section, labeling it *Victim # 2 Jacey Ward*. Beneath her name, she listed the details she knew to date then studied the photographs. Jacey had been wearing a UGA sweatshirt and one red boot was found not far from her body, the other missing.

The school colors for Brambletown High were red and black. So were the University of Georgia's. A lot of Georgians were Bulldog fans, so the sweatshirt didn't necessarily mean anything, but what if it did in this instance? What if Jacey and her boyfriend Cameron had been living in Athens or near the college?

She phoned Derrick. "I think we should go to Athens tomorrow and talk to the police there. Maybe Jacey and Cameron were staying somewhere around town."

"Good idea. We can coordinate with both the police department and campus police and use them to circulate posters, canvass businesses and access security cameras."

Ellie agreed. "If the killer abducted Jacey from Athens, we might catch a glimpse of him at a bar or restaurant. Let's also check footage at the gas stations around town and on route to the mountains for his car."

Her pulse jumped at the thought. Hopefully they'd get an image of the vehicle or the actual kidnapping.

SIXTY-NINE

Tilly didn't care if it was getting late in the evening. She'd waited years for answers and she refused to leave Brambletown without them.

She spotted Sheriff Clint Wallace's squad car in front of the precinct and was relieved he was there. Storm clouds hovered above, threatening a winter rain, and the traffic light swung back and forth in the wind gusts. She rushed up the steps and entered the building, then stopped at the front desk and asked to speak to the sheriff.

"What is this about?" the woman asked.

"The bodies found near Green Gardens Cemetery."

The woman straightened, her eyebrows raising. "You have helpful information?"

Tilly gave a little shrug. "I'd rather speak to the sheriff in person."

"All right." She punched a button on the phone and spoke into it. "Sheriff, there's a woman here who wants to speak to you about the bodies found at Green Gardens Cemetery."

"Be right there."

Tilly inhaled a deep breath and squared her shoulders for courage. She hadn't seen Clint Wallace since high school, but the minute he walked through the door she recognized him. He'd beefed up a little, but he was all muscle, sported a five o'clock shadow and his thick hair was still dark. Dammit, he was as handsome as ever.

His eyes skated over her, a smile crinkling the corners of his mouth.

"Well, Tilly Higgins. I thought I'd never see you back in Brambletown."

"I thought I'd never be back, but here I am. Still looking for answers about my missing sister."

His smile faded. "Let's go to my office." He glanced at the receptionist. "Why don't you go on home for the night?"

She nodded, grabbed her purse and darted to the door. The sheriff led Tilly through a doorway to an office on the right. He strode inside and gestured for her to take a seat.

"How are your parents?" he asked, surprising her.

"I don't know," she said honestly. "We've been estranged for years."

"They don't know you're here?"

She shook her head. "I saw the press conference. The detective and that FBI agent think those two girls' deaths were caused by the same person who took Ruth. Do you know why they believe that?"

He cut his eyes away from her. "It's just speculation for now."

"Come on, Clint. What do *you* think?"

His eyes hardened. "I think the Sylvester girl and Jacey Ward may be connected. I don't know about Ruth."

"What can you remember about my sister?" Tilly asked, her tone blunt. "You were an item back in the day."

"It was kids' stuff," he answered, his expression unreadable.

"But she broke up with you the day before she disappeared. You must have been angry about that."

Clint grunted. "Like I said it was kids' stuff. Ruth was always dramatic and had one of her tantrums, but I knew she'd come crawling back in a day or two."

Tilly gave him her resting bitch face. "She snuck out to meet someone that night. Was it you?"

"No. I was with my buddies." He folded his arms. "And for the record I don't appreciate an inquisition by you. For all we know your brother or father did something to Ruth and your family covered it up."

"Or your father lied to cover for you," Tilly said with a defiant lift of her chin.

Clint strode around the desk and grabbed Tilly's wrist, pinning her with an angry glare. "I'd be careful about throwing accusations, Tilly. You don't want to end up like those other girls."

His tone ticked her off, and she met his glare with her own, then jerked her arm away. "Is that a threat, Clint?"

He shrugged, a smirk on his face, then gestured to the door. "Take it however you want. Now get out. I have work to do."

Suspicions rose in her mind. As the sheriff, he had the perfect opportunity to make sure no one found Ruth.

If he had murdered her, had he been killing girls ever since and dumping them near the graveyard?

SEVENTY

Kat finally escaped dinner with her parents. Now Mama was busy cleaning the dishes and her daddy had retreated to his workshop which was off limits to her and anyone else who went nosing around. He claimed he was working on a secret project for her mother for her birthday, but Kat had never known him to be creative or surprise her mother with anything for any holiday.

She had a feeling he had a TV in the workshop—he called it his man cave—where he watched weird sci-fi flicks, along with a worn-out recliner and a stash of moonshine.

Once Mama finished the dishes and putting away the food, she'd settle onto the couch to watch her reality shows where she envied the rich families with money and expensive clothes, things Mama would never possess in her lifetime.

Guilt twinged at Kat's insides. Maybe if her mama hadn't gotten knocked up with her, she would have found a way to further her education or at least learn a trade. As it was, she was stuck here and dependent on her daddy's paycheck.

And he never let her forget it.

She vowed to do better, to never let a man rule her life, and when she decided she'd crawl in bed with some guy, *if ever*, she'd double up the birth control. Right now she had zero interest in *doing the nasty*—her mother's description when she'd had the big talk that every girl dreaded with their mother.

She settled back on her bed with a bag of chocolate chip cookies, bowing out of kitchen chores claiming she had a history project due, which gave her a valid excuse to be on the computer if one of her parents poked their head into her room to make sure she was tucked inside and behaving herself. Mama would be especially irate if she realized Kat was reading her high school journal.

Although it felt naughty to spy on her mama, she was enthralled to hear about her teenage antics.

Kat set her water bottle on the side table and opened Mama's laptop, keeping hers on the bed beside it in case she needed to do a quick switcharoo.

Leaning back against her giant stuffed bunny rabbit, she scrolled to another installment.

Today some of the kids at school decided to sneak over to the graveyard and Hetty and I crept outside and watched them as they spray painted the gravestones. Daddy was going to be mad because he was caretaker of the graveyard and headstones and would have to scrub and clean them off before the families came to visit.

He'd probably make me and Hetty do it. Or Joe who'd started working with him a while back. I don't understand why he took the job but I heard he lived with his grandma and probably needed the money.

Hetty and I hunkered in the shadows and tried to see who was up to all the shenanigans. Hunky Clint Wallace was one

*of them. Every girl in school has a crush on him. I wish I didn't
because he's so stuck up but I can't help it.*

*Then that bitch Ruth was there, laughing and talking
about me and Hetty being weirdos because we lived by the
graves.*

*"No wonder they're so pale," Ruth whispered. "I heard
their daddy makes them sleep in the freshly turned graves." She
sprayed the words devil's child in red paint across one of the
graves. "Maybe they're even vampires and drink the blood of
the dead."*

*"Most people are embalmed so they're blood has already
been drained from them," Jason, one of the baseball players,
pointed out.*

*"Then they're zombies," Ruth's friend Marnie said. "Espe-
cially that Hetty. I see her out here digging with her Uncle
Earl. My parents say she's touched in the head, that she might
have been poisoned by the toxins and that's why she's so
strange."*

*"Ida is the dumb one," another one of Ruth's friends said.
"You know she has a crush on you, Clint."*

Kat froze, her mind racing. Mama had had a crush on Clint
but Clint was Ruth Higgins' boyfriend? He was the sheriff
now? What had happened?

Hoping to find out, she continued reading.

*Clint pulled Ruth up to him, wrapped his arm around her and
gave her a lip lock. "But you're my girl, Ruth," he said as he
kissed her neck.*

*"I'm not worried," Ruth said with a giggle. "I know you'd
never go for white trash like Hetty or Ida Bramble."*

"That mean bitch," Hetty whispered. "We oughta kill her."

SEVENTY-ONE

Briar Ridge Mobile Homes

Tilly was still shaken from her confrontation with the sheriff as she drove away from the police station. She'd known coming back to Brambletown would be difficult, even dangerous, but if she uncovered the truth about what happened to her sister, it was worth the risk. Still, Clint's warning echoed in her head.

Night had set in, the winds picking up and beating at her car, and traffic was minimal. She made a snap decision to stop by Ida's house and point blank ask her where her father was. Although Clint's relationship with Ruth raised flags in her mind, Earl Bramble was and had always been the primary suspect in her sister's disappearance.

After Ruth went missing, two other girls in school told the sheriff that he'd been watching them and following them when they'd come to the cemetery to visit a family member. Ida and Hetty had admitted he was mean, and Tilly had heard the school counselor reported bruises on Hetty that she suspected came from Earl. Ms. Maeve claimed she saw him shove Hetty more than once when she took flowers to her beloved deceased husband's grave.

Tilly had never been to Ida's or Hetty's homes, and noting the state of the run-down mobile home park, she felt sorry for Ida.

She'd told her sister that Ida and Hetty's low-income lifestyle wasn't their fault and to be kinder to her, but Ruth was stuck on herself and savored the attention their father gave her, taking advantage of his wallet to keep herself decked out in expensive outfits, shoes, purses and makeup.

Tilly pulled into the graveled parking lot past three mobile homes until she found Ida's place. Mud streaked the side of the beige exterior and the yard was overgrown and unkempt. Obviously neither Ida nor her husband, Joe, were gardeners like Hetty.

Hoping Ida would open up to her seemed futile, but she had to take a stab at it. Taking a deep breath for courage, she walked up the graveled drive, climbed the two steps to the front door and knocked. The wind tossed her hair in her eyes, and she pushed the strands to the side and tapped her foot as she waited.

A noise sounded inside then the door squeaked open. Ida's husband, Joe, stood in the doorway, staring down at her. In high school, Joe had been fairly good-looking, but he'd gained about thirty pounds, his hair was receding and his belly hung over his faded blue jeans.

"What are you doing here, Tilly?" Joe barked.

Ida hurried up behind Joe, wringing her hands on a kitchen towel, her eyes wide with alarm. "Yes, why did you come?"

Tilly swallowed hard. "I wanted to talk to you about Ruth and the two girls they discovered at the graveyard."

Ida's glare could scorch butter. "You have a lot of nerve. Your family ruined my life."

Tilly offered her a tentative smile. "I'm sorry, Ida. I know

Ruth wasn't very nice to you and Hetty. Believe it or not, I tried to convince her to be more kind."

"Well, she wasn't," Ida snapped. "She was mean and sneaky and I hated her as much as she hated me."

"I know," Tilly said. Although at times she wondered if Ida or Hetty had hurt Ruth, she couldn't imagine them killing other young girls.

"Just answer one question," Tilly said. "Do you think your father killed Ruth?"

Joe shot her a venomous look. "You shouldn't have come here. None of us need that time dredged up again."

"I'm not the one dredging it up," Tilly said. "Whoever killed those girls is."

The door by the kitchen opened and Ida's daughter, Kat, appeared. "What's going on, Mama?"

"Go back to your room," Ida shouted.

Tilly pushed again. "Do you know where your father is, Ida? Do you think he killed my sister and that he's been murdering other girls?"

"I don't know where he is." Ida folded her arms across her chest. "Now get off my property and leave me and my family alone."

A second later, Joe pushed his way onto the porch. "You heard Ida, Tilly. Leave town. Nobody wants the likes of you here."

His words cut Tilly to the bone. But she lifted her chin and stood her ground. She had run fifteen years ago, but she wasn't running anymore.

And neither Ida nor Joe nor Clint Wallace would force her to.

"I'll be back," he shouted over his shoulder to Ida. "Gonna get some beer."

She hurried to her car, but Joe was on her heels. "Don't come back here, Tilly."

She slid inside, slammed the car door and locked it, then sped off as he climbed in his truck. Nerves clawed at her as she turned onto the highway.

Was he really going for beer or did he want to make sure she left his property?

SEVENTY-TWO

He traced his finger over the red cowboy boot, remembering the way it felt to slide it off Jacey's slender foot. While she lay still on the ground, he'd gently kissed her toes, admiring how delicate she was and reveling in his power over her.

The red scarf around her throat looked like a river of blood as he'd draped it over her neck and small breasts. Her fingernails were painted with alternating red and black, the UGA colors, although she would never be a student at the university.

Her time had come to an end.

Watching her take her last breath brought back the thrill of the kill and took him back to his mother. He had power over these girls. He'd had no power over his mother and her sick twisted boyfriends. Had been forced to watch through the crack in the closet doorway.

Time slipped away as the world blurred and he was five years old, huddled in the darkness.

A pair of his mother's red high heels were tucked in the closet. The heel of the red stilettos dug into his back.

He snagged the shoe, then gently touched the feathers with his fingers. Closing his eyes, he rubbed the soft feathers against his cheek, sniffing the shiny ribbon on the heel. He shut out the grunting sounds outside the closet, then threw off his sneakers and socks and slid the right shoe onto his foot. Next he slipped on the left one, then tried to stand.

Laughter bubbled inside him as he stood, teetering on the three-inch tiny heel and he wobbled and hit the wall. Pretending he was his mother, he righted himself and turned in a slow arc, smiling as the shoes clicked on the floor.

Suddenly the closet door swung open, and his mother stared down at him. She was half-naked, her eyes fuming, her breath puffing out like fire. "You sick little pervert!" She slapped him so hard his ears rang and tears stung his eyes, then she shoved him down and yanked off the shoes. "Don't ever touch my things again."

Then she closed the door and locked it and left him there for two days in the dark.

He jerked himself from the memory, his hand sweating as he walked to his trophy case and added Jacey's red boot to his collection. "You can't take them away from me now, Mama. No one can."

SEVENTY-THREE

DAY FOUR

Ellie and Derrick ate breakfast on the hour drive to Athens, which was the heart of the University of Georgia and home to approximately 37,000 students per year. The sheer number of dorms, apartments, fraternity and sorority houses, and rental properties would make finding a runaway more difficult, especially with off campus housing stretching for miles.

"Cameron would fit the median age for a freshman," Derrick said, "but Jacey was only fifteen and might garner attention if they'd frequented bars or if they'd lived on the streets."

"True," Ellie agreed. "We should check with real estate agents for a property they might have been living in."

"Let's hope they were in an apartment or house and not homeless like so many runaways," Derrick said with a scowl.

While she drove, Derrick compiled a list of real estate agents and started making phone calls.

Ellie's chest ached at the idea of a fifteen-year-old girl living on the streets. If Cameron and Jacey hadn't had jobs, they might have resorted to stealing to survive. There were other ways for a girl to make money, none of them which she wanted to contemplate. If Jacey was living with Cameron, they were probably sexually active but Laney hadn't mentioned sexual assault.

Derrick made call after call and texted each real estate agent a photo of both Jacey and Cameron, asking if they recognized either of them or had rented property to Cameron. Most rental properties didn't rent to minors but required an adult signature. Neither Jacey's nor Cameron's parents knew where they were so obviously had not cosigned for them.

Ellie heard the frustration in his tone as he seemed to be striking out.

Thirty minutes later, just as Ellie drove past the UGA arches, Derrick heaved a sigh. "So far nothing. Which could mean they're not in Athens. Although with so many young people in this town, they wouldn't have stuck out."

Ellie glanced around as students walked and rode bikes to class, backpacks slung over their shoulders, jackets pulled tight. Her adopted mother, Vera, had wanted her to attend college, not the police academy, although her father had been more supportive. Until she wanted to assume his job when he retired as sheriff. She'd been mad as hell when he'd supported Bryce Waters to replace him instead of her. But later she'd realized he simply wanted to protect her.

Cord's face taunted her. After leaving an abusive foster home, he'd run away and lived off the grid. "It's possible they were living with a group or on the streets," Ellie said. "Any word on Cameron's Pathfinder?" Ellie asked.

"Not yet," Derrick said. "But the police issued an APB for it."

She pulled into the police department's parking lot and they walked up to the entrance. They entered and introduced themselves to the desk sergeant.

He was a brawny man with thick gray hair and led them to

Detective Henry Willet's office. A younger man in a campus police unform identified himself as Paul Lansing.

"What makes you think Jacey Ward was in Athens?" the detective asked.

Ellie explained about her clothing, that she'd wanted to attend UGA and that Jacey's mother thought she'd run away with Cameron.

"People of all ages across the state wear UGA attire," Lansing said. "Do you have proof they even came to Athens?"

Ellie squared her shoulders. "I know it's a long shot, but Jacey lived in Watkinsville so not far from Athens."

A heartbeat passed. "We received the photos you circulated to law enforcement agencies," Detective Willet said. "I've already passed them around to our officers and instructed them to keep an eye out."

"We'd like for the local news stations to post them," Ellie said.

He nodded. "Done."

"And we need campus police's help as well," Ellie said.

Lansing nodded. "Will do."

"Thanks," Ellie said. "We'd like for you to have officers canvass local restaurants, bars, shops and gas stations. Agent Fox has reached out to real estate agents about a possible rental property where the kids could have lived."

The detective nodded although he looked skeptical that they'd turn up anything. If the kids hadn't rented something, they might be living with roommates and the place wasn't in their name.

Ellie's phone dinged and she checked the number. Her boss. "Excuse me, I have to take this." The room quieted as she answered the call.

"Detective Reeves, a call on the tip line from a woman outside Athens just came in. She says she may have seen Jacey Ward at the gas station where she works."

Ellie's pulse hammered. "Text me her name and address and we'll check it out."

She ended the call and stood. "A woman at a nearby gas station thinks she might have seen Jacey. We'll keep you posted. But please keep looking for Cameron. He may know what happened to Jacey." Or be responsible.

"I thought you were looking for a serial killer," Detective Willet said. "If Cameron's a teenager, he would have only been a toddler at the time that girl Ruth Higgins disappeared."

"True," Ellie agreed. "Although we can't rule out any lead." She pulled her keys from her pocket. "It's possible Cameron may have seen the man who abducted Jacey."

She headed to the door. They couldn't waste time. This gas attendant might be the lead they needed.

SEVENTY-FOUR

The convenience store/gas station was located less than two miles away on the main highway leading out of Athens. Ellie and Derrick met the store clerk inside, a chubby middle-aged woman with curly graying hair named Bertie. Two people stood in line so they waited until the customers left then identified themselves.

Bertie called another clerk to replace her then stepped aside to talk to them. "Thank you for calling in," Ellie said. "Can you tell us exactly what you saw."

"Well, it was gettin' kind of late so there weren't too many customers inside, a few folks filling up with gas at the pumps. Then I saw this young girl run into the parking lot."

Ellie showed her Jacey's photograph. "This girl?"

Bertie nodded. "Yeah, her hair was kind of scraggly and she looked too thin, but most of all what struck me was that she seemed nervous. She kept looking all around the parking lot like she was looking for someone."

"Like she was meeting someone?" Derrick asked.

Bertie shook her head. "No... it seemed more like she was scared and trying not to be seen. She kept her head down and darted into the store. She was out of breath and sweating and for a minute, she kind of hid behind the snack aisle. I thought she might be going to steal something, and I decided if she did, I would just let her cause she looked hungry and sad."

"That was very compassionate of you," Ellie said softly.

Bertie shrugged, her eyes softening. "She looked so lost I wanted to ask her if she was okay, but when my customer paid and left, the girl asked me if she could use the phone." Bertie fiddled with the collar of her blouse. "I asked if it was a local call and she said yes, so I let her use it."

"Do you know who she called?" Ellie asked.

"Said she needed to call her mama so I thought maybe her mama would come and get her. But I reckon she didn't answer, so the girl left a message saying she was coming home." Bertie sighed, her teeth worrying her lower lip. "I thought about offering her a ride myself, but then a family came in and I had to wait on them and while I was busy, the girl ducked outside." Her fingers toyed with her collar again. "After the family left, I looked for the girl and saw her again. She went into the alley. I lost sight of her then, but I got someone to watch the register and when I ran outside I saw her get into a truck parked on the side." Bertie's voice cracked with tears. "If she's the girl you found, I was right to be worried. I... should have stopped her from going with that man, b... but I was hoping it was her daddy."

Ellie's heart twinged at the guilt in the kind woman's voice. She squeezed her hand gently. "It's not your fault, Bertie. You couldn't have known something like this was going to happen."

"But I could tell she was scared." Tears glistened in Bertie's eyes. "I should have tried harder to talk to her."

"You let her use the phone," Ellie said. "And that message... and the fact that she called her mother meant she loved her. At least her mother can carry that with her, that and the sound of her voice on the recording."

Bertie nodded, then sniffed and dabbed at her damp cheeks.

"Can you describe the man?" Derrick asked.

Bertie's face fell. "Not really. I saw his back as he got in the truck. But I didn't see his face."

"Do you have camera footage inside and outside in the parking lot?" Derrick asked.

Bertie nodded. "I'll get the manager to show it to you."

SEVENTY-FIVE

Briar Ridge Mobile Homes

Kat woke to the sound of loud music blaring from the living room. She winced as she padded into the kitchen for cereal before getting dressed for school. Her daddy was lying on the couch snoring like a lion. She didn't understand why he turned the music up when he passed out or how her mama could possibly sleep with him. Then again, maybe she'd thrown him out of the bedroom and that's how he wound up on the sofa.

She rolled her shoulders to alleviate the kinks in her neck. Last night she'd stayed up too late reading her mama's journal. The games she and Hetty played in the graveyard were creepy, and Mama had hinted that they'd seen things they didn't want to talk about. That naughty things happened there.

So far she hadn't found the specifics but she was determined to keep digging.

Kat poured herself some cereal and milk, carried it back to her room then ate it while she gathered her homework for school. She worked hard to turn her assignments in on time and kept up her grades. The last thing she wanted was to be an uneducated pregnant teen like her mama had been, one who wound up in a dumpy trailer, shopped at thrift stores and fed her kids day-old food from the sale aisle at the grocery.

She intended to get out of this town, make something of herself and never come back.

Once she had her backpack ready, she took a quick shower and dressed in jeans and a sweatshirt then grabbed her backpack and headed to the living room.

Her mama had just crawled out from bed, her tangled brown hair ratty, her eyes tired as she blindly made coffee.

"You need breakfast?" Mama asked.

"Already had it." Kat rinsed her dish and put it in the drain. "Gotta go." She and Carrie Ann were meeting before homeroom to discuss her mama's journal.

A rumbling, then grunting sounded from the couch, and her father threw off the blanket he'd burrowed underneath, swung his stubby legs over the edge and stood, wobbling. He rubbed his eyes, then looked over at her with a frown.

"What the hell?" he growled.

"Just making coffee," Mama said. "I'll pour you a cup."

Kat rolled her eyes. Another thing she didn't intend to do, wait on a man hand and foot.

He scratched his belly, which was disgusting since his T-shirt rode up, revealing his hairy gut. Kat shuddered at the sight and started walking toward the back door, avoiding looking at him.

"Wait a minute, Kat. Where are you going?"

Kat froze, biting her tongue and striving for patience. She so did not want to get into a verbal battle with her father this morning. "School," she said then took another step toward the door.

"Not today," he growled.

She whirled around. "Yes, I am, Daddy. I have an Algebra test."

"No," he said. "You heard about that other girl being killed. You need to stay home today where you're safe."

"But, Daddy—"

"Joe, really," her mother said on a winded sigh. "She's just going to school."

"I'm her father and I'm just trying to protect my daughter." He turned on her mama. "Don't you care if she's safe? You want her to end up in that godforsaken graveyard like those other girls?"

"Of course not," Mama cried.

Kat gritted her teeth. *Just a couple more years and you'll be out of here.*

"Daddy, I'll go straight to school, I promise," she said, vowing to look for a summer job so she could save for college. She refused to miss a day of school or ruin her grade point average because he was being paranoid. "And I'll come right home afterward." Although she wanted to hang out with Carrie Ann.

She didn't wait for his response. She rushed out the door, forgetting her sack lunch and coat and promising herself she'd tough it out until she could leave this hellhole.

SEVENTY-SIX

Ellie and Derrick followed the manager of the convenience store into a back room where he set up the camera footage for them to view. They settled in with coffee and he rewound the tape to the day before. One camera focused on the interior of the store and another the exterior, so they first studied the exterior footage starting two hours before Bertie had seen Jacey.

People came and went, many stopping for gas, drinks and snacks, students running in for food, day workers and twenty-somethings carrying out twelve packs of beer and filling coolers with ice. Although the legal age for buying alcohol was eighteen, a lot of kids had fake IDs or managed to persuade an older student, friend or even a parent to purchase alcohol for them. The police did their best to curtail it by watching the local bars for inebriated kids as they left.

"I'll focus on looking for Jacey," Ellie said. "Derrick, narrow in on any vehicles or male drivers that might look suspicious."

"On it," he murmured.

The footage continued running and minutes later, Ellie

spotted a girl that looked like Jacey veering into the parking lot, her hair flying in the wind. Just as Bertie described, she kept glancing over her shoulder as if she was nervous. Had someone been following her?

"There she is," Ellie said. "Just like the store clerk stated, Jacey was definitely running from someone. And she looks scared."

Derrick nodded. "So far, I don't see anyone following her though."

"Now she's going in the store." She turned her gaze to the film of the interior of the store where Jacey hesitated in the snack aisle as Bertie described, then she ducked her head and inched her way to the counter. She spoke to Bertie and Bertie handed her the phone.

Ellie stiffened as she spotted bruises on Jacey's wrists as if she'd been restrained. Dammit, she couldn't see her arms or legs through her clothes, but the bruises indicated she'd endured violence at the hands of someone. Violence before she'd walked into the hands of a serial predator.

She pointed out the dark purple splotching to Derrick. "Did she get those bruises from Cameron or the killer?"

"The killer could have been holding her hostage and she escaped," Derrick suggested.

True. They really had no idea if or how long he kept them before strangling them.

Ellie's stomach knotted as she watched Jacey dart out the door and head into the alley. They lost sight of her there, but Ellie continued watching the footage, hoping she'd emerge and they'd spot her abductor.

Derrick cleared his throat. "There's been a good bit of traffic in and out of the store but look at that black pick-up truck. A man got out and filled up his tank, then pulled over into the corner of the parking lot. I can't see his plates, but watch."

Derrick rewound the tape and pointed out the truck.

"There. A man dressed in a dark jacket with a UGA cap gets out and takes a look around. Then he goes into the alley."

Ellie gasped. "The alley where Jacey went."

Their gazes locked. "Keep running it." Ellie said.

Derrick did and five minutes later, the same man exited the alley, keeping his face averted. Jacey walked beside him and climbed in the passenger side of the truck.

Ellie zoned in on her red boots. She was wearing both of them at the time.

Jacey hesitated to close the door but then shut it and the truck peeled from the parking lot.

"It looks like she went with him willingly," Ellie said.

"Maybe she knew him," Derrick said.

"Dammit, he must have been aware there were cameras and kept his face hidden, and his hand looked leathery with age, indicating he was a man, not a teen like Cameron—"

"We still need to find Cameron and that man," Ellie said. Although the unsub had never shown his face or even the front of his body. He'd hidden in the shadows of the alley and the truck was parked so close to it that he could just slide in without being seen.

Intentional.

Ellie's heart ached. Jacey had called her mother and told her she was coming home. But she'd just climbed in the vehicle with her killer.

"I'll send this footage to our people at the Bureau," Derrick said. "Their forensic analysis team might be able to narrow down the type of truck and more about it." He leaned closer. "Although it looks old to me, maybe a sixties model." He snapped his fingers. "That could help us."

Ellie's pulse jumped. "Let me look back at the original investigation notes."

Derrick's brows rose. "What are you thinking?"

Ellie took a breath. "That Earl Bramble drove a black sixties pick-up. I saw it in the photos. The sheriff at the time had it searched for evidence of Ruth."

"Maybe he is back," Derrick said. "And he's been hiding out or moving around all these years."

"Which means there may be other victims buried across the state." Ellie's heart hammered.

Dear God. How many more girls had he murdered?

SEVENTY-SEVEN

Kat settled in her homeroom class grateful she'd finished her homework the day before so she could read more of her mother's journal. She pulled her mama's computer from her backpack, booted it up and located the entries she'd bookmarked the night before.

She scrolled to the next entry and began to read:

Hetty had bruises on her arm yesterday. She was working with Daddy at the graveyard all afternoon, turning the ground for old Mr. Jenkins' burial on Saturday, and when I asked what happened she said it was an accident. That she tripped and fell over a shovel.

But I could tell she was lying. She's been acting weird lately, real quiet and moody and in gym class today, she ducked into a stall to change instead of changing in the locker room. She's always been shy but not with me, and I got the feeling she was hiding something. I've seen bruises on her arms before and she usually wears long sleeved shirts to cover them up. The other day her shirt rode up when she went to lift a sack of fertilizer and there were bruises on her back, too. I wish I had a mama to tell but she left when I was a baby.

When she came in from the graveyard, Hetty was covered in dirt and smelled like fertilizer so she took a bath. Then she put on her long-sleeved flannel gown and knee socks and refused to come to the supper table. I snuck her a piece of fried chicken and a biscuit, but she said she wasn't hungry and I heard her crying into her pillow.

I punched mine as I crawled in bed, hating the ugly thoughts I had about Daddy. That Earl Bramble was every bit as mean as people in town gossiped about. Maybe even meaner.

I was just about to fall asleep when a noise outside startled me. For a minute I lay there thinking it was a storm brewing, but I didn't hear thunder and I didn't see lightning.

It was New Year's Eve though and I figured there were fireworks. I wanted to go to a party tonight, but Daddy never lets me do anything. He always says nothing good happens to girls who go out at night.

But then... a scream pierced the air. This one so shrill I thought the bedroom window might shatter.

A shiver started deep inside me and wouldn't let go. Hetty rolled over in bed and jerked up, then startled awake.

She heard it, too.

Shivering, I eased aside the covers and planted my feet on the cold wood floor, then tiptoed toward the window. The curtain was flapping in the January wind that seeped through the cracks, an icy chill sweeping through the already chilly room.

Hetty tiptoed up behind me and clenched my arm. Her whisper came out in a puff, her eyes enormous in her pale thin face. "What was that?"

I had a bad feeling I knew. That this was real, not a figment of my imagination.

I caught the fluttering curtain and held it aside just enough to see out. Hetty stared over my shoulder, her bony body trembling against my back. The half-moon was barely visible through the winter clouds, leaving the woods and graveyard dark and filled with ominous shadows and sounds.

A curse echoed from the bushes and I squinted through the branches of the oaks, my stomach churning.

"Oh, God..." Hetty's voice rattled out.

My fingers dug into the windowsill as I saw a body being dragged from the bushes toward the deserted section of dead land bordering the graveyard.

Suddenly the figure in the dark coat and ski hat turned and stared at the house. At the window.

I grabbed Hetty's arm and pulled her down to hide. Did he see us?

Hetty hunkered into a ball and I curved my arms around her as if I could protect her.

Oh, God. I knew who that figure was. Daddy.

So did Hetty.

But if we tried to stop him, we'd end up in the ground just like that girl was going to.

SEVENTY-EIGHT

Brambletown

"Now we're back to treating Earl Bramble as our main suspect," Ellie said as she parked at Ida Bramble's house an hour later. "I feel like we're running in circles."

"Ditto," Derrick said. "But we have to chase every lead. And that camera footage points to a black truck that might have belonged to him." He gestured toward his iPad. "Sheriff Wallace's police report confirms that Earl drove a black sixties pick-up."

"That is suspicious. And worrisome that he killed Ruth and has escaped detection for a decade and a half."

Derrick tilted his head toward her with a conspiratorial look. "Makes you wonder if his daughter knew where he was all this time."

Ellie contemplated that possibility. "What if Earl knew Ruth was bullying Ida and killed her out of some misguided idea that he was protecting his child?"

Derrick's mouth turned downward into a frown. "Something to think about. But during the sheriff's interviews, locals painted Earl as a mean SOB. Not a caring father."

"He was also described as temperamental and had drinking issues. Maybe he just flew off the handle and snapped."

Derrick drummed his fingers on his thigh. "Possibly. Although if so, that murder would have been personal. These other murders aren't."

Ellie cut the engine and reached for the door handle. "True. Like most serial killers, he could have had psychological issues, past trauma or abuse that played into his actions. And once his appetite was whetted, he craved the euphoria he achieved during the kill."

"I'm still trying to understand why he'd come back to Brambletown now though," Derrick said. "Why not stay in hiding as he's been doing? People had forgotten about him, and no one had made the connection between Ruth and these other girls until I did."

"Maybe that's it. With the memorial being erected, perhaps he wanted to be in the limelight." Ellie slid from the Jeep. "Let's see what Ida has to say."

"We should question her husband, Joe, too." Derrick said. "In the original file, I read that he worked for Earl as a teenager. Maybe he has insight into Ida's father."

Ellie nodded and they walked up to the mobile home, the wind whipping around them and bringing the scent of impending rain. Storm clouds rumbled above, the sky gray as if the area was eternally cloaked in a dark fog of doom and gloom.

Ellie rapped on the door knocker and Derrick glanced around the grounds of the mobile home park. Seconds later, Ida opened the door. The rich scent of strong coffee, eggs, sausage and burned toast greeted them. Ida's cheeks flamed red from the heat of standing over the stove.

Over her shoulder, Ellie saw Ida's husband at the table, wolfing down biscuits and sausage gravy. He looked up and wiped his mouth with a paper towel, but his eyes looked blurry, his hair disheveled as if he hadn't showered.

"May we come in, Ida?" Derrick asked. "We need to talk to you and your husband."

Ida's flushed face paled slightly, and she waved her hand fanning herself. A nervous look passed between her and her husband, but she motioned them inside.

"Y'all want coffee?" she muttered although Ellie sensed it was the Southern hospitality she'd been raised on talking, that she knew this wasn't a friendly visit and was struggling to be polite. Or perhaps to bide herself time.

"Thanks, but we're good," Ellie said. "We picked up some on the way."

They followed her into the kitchen and settled into seats around the table.

"What now?" Ida asked. "We didn't know that girl you just found. Why keep harassing us?"

Ellie and Derrick exchanged curious looks at the way Ida's husband kept eating, seemingly undisturbed by their presence.

"I'm sorry for disrupting your morning," Ellie said, hoping to placate Ida. "But we have information about the latest victim, Jacey Ward's disappearance."

Joe sipped his coffee, wiped his mouth and set his coffee mug down. "What's that got to do with us? Ida told you we don't know that girl."

Derrick adopted a non-threatening tone. "Well, it's like this," he said. "Jacey disappeared from Athens last night. A witness claimed to have seen her get in a vehicle with a strange man and drive off. According to her and CCTV footage we viewed, Jacey looked frightened and nervous."

Ida fluttered a hand to her cheek but clamped her mouth shut.

"The man was driving a black sixties truck similar to the one your father drove," Ellie continued.

Ida made a small sound in her throat and Joe covered her hand with his. "It's okay, honey. Your daddy's wasn't the only black pick-up made in the sixties."

"We know the sheriff searched your father's truck when Ruth Higgins disappeared. You thought your father killed Ruth, didn't you?" Ellie asked.

Ida bit her lower lip, then gave a little nod. "I thought it was him I saw that night outside. But someone else could have done it. Ruth's brother could have killed her."

"Why would you say that?"

"He was a troublemaker, always starting fights. For someone with a rich daddy, he had a chip on his shoulder."

"Clint Wallace was pissed she broke up with him," Joe added. "He was one cocky SOB. Still is."

"His daddy let him get away with everything," Ida added.

Ellie considered the fact that they were offering other suspects. Having a chip on Hayden's shoulder and Clint being cocky or jealous was suspect but a far cry from murder.

Were they trying to divert suspicion from Earl?

"Ida, you told Sheriff Wallace that you saw a man in the graveyard that night, a man you thought was your father?" Ellie asked. "That he was wearing your father's clothes?"

"Yeah, I did." Fear flashed on Ida's face. "He even walked with a stoop like daddy did when he was drunk."

"I'm sure it was difficult to suspect your own father of such a crime," Ellie said gently.

Ida looked down at her fingernails. She'd chewed them down to the quick. "I guess so. But he was mean and drank too much and he used to lurk in the woods at night. Besides, two different girls came forward after Ruth went missing and said he'd followed them in the graveyard when they carried flowers to their loved ones."

"Did either of them claim he tried to grab them?" Ellie asked.

Ida shrugged. "One of them said he jumped out from behind a tree and spooked her. She ran and got away."

"Joe, you used to work with Earl, didn't you?" Ellie asked.

He clenched his jaw. "Yeah, way back in high school."

"What was your opinion of him? Did you ever see him exhibit violent tendencies?"

Joe sopped his biscuit into the gravy. "He had a temper when he was drinking."

"You have a daughter the same age as the victims we found," Derrick interjected. "You can protect her and the other teenagers in town by helping us."

Joe released a wary breath. "He was a hunter," Joe said. "Liked to stalk animals and kill them."

"You mean like deer?" Derrick asked.

"Yeah and rabbit. And one time I saw him kill a dog and bury it in the grave with someone."

Ellie's stomach turned. "Anything else?"

"He used to make comments about the young girls. Lewd comments. And... well, he was tough on Hetty and said he'd heard about Ruth, that she was a tramp like his own mother."

That could have been the trauma that resurfaced and triggered his rage toward her and young girls.

"Then he disappeared after Sheriff Wallace questioned him," Derrick said.

"Yes..." Ida whispered.

Joe shifted and squeezed Ida's hand again. "Look, my wife has been through hell because of all this. She doesn't need all this right now."

"We're almost finished." Ellie ignored Joe and focused on Ida. "What happened to your father's truck?"

Emotions flashed across Ida's face. "I... assumed he left town in it. I know the police looked for it but never found it."

Joe cleared his throat. "He probably had it painted or dumped it somewhere."

Ellie gave the couple a deadpan look. "That's possible. Have you seen him or heard anything from him lately or in the last fifteen years?"

"I already told you this," Ida said impatiently. "No, and I didn't look for him either. Hetty and I were glad he was gone and out of our lives."

"Did you think he was capable of murder, Joe?" Derrick asked.

Joe grunted and hugged Ida to his side. "I sure as hell did. I said good riddance to him so our family could finally live in peace."

SEVENTY-NINE

Kat was still contemplating the last journal entry as she left homeroom. Her mama did believe her father, Kat's grandfather, killed Ruth Higgins. She and Hetty had heard screams and seen him carrying a girl?

Had she told the police? Was that the reason everyone insisted he was guilty? Or had she kept silent out of fear?

Kat slunk into her English lit class, anxious to read more. But her teacher always had work for them to do. She read the assignment posted on the whiteboard.

"Today we're researching folklore surrounding death and the passing of a loved one."

"Why are we talking about this stuff?" Tory Griffin, a meek girl who hardly ever spoke up asked. "It's spooky and depressing."

"Because the South is historically known for its folklore, and with the attention to the history of our town and the memorial at the graveyard, I thought we should explore some of it."

Tory dropped her head but looked nervous. Others whispered and shifted, disturbed by the topic as well.

"Now get busy. I want a one-page paper by the end of class."

More complaints rumbled through the room, but everyone opened their laptops and reluctantly started to work.

Kat was inspired though. She'd heard whispers about black crows, that they were an omen of death to come. But she was more curious about what happened after someone passed. Where did they go? Was there a heaven? Angels? Could you connect with a deceased loved one?

Her grandfather Earl certainly wouldn't have been welcome in heaven. Instead, she was sure if he was dead, he was rotting in hell. Except now she'd heard rumors at the diner that some people thought he wasn't dead, that he'd been hiding out all these years and was killing again. That someone in North Georgia saw him buying cigarettes at a convenience store last week.

Fear ripped through her at the thought and she googled life after death, then found an article on signs from the afterlife. Seconds later she was intrigued by the topic and the various accounts written by individuals.

A woman named Laura Jean wrote:

My mother always loved butterflies and kept a butterfly garden that she treasured. At her graveside service, a beautiful butterfly suddenly fluttered above her coffin during the service. I knew it was my mother's way of letting me know she was at peace and happy.

A young girl named Bliss:

My father had a habit of finding loose coins, especially pennies when he was in the woods or in town on the sidewalk. He said they were presents from loved ones who'd passed sending a message that the loved one was okay and was watching over you.

Kat scratched her head. Her grandfather certainly hadn't sent butterflies or left any pennies. She read on:

In ancient times, people believed that the deceased needed coins to pay for passage across the River Styx.

"Thirty more minutes," the teacher announced. "Time to start composing your one pager."

Kat read one more entry, a piece from a woman named Heather:

I'm so broken right now. I lost my husband of fifty years and have a hole in my heart and life. I keep looking for signs he's at peace and in heaven. Today when I visited his grave, I saw one. While I was sitting beside him talking about all our wonderful memories and crying, I heard ducks in the pond by his grave. I looked up and this one duck stopped and preened his feathers, flapping them so loudly I felt like he wanted my attention. Then he sat still and stared at me for a long time. It was so odd I got a chill. The more he watched me, the more I sensed he was trying to tell me something.

Then he waddled up onto the bank and slowly came toward me. For a moment, he started to go toward the right but then stopped and turned back and stared at me again. Seconds later, he walked straight toward me, watching me pensively as he did. As he grew close, he stopped and stared at me again. Then suddenly he flapped his wings and swooped directly over my husband's grave, flying low the entire length of the grave.

Then he swooped to the ground at the head of the grave and started walking off.

I sat for a few more minutes then said goodbye to my husband and promised him I'd be back. When I reached my car, the duck was close by. As I slid into the driver's seat, he moved and stood directly in front of my car and stared at me again. A chill swept through me.

I had asked for a sign and I felt I'd just experienced one. A sense of peace overcame me, and I dried my tears and drove home.

My grandma once told me that seeing a duck at a gravesite was a sign from your loved one that he or she is at peace and they've crossed into another realm.

I realized I'd still miss my husband and there was a hole in my heart and life, but he had suffered and this was his way of telling me he was at peace and that he wanted me to find peace as well.

I promised him I'd try...

Kat's heart ached for the lonely woman who'd written that.

"Twenty more minutes," the teacher announced.

Kat quickly composed her thoughts and began her paper. But as she did, she decided to visit the graveyard again. Tonight.

Maybe she'd ask her mama if she'd seen any signs from her father that he was at peace. Or if he was still terrorizing the countryside by taking young girls' lives.

EIGHTY

Tilly had sent her first installment in the Brambletown series to her boss the night before. But nightmares of the morning after her sister's disappearance kept her awake half the night. The dead girls' faces stared at her as if asking for help. And the fact that she felt as if Clint Wallace and Ida and Joe had threatened her had caused her to jump at every sound.

Was one of them involved in Ruth's disappearance?

Although now the police suspected a possible serial killer, she couldn't imagine Ida or her husband repeatedly murdering teenagers, not when they had a teenage daughter of their own. She'd researched killers before and knew most serial killers were men in their twenties. Ida, Hetty and Joe had all been teenagers when Ruth disappeared.

Although Clint was a teen then, too, he was more likely the possibility. He worked in law enforcement and knew about collecting evidence and how to avoid detection.

Typically, she was a morning person, but after staring at the ceiling all night and hearing sounds outside, she hadn't fallen asleep until dawn.

But a noise startled her awake and she jerked up and

listened. There it was again. The wind shuddered through the eaves of the house, indicating a storm was on the way. She exhaled slowly, deciding her imagination was running wild because of the day before.

And all the ghosts around her, the ones living in her parents' house, the sad and painful memories. The ghosts in the graveyard. The dead girls' faces sneaking into her nightmares.

The floor creaked again, and she clutched the sheets in her fist. She hadn't imagined it. Footsteps echoed on the wood floor in the hall near her door.

Her heart hammered and she glanced around the room for something to use as protection. The room held nothing but some books and her suitcase of clothes. No umbrella or a bat to use as a weapon.

The door shook with the wind. Or was someone trying to open it?

She slipped from bed and grabbed one of her boots. Slowly she tiptoed to the closed door and hid behind it. Seconds later, the knob jiggled and the door slowly screeched open. Breathing echoed in the tense silence. She went still, bracing for a fight, then the floor squeaked again as a foot stepped into the room. Then another.

She waited until the man crossed the door threshold then jumped behind him and raised the heeled boot at his head. He must have sensed her presence because he spun around and before she could fight, he grabbed her and pushed her up against the wall.

She started to scream but he clamped his hand over her mouth and pressed his muscular body against hers, pinning her against the wall. Her scream died in her throat but she raised her leg to knee him in the groin.

"Don't fight," he growled.

Fear choked her then she looked into his face. Not Clint.

Shock momentarily trapped her in its clutches and she narrowed her eyes.

"It's me, Tilly," he murmured. "I'll let you go if you promise not to scream."

Terror mixed with confusion.

"Promise," he said gruffly. "I'm not here to hurt you. I just want to talk."

Her shoulders slumped although she was still wary.

"You know who I am, don't you?" he murmured.

Tears burned the backs of her eyelids, and she nodded. Slowly he released her, and she gasped for a breath, then anger hit her as she studied his features. He looked mature now, had gained muscle, his jaw had broadened and was covered in beard stubble. A scar crisscrossed his left cheek and the right corner of his lower lip.

Dear God. It was her missing brother.

EIGHTY-ONE

Just as they were leaving Ida's house, the detective from Athens called. Someone recognized Cameron from the photo they'd posted online and said he was living with a group of guys in a hostel on the edge of town. The detective had driven out to question him and found Cameron asleep, with drugs on the coffee table so had hauled him in and put him in a holding cell on possession charges.

Ellie parked at the police station and she and Derrick went in. The receptionist remembered them, informed the officer they were there, and he met them in the front of the station.

"Thanks for calling us," Derrick said. "Did Cameron mention Jacey?"

The officer shook his head. "No. He was pretty wasted, so I decided to wait until he sobered up a bit before questioning him."

"Smart thinking," Ellie said with a smile. Anything Cameron said while under the influence, even a confession, wouldn't be admissible in court.

"How is he now?" Derrick asked.

"Better. He slept a while. We got some food and coffee in him, and he's perked up. I'll bring him to an interrogation room."

They thanked him and followed him down the hall and settled into a small room on the right while the officer went to the holding cell to get Cameron.

Five minutes later, Cameron shuffled in looking wary, his eyes bloodshot, T-shirt rumpled and baggy jeans dirty. He reeked of sweat and drugs, indicating he probably hadn't showered in days. Cameron glanced at them then sank into the chair the detective pulled out for him and stared down at his shaking hands. He knew he was in trouble.

Ellie identified them. "Do you know why you're here, Cameron?"

He swallowed hard. "Yeah. Drugs." His voice quivered as if he might be on the verge of tears. "But I don't know why the fed's here. It's not like I was selling or anything like that."

"You were brought in on drug possession charges," Ellie said. "But that's not the only reason, Cameron."

A bewildered look crossed his face, and he swung a confused gaze at Ellie.

"Have you seen or heard the news in the last two days?" Derrick asked.

A frown pulled at the corners of his eyes, and he shook his head.

"How about your girlfriend, Jacey? Do you know where she is?"

He jerked his head up. "She left. Why? She say something bad about me?"

Tension built as Ellie let a heartbeat pass before she continued. He was still strung out. Obviously, Jacey had reason to leave him. "Just tell us when you last saw her."

He ran a shaky hand through his tousled brown hair. "A day

or two ago. I thought she was going on a food run, but she didn't come back."

"Is that what happened?" Derrick asked.

"Yeah."

"Were you two getting along?" he pushed.

Cameron shrugged. "I guess so."

"Then why would she leave and not come back?" Ellie asked.

He jiggled his leg up and down, then shrugged. "Hell, I don't know."

"Really?" Derrick asked, his tone curt. "I think you do. I think maybe you weren't getting along and you got in a fight and she ran away from you."

The boy released an agitated breath. "Naw, we didn't fight."

"Did you chase her when she left? Was she running from you?" Derrick continued.

Cameron shifted, his body going rigid. "No, I didn't go after her," he mumbled.

"Not even to make sure she was safe?" Ellie asked.

His cheeks reddened. "No. I... was tired and went back to sleep."

Ellie leaned forward, arms on the table. "Asleep or passed out, Cameron?"

"All right, all right. I took some pills and they knocked me out. I... ain't left the apartment since then." He cut his eyes toward the officer who was standing at the door, arms folded across his brawny chest, his big body poised as a barrier to the boy's escape if he tried to run.

"Cameron," Ellie said softly, regaining his attention. "Jacey was found dead in a town called Brambletown."

Cameron's face paled and he coughed and made a gagging sound. The detective grabbed the trash can and shoved it to him just in time to save the floor.

EIGHTY-TWO

Hetty clutched her phone in a white-knuckled grip, trembling at the fear in Ida's voice.

"I tell you, I'm scared to death," Ida said. "That detective and FBI agent were here earlier asking questions about Daddy. Remember his old pick-up truck?"

Like it was yesterday.

A dizzy spell assaulted Hetty as time rewound in her mind. How could she forget? Some of her worst nightmares had happened in that damn truck. "Of course I do. What about it?"

"They think a man driving it picked up that girl Jacey Ward at some convenience store in Athens then murdered her."

Hetty shook her head in denial, wiping perspiration from her neck with a rag. "There have to be other black pick-ups out there."

"Yeah. But they're pushing to find out if we know where Daddy is."

"Lord have mercy," Hetty whispered.

"They're combing the graveyard and that land now for

other bodies," Ida said brokenly. "Joe is upset, too. I think he's worried about Kat. She's the same age as those girls who were murdered."

"That is scary," Hetty agreed.

Panic lingered in the air between them. "What should we do?" Ida asked. "Maybe we should talk."

"No, I don't want to go to jail," Hetty cried.

"Me neither," Ida choked out. "What would poor Kat do if I was locked up?"

"Just keep your mouth shut," Hetty said, her tone full of horror. "We'll do whatever we have to do in order to keep our secrets buried."

"There's more," Ida said with a groan. "Tilly came to see me."

"Damn that girl," Hetty said. "I knew she was trouble when she rolled back into Brambletown."

"Like a dog with a bone. She wanted to know if we're hiding where Daddy is, too." Ida burst into tears. "I can't believe this is happening after all this time."

Hetty dropped her head into her hands, her head throbbing. "Don't worry, Ida. I'll handle Tilly."

"And Cord McClain?"

"Him, too." In fact, maybe she could convince him to help them. If the truth came out, he had almost as much to lose as they did.

EIGHTY-THREE

Tilly stared at her brother in shock. She barely recognized him. He was a man now, not a gangly teenager and at least a foot taller than her. His voice had changed and was deep and masculine, too. But his gray eyes were still just as deep and disturbing as she remembered.

For a brief second, she wanted to hug him and welcome him home and back into her life. But suspicions from the past lurked in the corners of her mind. And with two more girls' bodies discovered...

"Don't look at me like that," he said with narrowed eyes.

Tilly's chest heaved as she steadied her breathing. "You scared me," she said. "What are you doing breaking in here?"

"The same thing you're doing in this town," he said. "Now get dressed while I make coffee and we can talk." He paused at the door. "And please don't call the police on me, Tilly Willy."

Her heart melted as an image of Hayden riding her piggyback on the grass flashed back. They'd caught fireflies in mason jars and skipped stones in the pond and he'd even helped her with a school project when hers had fallen apart.

And he hadn't called her that nickname since they were children. "Okay," she murmured. She just hoped she didn't regret it.

He gave a nod, his expression softening slightly, then he left the room and closed the door behind him.

Tilly shoved her hair from her face, grabbed a pair of jeans and a sweatshirt, ran to the bathroom, splashed water on her face, brushed her teeth and combed the tangles from her hair. For a heartbeat, she saw herself as a teenager in the mirror, pretty Ruth standing beside her smiling as she dabbed on lip gloss. Ruth, the pretty, popular one. Her, the shy bookish girl with very few friends, always in the shadows.

Hayden, the troublemaker, acting out, arguing with their father, punching the wall when he was angry. Then the drinking.

Nerves twisted her stomach. *Get it together, Tilly. You're not that young girl anymore.*

She splashed cold water on her face, dried it with a hand towel, then inhaled several calming breaths like her therapist had taught her. She didn't know what to expect but if Hayden had wanted to hurt her, he could have done it while she was asleep.

Still, the painful memories clawed at her as she went into the kitchen. The heavenly aroma of coffee wafted toward her. Hayden stood at the counter with a mug in his hand, sipping it as he stared out the window. His look said he was a million miles away.

"I can't believe they kept this place," he murmured.

"I know. I guess they thought if Ruth was alive and came back looking for them, it would be here as a sign they hadn't given up. The landline is still intact with the same phone number."

"Figures." He closed his eyes for a second, released a disgruntled sigh, and scrubbed his hand over his face. She could feel the frustration and disappointment and pain in that sound.

Tilly gave him a moment to process the fact that he was back in their childhood home. She didn't know if it was cathartic or just agonizing. For her it was a mixture of both.

When he opened his eyes, he squared his shoulders as if trying to shake off the past. But she had a feeling they'd followed him just as hers had.

He pinned her with searching eyes. "Are you afraid of me, Tilly?"

Was she? "No," she said calmly. "But I do have questions."

He considered that for a moment then nodded. "Fair enough. Get some coffee and we'll sit down and talk." He stepped aside for her to reach the coffee maker then sat down at the kitchen table and waited quietly.

She stalled, dumping a pack of sweetener in her cup then carried it with her and seated herself across from him.

"How are you, sis?" he asked, genuine concern in his tone. "What have you been doing all this time?"

Small talk. She could manage that. "After you left, things were hard," she said. "I was mad at you for leaving me behind."

Regret flared in his eyes. "I'm sorry. I... was messed up in the head already. Then Dad turned on me and the police put me under the ringer, and I couldn't handle it."

Tilly sipped her coffee, grateful for the caffeine punch. "I know they were tough on you, Hayden. Dad pressured you to be perfect and wanted you to follow in his footsteps in politics and they doted on Ruth—"

"She could do no wrong," he agreed with a wry smile.

Tilly rolled her eyes. "Yeah, she was definitely the child they wanted." Although Ruth had had her sweet moments when they were younger. When Tilly was five and her mother was too busy to read to her at night, Tilly would cuddle with Ruth and her sister would read her story after story.

"I know they ignored you," Hayden said. It was a statement not a question.

"I could never measure up to her," Tilly said, erasing the bitterness from her voice. "I made peace with that a long time ago."

"Good." He leaned forward and gave her an earnest look. "They made us both feel like we weren't good enough," he said. "But you were, Tilly. You were twice as smart as Ruth and kinder and... I always knew you were going places in life. That you'd be the one to make a success out of yourself and prove to them they were wrong."

Tilly shrugged. "I tried to," she said. "Although nothing I did mattered. They didn't even attend my high school graduation much less my college one."

His heavy sigh filled the silence. "I'm sorry. You deserved better."

She shrugged again. Maybe so. But it still had hurt.

"I heard you're a writer now for the *AJC*."

His comment caught her off guard. "How do you know that?"

A smile tugged at his mouth, reminding her of the sweet but mischievous boy she'd known before he turned into an angry teenager and their lives had fallen apart.

"I joined the Army, which by the way was good for me, even though I resented Dad for pushing me to do it." He self-consciously touched the scar on his cheek, then dropped his hands back to his coffee mug. "Made me into a man. Taught me discipline and self-control. But... I saw things over in Afghanistan that changed me."

Again, the far-away anguished look. Tilly barely resisted reaching out and covering his hand with hers. But she wanted to hear what he had to say.

"Go on, Hay," she said, resorting to her childhood name for him.

He smiled at that, then his expression sobered. "Anyway, got caught in a landmine. But that wasn't the worst part. Saw an entire village get blown up. A few of the kids survived, but not all. Children, just children, killed for no reason." His voice cracked. "And the ones who did live... they instantly became orphans."

"That's awful," Tilly said. "How sad." At least she and he had family, even if they'd grown apart. "So, what did you do?"

"I was hospitalized for two months then went to rehab for physical therapy to learn to walk again. While I was there, I thought a lot about that explosion. I watched kids, injured like myself, fight to survive and I got to know some of them." His deep voice turned to gravel with emotion. "I made up my mind when I recovered and was discharged, that I'd find a way to give back to kids to atone for everything I'd done wrong."

Emotions gathered in Tilly's throat, filled with questions she didn't want to broach.

Finally he continued, "So if you want to know where I've been and I know the police are asking and looking for me, I stayed there and worked in the orphanages for a while then returned to the States and started a youth group/mentoring program for boys."

Tilly gasped softly. Not the answer she'd expected. "That's great, Hay. I'm proud of you."

Pain and sorrow streaked his eyes. "Don't be. I'm not innocent. Some of those kids who died... My unit had a part in it. Just like I did in our sister's disappearance. I... ran because it was my fault."

EIGHTY-FOUR

Athens

Ellie, Derrick and the detective silently agreed to give Cameron a moment to compose himself. They stepped from the room and returned a few minutes later with a wet paper towel and a soda for Cameron and coffee in hand for themselves.

Cameron sat slumped with his head in his hands, tears streaming down his gaunt, sunken cheeks. The kid couldn't be faking it. He was honestly surprised and grief-stricken by the news that Jacey was dead.

She and Derrick claimed their seats again, the air charged with questions.

Cameron wiped his face with the paper towel, popped open the soda and took a long drink. Finally he wiped his mouth and looked at them with glassy, haunted eyes. "W... what happened?"

Ellie licked her dry lips. "We were hoping you'd help us figure that out."

He stared at them blankly. "I... don't know," he mumbled. "Like I said, she left and I... thought she was coming back."

"You didn't follow her?" Derrick asked.

Cameron squeezed his eyes shut as if struggling to remember. Then he shook his head. "I told you no. I was too wasted."

At least his voice held remorse. Guilt, too. That he would have to live with.

"Had she been acting strangely the last few days?" Ellie asked.

He frowned. "What do you mean?"

Ellie cradled her coffee. "Had she been seeing someone else? Another guy maybe?"

His brows shot up. "No... I mean not that I know of. We... didn't have much money so sometimes she went out and..."

"And what?" Derrick said, his voice cold.

"And lifted food, you know, at the little stores." He traced a finger over the rim of his soda can, averting his eyes as if he was ashamed.

"And you didn't go with her?" Derrick pushed.

"Sometimes," he said. "But... not that day. I was..."

"Wasted," Ellie finished, unable to hide the disgust from her voice. "Tell me this, when she went out, did she meet up with someone? Maybe a man?"

Cameron jerked his head back toward them. "You mean like for money?"

"For that or just as a way to escape her situation?"

A small shrug lifted his bony shoulders. "She wouldn't do that," he said. "In fact she said she saw girls out there turning tricks but she refused to stoop that low."

Anger raged in Derrick's eyes. "But you wanted her to?"

His cheeks reddened. "Look, I was in a bad way."

Ellie wanted to knock the crap out of him. She sensed Derrick felt the same way because he stood and paced, his footsteps heavy. The officer's icy stare bored holes in Cameron's back.

Ellie reined in her temper. The boy obviously had a drug

problem. It didn't condone his behavior, but addicts often crossed the line and made choices they'd never make if they were clean. "Did she mention going home to her mother?"

His face crinkled. "I... don't know. Maybe. We... weren't talking much in those last days we were together."

"Well, this is what we know, Cameron," Ellie said, striving for patience. At least they had a general timeline now. "After Jacey left you that day, she ran to a convenience store, borrowed the clerk's phone and called her mother. She left a message saying she was coming home."

"She did?"

Ellie nodded. "But she never made it. She ended up catching a ride with a man driving an older model black pick-up."

Derrick returned, pulled his phone and the CCTV footage from the store parking lot. "This is her getting in that truck. Look at the vehicle and the man."

Pain contorted the boy's face as he watched, and he rocked back on his heels and cursed.

"Do you recognize him or the truck?" Derrick asked.

Cameron shook his head. "No, but... I should have gone after her. I... it's my fault she's dead."

Derrick sat down. "Cameron, look at me. Yeah, you made mistakes, son. You ran away, you've gotten mixed up with drugs. And you should have taken better care of your girlfriend, especially since she was a minor." He hesitated, breathing slightly heavy. "But you aren't responsible for her death. The man who abducted her and killed her is. And we're going to find him."

The guilt Derrick had harbored from his own little sister's disappearance years ago laced his voice. Derrick had only been a young teen then, but it had weighed him down for years.

He would be a great father one day. He probably already was to his godchildren.

"What's going to happen now?" Cameron asked, fear darkening his voice.

"That's up to you, son." Derrick folded his hands in front of him. "But we talked to your mother and we know she loves you. This might be your chance to get clean and make amends."

Doubts flashed in Cameron's eyes. "You think she'll talk to me?"

Derrick gave a noncommittal shrug. "There's only one way to find out. But if you call her and really want help, you'll have to play by her rules and commit to treatment."

"But it won't bring Jacey back." He choked out the words, guilt hitting him hard.

"No," Derrick said gently. "But you can turn your life around and make Jacey's death count for something."

"We'll find the guy who killed her," Ellie promised. "And make sure he goes to prison and never sees the light of day again."

EIGHTY-FIVE

Tilly held her breath as she waited for her brother to elaborate. Had he really caused Ruth's death?

"What do you mean?" she finally asked. "That it was your fault Ruth disappeared?"

Hayden pulled a hand down his chin, waited a beat, then released a pained sigh. "I was pissed at Ruth. She was such a brat and I... didn't like the way she treated you and... to be honest, those Bramble girls. They didn't deserve to be humiliated by her."

Tilly stared at him in surprise. "I didn't like it either," she admitted. "I told her they couldn't help how they were brought up or being poor or who their daddy was." Still, the Brambles hadn't been innocent either.

"Same," Hayden said. "But Ruth thought she was better cause Mom and Dad doted on her and she made all our lives hell."

Tension built in Tilly's chest at the resentment in his tone.

It took her a moment to summon the courage to ask. Did she really want to know? "Hayden, what did you do? You didn't—"

"No, I didn't kill her," he said quickly. "But I was mad and told her Clint was cheating on her," he said. "I just wanted to hurt her, to make her realize she couldn't have everything she wanted."

"Was he cheating?"

"Hell, I don't know. Clint was a player. He could have been."

"And she believed you? And that's why she broke up with him," Tilly said, connecting the dots.

"Yeah, and they had a fight. But she was going to meet him that night. At least she thought she was."

Confusion swirled in Tilly's brain. "What are you talking about?"

Hayden's breath wheezed out. "The guys I was with... we were drinking and I... sort of suggested that one of them leave her a note pretending to be Clint and ask her to meet that night."

Tilly gaped at him in stunned silence. "You what?"

"It was just a prank," he said. "I just wanted to teach her a lesson, that she could be dumped."

"But she told me she wasn't meeting Clint," Tilly said.

Hayden shrugged. "She lied. Maybe she was afraid you'd tell Mom and Dad and Clint would get in trouble."

Tilly massaged her temple. "Who left the note?"

"It doesn't matter," Hayden said. "We were all together and none of us left that night. That part is true."

"So Ruth went out to meet Clint who didn't show and... got abducted? Maybe by a stranger? Or did Clint know she was going out?"

"If Clint knew, we didn't tell him," Hayden said. "Although someone else may have. Or Ruth could have called him."

"Maybe."

The silence that ensued made Tilly's skin crawl. "Who else knew?" Tilly gripped her brother's arm and forced him to look at her. "Who, Hay?"

He closed his eyes, but not before she saw raw a seed of panic flash into them.

"Hayden, you're scaring me," she cried.

"Dad," he said in a tortured voice. "I called Dad and told him I knew she was sneaking out to hook up so she'd get in trouble. And he flew into a rage."

For a long moment, they simply stared at each other, questions hanging in the air. "Then why didn't he stop her?"

Hayden's eyes filled with misery and he shook his head. "I think he tried to find her." Hayden made an agonized sound. "When I got home later that night, he was gone."

"Oh, God, Dad lied to the police." A dizzy spell assaulted Tilly. She'd hoped by searching for the truth she'd be able to bring her family back together.

But if her father was involved in Ruth's disappearance, it would tear them apart forever.

EIGHTY-SIX

Green Gardens Cemetery

The memorial at the graveyard had been vandalized. Not only had it been spray painted with red paint, but someone had stuck a pitchfork in front of it as if to indicate the devil was present on the land.

There was opposition to the memorial and others in favor. Some locals claimed they didn't want it because it drew attention to the toxic land. Members of the community wanted folks to move back and help Brambletown get back on its feet.

Others wanted attention to the deaths and illnesses caused by the toxins as a reminder to the government that they'd abandoned the clean-up process and to take action.

But he hadn't come here to see it. Hetty had called and asked him to meet her. She didn't have to say exactly where.

He knew.

He walked past the old graves, his stomach twisting at the sight of two children's headstones. The fire had once wiped out entire families, the toxins killing others slowly with cancers, lung diseases and other illnesses. He stepped onto the land that had once been a forest of green but now looked brown and barren and wove along the unmarked path, hating the silence of the woods without forest creatures.

A cold breeze picked up, rustling dry brush and reminding him of death. He trudged on, his memories suffocating. Yet if he had to go back, he'd do the same thing all over again.

Another mile in and a sense of doom overcame him just as it used to when his foster father would go ape shit and beat the hell out of him for no good reason, except the old man talked with his fists and had a machine gun mouth that constantly hammered home how nobody wanted him or would ever love him because he was a sorry piece of shit.

Ellie loves you.

At least she loves the part of you that you've shown to her.

Would she still love him if he confessed his sins?

A noise ahead startled him and he saw movement. Hetty? Or was someone else in the woods?

The person who'd killed Ruth, Bonnie Sylvester and Jacey Ward?

The cold wind beat at the back of his neck as he spotted Hetty hunched with a shovel in her hands standing at the very spot they'd been fifteen years ago.

Twigs snapped beneath his boots and she turned as he approached, a sinister look in her eyes. Hetty had always seemed angry and a little off, but he knew the reason. They shared a connection that way.

Earl Bramble had taken her in which everyone thought seemed a nice thing to do, except he had gotten money from his brother's death in return. She hadn't been his daughter and he'd used her like Cord's foster father had used him, as a whipping post.

He glanced at the shovel clutched in her hands and noted she'd been shifting dirt and brush to make the area more natural.

Cord cleared his throat. "Why did you want to meet here? Don't you think it's dangerous?"

Hetty's lips thinned, and she clenched the shovel. "It is. But I wanted to make sure you keep your mouth shut. If you don't, I'll ruin you."

She raised the shovel as if to swing it toward his head, but he caught it with his hand and gave her an icy stare. "You can," he said. "But if you do, you'll take yourself and Ida along with me."

EIGHTY-SEVEN

Brambletown

The silence stretched thick with tension as Tilly processed her conversation with her brother. She'd known the police had questioned her father and that he had a temper, but he loved Ruth more than anything. She didn't think he'd actually hurt Ruth. Unless it was an accident.

Although if that happened he had no reason to kill others.

"Did you tell the police Dad went looking for her?"

Hayden shook his head no. "I... felt too guilty. Besides, he was our father and I didn't want to believe he'd hurt her. Although I did wonder."

"What?" Tilly asked. "Is there something else?"

Hayden pinched the bridge of his nose. "I heard him come in during the night. And he was all sweaty and went to the sink and washed his hands. They were dirty... and he seemed upset."

Tilly gaped at him, her thoughts running wild. "Did you ask him where he'd been?"

"No," Hayden said. "He was already on my case about everything and... I didn't have the nerve." He hesitated then poured himself another cup of coffee. "At that point, I didn't realize Ruth was in trouble." Guilt wrenched his voice. "And the next morning Mom was falling apart and so was Dad, then they called the police, and I decided Dad wouldn't call the police if he'd hurt Ruth."

"But he wasn't honest with them either," Tilly said. "Have you ever confronted him about that night?"

Hayden shook his head, and Tilly made a snap decision. "Well, it's about time we did. I'm going to find them and make Dad tell the truth."

A tiny smile tugged at the corner of Hayden's mouth. "I'm going with you."

Tilly's heart swelled with love for her brother. For the first in years, she didn't feel quite so alone.

EIGHTY-EIGHT

He clawed at his arms so hard he drew blood. The walls were closing around him. All these cops and that fucking fed snooping around. And Hetty and Ida were acting way too nervous like they might talk.

Then that bitch Tilly Higgins was back poking around. Her damn sister started it all. Well, maybe not *all*.

But she was the trigger fifteen years ago. The adrenaline of shutting her up sizzled in his veins, like the coal fire that burned underground. Steamy and hot but hidden.

Until now.

It would be stupid to take another girl tonight. Or go after Tilly.

Jacey Ward was barely cold in the ground. Well, she had been until that asshole ranger had found her. He was another problem to be taken care of.

But the ranger would have to get in line.

He had his priorities.

Still, the commotion at that graveyard was riling him up. All those stupid murder tourists. Crawling around taking pictures of the headstones, pictures of themselves for social media. The teenagers were flocking in groves. Some numbnut had posted a challenge to the kids to search for a relative buried there.

The whole post had caused a frenzy of newcomers tonight. Dusk was setting. The moon was just a sliver of light. Shadows danced across the sky, creating monsters out of storm clouds.

Someone had also desecrated the memorial.

Sweat dripped down his chin. Shit. It was only a matter of time before the whole freaking bunch of dead he'd had so much fun with over the years was uncovered. His secrets exposed. The people who actually admired him would see a different side.

A side that needed to remain in the dark.

Until then though... he'd enjoy the game. Silence as many players as he could. One by one, they'd fall like dominos until they all came tumbling down.

EIGHTY-NINE

Jimmy's Junkyard, Ballground

Ellie veered into the parking lot of the junkyard, a graveyard for broken vehicles, and parked behind a rusted Mustang which appeared to have been rolled. Dozens of run-down, beat-up cars and trucks, a wrecked school bus and two RVs had been dumped on the lot, most likely used for salvaging parts.

Captain Hale had called saying a black pick-up fitting the description of the one seen picking up Jacey Ward had been found here near Ballground, which was nestled in the foothills of the Appalachian Mountains and was known for its relaxing rural atmosphere and scenic mountain views, the opposite of the desolate half-dead area of Brambletown.

A police cruiser sat adjacent to a mud-coated cinder block building. Ellie and Derrick got out and found the policeman beside the black pick-up sandwiched between the two big rigs. He was peering through the window with a flashlight, brows furrowed.

Derrick identified them and the officer straightened. "I

haven't opened the door and examined the interior yet. If this is the truck you're looking for, I figured you'd want to do that and have a forensic team process and preserve evidence."

"Thanks," Derrick said. "Protocol is important, especially if this vehicle was used in an abduction/murder."

The officer nodded. "It was like this when I found it."

"Was anyone around when you arrived?" Ellie asked.

"No, no one." The office gestured toward the truck bed. "But I did notice it smells like fertilizer."

Which would fit with Earl Bramble and his work in the graveyard. Although he left town over a decade ago. So where had he kept the truck?

Maybe hidden in a barn or outbuilding somewhere?

Ellie surveyed the rural setting and two-lane road. "If the killer used this truck to abduct Jacey in Athens, then dumped her body in Brambletown, why leave the truck here?"

"Because he knew the police were looking for it?" the officer suggested.

Ellie gave a little nod. "Probably. He either had someone pick him up or he stashed another vehicle somewhere for his escape."

"There's an old, abandoned farm about a half mile from here," the officer said.

Derrick pulled his phone. "He could have been hiding out there. Do you know who owns that land?" Derrick asked.

The officer shook his head. "Don't think anyone's been there for a long time."

"See if your department can find out while I call an ERT," Derrick said.

Ellie pulled on latex gloves and opened the passenger door, then searched inside. "Nothing in here." She was hoping to find a shoe or scarf or blood but didn't see any.

She opened the glove compartment in search of the registration, but nothing was inside it either. Dammit.

Hopefully ERT would find DNA, maybe a hair or clothing fiber from the killer or Jacey to prove she'd been inside.

NINETY

Briar Ridge Mobile Homes

Kat had wanted to meet Carrie Ann after school to read more of the journal together, but she'd told her parents she'd come straight home and her father would kill her if she didn't.

So she secluded herself in her bedroom to dig deeper into her mother's past.

Her heart skipped a beat as she opened an entry and saw the first line.

Daddy's dangerous.

I saw more bruises on Hetty today and know what's been going on behind closed doors, I see all the little sneaky mean things he says and does. He's a monster.

Maybe that's why my mama left years ago.

Tonight, he was in a foul mood, stomping and cussing and drinking. I was afraid he'd come after Hetty. Sometimes he asks her to help him at the graveyard but when he goes late in the day, he makes me stay home. I used to think she didn't mind, but I was stupid. Hetty doesn't want to go and she hates

Daddy. But she has no other place to live, no relatives that want her.

Funny how everyone in town thinks he has a good side for taking her in. But Hetty and I know the truth. He got some money for giving her a place to live. Worse, I guess he needed a punching bag and poor skinny, orphan Hetty is perfect for that.

He has run-ins with other people in town all the time. Last week he pissed off the owner of the hardware store because he didn't like their prices. Another time, he yelled at the waitress at the diner and Daisy told him not to come back. Mr. Huntington, who'd lost his wife, accused Daddy of burying her in the same pine box as someone else. He even went to the law and had her body exhumed and it turned out he was right. Course Daddy claimed it was a mistake, but Mr. Huntington insisted Daddy did it to save money and he was probably right.

Daddy's still mad at the man cause he had to pay a fine, and I'm scared he'll do something to the old man to get revenge.

I want so bad to tell somebody that he's hurting Hetty, but I'm afraid of him and if I do, he'll probably make things worse for Hetty. Everyone in town thinks we're white trash anyway and whisper about us behind our backs. Mean old gossipy biddies.

This happened earlier tonight right when it got dark:

The back door slammed shut and I ran to the window in my bedroom and peered through the curtains. Daddy had on his old brown coat, a ski cap on his head and he was walking into his shed. He went inside for a minute and when he came out, he was carrying a shovel.

Hetty dragged on her pajamas. "What are you doing, Ida?"

"Daddy's up to something," I told Hetty. "He took his shovel from the shed." He usually dug graves or did maintenance work during the day. At night... well, I don't know exactly what he does. But at least he didn't make Hetty go with him.

Curiosity made my skin itch, and I changed into my clothes, then pulled on my thick coat, socks and boots and my hat. "What are you doing?" Hetty whispered as she clutched the bed quilt between her hands.

"To see what he's doing."

Hetty pulled the covers over her mouth and face so all I could see in the dark were the whites of her eyes. "Don't go out there," Hetty begged.

I walked back to the window. "Stay here. I won't let him see me."

My legs trembled though as I crawled through the window and dropped to the frosty ground. Gray snow clouds hid the moonlight and the starless night made it so dark I could hardly see as I darted from tree to tree following him. Twice he turned back as if he heard me, but I jumped behind a boulder, holding my breath until he moved on again.

Like a cat, I slithered a few feet behind until finally he stopped beneath a thin pine tree where brush and limbs were piled waist high. My nails dug into tree bark, and I hunched down and watched.

Seconds later, he dragged something heavy wrapped in a blanket from the pile. Tattered plastic stuck out from beneath the corner of the blanket. My pulse jumped and I shoved my fist to my mouth to keep from screaming.

The shovel hit rock as Daddy began to dig. I slunk a little closer then gasped as I saw a pair of red shoes peeking from the end of the blanket.

Daddy pulled one of them off, kissed it and laid it to the side, then rolled the lump into the hole.

My God. Daddy was burying a body. A girl's. But this one hadn't come from the morgue or a funeral.

NINETY-ONE

Finch Gardens, Sweetgum Lane

Tilly and Hayden made a joint decision not to call and tell their parents they were coming. Unlike fifteen years ago when they were kids, subjected to being treated as less than Ruth and divided by their own teenage pain, they formed a bond this evening as Tilly parked in front of the two-story Georgian home her parents had built after leaving Brambletown.

"You think Mom and Dad will tell us the truth?" Tilly asked.

Hayden tapped his fingers on his thigh. "Who knows. But it's time we get everything out in the open. We aren't kids anymore and this black cloud has hovered over our family for too long. It's the reason I joined the military."

Tilly gave him an understanding look. "I'm so sorry for what happened in Afghanistan," she said softly. "That must have been so awful."

"It was." Regret and pain deepened his voice. "But I saw a counselor and eventually decided not to go down the rabbit hole of addiction and vowed to atone for my mistakes by helping others."

"And you've been doing that," Tilly said, grateful to have earned his confidence. She'd been alone for so long she couldn't remember even having a close friend, not one who understood her family situation. It felt good to be comrades.

Hayden squeezed her hand. "As much as I can."

"Good for you," she said and squeezed his hand in return. "Now let's talk to the folks. No matter what they say, at least we have each other now."

"Yeah, we do."

She fought tears at his sincerity and reached for the door handle.

Like strangers, they rang the doorbell, the silence thickening with apprehension as they waited for someone to answer. The garage door was closed, but if they were home, it probably held a Mercedes or Beamer or some other expensive car her father drove. He had his standards.

The wind whirled around them, sending the windchimes on the front porch into a frenzy and echoing in the air, clashing and thrashing to the beat of Tilly's heart. The sky was darkening as the sun slid down and the moon had yet to appear, obliterated by the clouds above. An eerie chill washed over Tilly, sending her back to that horrible night Ruth sneaked out when she'd stared through the window and willed her sister to come home while she debated what to do. Be the tattle tale or face her sister's wrath. Even if she'd told, her parents would have defended Ruth and let her off with a talk.

Unless that wasn't what happened at all. Unless Ruth challenged her father to the point that he lost control. She'd only seen that once.

Shivering, she wrapped her arms around herself. She didn't want to relive that night or believe that her father was capable of violence.

But she'd seen what she'd seen and it was permanently imprinted in her brain. Her mother crying and screaming that her father had been ogling the teenage waitress at the restaurant where they'd had dinner.

The rage in her father's eyes, the sound of his fist hitting the coffee table and the wine glass shattering, Merlot streaming onto the floor like a river of blood.

NINETY-TWO

Kat's stomach churned. Her mama had witnessed her own father bury a girl's body in the graveyard.

But she'd been too afraid to tell the police. Was that body Ruth Higgins?

A knock sounded at the door and Kat covered the laptop with her pillow, as her mama cracked open the door. "Dinner's ready."

"Be right there." Kat waited until she closed the door, then stowed the laptop under her bed. She'd read more later.

She shuffled into the kitchen, saw the shepherd's pie and groaned. She used to like it, but Mama had made it so many times lately she was sick of it. Still, she sat, her mama's journal entry taunting her.

Mama placed water glasses on the table, then claimed the seat across from Kat.

"How was school, Kat?"

Kat took the opening. "Fine. Our English lit teacher talked

about the history of the town and the memorial and asked us to write a paper about folklore surrounding the dead."

Mama looked up at her, eyes narrowed. "That sounds like an odd topic for school."

Kat shrugged. "I read about signs people say they've seen after someone died. You know signs that their loved ones are trying to communicate."

Mama's hand trembled as she wiped her mouth with a napkin. "Maybe we should talk about something else."

"But you asked about school. Have you ever seen any signs from Granddaddy?"

"No," her mama snapped, her lips compressing into an angry line.

Kat wanted to ask about the girl in the graveyard, but then she'd have to admit she'd been reading the journal. "Some people say Granddaddy killed that girl Ruth."

Mama wiped sweat from her forehead with a paper towel. "Lord have mercy, Kat, I've been through this before."

"Do you think he did?" Kat asked.

The ice clinked in her mama's glass as she took a long drink of water. "Maybe," she finally admitted.

"So he was dangerous?" Kat asked.

Anger flashed on her mama's face. "Yes, Kat. He was a mean son of a bitch."

Kat forced down a bite of food. "Do you think he's back and that he's been killing those other girls?"

The color drained from her mama's face and she stood and pushed her plate away. "Enough talk about this. Now finish your dinner and go do your homework."

Mama picked up her plate, raked the leftovers in the trash, then went to the kitchen cabinet and pulled out a bottle of Jack Daniels. With a shaky hand, she poured herself a tumbler and stomped out on the back porch, slamming the door with a thud.

NINETY-THREE

"Have you spoken to Dad or Mom over the years?" Tilly asked as they waited on one of her parents to answer the door.

"No. I thought about calling when I was discharged, but I couldn't forget what Dad said to me after Ruth disappeared," Hayden said.

"What did he say?" Tilly asked.

"That it should have been me instead of her."

Tilly gasped. "I'm sorry, Hay. That was a horrible thing to say."

Hayden ran his fingers through his hair. "I was mad, but maybe he was right. I should have protected Ruth."

"It wasn't your fault," Tilly said.

Hayden rang the doorbell again, and Tilly glanced around the property. The house probably sat on two acres, the lawn was manicured, a pond with a flock of geese floating across the water. It looked so peaceful that she wondered if her parents had actually found any peace here. Her father had always wanted a stocked pond and claimed when he retired he'd fish every day.

She pictured him doing that and emotions choked her. They'd missed so many years together.

The door opened, and Tilly held her breath as her mother appeared. Surprise, confusion, then an awkward smile. "Well, you two were the last people I expected to show up here."

Tilly forced a smile, but Hayden shifted awkwardly. Her mother's soft brown hair was short and wavy and tinged with gray now, her eyes still haunted with sadness.

Behind her, their father appeared dressed in a golf shirt, his jaw set firmly. "I figured they'd crawl back sometime now that town is in the news again." He aimed a sharp look at Tilly. "Are you the one stirring it up?"

Anger destroyed Tilly's hope of a welcoming family reunion. "That's right, Dad. Instantly blame me like you always did. "

"Edward," her mother snapped. "Please, let's be civil."

Hayden squared his shoulders. "Dad, Tilly is not responsible for any of this. If you heard the news, you're aware two dead girls have been found in Brambletown. Those murders stirred up all the talk about Ruth."

Pain wrenched her mother's face.

"Well, maybe this time they'll find that bastard Earl Bramble and make him pay," her father snapped.

Tears filled her mother's eyes. "But it won't bring our precious daughter back."

"At least then we'd have closure," Tilly said softly. "And maybe we could all heal and move on."

"I'll never move on," her mother cried. "Ruth was everything to us."

"You have another daughter," Hayden bit out. "But you seem to have forgotten that or that you have a son."

"Our son was a problem," their father said. "We dismissed him a long time ago."

Anger heated Tilly's voice. "He was a kid and so was I when Ruth snuck out. What happened to her wasn't our fault and we needed you two. But you let us down."

Hayden tugged at her arm. "Come on, sis. It was a mistake to come here."

"Not yet." Tilly stood her ground. "Not until Dad answers our question." She crossed her arms. "We know you went after Ruth. What happened?"

Her father stiffened and threw back his shoulders. "You aren't suggesting I'd hurt Ruth?"

"Just tell us what happened," Tilly said sharply. "We deserve to know."

Fury darkened his expression. "I did go looking for her at the park and around town and every place I could think. But I couldn't find her." Bitterness filled his tone. "Finally I gave up and came home. I was hoping she'd already returned on her own."

But she hadn't.

"Now if your little inquisition is over, you two should get out of here."

Hurt felt like a knife digging in Tilly's heart.

"Don't worry, we won't bother you again." Hayden put his arm around Tilly's shoulders. "You two are the ones missing out because we're going to be a family. Without you."

Tilly gave her parents one last look, then turned and hurried down the steps. Seconds later, she peeled down the driveway and onto the highway. Neither of them spoke as she maneuvered the mountain road back toward Brambletown.

Night had fallen with the moonless sky dulling her mood. She'd come here to learn what happened to Ruth and reunite her family.

So far she'd failed at both.

By the time they neared Brambletown, her determination had mounted. Her parents could live in their fantasy world, frozen with grief and Ruth's ghost. She was going to get answers. Not for her parents but for her and Hayden.

Suddenly the sound of a vehicle racing up behind her broke into her thoughts then bright headlights blinded her. Tilly frowned and a minute later, the vehicle slammed into her rear bumper.

Hayden cursed and grabbed the dash, and she screamed as they careened onto the shoulder. She braked and tires screeched, then the car spun out of control and skidded. Metal crunched, glass shattered, and sparks flew as it flipped then rolled over and landed in the ditch.

NINETY-FOUR

Gus's Goat Farm

While Derrick stayed to oversee the initial search of the black pick-up, Ellie and two members of the ERT went to the farm to check out the house.

"No one has owned or run this farm for years. Belonged to the bank," the local officer said as he gestured to the house.

Lieutenant Williams, head of the ERT, assigned two investigators to search the outside of the farm and the barn, and she asked the officer to look for signs of another vehicle outside. If the killer had stashed an escape car here, knowing the make and model would enable them to issue an APB.

Ellie, the lieutenant and a crime tech named Phil pulled guns for the initial entry to clear the house, then ducked beneath the no trespassing tape over the door and divided up, sweeping the house and checking each room.

"I'll take the upstairs," Ellie said.

Williams nodded. "I'll see what I can find in the kitchen."

Paul began dusting the house for prints and she climbed the

staircase. Dust motes swirled in front of her, cobwebs evident in the corners. The rickety wood floor squeaked as she walked, a musty odor hanging heavy in the air. She peeked in the front two bedrooms and found them empty although as she entered, she noticed old blankets piled in the closet. She stowed her gun, then pulled on gloves and examined them, grateful not to find a body beneath. Knowing the blankets could have been used to wrap up a girl for transportation from the truck to the house and vice versa, she collected them for DNA.

Her breath caught as she spotted a couple of brown hairs on one of them. Jacey Ward had brown hair.

Had the killer kept her here for a while after he abducted her and before he dumped her in Brambletown? Ballground was between Athens and Brambletown so that was a possibility.

Would they find her DNA on those blankets? Or Bonnie Sylvester's?

Moving on, she walked down the hallway and found a larger room that was obviously the master bedroom. A rusted iron bed sat in the middle with rumpled bedding indicating someone could have been lying on it. Either one of the girls or the killer?

She searched the ancient wooden dresser, but it was empty; the killer hadn't left clothes here.

An antique wardrobe was perched in the corner and she moved to it next. It required a key so she searched the room for it but couldn't find one.

Things were often locked for a reason.

Pulling her Swiss army knife from her pocket, she flipped it open and used it to jiggle the lock. It took her a minute to pick the lock, but finally it turned and she opened the double doors of the wardrobe.

Her heart hammered as she realized what she was looking at. Several red scarves hung from hooks on the interior. And the shelves were lined with red shoes. A variety of styles ranging from sneakers to dress shoes to boots.

She recognized three of them—they were a match for the ones missing from their victims.

NINETY-FIVE

Tilly groaned, struggling to open her eyes. Confusion muddled her brain and fogged her vision. Where was she? What happened?

Her head hurt and so did her chest. And her legs... for a minute she couldn't feel them. Panic shot through her and she realized the air bag had exploded on impact but thankfully it had automatically deflated.

She heard rustling and turned her head to check on her brother. Blood dotted his forehead where glass had shattered, and he was slumped over in the seat unconscious. The passenger door was crushed and so was the dash. Could he have internal injuries?

Fear clogged her throat along with denial. She couldn't have just reunited with Hayden to lose him like this.

She pushed away the airbag and noticed a cut on her hand which was bleeding. The front dash was crunched and her leg was caught. Dammit.

With her other hand, she nudged her brother. "Hayden,

wake up." She shook his shoulder again, but he remained limp. "Please, Hayden. I don't want to lose you."

Again, no movement. Instead, blood trickled down his cheek and his arm was twisted at an odd angle. Probably broken. Terrified, she used two fingers to check for a pulse.

Please don't die on me, she silently cried as she waited. A second passed. Another. Five more.

Finally she felt a faint pulse. *Thank you, sweet Jesus.*

Still, she had to get help.

Frantic, she raked her hand across the seat until she snagged her purse. Inside, she found a tissue and pressed it to her cut to stem the bleeding then dug around for her phone. Not in the purse.

The floor maybe? It was so dark she couldn't see the floorboard and even if she could, with her leg pinned she couldn't reach it. Perspiration broke out on her forehead, and she wiggled and squirmed to free her leg but couldn't budge it. Dear God, she had to do something.

Checking to see if her phone had flown from her purse onto the seat, she raked her hand across it, digging between the seat edges, then peered down between the console and her seat. Something metallic glinted in the dark.

Her phone. Her breathing grew raspy as she angled her hand between the space and maneuvered her fingers until she finally grasped it. An inch at a time she managed to pull it up and clutched it in her sweating fingers. Trembling with fear, she entered her passcode then called 9-1-1.

"9-1-1, what is your emergency?"

"Accident, someone hit us," she cried. "We're trapped in the car."

"Who am I speaking with?"

"Tilly Higgins," she said shakily then named the highway where they'd crashed. "Please, hurry. My brother... unconscious."

"Are you injured yourself, Miss?"

Was she? "I'm okay. I think. Just a cut on my hand. And I… my leg is pinned under the steering wheel."

"I'm dispatching a team to you now. Please stay on the line until they arrive."

Terrified, she glanced at her brother again reliving the minutes before they'd crashed. She'd told the operator they had an accident. But it wasn't an accident.

Someone had intentionally run them off the road.

NINETY-SIX

Gus's Goat Farm

Ellie photographed the wardrobe with the shoes and scarves inside then hurried downstairs to relay her findings. Derrick was just stepping into the house.

"The killer has definitely been here," she told him. "Look at this." She showed him the pictures and Derrick clenched his jaw.

"His trophies," he said. "Just like you speculated, the sick bastard collects one of the shoes as a reminder of each victim."

"We found the scarves he used to kill Bonnie and Jacey with their bodies. But look how many scarves are here."

Derrick pulled a hand down his chin. "Damn. He's planning more victims."

Bile rose to Ellie's throat. "I counted eight pairs of shoes in there. But including Ruth, we've only identified three girls."

"Hopefully we find DNA or prints in the truck, in the house or on those items." Derrick shifted. "Fertilizer has definitely been hauled in the truck but the lab will have to determine how recently. We found a tiny button which I logged into evidence to be processed. I also sent a photo to the ME."

Ellie's pulse jumped. Maybe they were finally catching a break. "We have to work fast. He might be hunting his next victim at the moment."

Lieutenant Williams approached them, his expression earnest. "You guys need to see what I found."

Ellie and Derrick followed, hoping it was solid evidence to pinpoint the unsub. Williams led them to the coat closet near the kitchen and shined his light inside. The closet was empty, but he aimed the light against the side wall.

"Oh, God," Ellie gasped. "Those look like scratch marks." Her stomach twisted. "Someone was locked inside and tried to claw their way out."

"The unsub may have brought his victims here and kept them for a while before actually killing them." Derrick rubbed his chin. "There was no evidence of sexual assault though. So why keep the girls?"

"To instill fear," Ellie said. "I found blankets upstairs that he may have used to wrap them in to carry them inside. Or someone may have been onto him and he had to lay low before dumping the bodies."

Williams sprayed the wall with Luminol and several spots glowed a white-ish blue indicating blood. "We might get epidemiol cells off the interior of the closet from those scratch marks."

"I don't recall Dr. Whitefeather mentioning blood or DNA under the girls' nails. But I'll ask her to recheck."

"Be thorough collecting," Derrick told Williams. "With numerous victims, there might be multiple DNA and blood samples. And be sure to request any samples be compared to Earl Bramble's."

"Copy that." Williams shot Derrick an annoyed look. "And for the record, I'm always thorough."

Ellie stepped aside and phoned the ME. It took a minute to get patched through. "Laney, I'm at a farm where we think one or more of the victims might have been kept hostage. Forensics is collecting evidence and processing the house, and we also think we found the truck the unsub used in the abduction of Jacey Ward."

"Sounds like progress," Laney said.

"We found a closet bearing scratch marks on the wall where someone was obviously held. There's signs of bloodstains as if the person locked inside clawed the wall and door to get out. Did you find DNA beneath Bonnie's or Jacey's nails?"

"A couple of fiber particulates but no human DNA."

"How about wooden splinters? Even the tiniest sliver could verify they were here."

"Let me look at my report."

Ellie waited while Laney took a minute. Seconds later, she returned. "Not that I noted, but I can check again."

"Thanks. Let me know if you find something."

Adrenaline surged through Ellie. Hopefully the evidence they found here, the blood, DNA, scarves and shoes would help crack this case.

Her phone buzzed with her boss's name on the screen so she connected. "Hey, I was about to call you."

"I hope it's with a lead. But right now, I need you to go to the hospital. Tilly Higgins and her brother Hayden were involved in a car crash. Rescue workers are on the scene and going to transport them to Brambletown General."

"Are they hurt?"

"The brother is unconscious. But Tilly was semi alert." He paused, and she heard him chomping on a mint. "She claims someone intentionally ran them off the road."

"Will get over there ASAP."

"I'm sending ERT to the crash site."

"Good. I know Tilly was digging around to find the truth about her sister. She could have gotten too close to the truth and someone wanted her dead because of it."

NINETY-SEVEN

Ellie left Derrick with Williams' team to search the barn, exterior outbuildings and property, and she drove to the hospital to see Tilly and her brother. They'd been looking for Hayden, but he'd obviously resurfaced on his own.

It had been fifteen years so she didn't know what to expect. Sure, he'd had problems as a teen but his family life had also blown up in his face and he'd been questioned as a suspect in his sister's disappearance. He might still be bitter and angry or in fifteen years he could have matured and want answers like Tilly did.

She'd deal with whatever.

At the nurses' station, she asked about Tilly and Hayden and was told Hayden was undergoing tests and being evaluated. The hospitalist met Ellie in the waiting room and Ellie identified herself. The doctor was a young tall, balding guy in his thirties with a calming manner that must have instantly put his patients at ease.

"Ms. Higgins told the police that someone intentionally ran

her off the road and caused her crash," Ellie said. "I need to talk to her as soon as possible."

"I understand. We did a CT scan, and it was normal. She sustained some bruises and cuts, which we've treated. Her right leg was pinned beneath the steering wheel, but the rescue workers managed to extract her without damaging the leg." He folded his arms. "At the moment, the trauma of the incident is more serious than her physical injuries."

"That's the reason I need to speak to her." Ellie explained about the murder investigation.

"I see. You can visit for a few minutes but if she becomes agitated, you'll have to leave. She needs her rest."

"Understood." Although Ellie had a strong feeling Tilly would want to talk.

She followed the doctor to a room where Tilly lay covered in a blanket, clenching the sheets, worry on her face. Her eyes widened in recognition when she saw Ellie, then she seemed to relax slightly. But she addressed the doctor first, "How's my brother?"

"Still running tests," he said. "But his CT scan was normal as was yours. We think he has a minor concussion."

Relief softened the anxiety in Tilly's eyes.

The doctor addressed Ellie, "Please remember what I said, Detective."

Ellie nodded and he left the room. She walked over to the bed, pulled the chair up beside Tilly and sat down. "Sorry you've had a rough day."

Tilly sighed. "It has been. Even more than you know."

"Tell me about it," Ellie said gently. "We've been looking for your brother for questioning."

"He just showed up at the house," Tilly said. "But I can assure you, Detective, he had nothing to do with Ruth's death or these other victims. He was injured in the military and received an honorable discharge, then turned his life around and he's been mentoring young troubled boys since."

"You didn't know any of this before?"

Tilly shook her head. "No, but we had a long heart-to-heart at my house and decided to talk to our parents. They blamed us after Ruth disappeared."

"You know it wasn't your fault," Ellie said. "And you don't think Hayden was responsible?"

"No. He admitted he played a prank on Ruth by telling her that Clint cheated on her. Then one of his friends left a note for her pretending to be Clint and asked her to meet him, but it was just a joke. The guys were together all night as he first stated."

"And you believe him?"

"Yes."

"But you said Ruth told you she wasn't meeting Clint," Ellie said.

Tilly nodded miserably. "I should have figured she was lying, that she was afraid to get Clint in trouble if she got caught."

"Did Clint know the note was a set-up?"

"I don't think so."

"So if she went to meet Clint and he didn't show, she may have been being stalked or simply in the wrong place at the wrong time." Back to Earl Bramble.

Tilly sighed. "That would make sense."

"You told the officer who reported the accident that someone ran you off the road. Did you see the vehicle or can you describe it?"

Tilly shook her head. "No. I was driving and suddenly I heard a motor racing up behind me then bright lights blinded me before he slammed into my rear."

Hopefully they'd get paint from the other vehicle which could lead to the culprit. "Was it a car, a van, SUV or a truck?"

Tilly rubbed her forehead and winced, obviously agitated.

"I... don't know. But the lights were high off the ground and shined down totally blinding me. So maybe a truck or a van."

"You're doing great, Tilly." Ellie patted the woman's hand. "We're almost finished, then you can rest."

"I want to help," Tilly said. "I... it just happened so fast, and I was trying to regain control of the car, but we served and rolled and I couldn't stop us from slamming into the ditch."

Her voice grew raspy with agitation, and Ellie felt for her. Tilly would probably relive the event over and over in her head for a long time.

"Can we talk about what happened when you saw your parents?"

Tilly ran her fingers through her tangled hair. "Nothing good. They're still the same angry, bitter people who doted on Ruth. Hayden and I are done with them and that's fine."

Ellie's heart ached for her and her brother. "I know your father was questioned about Ruth. Do you think he had anything to do with her disappearance?"

Tilly thought about it for a second then shook her head. "Hayden said he told Dad she was sneaking out, and Dad admitted he went looking for her but couldn't find her. And even if he'd blown up and gotten angry with her, he wouldn't have hurt her."

"Do you have any idea who would hurt your sister?"

"I wish I did," Tilly said. "I came back for answers." She touched the bandage on her hand. "But I've obviously ticked off someone here."

"Do you have any idea who?"

Tilly huffed. "Ida and Hetty Bramble. Clint Wallace. And of course Earl Bramble, that is if he's still alive."

Considering they had information of sightings of Earl over the years and two recently, Ellie was beginning to think he was. And that he'd been preying on teenage girls for over a decade.

NINETY-EIGHT

Green Gardens Cemetery

Kat peeked into her mama's room. Finally, she'd turned in for the night and was sleeping like the dead. Her daddy was on a long-haul delivery and wouldn't be back till the next day and Kat had the night to herself. He was so protective he watched her like a hawk. Her mama probably liked it when he was gone, too. On those nights, sometimes they ordered pizza or had sandwiches instead of cooking all the stuff her daddy liked... and demanded.

Carrie Ann had texted that a group of kids were going out to the graveyard to hang out tonight, and Kat decided to join them. Maybe she and Carrie Ann could hunt for that grave where Mama had seen her grandfather.

If the girl he'd buried was the missing girl Ruth, maybe she could find her body and she'd be the hero and put an end to all the gossip about her mama and Hetty. If Mama thought her daddy was guilty of all these murders, why didn't she go to the police now?

People in town thought he was still alive though so maybe she was still afraid of him.

Kat had never met him but the thought of being a murderer's granddaughter was disturbing. A few of the kids at school had started talking about it, saying evil must run in her veins. Asking if she ever had the urge to kill somebody. If her mama helped him lure Ruth to her grave because of that big fight at the DQ.

Kat bundled up in her coat and ski hat, tiptoed through the hall to the kitchen, grabbed the flashlight from the drawer and ducked outside. The wind bit at her, and the sky was so dark that fear slithered through her.

Still, she snuck along the bushes of her backyard, then darted toward the graveyard. Weeds choked the path along the way and clawed at her legs, but she ran on, crossing the field and taking cover behind rocks and trees as she went. She spotted the little church at the top of the hill and a few people lingering in front of the memorial with candles and cameras. Some family members and friends had left flowers and gifts, even small toys, to honor the men, women and kids who were buried there and also for those named on the memorial whose bodies had never been recovered.

The tall trees on the edge of the woods beyond it were still mysterious and she wondered if some of the dead who hadn't been recovered were buried there or if their bodies had disintegrated into bones and dust. At one time, she was squeamish, but after biology class she'd overcome it and decided she wanted to be a doctor.

Some areas had deep ridges and gulleys that reminded her of sink holes or quicksand. A foul odor usually clogged the air but tonight she smelled the pungent odor of pot.

Kat had tasted beer before, but she'd seen her daddy act stupid when he drank too much, so she steered clear of it now. The acrid scent of marijuana made her feel ill, so she hadn't dabbled in that either. Low voices echoed a few hundred feet in, and the glow of a small campfire sparkled against the inky night. A noise sounded behind her and a twig snapped. But when she turned to see if anyone was there, there was no one.

Heart hammering, she crossed to the group of teens huddled by the fire. Carrie Anne was already there in a short skirt and red boots which seemed ridiculous to Kat since it was forty-five degrees tonight.

"Look who's here, the graveyard girl," one of the boys named Woody said with a laugh.

Kat glared at him, irritated to be dubbed the same nickname as her mama and Hetty. Was she doomed to relive her mother's life?

"Better watch out," one of the soccer players said. "If her grandfather's killing these girls she may know where he is."

Everybody laughed and Kat bit her tongue to contain a smart-ass remark. She slipped around the circle and seated herself on the ground beside Carrie Ann. Raphael, a jock with a cocky attitude took a toke of the joint and passed it to Carrie Ann. She inhaled a long drag, then handed it to Kat.

But Kat passed it along to a girl named Bebe Butterworth on her left.

"Graveyard girl too stuck up to take a hit?" Woody said with a snide look.

Kat gave him a sour smile. "It's not my thing," she said although Carrie Ann nudged her as if to say she should just go along.

Maybe this was a mistake.

"Tell us about your murdering grandfather," Bebe said.

"Never met the man."

"Did your mom know he was a psychopath?" Raphael asked.

Anger sent Kat up from her seat on the ground and sympathy for her mother followed. Why had Mama stayed around this Podunk town and put up with this shit her whole life?

She didn't intend to. She'd hightail it out of Brambletown as soon as her diploma was in hand.

Frustrated because she wanted to tell Carrie Ann about the journal entry and convince her to help search for that grave, she decided to challenge the group.

"You talk like a big guy," she said, addressing Woody. "If that girl Ruth was buried out here fifteen years ago, prove how brave you are and help me look for it."

NINETY-NINE

That little black skirt and those red cowboy boots were his undoing. Still, he hid in the shadows of some pines that stood so closely together they looked entwined like one giant tree.

The voices screamed inside his head, over and over, calling her vile names and ordering him to get rid of her. Sometimes he tried to silence the voices but the more he protested the louder they shouted, dominating his mind and sometimes blurring his vision until he obeyed and did what they said.

Another voice from his childhood taunted him.

You're worthless. Evil.

He covered his ears with his hands. *Shut up, shut up, shut up.*

Sweat dribbled down the back of his neck into his shirt. His breathing quickened. *Her* shrill laughter pierced his eardrums. He had to make *her* shut up.

She's gone now. In the past. She can't hurt you anymore. Focus on the present.

He peered at the group of teens, silently laughing at their

stupidity. That girl Carrie Ann though... he couldn't take his eyes off her. His rational side insisted he stay away from her.

But she'd been sneaking out of her house to meet her friends so they could party in the woods a lot. Another girl he didn't know and two boys, who looked like jocks but talked like druggies, were passing a joint around. Carrie Ann's best friend Kat was with her, too.

Earlier, the teens snapped photos for their Instagram posts in front of the little white church that had once seemed quaint and charming but now stood rotting and empty, the interior so hollow only the sounds of lost voices singing old time gospel tunes echoed from the eaves.

The parched, dry land had been deserted for years, and the burial ground held more bodies than anyone knew about. That fact gave him secret pleasure.

A smile curved his mouth as he remembered the first girl he'd buried here. That had been sweet. Personal. Watching her gasp for her last breath and claw at his hands to release her had brought a calm to the gnawing craving for murder that possessed him. That calm had lingered for a while but just like the underground fire, it had a life of its own.

The beast needed feeding. And the little blond with those red cowboy boots would be his late-night dinner.

He listened for sounds of wildlife but as usual, it was quiet. Just like the trees and grass, the wild animals couldn't survive on the toxic land.

As if that was something to celebrate, some fool had erected that dumbass memorial for the dead who'd lost their lives in the coal mountain fire years ago.

Laughter erupted from the campfire the little idiots had set, and the teens were laughing and teasing Kat about being a graveyard girl like her mama.

He waited patiently to see what the group would do next. Kat challenged them to look for that missing girl Ruth Higgins.

There was no way they would find her though.

So far though the others had ignored Kat's challenge. All talk, that's what they were.

The weed was making Carrie Ann loose and in a party mood. Her defenses were down.

Perfect. She'd be too messed up to fight him. Ticked him off though because he did like a girl with spunk. She had it or she wouldn't be out here in the dark with all the ghosts surrounding her.

He couldn't take Carrie Ann though until her friends either passed out or left her alone. Or she decided to leave on her own. Knowing he had time, he followed the path to the spot he'd chosen for her eternal resting place. Far enough from the camp site that if the police checked out the area, they wouldn't find her grave. Deep in the ravine, he'd bury her so she wouldn't be found as quickly as Jacey Ward had.

It's dangerous to take a local girl, he reminded himself. But he drowned out that voice. He couldn't resist this one. Those red boots were calling his name.

He was surprised the police hadn't mentioned the red shoes in their press conference. But he'd watched enough crime shows to know that sometimes they omitted details from the public in order to catch a suspect off guard during an interrogation.

Hell, he enjoyed shoving his skill down everyone in this town's throat by wandering the streets while going noticed. A bonus was watching the law run in circles trying to figure out his identity.

For years now he'd had to hunt in other towns, but the memorial had brought a new wave of curious morbid seekers to feast on the unsightly graves, small-town gossip and suspicions.

He laid his shovel next to the grave he'd already dug, then returned to the trees where he'd been standing to watch the teens and settled in to watch.

He'd heard Carrie Ann say she had to be home by

midnight. The others groaned and moaned about how strict her parents were.

Not strict enough because she was here. After she'd arrived, he'd snuck over to her car and punctured her tire to create a slow leak as she drove home. He'd follow her until the tire went flat, then he'd roll up and offer his gentlemanly assistance.

Then she'd be his.

ONE HUNDRED

Kat was pissed at Carrie Ann. They'd been besties since kindergarten and Carrie Ann had never minded that Kat lived in a trailer and that gossip swarmed around her and her family like gnats on a muggy night. In fact, sometimes she'd thought Carrie Ann was intrigued by the mystery and kept hoping Kat would admit that her grandfather was alive and that her mama had been covering for him all this time.

Knowing she and the whole group were high now, she fisted her hands on her hips and shot them another challenging look. "So y'all going to just get stupid all night or are you gonna help look for bodies out here?"

"You're crazy," Bebe said.

Woody picked up a stick and drew a big X in the dirt. "Is your grandaddy hiding out here?"

Raphael raised his dark brows. "Yeah, are you setting us up?"

Kat laughed. "Are you chicken?"

Carrie Ann glared at her as if to ask why she was being so weird.

Raphael lurched up, his teeth gritted. "I'm not chicken."

Woody squared his shoulders and clutched the stick as he stood. "Me neither."

Bebe rubbed her arms with her hands as if she was freezing or nervous. "He's not out here is he, Kat?"

Kat wiggled her brows. "Of course not. He'd be a moron to make a move with the cops crawling all over Brambletown."

Bebe gave a tiny nod then pushed to her feet and grabbed the biggest stick she could find.

Kat cut her gaze toward her best friend. "Carrie Ann, you gonna stay here by yourself?"

Carrie Ann bit down on her lower lip. "You really think there're more bodies out here?"

Kat didn't know. But she wanted to see the spot where her mama had watched her granddaddy haul that girl and she didn't really want to go alone.

"Never mind, Carrie Ann. Stay here or go home. I don't care."

She whirled around and shined her flashlight into the woods to light a path. Behind her, she heard grumbling but everyone except Carrie Ann followed her. The others whispered as they hiked.

"It's so dark," Bebe said in a tiny voice.

Woody flipped on a flashlight. "Stay close to me, Bebe. I'll protect you."

Raphael shined his own light around as they walked, pushing brush away with his gloved hands.

Kat thought she knew the general place her mama had talked about in her journal and stayed razor focused as she climbed over rotting tree stumps and maneuvered through patches of knee-high weeds.

She scoured the land for the rock formation her mother had described.

They must have walked at least three miles, and Bebe was complaining about her legs hurting. "Let's go back," she begged.

"I'm cold and tired. I thought we came to party, not ghost hunt in the dark."

"I'm with Bebe," Woody said. "I want another beer."

"Go back if you want," Kat said, annoyed with the whining. Besides, she felt bad for leaving Carrie Ann alone.

A killer was on the loose and they should have stayed together.

Raphael suddenly halted at the edge of a ravine. "Look, guys, there's a shovel."

Kat rushed up beside him and stared at the shovel which had been tossed in the brush. She didn't dare touch it, but she and Raphael both stooped down and pushed away some weeds.

Raphael's breathing quickened and Kat sensed Bebe and Woody inch up behind them and look over their shoulders.

"There's an old hat stuck in the dirt," Raphael said.

Kat leaned closer, saw the brim of a baseball cap and gasped.

She'd seen that hat before. In the pictures in her mama's old photo album.

That hat belonged to Kat's grandfather.

"We should get out of here," Bebe cried.

Kat held her breath as she spotted a section that looked as if a dog had been digging in the dirt.

"Shit," Raphael muttered. "That looks like a bone."

Bebe screamed and everyone turned to run.

Kat stared at the bone in horror. *Was* Ruth Higgins buried here?

ONE HUNDRED ONE

Brambletown Police Station

After leaving Tilly, Ellie made a phone call and confirmed that Hayden Higgins had been working with a mentorship program for boys. The director of the program sang Hayden's praises, claimed he was one of their most effective leaders, and that he hadn't traveled to any of the cities where the girls went missing.

She hung up, satisfied to dismiss him as a suspect, then drove straight to the sheriff's office and asked to speak to Clint Wallace.

While she waited, she surveyed the bulletin board in the bullpen area and noted a few fliers for missing and wanted people. A couple were outdated, the criminal caught, and two of the missing were old photos; one of an elderly woman and another of an infant who was believed to have been taken by his father in a domestic dispute.

When Clint finally appeared, his look was guarded. Ellie wondered if he'd intentionally stalled just to annoy her but decided not to ask. She had more urgent questions on her mind.

"What are you doing here?" he asked.

"Tonight, Tilly Higgins and her brother were run off the road by another vehicle. I just came from the hospital."

"You found Hayden Higgins?"

"Actually he came to see Tilly willingly. Apparently, he's been running a kids' program to mentor young boys and teenagers."

"You sure we're talking about the same guy, the one who was always in trouble?" Clint asked, his tone skeptical.

Ellie nodded. "I verified his job and home location and spoke to the head of the program. Tilly also vouched for him."

"She's his sister. Don't you think she'd lie for him?"

"I think she came here looking for answers and since she and her family have been estranged for years, that if she thought he killed Ruth, she would turn him in." She waited a beat. "How about you? Your father lie for you back then?"

Outrage slashed his face as he tightened his jaw. "Hell, no. He was a hard ass."

Ellie still didn't know if she believed that. "I think whoever ran Tilly and her brother off the road is probably the killer we're looking for." She debated how to approach him but decided not to mince words. "You didn't know about their accident?"

His eyes turned steely. "No, must have missed that call."

Ellie raised a brow in question. "Where were you tonight?"

He spewed a litany of colorful words. "Not that I have to answer to you, but I was investigating the vandalism at the memorial. Turned out like I thought, a bunch of teens."

That answered that question.

"I called their folks and gave them a warning. But they'll have to clean it up."

"Sounds fair," Ellie said. "I do have news about the case. We found the pick-up we believe our unsub drove in the abduction of Jacey Ward. ERT is processing it and some items we found inside. We also searched a farm nearby where we think the unsub may have been staying and found these." She pulled her phone and showed him pictures of the scarves and red shoes. "He takes the shoes as souvenirs which suggests he may have a shoe fetish."

The sheriff's face paled slightly.

"Sheriff, what is it?" Ellie asked.

"Where did you say you found those?"

"A farm not too far from here. Do you know of it?"

"My father talked about searching a farm when Ruth disappeared." He released a shaky breath. "But he didn't find anything."

"The killer might have not been using it at the time."

"But Earl Bramble could have been hiding out there for years right under my nose."

Ellie gave a little nod. "We'll know more when we get forensic results from the truck and the house."

The sheriff cleared his throat. "Then we can find the bastard and lock him up for good."

ONE HUNDRED TWO

Luck was on his side tonight. Carrie Ann had been too scared to hunt for bodies in No Man's Land in the dark. Bodies they wouldn't find because he'd hidden them well.

But stupid girl—didn't she realize that staying back alone meant she was vulnerable?

Laughter bubbled in his throat as he trailed her little Honda onto the highway. Careful to stay far enough behind her so she wouldn't realize he was on her tail, he whistled, letting her enjoy her last few minutes before she realized she was going to die.

It was so silent outside on the winding country road that it reminded him of the quiet before a storm. The fucking idiots in this town had no idea they were going to lose another member of their community tonight, that there would be one less young girl around.

That tomorrow he'd go about his business like he always did and no one would suspect him of anything.

They didn't know about his hideout or his trophies yet.

Hopefully they never would.

He pulled the red scarf from the console and wrapped it around his gloved hand. Dammit, he wanted to feel the silk with his fingers but that would leave prints or DNA from his sweat and he couldn't risk that.

Just as he'd planned, about four miles from the graveyard her rear tire had leaked to the point that her car began to rumble and was off balance. She slowed, fighting the steering until she reached a turn off to a side road around a bend. His breath quickened as she rolled to a stop.

He slowed and watched as she got out to assess the damage. He hoped she didn't call her parents for help but had banked on the fact that if she did, she'd have to tell them where she'd been and what she was doing. Before she had the chance to pull her phone, he rolled to a stop behind her.

For a moment, she looked panicked then relief stretched across her face when she recognized him.

"Looks like you've got car trouble." He glanced around the deserted area. "Let me give you a ride and get you home safely."

She hesitated but finally nodded. "Thanks, I appreciate it. My folks will kill me if they wake up and I'm not home." She grabbed her backpack and slid from her vehicle and locked the door.

He could barely contain his laughter as she settled in the front seat.

He was tempted to do her right here on the spot. But he headed down the side road she'd turned onto.

"Where are we going?" she asked.

"Down here a bit so I can turn around."

She nodded, chewed on her bottom lip and fidgeted. But he had a feeling she wasn't afraid of him. She was planning how she'd explain where her car was to her parents. Making up some story. Going to sneak in tonight and wait until the dope wore off and she wasn't high.

Only she wouldn't be there in the morning to tell her story because her story was about to end.

ONE HUNDRED THREE

Kat's head spun in circles. They should call the police. Let them know they found a body.

But if she did, her parents would know she'd been in the woods and they'd go ape shit that she'd been out there at night. Especially with a killer targeting teenage girls.

A killer who might be her grandfather.

Would he kill her if he knew she was here and might have exposed Ruth Higgins' body?

Brush crackled and twigs and branches snapped, brittle in the silence, as her friends raced back to camp. A chill whipped through her, and she shivered then ran back to talk to the others. Shadows seemed to lurk everywhere in the woods. A wild animal howled somewhere in the distance, odd since wildlife and vegetation rarely survived in the area.

She picked up her pace. Her sneakers pounded the dry ground and she paused every few feet to check over her shoulder. At one point, she thought she saw eyes peering at her and heard someone whispering her name.

Terrified, she ran faster. She stumbled over a rotten tree stump, fell on her knees and pine cones stabbed at her legs. Gasping for a breath, she peered all around her, then pushed up, determined to reach their camp.

But as she rounded the corner to the pit Raphael had dug in the ground, the fire was out and the others were digging a hole to hide the weed.

"We have to tell someone," she rasped.

"No way," Woody screeched. "We'll get arrested."

"My parents would freaking ground me for life," Bebe said on a sob.

Raphael touched her arm. "They're right, Kat. We'd get in so much trouble."

"But it's not right," Kat said in a tortured whisper.

"You want the police to come down on us like they did your family fifteen years ago?" Woody hissed.

Kat's heart pounded. In her mother's journal, she'd sounded so traumatized by everything that happened. All the gossip about the Graveyard Girls. Them being white trash. Her father a murderer.

Mama had wanted to be free of it.

As many issues as she had with her mama, could she start that shitshow all over again? And ruin her own reputation at school?

She wanted desperately to escape Brambletown and her family's reputation.

Tears blurred her vision, then she glanced around and realized her best friend was gone. "Oh, God, where's Carrie Ann?"

"She seemed pretty freaked. She probably left the minute we hiked into the woods," Woody said.

Kat nodded. He was right. Carrie Ann had her car and was probably safe at home right now.

ONE HUNDRED FOUR

Gus's Goat Farm

He savored the sound of Carrie Ann's muffled screams from the back of the truck where he'd secured and gagged her. Just as he'd thought he could finish her off on that winding deserted road, a fucking car had driven by.

Seeing a truck like his might have alerted the driver that he was out of place, so he hauled ass the other way and decided to prolong his pleasure and her pain/fear by carrying her to the farm. With some of his victims, he'd made it swift and fast and unemotional, but he might play some games with her.

The thought excited him to no end.

After all, his life had become dull and routine. Meaningless except to kill.

A banging noise echoed from the back, feet on metal, and he realized she was kicking the sides of the truck. She was a feisty one, all right.

Just like Ruth had been.

And the first one... well that sick bitch had never seen it coming. Had thought she was in control.

He'd shown her different. She got what she deserved. And he was damn proud of that.

The truck bounced over the ruts in the road, and he rounded the corner and noticed the pick-up was gone. Shit, they'd found it.

Not to worry though. He'd wiped his prints free and planted the ones that needed to be there.

Pride made his chest puff up. No one in Brambletown knew how smart he was. Maybe one day they would.

He barreled on, but when he approached the turn-off for the farm, he spotted lights flickering across the field. And another light at the barn.

Shit, shit, shit. The damn police had found his place.

Panic made his pulse hammer, and he punched the gas and sped by. A mile down the road and he forced himself to slow in case another cop was watching the area. He couldn't get pulled over on some routine surveillance.

No, no, no, not him.

He breathed in and out to calm himself, then clawed at his skin the way he used to claw at the walls of the closet he'd been locked in as a child.

A smile calmed his panic as he envisioned wrapping the red scarf around her neck. He already had her grave dug.

By now, hopefully her friends were gone and he could put her in the ground.

Then he'd watch the town and the cops get in an uproar in the morning when they realized he'd struck again.

ONE HUNDRED FIVE
DAY FIVE

Briar Ridge Mobile Homes

Kat snuck back into the house, grateful her mama was in her room still asleep. She should be; it was already past midnight.

Her stomach knotted though as she slipped into her bedroom and closed the door. She felt dirty all over from being in the woods but didn't dare shower for fear she'd wake her mama.

But the image of that grave and the bone and her granddaddy's hat haunted her. If he'd buried Ruth Higgins there or another girl, she had to tell. Maybe her mama and Hetty could keep a secret like the one they'd kept for over a decade, but her conscience wouldn't let her.

She paced the room, rubbing her arms with her hands, anxiety clawing at her. She had to do something. She couldn't go to bed and sleep, not knowing she might have just found the girl the whole town had been looking for for the last decade and a half.

Shoving her hair behind her ears, she dropped onto her bed and opened her laptop. She googled the number for that tip line the detective had mentioned on the news. Her breathing quickened, her heart beating so fast she could hear the blood roaring in her ears.

She could call in an anonymous tip. She didn't have to leave her name. No one would know it was her, especially not her parents.

Blowing out a shaky breath, she pulled her cell phone from her pocket and called the number for Crooked Creek's Police Department. A man answered and identified himself as Deputy Landrum.

Before he could ask anything else, she blurted, "There's a body in the woods by the graveyard. About three miles to the north at the ravine."

"You saw this body?"

"A hat and... bones poking through the brush."

"May I ask who's calling?"

She didn't respond. She hung up, her hands trembling as she stripped her clothes, then put on her pjs.

Hoping she did the right thing, she crawled into bed and yanked the covers over her head to block out the night and the image of her grandaddy's hat beside that grave.

ONE HUNDRED SIX

Ellie and Derrick were heading back to Crooked Creek for some R & R when Deputy Landrum phoned. She put him on speaker.

"Detective Reeves, a tip just came in about a body in the woods near that graveyard."

Ellie groaned. "At this time of night?"

"Afraid so."

Ellie's pulse jumped. "Do you think it's legit?"

"I don't know. It was a young girl so it could be a teen prank. But she sounded shaken up. When I asked her name, she hung up."

Ellie rolled her shoulders to loosen the kink in her neck. It had been a long day already. But if this lead was legitimate, they had to check it out.

"Can you trace the number the girl called from?" Ellie asked.

"Already done it," the deputy answered. "The phone belongs to Kat Jones."

Dammit.

Ellie and Derrick traded a look. "Thanks, Deputy. We'll talk to her and check it out." Ellie ended the call and swung the Jeep toward Ida Bramble's mobile home park.

Derrick scrubbed his hand over his face. "It's late, Ellie. You think we should wait until tomorrow?"

"No," Ellie said. "If this is legit, the killer might move the body by morning."

"You're right," Derrick said. "We can't waste time."

Ellie sped up and they rode the next few miles in silence. When she reached Ida's trailer she veered into the driveway. A lamp burned in the living room indicating someone was home. They made their way to the front door and Derrick rang the bell.

Tension thickened and a stiff wind blew through bringing the scent of garbage. A cat screeched from the neighbor's yard, and she realized it was tearing into someone's trash. Derrick punched the bell a second time and finally Ellie saw Ida walking through the living room toward the door wearing a pair of flannel pajamas. Her hair was rumpled, and she yawned as she opened the door. Jesus, they'd woken her up.

"What are y'all doing here this time of night?" Ida grumbled.

"Sorry to bother you so late, but it's important," Ellie said. "We need to speak to your daughter."

Ida's brows shot up. "Kat? Why?"

"Is she here?" Derrick asked.

"Of course she is. She's not allowed to go out at night with that killer on the loose."

Ellie offered her an understanding smile. Obviously, Ida was unaware Kat had called the tip line. "I don't blame you. But someone using her phone called us and we really have to talk to her. With you present, of course."

Ida toyed with the top button of her pajamas. "Can't this wait until tomorrow?"

"I'm afraid not," Ellie said.

"We can either do it here or at the police station," Derrick said.

Ida sputtered a nervous sound, then threw her shoulders back and walked down the hall. She called Kat's name as she banged on the door then opened it.

"Get up, Kat, the police are here and need to talk to you."

Ellie and Derrick waited in the living room until Kat appeared. She was wearing pajama pants and a sweatshirt and looked terrified.

"Kat," Ellie said gently. "We received a tip call from your phone tonight about a body in the woods by the graveyard. It was you that called, wasn't it?"

The girl's pallor turned a ghostly white.

"That's impossible," Ida snapped. "Kat was here all night. I told you we don't let her go out, especially in the woods."

Kat's lower lip trembled, and she tugged the ends of her sleeves to cover her fingers.

Ida fisted her hands on her hips. "Tell them, Kat. You were here all night."

"We can check your phone," Derrick cut in.

Tears filled Kat's eyes. "I'm sorry, Mama."

Ida gasped and sank into the club chair by the fireplace. "Lord have mercy, Kat. What did you do?"

Kat covered her face with her hands and dropped onto the sofa.

Ellie slid down beside her and rubbed her back. "Listen, Kat, you aren't in trouble. But we need to know what happened tonight. Why you made that call."

Ida looked stricken with shock. "Did you go to that graveyard?"

Kat gave a quick nod and wiped at her damp cheeks. "Some of the kids wanted to go so I met them there."

"Then what happened?" Ellie asked gently.

Kat picked up the throw pillow on the couch and hugged it like a teddy bear. "We went into the woods and... one of the guys saw a hat and then some brush was piled up by the ravine and... it looked like a dog had been digging there."

"Go on," Ellie said.

"Then we saw a bone," Kat said.

"Did you touch it or dig around?" Ellie asked.

"No... everyone got freaked out and ran back to the camp."

"Did you see anyone else in the woods?"

Kat shook her head no.

"You told the deputy on the phone the general area where you saw the bones. Can you be more specific about the location?"

Kat gave a small shrug. "No. But I could show you."

"She's not going out there in the night," Ida cut in. "She's just a child."

"If she saw a body, then we need her to take us to the location," Derrick said.

"We'll be with her every minute," Ellie promised. "And we'll protect her."

"No," Ida said. "Absolutely not."

"I can draw you a map," Kat offered.

Ellie glanced at Derrick and he nodded. "That will work. Can you do that for us now?"

"I'll get a notepad." Kat rose, walked to the kitchen desk, removed a legal pad, sat down and began to draw.

Ellie called Cord and explained about Kat's discovery and asked him to meet her and Derrick at the graveyard.

Five minutes later, Kat handed the map to Ellie. "Thank you for being brave enough to call about this," Ellie said. "We want to catch this killer before he hurts anyone else."

Kat swallowed hard. "There's something else."

"What is it?" Ellie asked.

Kat stooped in front of Ida. "Mama, the hat I saw there. It... was Granddaddy's."

Ida made a strangled sound then stared into space but said nothing.

ONE HUNDRED SEVEN

Panic overcame Ida as the detective and fed left.

This couldn't be happening. Her own daughter had been in the woods and had drawn a map for the police.

In spite of everything she and Hetty had done to protect the past, it was totally unraveling.

"I'm sorry, Mama," Kat whispered.

Ida wanted to shake her daughter for sneaking out. For disobeying. For telling the police where to look. Once they found the body, they might put all the pieces together.

"Mama?"

"Go to bed, Kat. I don't want to talk to you now." *You've ruined everything.*

Kat gave her a small hug, but Ida couldn't bring herself to return it. Teary-eyed, Kat hurried back to her bedroom and shut the door.

Ida's legs buckled as she stood, and she had to hold onto the wall to make it to her bedroom and her phone. Chest aching with fear, she pressed Hetty's number. The phone rang three times before she answered.

"Ida?"

A sob caught in her throat. "It's happening," she cried.

"What do you mean?"

"Kat and some of her friends were in the woods tonight and found a body. And Daddy's hat was there."

Hetty screamed into the phone and Ida pressed her fist to her mouth to keep from joining her.

ONE HUNDRED EIGHT

No Man's Land

Cord was waiting at the graveyard when Ellie and Derrick arrived. His expression was closed, his posture rigid, his eyes somber.

Ellie showed him the map Kat had drawn and his jaw tightened.

"Can you help us find this place?" she asked.

His gaze met hers and she saw something disturbing in his eyes, something she didn't understand.

"Cord?"

"Yeah, follow me." He handed them flashlights and they followed as he guided them through the woods. An eerie quiet filled the air, the silence deafening, a reminder of why they were here. Dread mingled with hope that after all these years, they might finally find Ruth Higgins and get justice for her.

Tension built but no one spoke, each scanning the woods with their flashlights and maneuvering around rotten foliage and fallen trees. They found the spot where the kids had built a campfire and paused to look around.

"At least they put dirt on the fire to snuff it out," Cord said.

Ellie nodded. "Good. At least they were smart enough to do that."

Cord consulted Kat's map and aimed his flashlight to the north. "This way."

Ellie and Derrick followed. About three miles in, Cord halted, his heavy sigh breaking the quiet.

"There's the ravine," Derrick said.

Ellie inched closer, stooping to look through the brush and spotted the hat Kat had described. She pulled her phone and snapped photographs of the area as Derrick looked around.

"There's a shovel." He took a picture of it then with gloved hands dragged it from the brush. Ellie lifted the hat to send to forensics and saw a bone jutting through the soil. "Kat was right," she said. "A body is buried here."

She stood, called her boss, requested an ERT then called the ME.

"Bring your forensic anthropologist," Ellie said. "This one may have been here a while."

"Will be there ASAP," Laney said.

Cord ran his fingers through his hair, ruffling the shaggy strands. "I'll go back and meet them then lead them here."

"Thanks, Cord," Ellie said although he seemed disturbed as he looked back at the makeshift grave. Dammit, something was going on with him, and when this case was solved, she intended to get to the bottom of it.

While he hiked back to the graveyard, she and Derrick searched the area. Hopefully the shovel had prints on it and Kat said the hat belonged to Earl Bramble. If it matched the prints and DNA on the scarves, this might be the evidence they needed to connect him to this murder and the others.

ONE HUNDRED NINE

Somewhere on the AT

He clenched the steering wheel in a white-knuckled grip as he passed the graveyard. Dammit, dammit, dammit. He was tired and needed sleep.

But the cops were there again.

Blue lights swirled against the night sky and he spotted the ME's vehicle. They must have found something. One of the girls' bodies?

Sweat beaded on his skin. Panic robbed his breath. Which one had they uncovered?

The banging in the back had stopped for a minute. Carrie Ann must be exhausted. He should just put her out of her misery. But he wanted to make a point this time. Teach the young girl a lesson.

That the woods were dangerous. That girls were stupid to venture out there alone.

In an effort not to be seen, he cut his lights as he drove past the graveyard. By the time he made the turn off onto the main road, he punched them back on. The winding road wrapped around the mountain. He took a switchback on two wheels, then the banging started again.

What was he going to do? He couldn't go back to the farm. Or the cemetery tonight.

He had to find a place and lay low. He could grab some sleep in the truck while she stayed locked in the back. But he couldn't park in plain sight for fear someone would see him or hear her kicking the walls of the truck.

An idea struck him and he grinned and sped toward the one place he felt safe. Where no one suspected him of anything. Where he got respect.

Once the police left in the morning, he'd bury her with the others.

Recovering the remains in the brush was a tedious process. Evidence had to be preserved. The autopsy would be key to confirming this body was related to their current case.

"I don't see a scarf," she said.

"It looks like a dog or animal has been digging here," Derrick pointed out. "The animal could have dragged it off."

"Hopefully ERT will find it." She shined her light across the ground. "Have you recovered a shoe in the grave?"

"Not yet." Laney said as she angled her head toward Ellie. "But there's something else. This body is not a female. Judging from bone structure, size and aging, it's not even a teenager."

Ellie narrowed her eyes as she studied the skull. "What? Are you sure?"

Laney pointed to cranial structure. "Yes. The autopsy will give us more insight into cause of death and timing, but I'd estimate he's been dead for years, perhaps a decade."

Ellie's thoughts raced back to everything they'd learned so far. "This man's death could have occurred around the time Ruth disappeared."

"It's possible," Laney agreed as she examined the back of

the skull. "He certainly wasn't strangled. It looks like he died of blunt force trauma to the head."

Ellie contemplated that information. Derrick squatted down and examined the crack in the skull. Cord's eyes cut to the bones then across the woods then back, a vein throbbing his neck.

"Earl Bramble supposedly disappeared around that time, which made him appear guilty," Ellie said, her mind shifting to piece together the puzzle. "What if he didn't leave town?"

"We thought he's been hiding out, traveling around, killing other girls," Derrick said.

"That was our theory." Ellie's stomach twisted. "What if we were wrong? What if this is Earl and someone killed him?"

Cord shifted, sending loose rocks skittering down the hill.

"But who would kill him?" she asked out loud.

Derrick cleared his throat. "Someone who thought he murdered Ruth and wanted him to pay."

"The Higgins men had motive," Ellie said with a knot in her stomach.

Derrick nodded. "They did."

"I'll pull Bramble's medical and dental records and run his DNA," Laney said. "Hopefully we'll have a definitive ID by mid-morning."

ONE HUNDRED ELEVEN

Crooked Creek

Ellie and the team had worked into the early hours of the morning, but she'd eventually convinced Cord to come home with her to get some rest. Both dirty from the hike in the woods and body recovery, they showered, then fell into bed and made love, a silent agreement to cease discussion of the case for some rest.

Just good physical exertion and honest love—at least on her part.

The little voice inside her head whispered that he was still keeping something from her, but she hushed it and snuggled into his arms. She would ask him about it.

But not now. No... not at the moment.

She wanted to curl in his arms and forget that parents were terrified and girls were in danger, and at this point she still didn't have the killer in custody.

For all she knew, he could be ending another innocent girl's life at that moment.

Fear and doubts assailed her. Would she fail her as she had the others?

Tormented, she punched her pillow. Rolled over and over. Cursed herself and sorted through the details of the case. They might have found Earl Bramble's body. Which meant someone else had murdered the girls and perhaps Earl. They'd need to talk to the Higgins family again.

Look for other suspects. But if Mr. Higgins had killed Earl, it had been personal. He could have been trying to force him to admit where Ruth was.

But why would he kill again?

It didn't make sense that he'd murder other teenage girls or if he had, that his wife wouldn't have known.

What were they missing?

ONE HUNDRED TWELVE

Briar Ridge Mobile Homes

Kat barely slept. She was so stupid. She should have known the police would trace her number.

And now Mama was mad as heck at her.

It was the right thing to do though. If that body was Ruth, her parents needed to know she'd been found.

She stared at a spider crawling across her ceiling, spinning its web. A shiver went through her as she remembered the night before. That grave. The bone.

She blinked to clear the images.

Thank goodness it was Saturday and she didn't have to go to school or face the other kids.

She rolled to her side, wishing she'd never read her mama's journal.

There's still more to read.

The clock ticked in the silence. Minutes passed. It was only six a.m. and she was so exhausted. And afraid to face her mama. Had she called her daddy and told him what happened?

Suddenly a loud knock sounded at the door and her mama

shoved it open. She stormed inside and stopped beside Kat's bed, her arms folded. "Kat, Carrie Ann's mother is on the phone and she's frantic."

Kat jerked to a sitting position. "What?"

"She says Carrie Ann snuck out sometime last night, took her car and she isn't home yet."

Kat's heart pounded with fear. "What? But..."

"Was she with you and those other kids?"

Kat dug her fingers in the covers on her bed.

"Was she, Kat?"

Tears burned the back of Kat's throat. There was no use lying. If Carrie Ann was in trouble, she had to talk. "Yes. But... she was freaked out and didn't go with us into the w... woods. When... we got back to the campfire she'd... already left."

Terror gripped Kat. Had that monster murdering teenage girls taken her?

She clutched her stomach. She was going to hurl.

"Lord have mercy," her mama muttered as she pressed her phone back to her ear. "Kat says Carrie Ann was with her and some other kids at the graveyard." Mama thrust the phone toward Kat. "Talk to her and tell her what you told me."

The furious look her mama sent Kat could melt butter. Kat's hand trembled as she took the phone. "Hello."

"Where's Carrie Ann?"

Kat pinched the bridge of her nose to stem the tears. "I... don't know. I thought she went straight home last night."

"What do you mean?"

Some of us went to the graveyard to hang out, then into the woods. But Carrie Ann didn't want to go in the woods, and when we got back to the camp she was gone."

"What time was that?" Carrie Ann's mother said.

"Around eleven," Kat answered.

"How could you guys be so stupid and go up there with a killer on the loose?" Carrie Ann's mama screamed.

Kat burst into tears and her mama took the phone. "It was stupid and the police were here during the night but they didn't mention Carrie Ann. I'll deal with Kat. Now hang up now, Phyllis, and call the police."

A minute later, her mama stomped out. Kat buried her head in her pillow, terror seizing her. She never should have left Carrie Ann at the camp alone.

If something bad happened to her best friend, it was all her fault.

ONE HUNDRED THIRTEEN

At seven-fifteen, Ellie jerked awake, her anxiety already rising to a fever pitch. Today hopefully they'd find the ID of the dead man in No Man's Land and get results for DNA on the scarves and shoes.

Then they'd be one step closer to identifying the teenage killer.

She rubbed her eyes and pushed her tangled hair from her face, then glanced up to see Cord standing at the window staring out. He was so still and somber, his body wracked with tension, that her breath stalled in her chest.

She swallowed hard, the sense that something was really wrong making her heart stutter.

Then he turned to her and she saw pain and... what looked like fear in his deep brown eyes. She'd never seen Cord look afraid before. What the hell was going on?

"I need to tell you something," he said in a deep gravelly voice.

Ellie was not a crier. But tears blurred her vision and she was too choked up to speak so she simply waited.

Tension simmered in the silence.

The doorbell rang, the sound cutting through the air like a gong. She and Cord froze, locking gazes.

The bell rang again.

Ellie took a deep breath, pushed away the covers, grabbed her robe from the end of the bed and dragged it on. She tied the belt and padded to the living room, wondering who was at her door this time of the morning. Laney would have called with lab results and so would her boss, not shown up at her house.

Anxiety needling her, she checked through the peephole and saw Derrick standing on her front porch pacing back and forth.

She smoothed down her hair as best she could, then unlocked the door. "Derrick?"

His eyes darkened as he looked past her. "Is McClain here?"

The look on his face unnerved her. "Yes. What's wrong?"

He released a loud sigh. "Just get him, okay?"

She narrowed her eyes but gave a nod. What in the world was going on? Before she could walk back to the bedroom, Cord appeared, dressed, his shoulders rigid, his expression so disturbing that Ellie's stomach roiled.

Derrick cleared his throat. "McClain, I need you to come with me to the station."

Ellie stared at him in shock. "What's going on, Derrick?"

"It's fine, Ellie," Cord said gruffly.

"No, it's not," Ellie said. "Tell me what's going on."

"Ask McClain," Derrick said.

"Ask him what?" Ellie snapped.

The silence that stretched raised Ellie's anxiety even more.

Derrick stepped inside. "Why his prints were on the shovel found in that grave last night."

Dammit, Cord knew his prints were on file from his juvie days.

And he'd known his day of reckoning was coming. But even though he'd been a kid himself fifteen years ago, he had no regrets about what he'd done.

Except for hurting Ellie. And that she'd be disappointed in him.

"Cord?" Ellie said in a pained whisper.

"It's okay. I'll go with him. Just keep working the case."

"Tell me what's going on," Ellie said, her eyes filled with questions.

Before he could respond, Ellie's phone dinged. She glanced at the number. "Dammit, it's Captain Hale."

"Answer it," Cord said, needing to buy himself time. Ellie would beat herself up if she didn't solve this crime.

She connected the call. "Yeah, I'm here."

He and Fox waited silently, both on edge.

A second later, she hung up, her expression drawn. "Another girl is missing. Kat Jones's best friend Carrie Ann Parker. We need to go."

Derrick scowled at Cord. "I have to deal with this first."

Anger flared in Ellie's eyes. "Deal with what?"

"Go about the girl," Cord said through clenched teeth.

"Captain said Deputy Eastwood answered the call and questioned the parents. Apparently, they didn't realize she'd snuck out and didn't come home until this morning. She's issued an APB for her car and Sheriff Wallace has his deputies searching abandoned properties. Sheriff Waters is circulating her picture and information to all law enforcement agencies, and he's already notified Angelica Gomez to air the story." Pain and fear wrenched Ellie's eyes. "Carrie Ann's parents have requested a camera interview and plan to offer a reward for information that might help find her."

"I followed up with the ME and lab this morning," Derrick said. "Dr. Whitefeather must have worked through the night. She already IDed the body those kids found."

Ellie's breath caught. "Who was it?"

"Just as you speculated, Earl Bramble."

Cord could barely look at Ellie because he knew Bramble was dead and had kept it from her. And his prints on that shovel were evidence against him, and soon she would know the truth.

ONE HUNDRED FIFTEEN

Ellie's head spun. "Earl Bramble... dead?"

"Yes," Derrick said. "The ME is a hundred percent. Said she double-checked DNA, medical and dental records."

"But if he's been dead for years, even if he killed Ruth, he's not our unsub."

"No," Derrick said. "That's the reason I need to talk to McClain." He tilted his head toward Cord. "About those prints on the shovel, McClain. Care to explain how they got there?"

A muscle ticked in Cord's jaw. "I can't."

"Why not?" Ellie rasped.

"It's not what you think," he said gruffly.

Derrick crossed his arms. "Then what is it?"

A tense beat followed but Cord simply shook his head.

"Cord," Ellie said shrilly. "There has to be a logical explanation. Tell us what happened."

"It's not my story to tell," he said.

Derrick pulled handcuffs from his pocket. "Maybe sitting in a cell for a while will loosen your tongue."

Horror washed over Ellie as Derrick jerked Cord's arms behind him and snapped the cuffs in place. Then he pushed

Cord toward her front door. Cord gave her a forlorn look and mouthed, "I'm sorry," then dropped his shoulders as Derrick escorted him to his car.

For a moment, Ellie was too stunned to move or speak.

She knew Cord had secrets. A checkered past that included abuse. She suspected he'd fought his foster father. But in self-defense.

The past few days working this case he'd been brooding. She'd sensed something was wrong.

If he'd known Earl Bramble was dead, why hadn't he said something?

Hurt and anger bled through her. They'd suspected Bramble of all these murders and been searching for him, and Cord allowed her to believe that, let them chase their tails blindly. Let them waste time.

And now another girl was in danger and might die because of his silence.

ONE HUNDRED SIXTEEN

Derrick pushed Cord into an interrogation room and slammed the door. Furious with the bastard for withholding information, he walked down the hall, grabbed a cup of coffee and took it to Ellie's office where he worked when he was in town.

He needed to calm down. Treat this like any other case. As if McClain was any other suspect.

But it wasn't any other case. Girls were dead and another one missing. McClain might have answers. Worse, he'd conned Ellie into believing he was a good guy.

Derrick had even started to think so himself.

He drummed his fingers on the desk then ran a background check on Cord. He'd done it when they'd first met, but maybe he'd missed something.

He would have been a teenager when Ruth disappeared. Had been abused. Had a juvie record, although it had been sealed.

With his past, he could fit the profile of a serial killer.

Indecision played through his mind as he recalled the

rescue and recovery missions McClain had worked through SAR and FEMA. The courage and skill he'd shown working on the task force. The lives he'd helped save.

He'd been instrumental in saving Ellie's life more than once and even in saving Derrick.

Determined to get to the bottom of the situation, he stood and headed down the hall to knock some sense into the man. But he bumped into Ellie as she made a beeline for her office. She was panting for a breath, her eyes blazing with anger.

At McClain or at him? Probably both?

"What are you doing here?" Derrick asked. "I thought you'd be working to find Carrie Ann."

"I talked to her parents on the way here. I'll talk to Kat next. But I want to know what Cord has to say."

Derrick gritted his teeth. Good god, Ellie was stubborn. "I was on my way to question him."

"Let me," Ellie said.

"You're too close to this, to him," he said matter-of-factly.

"But—"

"You know I'm right, Ellie. I can't let you compromise the case."

Not when McClain already has.

"Please, Derrick…"

"If he intended to tell you something, don't you think he already would have?"

She released a wary sigh. "All right. But I want to watch the interview."

He conceded to that, and she slipped into the monitor room to view his conversation with McClain.

Derrick ducked into the interrogation room where he'd left the ranger. McClain looked stony faced, his posture on edge as he stared at the table. Derrick claimed the chair on the opposite side and folded his arms. "You ready to talk?"

"I don't have an answer for you."

Derrick's temper flared. "You realize your silence cost us valuable time in hunting the maniac killing these girls?"

Regret flickered in Cord's pensive brown eyes. "That wasn't my intention. I've been trying to find the killer. And if you let me go, I'll comb every inch of No Man's Land to find that girl Carrie Ann."

"First tell me how your prints got on the shovel where Earl Bramble's remains were found."

"I didn't kill him, if that's what you want to know."

"Then who did?"

Cord pulled a hand down his chin. "That I can't tell you."

Suddenly the door opened and Ellie stormed in. She crossed the room, planted her hands on the table and stared McClain in the eyes. "Can't or won't, Cord?"

He closed his eyes for a brief second, then looked up at her with a contrite expression. "I'm sorry, Ellie. I wish I could help but I can't."

"Why are you being so damn obstinate?" Ellie snapped. "Do you want to go to jail?"

Anguish darkened his eyes. "That's the last thing I want."

"Then explain about your prints. Did you know Earl Bramble? Were you with him the night he died?"

ONE HUNDRED SEVENTEEN

Ellie barely resisted grabbing Cord by the shoulders and shaking the truth out of him. But she reined in her emotions and decided not to go there. She loved the infuriating man. "Then trust me," she said softly.

"Ellie, we talked about this. You don't need to be in here." Derrick turned to Cord. "Are you going to jeopardize her reputation to protect yourself?"

A thick silence filled the room, and the truth dawned on Ellie. "You aren't protecting yourself, are you, Cord? You're covering for someone else, aren't you?"

His only reaction was to avert his eyes.

Ellie's phone dinged and she checked her phone. "It's the lab." Her pulse jumped and she connected. "Detective Reeves."

"It's Williams. I thought you'd want to know the results ASAP."

"Definitely. Another girl is missing." She massaged her temple where a headache pulsed.

"Dr. Whitefeather identified the body we found as Earl Bramble."

"I know. Agent Fox already told me that. Were his prints on any of the items or in the house at the farm?"

"No. But we have the results on the DNA and prints from the scarves and truck. A male's."

"Hayden or Edward Higgins? Or Clint Wallace's?"

"No."

He'd said a male. Who could he be talking about? "Spit it out, Lieutenant."

"Someone close to the Bramble women. Someone who also worked at the graveyard when he was a teenager and attended school with Ruth Higgins."

"Clint and Hayden were the only teenagers considered as suspects. Was it one of their friends?"

"I don't know if they were friends, but the prints we found belong to Joe Jones."

Ellie swallowed hard. "Oh, my God, that's Ida's husband." When she'd met him, he'd seemed worried about the safety of his daughter. He'd also been living in Brambletown for years. And no one ever suspected him.

Did he have Carrie Ann now?

She thanked him and hung up. "Derrick, we have to go."

"What's happened?"

"I'll explain in the car." She pocketed her phone and pulled her keys. "I'll drive."

Cord's chair rattled as he shifted. "Uncuff me and let me help."

"Only if you're ready to talk, McClain," Derrick said.

Ellie gave him an imploring look. Why in the world would he cover for Joe Jones? Had he known him as a teen? Did he owe him something? "Cord?"

His heavy sigh answered her question. He wasn't going to talk.

Heart hammering, she turned and walked out the door.

Now they knew who to look for. If Carrie Ann was still alive, maybe they could save her.

ONE HUNDRED EIGHTEEN

Briar Ridge Mobile Homes

Kat had cried her heart out all morning.

Carrie Ann had been her best friend since they were five. She didn't want to lose her, especially to some monster.

The police hadn't said exactly what he was doing to the girls he took and killed. But her imagination had gone wild. She never should have left her friend alone in the woods. That was so stupid and selfish.

But she'd been obsessed with her mama's journal.

She paced her bedroom then stared out the window, swiping at more tears that seemed to fall like rain. Gray clouds filled the sky, blocking out the midday sun. Thunder rumbled in the distance and lightning zigzagged across the treetops.

Fear clawing at her, she thought about the journal again. Maybe there was something in there about what happened to her granddaddy. Something to tell her where he might be or where he might have taken Carrie Ann if he had her.

She blew her nose on a tissue, returned to her bed and opened up her mother's laptop, then scanned the entries. She vaguely knew the date her grandaddy was supposed to have run off.

She scrolled the entries in between the time Ruth disappeared and he left and found an entry that made the hair on the back of her neck stand on end.

Daddy's been so awful that me and Hetty hide from him. He used to just take out his anger on her but ever since that bitchy Ruth disappeared, he's flipped a switch and takes his rage out on me, too. At night, he tears through the house roaring like a lion. Yesterday he threw the supper dishes against the wall and broke them and the hamburger stroganoff I made splattered all over the walls. Then he made me scrub it clean with bleach. I thought I was going to pass out from the smell and my fingers are raw.

He's been diving into the brown whiskey morning, noon and night and twice me and Hetty woke up and he was standing in our room like a zombie, one time with a butcher knife in his hand and the last time with a shovel.

Hetty was so scared she wet herself. I was terrified too and my legs fell beneath me when I tried to get up and run. Daddy screamed at us both, then grabbed Hetty by the hair and dragged her outside. She was screaming and he slapped her, and I wanted to call the police, but Daddy told me I better stay inside or he'd put me in one of the pine boxes he'd been building and he'd leave me there forever.

I hate the dark. And I hate closed in places like elevators, small rooms, caves and the mines all over the mountains. Even when Hetty and I played in the graveyard and she'd climb in one and hide, I couldn't go in after her. I pictured myself lying there in the hole with the dirt being poured over me, filling my eyes and mouth and nose.

Panic sent me into such a doggone stir that for a minute I thought I was having a heart attack, but fear for Hetty finally overcame the panic, and I managed to crawl from bed and leave the room. I knew if he caught me I'd get it. But when I stepped outside, Hetty's screams echoed from the woods, and I saw where he was taking her.

No Man's Land. That's what the locals called it because no man could survive there.

Poor scrawny Hetty sure couldn't.

I saw the track marks her feet were leaving as he dragged her, and my temper exploded and I screamed at him to stop. It felt like evil burning inside me, but I had to save Hetty.

She was my cousin. She was my best friend, too. And if he killed her, I'd be left alone with that monster.

Digging my heels in at all the times he'd been mean to me and Hetty, I remembered Daddy's shed and ran toward it. Inside, he kept gardening and woodworking tools. Machines for the digging process were becoming all the rage, but he still liked to get his hands in the dirt.

My stomach heaved. Then I wrapped my hand around the shovel handle, swung it over my shoulder and chased after Daddy.

Ellie parked at Ida's trailer, surveying the property. Ida's car was in the drive but it was the only one. On the drive, Derrick had researched Joe and learned he drove a delivery truck for a discount store called Ten Below, giving him ease in moving from one city to the next. He had deliveries in the towns where Jacey and Bonnie lived.

"No truck here," Derrick said. "I'll call the company and find out his schedule while you talk to Ida."

Things had been on edge between her and Derrick ever since he'd barged into her home and dragged Cord in for questioning.

Although she had to admit, she couldn't blame him for doing his job. Damn Cord for shutting down. He had to be protecting someone. That was the only explanation that made sense to her.

But who? Joe? It didn't make sense. Unless Cord knew him from the foster system. "Did Joe grow up in foster care?" Ellie asked.

Derrick consulted his tablet. "Looks like he lost his mother when he was twelve and moved in with his grandmother in Brambletown. But he did spend a few months in the system while she petitioned for custody."

Dammit, Cord could have met him during that time. But Cord wasn't some narcissistic jerk who didn't care about others. He was especially protective of children and women. Just as he had been with her.

Still, even if he had some misguided loyalty toward Joe, she couldn't imagine Cord covering for a predator who targeted teenage girls.

"Ellie?" Derrick said.

She jerked her mind back to reality. She'd deal with Cord later. Right now, she had a girl to save.

Focus on that.

"Yeah, I'm going in." She opened the Jeep door, braced herself for whatever she found—did Ida know her father was dead? That Joe's prints were on the scarves and shoes connected to the dead girls?

That her husband might actually be a killer.

All along they'd wondered if she'd covered for her father. What if she'd covered for her boyfriend back then? And her husband now?

She didn't want to believe it. Ida had a teenage daughter. Would she really keep quiet if she knew her own husband was targeting other teens? Especially Kat's friend?

Or could Ida be blind to it all?

Ellie inhaled a sharp breath and walked to the door while Derrick called the trucking company. With a heavy fist, she knocked. Inside, a tea kettle whistled. A light flickered on in the kitchen. Feet shuffled.

By the time the door squeaked open, Derrick appeared behind her. Ida stared at them, her eyes red rimmed, her face puffy as if she hadn't slept all night. Or she'd been upset.

"Ida, we need to talk."

Ida nodded as if she'd been expecting them. Maybe she did know about Joe. But if Ida had covered for him, she was complicit, too.

Ida waved them in and gestured to the kitchen table, then poured everyone a cup of hot tea and brought it to them. She set sugar and milk on the table. Ellie took sugar but Derrick shook his head in offering.

She swallowed a sip, then began. "Ida, we found your father's body last night. It looks like he's been dead for years, maybe since he supposedly left town."

Ida's spoon rattled in her tea cup as she stirred a mountain of sugar into it. She didn't speak, but her glazed eyes showed no surprise.

"Did you know he was dead?" Ellie asked softly.

Ida lowered her head face down into her hands on a moan.

Ellie gave her a moment to compose herself, then asked. "You were dating Joe back then, weren't you?"

Ida's eyes widened and she nodded, confusion clouding her face.

"Did Joe kill your father because your father murdered Ruth?"

"W... what? N... no."

Kat suddenly burst into the room. "It's not Daddy's fault," she cried. "Grandaddy abused Hetty and he dragged her into the woods and was going to kill her that night."

Ellie's gaze swung from Ida to Kat. "You mean Joe killed Earl because he abused Hetty?"

"No..." Kat whispered. "It wasn't—"

"Be quiet, Kat!" Ida yelled.

"But, Mama, the police will understand. You were protecting Hetty..."

Ida shot daggers with her eyes toward Kat. "How do you know about that, Kat?"

Fear wrenched Kat's face. "I found your journal, the one on your computer that you wrote back then."

Ellie's pulse quickened. She hadn't seen that coming. If it was true though, she'd need the computer for evidence. "You killed your father, Ida?"

She moaned as tears spilled over. "He was so awful to Hetty, and everyone was sure he killed Ruth and... I couldn't walk outside without some reporter taking my picture or asking questions and the kids at school were horrible." Her sob wrenched the air. "He was getting more and more violent, and Hetty and I would hide in our room to get away from him. When he grabbed Hetty by the hair that night and dragged her to one of the graves he'd dug, I knew he was going to kill her..." Her voice cracked. "I had to save her."

Kat inched toward her mother and curved her arm around her. "It's okay, Mama. It's okay. Now everyone will find out what a monster he was."

"Yes, the truth will come out," Ellie said. "But there's more, Ida. How was Joe involved that night?"

Ida shook her head. "He wasn't. He... didn't know what happened. I... never told him." She wiped at her tears. "He thought Daddy was guilty of killing Ruth and he was relieved Daddy was gone so the gossip could die down."

Ellie was beginning to see the picture. "Ida, we don't think your father killed Ruth."

Ida and Kat both gaped at her. "What? Of course he did," Ida said in a raw whisper.

Ellie shook her head. Ida's conviction sounded real.

"I'm sorry," Ellie said gently. "But we have evidence connecting your husband to the recent crimes and to Ruth."

The color drained from Ida's face, and she sank back in the chair as if she was folding in on herself. "That's ludicrous. Joe... why would he have killed Ruth?"

"His prints and DNA are on items we found that belonged

to the dead girls," Derrick cut in. "We even found the truck that was used to abduct Jacey Ward from Athens and the farm where he took the girls and hid out to escape being caught."

"I don't believe it," Ida gasped.

"No," Kat screeched. "My daddy wouldn't kill anyone. And he wouldn't take Carrie Ann. She's my best friend."

Either Ida and her daughter were in denial or they were oblivious to everything Joe had done.

"Where's your husband now?" Derrick asked.

Ida pressed her hands to the sides of her head, her eyes glazed with shock. "Work."

"He had a delivery," Kat said in a shaky voice.

"Do you know where he was supposed to go today?" Derrick asked.

Ida shook her head. "He delivers all over North Georgia, even in Tennessee."

His job had given him access to target girls in various cities where teenage girls had disappeared.

"We'll find him and get to the bottom of this." Ellie debated on whether to charge Ida. She'd basically confessed to murder. She also needed to bring Hetty in for a statement as well. Although, it sounded as if Ida and Hetty had a solid case for self-defense.

"You told the police you saw your father in the graveyard the night Ruth died," Ellie said. "You said he was wearing your father's hat and coat. Did you actually see his face?"

Ida chewed on her thumbnail.

"Ida?"

"N... no," she mumbled. "It was dark and I was so shocked and... I mean I thought it was him."

"Is it possible that Joe was wearing your father's coat and hat?"

Tears trickled down Ida's reddening cheeks. "M... maybe. But I... don't understand why Joe would kill Ruth."

"Maybe he was being protective of you," Ellie offered.

Ida shrugged. "Even if that was so, he's been overprotective of Kat, especially since those bodies were found. He ordered her not to go in the woods and repeatedly warned her it was dangerous."

Or perhaps he didn't want her to find him.

"Kat, please get the computer with that journal on it," Derrick said. "We need to take your mother to the station and record her statement."

"I'll send Deputy Eastman to pick up Hetty," Ellie said. "She's worked with domestic violence victims before."

"Ida, do you know where Joe is now?" Ellie asked.

"Like Kat said, he went on a delivery last night. He should be home sometime tonight."

"I called the trucking company and left a message," Derrick said. "Hopefully they'll call me back with his location."

"I'll call an ERT to come here," Ellie said.

Derrick gave a nod. "I'll search the grounds in case Carrie Ann is somewhere on the property."

Kat clutched her stomach as if she might be sick, and Ida choked back a protest of denial. Ellie bit down on her lower lip. Normally she'd call Cord to lead the search but considering his questionable involvement in the case, she couldn't include him.

Ellie gestured to Ida's daughter. "Kat, you need to come with me and your mother."

"You can't arrest my daughter," Ida snapped. "She's just a child. And she had nothing to do with any of this."

"I realize that," Ellie said. "And I'm not arresting anyone at the moment. It's for your protection, Kat. If Joe decides to come home, neither of you should be here."

Ida choked back more tears and Kat's chin quivered.

Derrick gestured to Kat. "Please retrieve that computer."

Ida gestured for her daughter to do as Ellie asked and Kat

rushed from the room. She returned a few minutes later, looking contrite at Ida's disapproving look.

As the three of them walked to the car, Ellie thought about Cord's reaction to her questions. His denial of killing Earl but his refusal to offer information.

He wasn't protecting Joe. He was protecting Ida and Hetty Bramble.

"Please let me call Hetty and warn her that deputy is coming," Ida begged as she and Kat settled into the back of Ellie's Jeep. "She's gonna be scared to death."

Ellie slid into the driver's seat and locked the doors. "I'm sorry, Ida, but we can't do that," she said softly. For all she knew, Hetty would take off and run. "But you both have the right to an attorney, if that's what you want."

"You can't arrest Mama and Hetty," Kat cried in distress. "They acted in self-defense."

Ellie's heart squeezed for all of them. "We need Hetty's statement, and after we look at the journal, we'll discuss how to move forward." Considering the time lapse, their accounts of the night Earl died, and statements about Earl from locals, she had a feeling the prosecutor wouldn't press charges. But she couldn't promise anything yet.

Kat slid her arm around her mother and hugged her. "It's okay, Mama. Everything's gonna be all right."

Except nothing was all right.

They needed to find Joe. If he hadn't killed Carrie Ann, maybe they could save her.

Then the cloud of suspicion and gossip would start all over again for Ida and her daughter. For years people had wondered if Ida and Hetty had covered for their father.

Now they would question if Ida had covered for Joe.

Even if she denied it, people would wonder how she could possibly be unaware she was living with a serial killer.

ONE HUNDRED TWENTY-ONE

Briar Ridge Mobile Homes

While he waited on the ERT, Derrick conducted an initial sweep of the property in case Joe was somewhere on the premises or he'd left Carrie Ann's body on the land.

Woods backed the trailer park and would require manpower, but he found one tool shed out back housing tools but another locked tool shed nestled between some trees and broke the lock. As soon as he opened the door, his gut tightened. A brown leather sofa sat along one wall facing what he guessed to be a fifty-four-inch TV.

The wall to the left was covered in pictures of teenage girls. Derrick pulled on latex gloves and walked over to the shelf beside the TV where CDs were stacked by an old CD player. He ground his teeth as he read the titles—all teenage porn and S&M.

Sick bastard. Although looking at these made Derrick question why Joe hadn't committed sexual assault on his victims.

His brain rattled off answers. Perhaps he was impotent. Or

the only way he could get off was porn and that may have stopped working, so he graduated to strangulation. Predators often experienced release by committing violence.

He saw a closed storage closet and opened it. Instead of photographs of teenage girls, this one held pictures of a grown woman, half naked, wearing a pair of red stilettos.

That woman must have been someone he'd known. Maybe his mother? Or a hooker who'd first taught him about sex? Or a woman who'd possibly abused him?

A car engine rumbled from the driveway, and he stepped outside and saw the ERT van parking. He rushed to fill them in and they divided up, one agent going inside to search while two went into the woods and another began processing the shed.

Derrick returned to the front steps of the mobile home, then called Ten Below again and got through this time so he asked to speak to the manager.

"This is Special Agent Derrick Fox," he said. "I'm looking for one of your employees Joe Jones. I was told he was on a delivery last night."

"That's odd," Joe's boss said. "Joe wasn't on the schedule yesterday or today. And he hasn't called in. In fact, he hasn't returned the delivery truck he drives."

"So he still has the truck?" Derrick asked.

"He must, which is against the rules. When he does get back, I intend to fire him."

"Can you trace the location of his truck?" Derrick asked.

"Yeah, hold on."

A minute later, the manager returned and gave him the address for a house on Bush Road. "Thank you for the information. If he checks in, please call me on this number. And don't tell him that I was asking about him."

"What's going on, Special Agent Fox?"

"I'm not at liberty to say, but I will warn you that he might be dangerous so like I said, don't let on that I'm looking for him."

"All right."

Derrick ended the call. If Joe was at the address his manager had given him, they might have a chance to save Carrie Ann.

ONE HUNDRED TWENTY-TWO

Ellie left a nervous Ida and Kat at the station with Deputy Landrum to record their statements. Deputy Eastwood was on her way to the station with Hetty who would be held in a separate interrogation room from Ida to prevent the women from comparing stories. She sympathized with them, but she had to run this investigation by the book.

Everyone had kept too many secrets. Including Cord.

Dammit. Disappointment mingled with worry.

She had to have a conversation with him when they returned. Then they'd talk to the DA and decide if charges should be brought against Ida and Hetty and Cord for obstruction of justice.

But first they needed to find Joe. Carrie Ann's life depended on it.

Derrick had called with a lead, so she drove back to Ida's to pick him up. He quickly filled her in on what he'd found in Joe's shed. The idea of Joe watching teen porn made her stomach sour.

"Do you believe Ida?" Derrick asked as Ellie pulled to a stop, and he climbed in her Jeep.

Ellie nodded. "Two teenage girls living with an abusive Earl? Yeah. Everyone in town believed Earl was guilty which supports their story about his violent behavior." She imagined the girls hiding in their rooms out of fear, and compassion swelled inside her. If Cord had known the Bramble girls were being abused or had seen what happened, obviously his protective side had emerged and he'd kept silent to protect them, thinking the Bramble girls had been through enough. That Earl's death meant they had a chance at life.

"What do you want to do about McClain?" Derrick asked, his tone deep.

Ellie cut her eyes toward him. She was still pissed at the way he'd handled the situation. "I don't know yet. But you should have come to me first."

His jaw hardened. "I was just doing my job and following the leads."

Was that all it had been? He and Cord had butted heads in the beginning, but during the cases they'd worked, they'd settled into a cordial relationship and developed mutual respect. Things might have been turned on their heads now. Time would tell.

Thunder rumbled and dark clouds cast eerie shadows across the sharp peaks and ridges of the mountain. Ellie turned onto a narrow winding road that looked as if it went nowhere. Overgrown bushes choked the shoulder of the road, and the graveled surface was pocked with potholes.

"I see why he'd choose this area," Derrick said.

"Off the grid."

Derrick glanced up from his tablet where he'd been researching Joe's background. "It looks like Joe and his mother lived here before they moved to that farm." He rubbed a hand across his beard stubble. "She was definitely the woman in those photos I saw, the one dressed like a hooker and wearing red stilettos."

"Where is she now?"

"According to this, she abandoned him when he was twelve. DFACS found him alone at the house after a teacher reported his absence from school for seven days. They sent him to live with a grandmother who lived in Brambletown. She died when he was seventeen and by then, he'd aged out of the system. At fourteen, he started helping out at the cemetery doing lawn maintenance."

Gravel spewed from her tires as the Jeep chugged up the unpaved road. Around a bend, she spotted a long driveway flanked with pines and more bushes and barreled up it hoping they weren't too late for Carrie Ann.

ONE HUNDRED TWENTY-THREE

Bush Road

Memories of this godawful house bombarded him as he dragged Carrie Ann from the back of the truck. Her eyes were practically swollen shut from crying and her fingers looked raw and had been bleeding from clawing at the sides of the truck.

"It'll be over soon," he murmured as he yanked her hair and threw her over his shoulder.

She kicked and beat at him with her bound hands and feet, but he simply laughed. She was a scrawny girl although she and Kat wolfed down fries like they hadn't eaten in months. It showed on Kat just like it did Ida, but either Carrie Ann had good genes or she was one of those teenagers who puked after a meal just to look like a twig.

As he walked past the rotting house, he was swept back in time. He could hear the floor squeaking inside as his mother's friends showed up. Could see the closet where he'd been locked and the light that had burned out overhead, pitching him in darkness for hours while he listened to his mother and her lover bang the walls with the bed or the table as he ground inside her.

Carrie Ann whimpered through the gag, but she could cry and scream for all he cared. No one was close enough to hear her. Just like no one knew he'd spent the worst years of his life on this land.

Where he'd actually killed his first victim. Where he'd brought his second.

A noise sounded in the distance. He froze. Carrie Ann slugged him in the middle of the back and that pissed him off. The noise again... A car motor... gravel slinging.

Shit. Someone was coming. Who the hell?

He shuffled toward the shed out back, opened the door and started to toss Carrie Ann inside. She cried out but he slapped her so hard her head lolled back, and she passed out. If the police had found him, the shed was one of the first places they'd look. Breath panting out, he hauled the girl into the woods. A mile in and he spotted the pond he'd fished in as a kid.

Scum floated on the top and sticks protruded from the water. Behind him, car doors slammed. Voices filtered through the woods.

"Police," the female detective shouted. "We know you're here, Jones, and you have Carrie Ann. Make it easy on yourself and put an end to this now."

He'd put an end to it. He wanted to slide the scarf around Carrie Ann's neck and watch her eyes bulge as she struggled to breathe.

But he didn't have time to take it slow.

The pond beckoned. Frogs chirped. A water moccasin slithered across the surface. The murky stench of pond scum wafted in the air.

He crossed to the pond and tossed the girl inside. Bound, gagged and unconscious, she began to sink below the dirty water.

Dammit, he'd forgotten to take her shoe. Those glorious red boots. He couldn't leave without one.

He dragged her by one foot and yanked off the boot, then made a run for it through the woods while her body slipped below the water. His mother's old car remained hidden in the woods where he'd covered it with brush.

He'd been hiding out along the trail for years now. He knew where he'd go to lie low until he could get away.

Ida's and Kat's faces taunted him. Ida hadn't been his first choice. He'd only married her because she'd gotten knocked up.

It was the other girl Ruth he'd wanted. Not only had she turned him down, but she'd laughed at him. Laughed for fuck's sake.

She'd paid for that. He'd had to kill her.

ONE HUNDRED TWENTY-FOUR

Guns drawn, Ellie darted through the woods while Derrick charged toward the house in case Joe stashed Carrie Ann's body inside.

Please let her be alive.

A boom of thunder startled her, and lightning flashed in the distance. Ahead she heard water lapping at the bank and veered toward the sound, searching the brush as she ran. Around trees and through thick foliage, over puddles then the swampy odor of stagnant water.

There it was. A pond.

"Joe, give it up!" she shouted. "Save Carrie Ann and it'll look better for you!"

Even as she said it, she darted to the edge of the pond, searching for a floating body. "Carrie Ann!"

Somewhere in the distance, tree limbs snapped in the blustery wind, but she had a bad feeling the girl was drowning in that murky water. Yanking a flashlight from her pocket, she shined it across the pond then the embankment. Footprints. Large. A man's boots.

Derrick's voice bounced through the trees then he was a few feet away. "House and shed are clear."

"I think he dumped her in the pond. He's headed north. Go after him!"

Derrick ran past her, and she laid her gun behind a boulder, draped her jacket over it, removed her boots then dove into the pond.

ONE HUNDRED TWENTY-FIVE

This bastard was not going to get away.

Derrick wouldn't stop until he obtained a list of all his victims and where they were buried.

The families deserved that closure. He'd given it to his own mother, and he'd do the same for these teenagers' families.

Derrick spotted a dark figure ahead a few hundred feet as he climbed a hill and he picked up his pace. Since his back injury he hadn't been able to lift weights or run like he had before, but he was healing now, and no way did he intend to lose the chase to a short man with a paunch who probably downed a six pack or a fifth of liquor a night.

A wild animal howled, and forest creatures roamed the woods, the sound of feral cats whining into the night. He raced around a boulder and through patchy brush then a gunshot boomeranged and a bullet whizzed by his head. He ducked and dashed behind a tree, then scanned the area where it had come from.

Joe peered around the tree, his shotgun raised and fired again. Derrick gripped his weapon and released a bullet. Using a tree as cover, Joe managed to dodge it and they exchanged another round. Derrick threw a stick to the left as a distraction and Joe shot at it. Another rock to the opposite side, biding his time until Joe ran out of bullets. When he paused to reload, Derrick made his move.

Stealthy as a cat in the dark, he maneuvered his way toward Joe until he could circle around and sneak up behind him. The wind picked up, rustling the trees. The cat's whine turned into a full-fledged cat fight. Teeth gritted, Derrick inched up behind him and pressed the barrel of his Glock to the back of Joe's head.

"Drop it," Derrick ordered.

Joe went still, then had the nerve to quickly pivot as if to fight Derrick. Big mistake.

The faces of the dead girls flashed behind Derrick's eyes, and his finger tightened on the trigger. But reason and training kicked in. He wanted answers, names and locations more than he wanted to see the man's blood spill over.

"I said drop it, Joe. It's over."

Joe had the gall to laugh.

Derrick gave him a sardonic smile. "You won't be laughing when you're some man's bitch in prison."

Anger radiated in Joe's growl, but Derrick didn't give him time to react or escape. He knocked the shotgun from Joe's hand, then kicked it into the brush, jerked the bastard's arms behind his back and cuffed him.

Joe cursed and Derrick shoved him forward through the woods. By the time they reached the pond, Ellie was dragging Carrie Ann out.

Derrick watched as she hauled the girl to the ground and started CPR.

"Come on, Carrie Ann," Ellie pleaded. "Breathe for me."

Joe stood stoic, a tiny smile tugging at his mouth as if he thought she was already dead.

Ellie did compressions, counting and talking to the girl.

"Your parents want to see you and so does Kat," Ellie said softly. "You need to come back to them."

Seconds later, the girl coughed then spit water, choking on it. Ellie quickly tilted the girl's head to the side and patted her back to help her purge the pond scum. Carrie Ann's eyes flew open and she gasped, disoriented, but Ellie cradled her in her arms and rocked her. "You're okay, sweetie. You're okay now. I've got you."

Relief filled Derrick and he shoved Joe to a rock, kept his gun aimed on him and called 9-1-1.

ONE HUNDRED TWENTY-SIX

Ellie and Derrick left the ERT to search and process the house where Joe had held Carrie Ann and rescue and recovery teams combed the woods beyond for other bodies.

Derrick took Ellie's Jeep to drive Joe to the police station and she rode in the ambulance with a shaken and traumatized Carrie Ann. "You're going to be okay, honey," Ellie assured her. "I know you're scared but I'm calling your mom to meet you at the hospital."

Tears rolled down Carrie Ann's cheeks as the medic started an IV to help with dehydration. Ellie called Mrs. Parker's number.

"Hello," the woman answered in a frightened voice.

"Mrs. Parker, this is Detective Reeves calling about your daughter."

A heartbeat passed, and Ellie heard the woman's breathing grow loud and raspy. "Did you find her? Is she okay?"

"We did find her and she's shaken and scared but alive. I'm

in the ambulance with her and we're on the way to the hospital now."

"Thank God," she cried. "What happened?"

Ellie didn't want to go into details with Carrie Ann listening. "We apprehended the man who abducted her and he's on the way to the police station for booking now. I'll fill you in on everything later. But Carrie Ann is safe now, and the man will go to prison."

A choked sound echoed over the line. "Can I talk to my little girl?"

Ellie glanced at Carrie Ann who was trembling beneath the blanket. "Your mom wants to speak to you."

Carrie Ann nodded and reached for the phone. "Mom?" she whispered.

"Oh, my God, sweetie, I've been so worried about you. Are you okay?"

"I'm s... sorry, Mom..."

Another tense second passed and the woman gulped. "Shh... It's okay, sweetie, as long as you're all right. I'll meet you at the hospital."

Carrie Ann began to sob, and Ellie heard her mother do the same.

"I'll be there as soon as I can," Mrs. Parker cried. "Hang in there, sweetie. I'll see you soon."

Mrs. Parker ended the call and Carrie Ann handed the phone to Ellie. Then the girl turned on her side and curled into a ball, her body shaking with tears. Ellie patted her back and soothed her, her heart aching for the girl. But relief also filled her.

They had saved her. And Joe was on his way to the police station.

The siren squealed into the night as they raced around the mountain. They careened around a curve, then stopped at a traffic light, sped up and minutes later veered into the hospital ER entrance.

The medic opened the ambulance door, and the EMT joined him at the rear as they moved Carrie Ann from the ambulance. A nurse met them as they wheeled her in.

"Don't leave," Carrie Ann screeched to Ellie.

"I won't, honey. I'll stay with you until your mom gets here." Ellie hurried along beside her and held her hand as they rolled her into the ER waiting room, then through a set of double doors to an exam room. Ellie explained to the doctor about the abduction and attempted murder and asked for a psychologist to evaluate Carrie Ann.

Just as they were about to take Kat for a CAT scan and lung X-ray, her mother raced into the room, teary-eyed and terrified.

"Mom," Carried Ann cried. "Mom!"

Her mother hurried to her, pulled her into her arms and the two sobbed together as Mrs. Parker rocked her daughter and comforted her.

Ellie slipped out of the room and left them together with the medical staff to take care of them.

She had to tie up this case and make sure Joe Jones never saw the light of day again.

ONE HUNDRED TWENTY-SEVEN

Crooked Creek Police Station

When Ellie arrived at the police station. Derrick had booked Joe who'd clammed up, then Derrick put him into a holding cell.

"I'll collect all the evidence we have against him and we'll confront him together," Derrick told Ellie.

"While you do that, I'll interview Hetty."

They agreed and she found Hetty in the second interrogation room.

Sweat drenched Hetty's hair and clothes and she paced the room, wringing her hands together. When she saw Ellie, Hetty froze and her pale face turned a sickly yellow.

"Am I under arrest?" Hetty asked. "Because if I am, I want a lawyer."

"You're not under arrest," Ellie said. "But please sit down, Hetty. We need to talk."

Hetty sighed wearily, dark circles beneath her sunken eyes. Ellie imagined her as the young girl suffering from Earl Bramble's abuse, and sympathy filled her. Hetty had lived in fear during her younger years, and if Ida's story was true, they'd both lived in fear the past fifteen years, keeping their secret and terrified of going to prison.

"Can I see Ida?" Hetty asked.

"Once I take your statement, we'll see about that."

Hetty's lips pressed into a tight line. "What did she tell you?"

"I'm not at liberty to disclose that at the moment," Ellie said, striving to handle the interview by the book. "We found Earl Bramble's body," Ellie said.

Hetty squeezed her eyes closed for a moment and began to tremble. When she finally looked at Ellie, her shoulders sagged in defeat. "And she told you what happened?"

"Her version," Ellie said. "I need to know yours."

Panic flashed on Hetty's face, then resignation. "I guess the truth had to come out some time."

"It usually does," Ellie said softly. "Sometimes it's a relief to unburden yourself."

"I don't want Ida to be in trouble," Hetty said. "She was protecting me."

"Protecting you from what? Or whom?" Ellie asked.

"Her daddy," Hetty admitted. "Everyone thought he was doing me a favor by taking me in, b... but he wanted my father's money, and he..."

"He what?" Ellie asked, treading gently.

"He used to hit me," Hetty spit out. "That and make me work in the graveyard half the night and get up at dawn and help him again and if I complained he'd... beat me."

"Why didn't you tell someone?" Ellie asked.

Hetty heaved a labored breath. "Because he said if I did, he'll start up on Ida."

Anger for Ida and Hetty burned Ellie's throat. "So you were protecting each other?"'

Hetty emitted a little cry of distress then nodded. "She was all I had."

Ellie wanted to pull her into a hug. "I'm sorry that happened to you," she said. "But there's more," Ellie said, needing to see Hetty's reaction. "We have evidence that Ida's husband, Joe, killed Ruth Higgins and the other victims we've found dead in Brambletown."

Shock widened Hetty's eyes. "What are you talking about? Joe a killer?" She dabbed sweat from her forehead with her fingers. "That can't be so."

"It is," Ellie said. "Do you think Ida knew he murdered Ruth?"

Hetty shook her head no. "Oh, God, no. We both thought her daddy killed Ruth. And if Ida knew about Joe, she would have gotten Kat away from him."

Ellie studied her for a moment. Hetty's reaction seemed sincere. "Go on. About the reason you didn't tell on Earl?"

"We thought he was a murderer and got what he deserved. That with him gone, we'd all be safe."

With all Ellie knew about Earl Bramble, and the fact that he'd abused Hetty, their rationale made sense.

"But when other girls started showing up dead, you knew Earl couldn't have done it," Ellie said. "Why didn't you come forward then?"

Guilt streaked Hetty's eyes and her lower lip quivered. "We were afraid," she said in a ragged whisper.

Ellie gave a nod of acceptance. Ida and Hetty were minors when Earl died and living in terror. She understood their fear. But it angered her that folks in town didn't recognize the abuse or if they had, they'd turned a blind eye. Someone should have protected them.

"I'll be right back." She left the room and returned with a notepad and pen. "Hetty, I believe you, but I need you to write down everything that happened. The more details you offer the better, especially details of your abuse."

"Are we going to jail?" Hetty asked.

Not if she could help it. "You were both minors. And you were abused and acted in self-defense," she said gently. "I'll explain that to the DA and do my best to convince him not to press charges."

Hetty shifted nervously but picked up the pen and began to write.

ONE HUNDRED TWENTY-EIGHT

Ellie knew Ida was fretting and Kat was worried sick about her friend, so she joined them to offer an update.

Ida still looked shell-shocked from the accusations against Joe and Kat was biting her nails down to the quick like her mother did.

They both looked up at her with expectant but nervous expressions, then Kat clung to Ida's hand. Or was it the other way around?

Ellie decided to be direct. "We found Carrie Ann and she's shaken but alive."

Kat released a relieved cry and Ida nodded, emotions coloring her face.

"Where is she?" Kat asked.

"At the hospital with her mother. She's bruised and traumatized, but the doctors are taking good care of her and she should recover. Although she probably will need some counseling."

Kat's face crumpled.

"And?" Ida choked out. "Was it... Joe?"

Ellie gave her a sympathetic look. "I'm sorry, Ida, Kat. But yes, it was. We apprehended him at the scene where he had dumped Carrie Ann in a pond. He's in custody now here at the station and being booked on multiple accounts of homicide."

"This can't be happening," Ida said in an anguished voice. "How could I have lived under the same roof with him and not realized he was that sick and dangerous?"

"My daddy…" Kat sobbed. "I can't believe he tried to kill my best friend."

"I understand this is shocking," Ellie said. "But we have irrefutable evidence against him and caught him red-handed with Carrie Ann."

"Can I see him?" Ida asked.

Ellie shook her head no. "I'm sorry, but not now. We still have to interrogate him. And right now we're busy collecting evidence."

"I don't want to see him," Kat said shrilly. "Not ever again."

Ellie understood the girl's anger. She and Ida had a hard road ahead of them.

Kat glanced at Ida. "What's gonna happen to my mom?"

Ellie offered her a tentative smile. "I spoke to Hetty and she's writing down a detailed account of what happened with the abuse and the night Earl died. I can't promise for certain, but considering you were both minors, Ida, and the abuse. I don't think the DA will press charges."

Ida slumped in relief and Kat pulled her mother into her arms. "Don't worry, Mama, we're going to be okay."

Ida pushed her tangled damp hair from her wet cheeks then lifted her chin, and cupped Kat's face with her hands. "We will," she said firmly. "But I'm not gonna let you suffer like I did the last decade and a half. When I'm clear, we're packing our bags and leaving this town for good. We'll find a small place somewhere and start over."

A smile tilted Kat's lips. "I'd like that, Mama."

"I love you, girl," Ida whispered.

"I love you, too," Kat said brokenly.

Ellie smiled and left them hugging each other, then went to collect Hetty's statement and call the DA's office.

Ida and Hetty and Kat had been through enough. She didn't want them to suffer a minute longer.

ONE HUNDRED TWENTY-NINE

Ellie's phone call to the DA went exactly as she'd hoped. He would not press charges against Ida and Hetty and was happy they'd solved the teenage murder cases.

She hurried and told Ida, Kat and Hetty and they had a tearful reunion.

"I want to see Carrie Ann," Kat said. "I have to, Mama."

"Just be warned, Kat, that she and her mother may not take it well," Ida said.

Kat nodded. "I know. But it's the right thing to do."

Ida agreed, and Ellie arranged for Deputy Landrum to drive them to Ida's to retrieve her car and take Hetty home as well.

Then she went to meet with Derrick. He stood, raking photographs and notes into a stack and said, "ERT found two bodies on the premises of the house where Joe grew up. Laney already identified them as Ruth Higgins and Joe's mother."

Ellie's stomach clenched. She wasn't surprised but dreaded telling Tilly.

"Let's interrogate that animal," Derrick said. "We can use the evidence to pressure him into telling us where the other victims are."

"Hopefully that will work," Ellie said. "Then we can put this one to rest. But we have to tell Tilly."

Derrick's jaw tightened. "I'll handle that. I know you have to deal with McClain."

His words sucked the wind from her, but he was right.

She walked to the third interrogation room while Derrick retrieved Joe from the holding cell. He looked rough around the edges, pissed, and smelled like sweat and dirt.

Joe grunted as Derrick pushed him into a chair and hand-cuffed him to the metal table in the middle of the room. Ellie seated herself opposite him while Derrick stood, towering over the short squatty man.

"We have you dead to rights," Derrick said matter-of-factly. "So don't bother to deny anything. We caught you red-handed after dumping Carrie Ann Parker in that pond."

Joe's chubby cheeks reddened, and he stretched out his legs as if to indicate he wasn't worried.

Fool. He damned well should be worried.

"We also have collected numerous pieces of evidence with your DNA and prints which puts you at the murder sites and chronicled your delivery schedule to locations where other victims were abducted."

"Joe," Ellie interjected. "We also have the scarves you used to strangle your victims and the shoes you collected."

Derrick spread photographs of the items across the table.

"In addition, your fingerprints and DNA were all over the closet where your mother locked you as a child." Derrick leaned forward. "That would have been when you were forced to watch her entertain her johns, wasn't it?"

He added photos of the closet and the lab results in front of Joe, then a photo of Joe's mother. Joe squirmed and averted his eyes but a myriad of emotions streaked his face.

"We also found your mother's body and Ruth Higgins' remains on your property."

Joe groaned as his gaze moved from his mother's picture to Ruth's. "I loved Ruth," he admitted. "But she wouldn't have anything to do with me."

His gaze traveled to the shoes they believed belonged to his mother.

And Ellie knew they had him.

The son of a bitch's face twisted into a smile. "They all got what they deserved just like she did."

"Then you admit to killing your mother and Ruth and the other girls we recovered," Derrick said between gritted teeth.

Joe traced his finger over the photograph of his mother's red stilettos. "That bitch was a monster."

And she'd raised another one, Ellie thought.

"What we need is for you to tell us who these other shoes belonged to," Derrick said as he tapped the photos of the shoes they'd yet to identify.

Joe clenched his beefy hands on the table, the handcuffs rattling. "What's in it for me?"

Derrick and Ellie exchanged a conspiratorial look, then Derrick responded. "We'll see if we can take the death penalty off the table."

Joe stared at the blunt ends of his dirty fingernails, then smiled when he looked up as if he was in control. "All right."

Derrick shoved a pen and pad in front of him. "We also want names, locations or drawings of where their bodies are buried, and for you to match each one with one of these shoes from your collection."

Joe bared his teeth in another evil smile then picked up the pen and got to work.

ONE HUNDRED THIRTY

Kat and Ida received a hostile welcome from Carrie Ann's mother.

"Did you know your husband was a killer?" Mrs. Parker asked.

Ida shook her head. "Of course not. If I had, I would have stopped him. And I sure as hell would have gotten my own daughter away from him. Besides, Kat loves your daughter and I wouldn't let him hurt her either."

"I do love her," Kat said, tears streaming down her cheeks.

"But you left her alone in those woods," Mrs. Parker snapped.

Kat bit her lower lip. "I know and I'm sorry. I'm so... sorry. I thought she went home." Kat scrubbed her face with her hands to dry the tears. "I can't believe my daddy did this."

For a brief second Carrie Ann's mother softened.

"Please, can I see her?" Kat said. "I have to tell her I didn't know. I never would have left her or let my daddy hurt her. I swear."

Ida spoke up. "Please, Phyllis, you can hate me if you want, but Kat is a kid and she and Carrie Ann have been friends since kindergarten. She's hurting, too."

Mrs. Parker wiped tears from her eyes then gave a reluctant nod. "Just don't upset her any more. She's been through enough."

Kat nodded, gulping back more tears. "I promise. I just have to tell her I'm sorry and say goodbye."

Mrs. Parker motioned to the nurse that it was okay, and Kat followed her through the doors to the ER exam room.

Mrs. Parker crossed her arms and faced Ida. "She's saying goodbye?"

Ida nodded. "We're leaving town as soon as we can pack up. I won't subject Kat to the same life I had growing up."

Carrie Ann's mother murmured that she understood. Then she pulled Ida into a hug.

ONE HUNDRED THIRTY-ONE

Kat hesitated at the doorway to the ER exam room, her heart aching as she saw Carrie Ann, bruised and pale lying in the bed looking shocked and scared.

Would Carrie Ann even want to see her? Did she hate her? Would she ever forgive her?

As if her friend knew she was there, she turned her head toward the door and their gazes met. Pain and fear darkened Carrie Ann's eyes, then she slowly reached out a shaky hand.

Kat choked back a sob and rushed toward her. "Oh, God, Carrie Ann, I had no idea. I'm so... sorry."

"I... kn... ow," Carrie Ann whispered. "Come here."

Kat fell into her best friend's arms, and time faded as if they were five years old again, eating popsicles, wading in the creek and catching fireflies in mayonnaise jars in their backyards.

ONE HUNDRED THIRTY-TWO

While Ellie arranged the press conference for the next day to inform the public they'd caught the teenager strangler and the young girls in Brambletown and across North Georgia were safe, Derrick drove to Tilly's. They'd decided to hold off releasing news to the public until the next day to give them time to locate Joe's other victims and inform their families. Sheriff Wallace had volunteered to visit the Higgins' family himself and relay the news, and Derrick and Ellie agreed.

Derrick didn't want Tilly to hear about Ruth on the news either. She deserved more than that.

He knocked on the door, and she answered, immediately inhaling a deep breath as if she knew he had bad news.

She gestured for him to come in and he followed her to the kitchen. "You have news about Ruth, don't you?"

"How did you know?"

"Just a feeling." He saw an open bottle of scotch and she poured two fingers into high ball glasses and handed him one. Then she led him to the living room where a fire crackled in the fireplace, the glow of the embers adding a warmth to the room that couldn't begin to erase the chill of his news.

She sank into the club chair by the fire and took a sip of her scotch. "You solved the case?"

"Yes," he said. "Detective Reeves is going to hold a press conference tomorrow. But I wanted you to hear the truth from me."

Pain wrenched her face. "Thank you, Agent Fox. I had a feeling you understood."

"I do." He sipped his own drink then sat beside her in the matching chair. "We found your sister's body."

A tiny moan escaped her. "Where? Did Earl Bramble do this?"

He shook his head then explained about Jones. Surprise flashed in her eyes, then resignation. "My God, Joe killed Ruth. Did Ida or Hetty know?"

"No, they were as shocked as you."

"Why would Joe kill Ruth?" Tilly asked with a puzzled frown.

"Apparently, he was traumatized when he was young by his mother. He also had a crush on Ruth and he said she wouldn't have anything to do with him."

Tilly stared into her drink. "She probably was harsh to him. But that doesn't seem like a reason to kill her or those other girls."

"Like I said, he was traumatized as a child. We'll have a psychiatrist evaluate him, but he may have had a psychotic break when he was younger." Derrick didn't want to share details at this point.

A shudder rippled through Tilly and Derrick wanted to pull her in his arms.

"Thank you for telling me. I need to call my brother and parents and let them know."

Her tormented gaze met his. "Under the circumstances, Sheriff Wallace offered to inform your parents."

"Thanks," she murmured. "I really don't want anything else to do with them."

"I figured," Derrick said. "And I'm sorry. Do you want me to tell your brother?"

She tossed back the rest of her drink. "No. Hayden and I made peace with each other. I'll talk to him. I owe him that much."

"Of course." He knew he should go, but didn't want to leave her yet. Not when she looked so vulnerable. "Why don't you call him, and I'll wait around if you want to talk."

A slow smile lifted her lips, and she squeezed his hand. "I'd like that, Agent Fox."

"It's Derrick," he murmured. "Please call me Derrick."

"All right, Derrick," she murmured with a tiny smile. "I'll be right back." She stood and walked to the kitchen, then he heard her talking to her brother. A minute later, she returned with the bottle of scotch.

"How is your brother?" Derrick asked.

She shrugged. "Sad, but relieved to finally know the truth."

"I understand."

"I guess you do." Tilly wiped at a tear. "It's hard to let go, but it's time."

Derrick nodded. "Closure does help. Eventually."

She refilled both their glasses. "I followed up with Emanuel Black and the governor on the toxin cleanup on the land by Green Gardens Cemetery," Tilly said, surprising him by changing the subject. "Looks like the protests and publicity lit a fire with the governor. He has a committee working on it. Their goal is to have it cleaned up and environmentally safe within a year."

"That's great news," Derrick said. "I've read some of your articles. You're an amazing writer."

She spread a blanket on the floor in front of the fire, sat down and patted the seat beside her. He smiled and joined her, and for a long moment, they just sat quietly and stared into the flames.

As they sipped their drinks, she slowly reached for his hand, and he clasped hers and squeezed it. He'd felt a connection with her the first time they met. He admired her investigative writing, her tenacity in searching for the truth and her love for her brother.

She also possessed a quiet kind of beauty that drew him to her. A spark of something was happening between them, and Derrick decided to embrace it.

ONE HUNDRED THIRTY-THREE

Ellie was satisfied that Ida, Kat and Hetty would eventually be okay. They were survivors.

She didn't blame Ida for deciding to take Kat and leave town and hoped they could start a new life. Hetty had even decided to go with them and start a gardening center somewhere else.

She hoped they'd find happiness and peace and put the past behind them. Although overcoming the fact that they'd trusted Joe and he'd deceived them would be difficult for Ida and Kat. How did one reconcile the fact that a serial killer had lived right under their own roof and they'd been oblivious to it?

Then again, she understood how love could make you blind to someone's secrets.

Resigned that she had to face Cord, she walked to the interview room and opened the door. When he looked up at her with tortured eyes, her heart melted, anger disintegrating into the abyss of her love for him.

"We found the killer. It was Ida's husband, Joe."

Surprise flickered on his face.

"All the evidence confirms it. We also caught him red-handed with Carrie Ann Parker, but we saved her and she's at the hospital with her mother now."

"He confessed?"

She nodded. "He had no choice. Derrick offered to take the death penalty off the table if he revealed the names of all his victims and where he buried him. Federal agents are searching for the bodies now so we can contact families. We also found Joe's mother, who was his first victim, and Ruth's remains buried on the property where he lived as a child."

Cord shook his head. "No one suspected Joe."

"No, but it all fits." She cleared her throat. "He was traumatized as a child by his mother. And his job as a delivery man gave him opportunity. He had access to each of the cities where girls disappeared."

Cord digested that for a moment, and she continued. "I know who you were covering for, Cord."

His gaze shot to hers, a war of emotions in his eyes.

"Ida and Hetty explained everything."

"You aren't sending them to jail, are you? Because it was self-defense. Earl Bramble was—"

"Abusive, I know that now." She sighed. "They're being released, Cord. No charges against them or you."

Relief softened his strong features. "Good. They suffered enough."

His protective tone tugged at Ellie. In spite of his secrets, deep down Cord was a good and honorable man.

"I understand why you did what you did," she said softly. "What I don't understand is why you didn't confide in me."

Cord released a wary breath. "Because I didn't want to compromise your job. I figured knowing would put you in a difficult position and I knew Ida and Hetty didn't kill Ruth."

"But you knew they killed Earl and that he was dead, and

we wasted time looking for him." Betrayal laced her voice. "You could have saved us time and manpower and helped us focus on other suspects."

Cord's expression looked tormented, but he didn't argue.

"If you have to charge me with obstruction, I understand, El."

Ellie vacillated. Maybe they would have found Joe sooner. Maybe not.

"I'm not pressing charges," she said. "But... I need time, Cord. I have to be able to trust you. How can I do that if you don't trust me?"

"I do trust you," he said gruffly.

Emotions gathered in Ellie's throat. "I mean totally trust me, Cord. No more secrets. Talk to me about your past." She swallowed hard. "Let me see you. I mean really see you, not just touch you in the dark."

He ran his fingers through his hair but slowly shook his head. "You won't like what you see."

"That's exactly what I mean," Ellie said, disappointment heavy in her heart. "You don't trust in me or our feelings toward each other." She turned and walked to the door. "You're free to go. I... need some space to think. Deputy Landrum can drive you home."

Frustration mingled with hurt as she left the room.

ONE HUNDRED THIRTY-FOUR

Cord watched Ellie go with a sinking heart.

He wanted to trust her. He really did.

But fear kept a stranglehold on him.

Deputy Landrum was waiting on him and drove him home in silence. Cord wondered what the deputy thought but it didn't really matter.

Ellie was the only one who mattered. And he'd royally messed that up.

"Thanks for the ride," he said as Landrum dropped him off.

"No problem."

Cord hunched his shoulders in the wind as he let himself inside his cabin. He walked through the living room in the dark, crossed to the bathroom and showered with only a low light burning. He despised looking at his scars in the mirror.

How could he expect Ellie to not be repulsed?

He scrubbed his body then rinsed and dried off. Regret for all his wrongdoings haunted him. Shame for being a victim. He'd tried so hard to overcome that through his work with SAR.

Ellie was the bright spot in his life. The sunshine that lit up the darkness.

But he'd hurt her.

Stop being a coward, man.

Sucking in a deep breath, he flipped on the light and stared at himself in the mirror, counting the scars and remembering how he'd gotten them.

ONE HUNDRED THIRTY-FIVE

Crooked Creek

Ellie had a good cry while she showered. And she hated to cry.

In fact, she *never* cried.

Exasperated with herself, she dressed in a T-shirt and pajama pants, then padded to the living room, started the fire then poured herself a finger of Ketel One. The citrussy rich flavor slid down her throat, taking the edge off her nerves, and she finished it then poured herself another one. Her stomach growled, and she gathered a plate of cheese and crackers and carried it to her sofa. She curled beneath the blanket and nibbled on the snacks as she sipped her vodka.

The flames danced and glowed in the dim light and a mellow feeling swept over her. She'd solved a case. Girls in Brambletown were safe. And parents could sleep again tonight.

She'd done her job.

But she'd lost the man she loved.

The doorbell rang, breaking into her thoughts, and she set her drink on the coffee table and went to the door. Hoping it wasn't another case, she checked the peephole.

Cord.

Her breath caught. He looked freshly showered in a denim button down shirt and jeans that hugged his muscular body. She couldn't quite read his expression, but his jaw was tight, accentuating his sharp cheekbones.

God. He was so ruggedly handsome.

He knocked and Ellie whipped herself into some semblance of a normal heartrate. But when she opened the door, the scent of fresh soap on him and his sexy eyes nearly brought her to her knees.

"Can I come in?" he asked gruffly.

She could not say no to this man, so she waved him in then closed the door. When she turned back to him, a hungry look burned in his eyes.

He swallowed hard. "I do trust you," he said.

Ellie titled her head to the side with an eyebrow raise.

"More than I've ever trusted anyone. It's... just hard for me."

Her anger faded. "I understand that, Cord. But I need it."

He stared at her for a long moment, emotions crossing his face. Fear. Regret. Desire. Love?

Then he reached for the buttons on his shirt and began to unbutton them one by one.

"What are you doing?" she asked breathlessly.

"Going to show you who I really am."

She couldn't breathe. Couldn't move. She was mesmerized by the deep amber flecks in his eyes and the sight of his bronzed chest. Then the scars. A few on his torso, then he inhaled and turned his back to her. Slowly he slid down his shirt and let it fall to the floor.

She drank in the sight of him. Strong. Bold. Courageous.

And so many scars. Deep, puckered, dark red and purple, jagged and rigid ones, cigarette burns, whip marks; a collection of the pain and abuse he'd endured. A sign of his strength in overcoming trauma and building a selfless life with SAR saving others.

Tears burned the backs of her eyes, and she wanted to lay down at his feet and sob like a baby.

But she blinked the tears away. She refused to let his scars intimidate her or show how much it hurt her to think that he'd suffered such cruelty.

In fact, she loved him even more for surviving them.

Desperate to hold him, she stepped closer to him, then traced her finger along the rigid flesh of one long jagged scar and kissed the puckered skin. A shudder rippled through him, and she moved to the next scar, then the next. Except for a slight tremble of his body and his breathing growing rapid, he stood ramrod still.

"This is who I am," he said, his voice thick with emotions.

His breath whooshed out, and he spun around, and looked into her eyes, studying her intently. Searching for a sign she was repulsed.

She lifted her hands and cradled his face between them. "I love the man you are," she said softly.

Emotions tinged his eyes, then a nervous smile.

"I love you just the way you are, inside and out."

His face crinkled with emotions, and he groaned then scooped her up and carried her to the bedroom.

She kissed him thoroughly as he laid her on the bed and pulled her in his arms.

Thank you so much for reading my Detective Ellie Reeves novels! If you're new to the series, don't worry—each book is a standalone novel so I'm happy you're following her journey both professionally and personally. If you'd like to keep up with all of my latest releases, you can sign up at the following link. Your email address will never be shared, and you can unsubscribe at any time.

www.bookouture.com/ritaherron

The Graveyard Girls is the eleventh installment in the series and was a challenge to write because, after a long battle with cancer, I lost my precious husband of fifty years in July. Part of me died that day with him, and at times the grief has been unbearable. But thirty years ago, when I admitted to him I wanted to write, he was the first person in my life to encourage me.

The voice of *The Graveyard Girls* came to me before the loss though, and the girls continued whispering in my head afterward, begging me to write their story. So, I finally picked up a pen and my laptop and put their voices on paper and brought the town of Brambletown to life.

The town is haunted by the mystery of a fifteen-year-old girl's disappearance, suspicions and rumors surrounding the locals, a coal mountain fire that still burns below the grounds surrounding the graveyard, and plenty of secrets that should keep you guessing until the end.

I hope you enjoy the twists and turns as well as Ellie, Cord and Derrick's continuing journey.

With a madman on the loose and other teenage girls' lives in jeopardy, the three must once again work together to keep him from taking more victims.

I love to hear from readers so you can find me on social media or my website.

Happy Reading!

Rita

www.ritaherron.com

 facebook.com/authorritaherron

 x.com/ritaherron

 instagram.com/ritaherronauthor

ACKNOWLEDGMENTS

I owe this book to my Monday night Zoom girls—I couldn't have finished it, or even started it without your support. We began our writing journey thirty years ago at the Georgia Romance Writers monthly meetings and through the years, have seen each other through the highs and lows: rejections, publication, personal problems and career planning. You are a great and talented group of writers and also my best friends.

1. To Stephanie Bond, my longtime critique partner for always being there for me to brainstorm, hash out plot points and ideas and for encouraging me to write, even during the dark times of the last two years. Your work ethic and professionalism are an inspiration. Your suggestion about the red shoes added the twist I needed and became instrumental in the killer's MO.
2. To Dorene Graham—I'm so excited to see you developing another series. Your tarot readings helped give me insight and food for thought for my characters. Listening to you discuss The Hero's Journey was a reminder of how to develop goals, conflict and growth for the main characters.
3. To Jenni Grizzle (aka Jennifer St. Giles)—who always adds to plot ideas and understands my brain with its dark twists and turns.

4. To Susan Goggins—thanks for telling me about the coal mountain fire. It became the inspiration for the setting in this book and added the atmospheric element and backdrop for *The Graveyard Girls*.

I also owe thanks to my two amazing daughters, Elizabeth and Emily, whose strength, courage, love and support surrounded me during the hardest season of my life. They feel the loss of their father deeply, and I pray for their healing and happiness every day.

A huge thanks to Sean Linton, who read and edited final proofs for the book when my eyes and brain were burned out from reading the manuscript so many times. Congrats on your wedding!

Another big thanks to the entire Bookouture team for their patience and support while I took the time to grieve the loss of my husband. To my amazing editor Lydia for prodding me just enough and for your insight and suggestions to improve my story.

Also, thanks to the supporting editors, to the team for the amazing cover and for all the efforts to promote the Detective Ellie Reeves series. I feel amazingly lucky to be part of Bookouture!

www.ingramcontent.com/pod-product-compliance
Lightning Source LLC
Chambersburg PA
CBHW031737180726
48283CB00005B/1544